BOTANICA DELIRA

BOTANICA DELIRA

MORE STORIES OF STRANGE, UNDISCOVERED, AND MURDEROUS VEGETATION

Chad Arment, Editor

COACHWHIP PUBLICATIONS
Landisville, Pennsylvania

Botanica Delira, edited by Chad Arment
Copyright © 2010 Coachwhip Publications
No claims made on public domain material.

ISBN 1-61646-025-3
ISBN-13 978-1-61646-025-9

   Cover: Orchid© Ingrid Taylar

   "The Devil Tree," (1883) includes minor editing due to incomplete
   source material.

CoachwhipBooks.com

CONTENTS

NEWSPAPER HOAXES

PREFACE

Tall tales of strange plants may never have been as common as those of a zoological bent, but there are still quite a number of stories that can be gleaned from early newspapers and magazines. These tales of botanical marvels sought to entertain and thrill the readers with rarely more than a wink and a nod at the truth. Occasionally, an enterprising writer would include mention of recognized species of unusual flora (carnivorous plants, sensitive plants, etc.) in an attempt to impress the reader with a scientific foundation for wild assertions, but the characteristics of known species were not immune from exaggeration for the sake of a good story.

Newspaper paragraphers (inserting brief notes to fill out newspaper columns) mentioned strange plants like the Venus flytrap and the "deadly" Upas tree as far back as the 1700s. Deliberate newspaper hoaxing of botanical wonders (or, more often, horrors) doesn't seem to have caught on until the 1870s, when stories of man-eating trees begin to appear. (The most popular tale, "The Man-Eating Tree" originally appeared in short story form, so is reprinted in the second section of this volume.) Writers submitted the yarns, and they were printed and reprinted (usually with changes in details or story structure) in various newspapers over several years. One year the devil tree might be located in Madagascar, and in other years it would crop up in Ceylon, Sumatra, Australia, or Nicaragua.

One positive aspect to these stories is that they influenced the development of a fascinating subgenre of speculative fiction. Of

9

course, there is a wide range of quality in cryptobotanical fiction, but more often than not, the cheaper thrills came from newspapers themselves, as they paid authors for more extensive stories carrying along the themes their readers already knew.

I'm aware of at least one case where this process was reversed. The 1883 short story "The Devil Tree," collected in this volume, was published in magazine *Frank Leslie's Pleasant Hours*. Just a few years later, a stripped-down version of the story without the revenge motif was reprinted as a hoax tale in various newspapers. While anonymous in both versions, a February 18, 1901, Galveston, Texas, *Daily News* article credited well-known hoaxer Joseph Mulhattan as the likely author. This assumption may not be justified, as I have seen no corroboration that Mulhattan ever wrote true short stories.

What follows in this first section is a selection of tall tales and exaggerated stories found in early newspapers, purporting to relate nature's marvels. It also includes an editorial from a botanical journal that had something to say about such stories that were prolific at the time. It's no surprise that as scientific education developed, deliberate hoaxing died out, though the journalistic desire to bring strange new plants and animals to public attention still goes on.

Still, the authors of the short stories found in the second section of this book, and in my first anthology of strange botanical fiction, *Flora Curiosa*, owe a debt of gratitude to these journalistic fancies, for stimulating ideas and developing an audience that continues to the present day.

The Electric Tree of New Guinea

The following is going the round of the papers at present, and we give it for what it is worth, merely remarking that it is too much on a par with many other unrealized wonders of New Guinea for us to accept without reserve. It has a Munchawsenish smack with it, and we shall wait with patience further developments regarding this to our mind somewhat uncanny tree. The fact that "Dr. Kummel is much puzzled to account for the existence of this singular tree by any process of natural selection," is very interesting as reflecting on the doctor's facility for being puzzled. One would naturally think that his own experience with a little bit of "core," would have suggested to him the process by which his newly discovered tree has been selected by nature as the fittest in the region it occupies. The tree that could send a German doctor rolling and yelling on the ground, and cause him to lose his spectacles, appears to us to be eminently capable of taking care of itself, and of holding its own in the struggle for existence:—

"One of the German expeditions to New Guinea has just made a startling discovery. It has, of course, been perfectly well known, and is indeed one of the great principles of modern science, that force, or energy, is not only indestructible, but transformable, as, for instance, the heat energy of steam is transformed into the energy of visible motion by the steam engine, and that again into the form of energy which we call electricity, by the dynamo. So, again, it is of course familiar that the peculiar force, whatever it is, which we call vital is partly transformed into weak electric

currents along the nerves of men and other animals, an extreme
instance occurring in the well-known electric eel which gives a
really powerful discharge of electricity. Now, hitherto in plant-life
nothing of the sort, however possible, has been proved to exist,
and the New Guinea discovery is neither more nor less than a
gigantic vegetable gymnotus. The scientific interest of the find is
immense, and not less, probably, its future practical bearing on
the lives of our descendants. The electric eel could scarcely be used
as a regular source of electric currents, but the *Elsassia electrica*,
as Dr. Kummel has patriotically named it, can, to all appearance,
be readily acclimatized and cultivated, and, if not overdrawn on,
will give, if one may use the expression, a steady crop of energy
available for all the multitudinous uses for which modern civilization now uses the dynamo or the battery. It is true that the current
given by one tree is, though considerable in quantity, of much lower
intensity than is wanted for many purposes; but even if it is found
that this defect cannot be remedied by coupling up a number of
trees in series without damaging them, science has methods of
transforming, with little loss, larger weak currents into smaller
strong ones, and there need be no difficulty on this score. The out-
look is immense: parks which will form a pleasant recreation-
ground to the citizens will light our cities almost free of cost or
care; our gardens will themselves illuminate the villages of their
owners, whilst the very hedgerow trees on our farms will supply
the power for agricultural operations in the fields which they
surround. I purposely refrain from the greater question of the
application of electricity from this source to the general super-
session of steam and other motors, but that it will come I have
little doubt. However, I have said enough both on the theory and
the prospects of the discovery, and cannot now do better than relate in his own words the account given me by Lieutenant von
Immer Gassende, the fortunate discoverer, who is now on his way
to Sydney, where he catches the French mail steamer, the *Salazie*,
on the 6th October and proceeds to Europe. The Lieutenant, though
much pulled down by the dangerous fever he has had, and which
is indeed the cause of his return home, is anxious to be again in

New Guinea, and to pursue those explorations which have been already so fruitful in result. He is a fine type of the German gentleman and sailor. He said: 'It is unnecessary to trouble you with many details of our journey. Dr. Kummel and I, with some half-a-dozen men, left the ship at anchor in a small bay to the east of Cape Della Torre, and at once commenced working our way, as nearly due south as we could manage, over the low jungle-covered range which here skirts the coast. We saw for the first two days a few natives of the type prevalent in this part of Papua, with small patches of bananas and other cultivated ground; we were not, however, molested by them, and farther on the country seemed absolutely without inhabitants. When we had got some 100 miles inland, a journey which took no less than twelve days' hard work, and had reached an elevation of about 5000 feet, being, in fact, on one of the northern spurs of the great central range, we encamped for the night in a more open country than we had hitherto seen. Our way in the morning was on an ever-ascending slope through park-like scenery, not only beautiful in itself, but a very refreshing change from our previous experiences. Towards noon I stopped under a large tree which seemed to particularly attract the attention of Kummel, who had been finding all kinds of novelties the whole morning, to take the exact bearings of a high peak which was visible through an opening in front of us. To my surprise, the compass seemed utterly drunk, varying in all directions in the roost capricious manner at each movement I took. I called Kummel's attention to this, and he said jokingly that we must have arrived at Sinbad's loadstone rock. I tried a variety of experiments, and found that, on walking into the open, the disturbances became feebler, but did not entirely cease for some distance. Whilst we were discussing the matter, one of the men, who carried a heavy cutlass or machete for clearing the path, struck one of a number of peculiar buttresses which ran up the outside of the tree, splitting off a large slice, and severing a curious-looking black core some half an inch thick, which formed the centre. Kummel, in his scientific curiosity, ran up, placed his hands on the two ends of the core to look at it more closely, and instantly, to my utter astonishment, gave a yell and rolled head over heels, getting up without his spectacles, and stammering to me that he had had a severe electric shock. One of the men was induced to repeat the experiment with similar results. I had no galvanometer, but improvised one with a length of copper wire, the centre of which I formed into an open spiral round my compass, and on inserting the ends of the wire into the opposite sides of the black matter, the needle was violently deflected, showing conclusively that a very considerable current was passing. Every branch and every twig of the tree, which I can assure you we treated with much respect, presented similar ridges and cores, with the addition of a thicker central one, and I quickly proved that the current circulated through the entire system. How it is kept up, no one can at present tell; but there it is. I am not able to say what the intensity or the quantity of the current might have been, but it was enough to knock you down in a very unpleasant way. We made a lot of more experiments on the tree, and would have cut it down, but it seemed a dangerous job to undertake. We saw a great many more of the same kind farther on, quite a forest, in fact; but I was that night attacked with very severe fever, and, after stopping several days to rest, I found myself obliged to return to the ship, and was then invalided home as my only chance. Dr. Kummel has returned with instruments to take proper measurements of the current, and to satisfy himself as to a number of points. In the meantime, I take home a preliminary memoir, pieces of the wood and core, etc., and seeds which we were fortunate enough to obtain. I am sorry I cannot show you them, as they are in my boxes on the steamer. The chemist on board says the black substance is a very pure amorphous carbon, giving hardly a trace of ash. Dr. Kummel is much puzzled to account for the existence of this singular tree by any process of natural selection. He says he cannot see how the possession of this system of electric currents could have benefited it. It has certainly, however, cleared out nearly every other species of forest tree from its habitat. Yes, I sincerely hope *Elsassia electrica* will grow in other countries; it would be a great thing, would it not?'"

A Strange Vegetable Production

A correspondent writing to a St. Louis paper from Mexico, says: "I have taken much interest in the study of botany during my sojourn in this country, the flora of which presents one of the richest fields for the scientists in the world, and have wandered some distance from the town on several occasions in my search for specimens. On one of these expeditions I noticed a dark object on one of the outlying spurs of the Sierra Madre Mountains, which object excited my curiosity so much that I examined it carefully through my field glass. This revealed that the object was a tree or shrub of such an unusual appearance that I resolved to visit the spot.

"I rode to the mountain, the sides of which sloped sufficiently for me to make my way on horseback within a few rods of the summit. But here I was stopped by an abrupt rise so steep that I despaired of reaching it even on foot. I went around it several times seeking for some way to climb up, but the jagged rocks afforded not the slightest foothold. On top of this knob stands the tree I had seen. From the spot on which I now stood I could see that it somewhat resembled in form the weeping willow, but the long, drooping, whip-like limbs were of dark and apparently slimy appearance and seemed possessed of a horrible life-like power of coiling and uncoiling. Occasionally the whole tree would seem a writhing, squirming mass.

"My desire to investigate this strange vegetable product increased on each of the many expeditions I made to the spot, and at

15

last I had discovered an unheard-of thing. A bird which I had watched circling about for some time finally settled on the top of the tree, when the branches began to awaken, as it were, and to curl upward. They twined and twisted like snakes about the bird, which began to scream, and drew it down in their fearful embrace until I lost sight of it. Horror stricken, I seized the nearest rock in an attempt to climb the knob. I had so often tried in vain to do this that I was not surprised when I fell back, but the rock was loosened and fell also. It narrowly missed me, but I sprang up unhurt, and saw that the fallen rock had left a considerable cavity.

"I put my face to it and looked in. Something like a cavern, the floor of which had an upward tendency, met my sight, and I felt a current of fresh air blowing on me with a dry, earthy smell. Evidently there was another opening somewhere, undoubtedly at the summit. Using my trowel, which I always carried on my botanizing expeditions, I enlarged the hole and then pushed my way up through the passage. When I had nearly reached the top I looked out cautiously to see if I should emerge within reach of that diabolical tree. But I found it nowhere near the aperture, so I sprang out. I was just in time to see the flattened carcass of the bird drop to the ground, which was covered with bones and feathers.

"I approached as closely as I dared and examined the tree. It was low in size, not more than twenty feet, but covering a great area. Its trunk was of prodigious thickness, knotted and scaly. From the top of the trunk, a few feet from the ground, its slimy branches curved upward and downward, nearly touching the ground with their tapering tips. Its appearance was that of a gigantic tarantula awaiting its prey. On my venturing to lightly touch one of the limbs, it closed upon my hand with such force that when I tore it loose the skin came with it. I descended then, and closing the passage returned home.

"I went back next day carrying half a dozen chickens with which to feed the tree. The moment I tossed it the fowls, a violent agitation shook its branches, which swayed to and fro with a sinuous snaky motion. After devouring the fowls, these branches, fully gorged, dropped to their former positions, and the tree, giving no sign of animation, I dared approach it and take the limbs in my hand. They were covered with suckers, resembling the tentacles of an octopus. The blood of the fowls had been absorbed by these suckers, leaving crimson stains on the dark surface. There was no foliage, of course, of any kind.

"Without speaking of my discovery to anyone about, I wrote an account of it to the world-famous botanist, Professor Wordenhaupt, of the University of Heidelberg. His reply states that my tree is the Arbor Diaboli, only two specimens of which have ever been known—one on a peak of the Himalayas and the other on the Island of Sumatra. Mine is the third. Professor Wordenhaupt says that the Arbor Diaboli and the plant known as Venus fly-trap are the only known specimens, growing on the land, of those forms of life which partake of the nature of both the animal and vegetable kingdoms, although there are instances too numerous to mention of this class in the sea. The Portuguese man-of-war may be mentioned, however, as one, and the sponge as the best known specimen."

A Metal Eating Plant

Professor Schelwisch, the well known naturalist of Bavaria, while traveling with the Stanley expedition in the heart of Africa for the purpose of studying the flora and fauna of the dark continent, was the first white man to discover this strange plant.

One day while resting at a small village near the foot of Mount Milosis, in the Umbopo region, Professor Schelwisch noticed a plant with a peculiar steel colored foliage, and on examination it was found that the shrub, although growing like other plants from the soil, was practically composed of iron. The leaves, though very thin, were bent with great difficulty, and the twigs and branches resisted pressure with a force about equal to the same amount of iron, and to secure a leaf it was found to be necessary to separate it from the bush with a file.

While Professor Schelwisch was digging at the base of this plant for the purpose of making an examination of its roots, the natives crowded around him in great numbers, gesticulating in a menacing manner. The professor desisted from his work and the interpreter was sent for. He explained that this was a holy tree and worshiped by the natives in their fetich religion as a God plant, and that to dig one up would bring ruin and desolation upon the whole village and surrounding country.

Professor Schelwisch offered to buy the plant, and, taking out a handful of copper coins, gave them to the savages, who gladly accepted the money and distributed it among themselves. The professor then returned to the work of digging up the unique plant,

18

but had not made any great progress when the natives again set upon him. Through the interpreter the professor informed them that he had legally bought the plant and intended to remove it. As soon as this message was made known to the savages every one who had received a coin came and dropped it in the hole at the base of the shrub. Professor Schelwisch allowed the coins to remain in the hole and walked away toward the mountain to hunt another specimen.

Its Strange Properties Discovered

Next day, as the party were preparing to continue the march, the professor was curious to know if the coins had remained undisturbed during the night by the superstitious natives, and on approaching the metal plant was astonished to find it had changed its color completely. Instead of being a beautiful steel color, the stem, leaves and what was exposed of the roots presented the appearance of newly coined copper coins and glittered in the morning sunlight like polished gold. Upon examination it was ascertained that during the night the strange plant had absorbed nearly all the copper coins, with the result of completely changing its color. What was left of the coins in the hole showed that they were more than half eaten away or absorbed by the roots of the metal plant. Not only was the color changed, but the texture of the plant had undergone a similar transformation. It was found that the thin ivy shaped leaves were now easily bent around the fingers, would retain any shape given them and could be readily cut with an ordinary pair of scissors.

Professor Schelwisch succeeded in surreptitiously securing several branches of this wonderful metal eating plant, and was also successful in obtaining a good photograph of it. No further trace of the existence of the metal plant was found until the expedition reached the Uniamesi country, when at the base of the Nkomabakosi mountains a perfect forest of this curious plant was found. This being an uninhabited region no difficulty was encountered in securing specimens to take back to England.

FIRE DOES NOT AFFECT IT

While in this locality ample opportunity was afforded the members of the expedition to make an exhaustive study of the habits and peculiarities of this most remarkable of all species of the vegetable kingdom. By a series of carefully conducted experiments it was found that this plant would feed on any kind of metal placed at its roots and in a few days take on the characteristics of that metal, and in the case of the softer metals often but a few hours were required to effect a complete metamorphosis of its fiber and color.

Being curious to know how fire would affect a growing plant of this species, preparations were made for the test. Large quantities of seasoned wood were procured and piled in a long row covering about thirty of the metal plants and a fire kindled at the windward end. Stanley and his entire party watched the experiment, and had the satisfaction of demonstrating that, beyond the blackening of the foliage by smoke, the intense heat to which the metal plant had been subjected had done no harm to the plant itself. At the expiration of a week it was found that the rain had removed nearly all traces of the fire and the plants were apparently as healthy as ever.

The roots present peculiarities not found in other plants. They branch out from the trunk on all sides like a vine and are usually from six to eight inches beneath the surface of the soil. Regularly at every seven or eight inches the root branches and at this juncture grows a peculiar pair of round, slightly concaved discs, hinged together like the shells of a clam at the point of juncture with the root. These discs leave their convex sides outward and usually remain about half open until they encounter metal or metal ore, when they gradually close around it and a process supposed to be similar to electro-plating goes on, the metal being rapidly absorbed by the plant.

Vegetable Boa Constrictors

Portions of the South Pacific ocean produce a wonderful species of the seaweed called the "vegetable boa constrictor." They are likely to be met with at any point between the lower point of southern California and the Sandwich Islands on the other side and between Chili and Australia on the other. These vine-like stranglers are frequently found tightly entwined about the body of a dead whale, shark or porpoise, but whether they had fastened upon the bodies of these dead sea animals before life has become extinct or had only ventured to attack the remains after the vital spark had fled are conundrums which of course cannot be answered. Experiments made with this curious vine and the carcass of a porpoise washed ashore in the harbor at Apia tend to prove that the vine, like that of our common bean, will not entwine itself around anything dead, whether that thing be of vegetable of animal creation.

Dr. Chadbourne, in his "Annals of the Caroline Islands," says: "I have often seen monster specimens of macricystis (the giant seaweed) with every vestige of life squeezed out of them by that ocean demon, the constrictor vine, which is itself a species of seaweed. Macricystis often grows to be from 20 to 30 inches in diameter and 1,500 to 3,000 feet in length, while the constrictor vine seldom exceeds 100 feet in length and is never larger in diameter than a pound and a half salmon can. It is the "squeeze snake" of the ocean, however, and woe to the unlucky man, animal or plant that comes within its reach."

An Arizona Yarn

"There are more queer things to the acre in Arizona than in any other part of this wide land," said Col. Brace Dion, of Houck's Tank, Apache county, "and, according to my idea, and I know pretty near what queer things are, the queerest thing in all Arizona is the tree that has a temper worse than a blonde comic opera prima donna's, and gets its dander up with just as small provocation. They tell me out there that this tree belongs to the coniferous species. It grows to be something like twenty-five feet high and then stops. Its leaves are long, slender and pointed, like porcupine quills. When this tree is in good humor these leaves lie close to the branches, and it spreads a pleasant aromatic odor all around. But when it is angry every leaf on the tree rises up on end, and the aspect of that particular piece of timber is about as fierce and threatening to look at. The pleasant resinous odor the tree sends forth in its peaceful mood gives way to an odor that will put wings on your feet to place as much distance as you can between the offensive tree and yourself.

"This tree is especially touchy on the subject of dogs, and the coming of a canine anywhere near it will instantly make it furious. Yet a wolf, a grizzly bear, or a mountain lion never ruffles the temper of this tree if these animals do not presume on too great familiarity with it. They may lie around it as long as they care to, but if one of them so far forgets itself as to rub or scratch the trunk of the tree, the hot-tempered thing will fly into one of its tantrums instantly, and the way Mr. Bear, Wolf, or Lion will make himself

22

scarce in those parts is a whole circus to see. Nothing will work this tree up to a concert pitch, though, so quick and effectually as throwing stones at it. Then it will actually rip and tear, and no living thing would think of going within gunshot of it. Some folks out at Houck's Tank call this tree the porcupine tree, and some say its right name is skunk tree. I call it the holy terror tree. But, no matter what you call it, it is a queer job of nature, and Arizona claims it as her own."

Rather Uncanny

The following peculiar experience is said to have befallen an Englishman some few years since while on a botanising expedition in the northern part of Hawaii. Though we know nothing against the narrator's veracity, we are hardly prepared to vouch for the absolute accuracy of every detail of the story.

During his rambles he came to a certain ravine which his native guide showed a strange disinclination to enter. The botanist, however, pushed on, and suddenly found himself in front of a circular space of about 100yds in diameter, thickly covered with the bleached remains of birds, animals and human beings, apparently arranged with the smallest bones no the outside of the ghastly circle.

In the centre was a well-like opening in the ground, from which emanated a sickening odour. No vegetation grew within 50 ft of the cavity, and the explorer asserted that he saw a luminous column of smoke or gas arising from it.

Darkness, and the native's obvious terror, prevented further exploration for a time; but later on the botanist returned to the place. The guide, after vainly trying to turn him from his purpose, performed some mystic incantations to endeavour to ensure his safety.

Nothing happened until Mr. C— had gone about a mile up the ravine, when his progress was stopped by a wall of lava, about which waved a strange mass of sea-green foliage, resembling a bunch of seaweed, about 12ft high, edged with fine streamers that radiated in all directions, which a movement on the spectator's part caused to point directly at him.

Just then he slipped and fell, but not before something struck him with a hissing noise so violently on the crown of his heavy felt hat that he lost consciousness. When he recovered, the wall above was stripped of its verdure, and he saw a long snake-like object twisting and curling on the rocks. It had missed its prey, and a low angry hum filled the air.

What connection it had with the circular space he had discovered on his previous visit, or the mass of apparent foliage, he did not stop to inquire; but, without ascertaining whether the demon of the ravine was of animal or vegetable origin, the explorer made his way back to safer parts with all possible despatch.

The Land Octopus

Naturalists are familiar with a number or carnivorous or flesh-eating or flesh-destroying plants, and they are very curious in their operation. Usually they are of small dimensions and confine their homicidal tendency to insignificant insects. The most remarkable in size and strength is that described by M. Fabiani Carlo, who tells of a naturalist named Dunstan who, while traveling with his dog on the shores of Lake Nicaragua, heard the animal give vent to cries of pain. Going to the spot he found his dog held by three black, sticky bands, under which the skin was bleeding from chafing even in the few minutes that had elapsed. These bands were the branches of a new and gigantic carnivorous plant, which Dunstan calls the "land-octopus," and which apparently is about as formidable as his twin brother of the sea. These branches are flexible, polished, black, without leaves, secreting a viscous fluid and furnished with a great number of suckers by which the "land-octopus" attaches itself to its victims. Dunstan, with great difficulty, cut away the branches after having his hands severely injured by the tentacles of the "land-octopus." Under the circumstances close investigation of this plant monster was not very convenient or comfortable, but Dunstan proved that the fetid odor attracted the prey, while the sucker tentacles secured and destroyed it. After sucking out the nutritive elements of the captured animal the land-octopus cast it way. The natives of Central America, very appropriately call this blood-thirsty plant the "Devil's Noose."

Demon Flowers

Charles Fosterman, of San Diego, whose death has recently been recorded, is reputed to have been a great collector of orchids in South America at one time, and appears to have been fond of a joke on the average newspaper reporter, one of whom gives away the following, evidently played off on him by the Mr. Fosterman aforesaid:

"He said he landed once on the coast of Brazil, a few degrees south of the equator, where he met a native chief, who told him of a 'village of the demon flowers' to the westward. Further questioning convinced him that the 'demon flowers' were orchids of the rarest and most wonderful kind, so he decided to find this 'village' at any cost.

"He had traveled through forests about six weeks, and was calculating that in a fortnight more he would be in the neighborhood of the 'village of the demon flowers' when, one afternoon, three of his forward guards threw up their arms, and, with a cry, fell senseless to the ground. He had noticed a peculiar sickening odor pervading the heavy, heated air, and quickly gave the order for the other men to advance with caution and drag back the fallen ones from the spot where they lay. They did so, and, returning, reported that they had seen through this dense forest a little further on, the vast 'village of the demon flowers.'

"Accompanied only by a Portuguese interpreter, the orchid-seekers started forward, their mouths and noses muffled as a safe-guard against the awful odor. They managed to reach the spot

27

where the three men had been stricken down, but could go no further. They could see, a hundred yards ahead of them, a great mass
of orchids. Trees, undergrowth, and everything was loaded down
with them. They were of hues more brilliant than he had ever seen
or dreamed of seeing. But, like a barrier, the wall of awful, sickening, overpowering odor rose between."

This is something like the wonderful Upas tree of Java all over
again—a tree under which a veracious traveler found heaps of skulls
of those who, sleeping under it, had died. The skulls did not
frighten the newly arrived traveler, whose fate was to be next, nor
excite a thought as to how they died. In this case the "forward
guards" would seem to know how deadly the orchid was, but were
going to their death to get some at any rate. How self-sacrificing
for the good of science!

EDITORIAL, *AMERICAN BOTANIST*

On many occasions we have been led to comment upon the propensity of the average newspaper reporter to build an impressive story about plants upon an exceedingly tenuous basis of fact, but our astonishment at such feats of the pen is as nothing to our admiration of the reporter's ability in getting some of these stories past the editor who is usually supposed to be a man of some brains and ordinary common sense. Time and again in the lay press we come upon bloodcurdling stories of plants that deal out death to all who approach—Upas trees, man-eating plants, the vulture lily of the East Indies and many others that fail to impress the botanist but which appeal to the credulity of the general reader and by catering to this belief in the marvellous spoil his appreciation for the wonderful things about plants that are true. The latest contribution to the pseudo-science of botany is entitled the "Death Orchid" and runs as follows: "Three years ago, an orchid hunter, Grayson set out to find 'El Lugor de los Flores Venenosos,' that is 'The Place of the Poisonous Flowers,' which was said to be located in the dense and pathless wilderness occupying the vast stretches between the head waters of the Orinoco and the Andes. One morning there was a perceptible smell of flowers in the air. When the orchid hunter and his Indians camped that night the jungle smell had been entirely lost in the cloying scent. Many of the band refused to go further. As Grayson and the others proceeded the rankly sweet and oppressive odor became stronger, attacking the senses like a narcotic. The orchid hunter felt as if he were being attacked

29

by the insidious power of opium, but retained enough consciousness to become aware that, gleaming through the trees ahead he
saw flowers of huge size and vivid colors; many hued clusters of
them hanging in trails. It was the death orchid! When he recovered his senses, he found himself being carried back to camp where
the rest of his porters had remained. Many of the band were
severely sick and many half witted with the continued effect of the
scent." The botanist who reads this account is likely to wonder
whether the story was not written up by one of those half-witted
members of the party. It would have required some such condition of mind, we are inclined to think, to perceive the headwaters
of the Andes. But the query which sticks longest in mind is, why
should anybody take the trouble to make up such preposterous
stories when a multitude of the wonders of the plant world are still
to be adequately described.

PLANTS THAT FIGHT

N. TOURNEUR

There is nothing more striking in nature than the means which certain plants possess for defence against their natural enemies.

Death-dealing in its powers of self-protection is the vulture lily of the East Indies, that for a long time was considered to be a traveller's myth, till in recent years its existence was verified in Borneo and Sumatra. The French explorer who discovered the plant in Sumatra had been told by the natives of a lily of immense size, to be found in the forests of the interior, that sent forth death-dealing fumes, and after a long search he discovered several. The largest covered an area of sixty feet with its evil-smelling growth. Its spadix was over six feet high, and the spike-shaped leaves were from ten to twelve feet long. At sunset and about an hour before sunrise its poisonous fumes were found to be most powerful. A dog, a goat, and other small animals tethered near the plant were picked up dead in the morning. The Frenchman himself was taken so violently ill while examining this vulture lily, that he had to return hurriedly to the coast.

The so-called deadly properties of the upas-tree of Java and of the spider-plant of Madagascar, which also is reputed to entice its human prey, have not been verified as realities; but in the vast stretches of wilderness that lie between the headwaters of the Orinoco and the Andes, there has been discovered a growth of the orchid genus, the flowers of which give out a musky odour, which is so stupefying and poisonous in its effects that, as yet, no human beings, natives or white men, have approached near enough even

31

to pick any of the huge, clustered, many-hued flowers gleaming enticingly through the jungle trees, or to attack its roots.

Some plants protect themselves by presenting attitudes that scare the enemy, just as certain insects do. One of the most common instances is that of the sensitive plant and its movements when touched. A creature, on coming near during its browsing, is afraid to nibble a plant that moves so mysteriously. The squirting cucumber of the Mediterranean also alarms goats and other animals, when they touch it, by discharging its ripe seeds into their faces. It also contains a very pungent juice which it spits on to the skin or face of its opponent, and the smarting pain that results is very difficult to endure for some minutes.

In the dry regions of South Africa, where all green things are nibbled down during the rainless season, certain ice-plants and milk-weeds have the trick of forming tubers, or stems, exactly similar in appearance to the pebbles or soil around them, so that when the leaves of these plants die down during the dry season, the tubers remain undetected by animals.

In South Africa there is a species of acacia much resembling the sensitive plant in general appearance, which maintains a standing army of ants for defensive purposes, and provides them with food and lodging. In this singular growth there are two large thorns at the base inhabited by colonies of the ants, which bore into the thorns and make a home for themselves by eating out the soft inner tissue. On the leaf-stalks there are honey glands, and at the tip of each leaf there is a sausage-shaped body, about as large as a pin's head, consisting of albuminous food. The ants sip the honey and eat the solid food-bodies, and being content with their lot, remain on the acacia without doing it any injury. When the plant is threatened by an invasion of the leaf-cutting ants that would destroy it, the ants forming the acacia's army rush out and repel the invaders. Many other similar arrangements are to be observed in tropical vegetation.

SHORT STORIES

Lost in a Pyramid, or the Mummy's Curse
Louisa May Alcott

I

"And what are these, Paul?" asked Evelyn, opening a tarnished gold box and examining its contents curiously.

"Seeds of some unknown Egyptian plant," replied Forsyth, with a sudden shadow on his dark face, as he looked down at the three scarlet grains lying in the white hand lifted to him.

"Where did you get them?" asked the girl.

"That is a weird story, which will only haunt you if I tell it," said Forsyth, with an absent expression that strongly excited the girl's curiosity.

"Please tell it, I like weird tales, and they never trouble me. Ah, do tell it; your stories are always so interesting," she cried, looking up with such a pretty blending of entreaty and command in her charming face, that refusal was impossible.

"You'll be sorry for it, and so shall I, perhaps; I warn you before-hand, that harm is foretold to the possessor of those mysterious seeds," said Forsyth, smiling, even while he knit his black brows, and regarded the blooming creature before him with a fond yet foreboding glance.

"Tell on, I'm not afraid of these pretty atoms," she answered, with an imperious nod.

"To hear is to obey. Let me read the facts, and then I will begin," returned Forsyth, pacing to and fro with the far-off look of one who turns the pages of the past.

Evelyn watched him a moment, and then returned to her work, or play, rather, for the task seemed well suited to the vivacious little creature, half-child, half-woman.

"While in Egypt," commenced Forsyth, slowly, "I went one day with my guide and Professor Niles, to explore the Cheops. Niles had a mania for antiquities of all sorts, and forgot time, danger and fatigue in the ardor of his pursuit. We rummaged up and down the narrow passages, half choked with dust and close air; reading inscriptions on the walls, stumbling over shattered mummy-cases, or coming face to face with some shriveled specimen perched like a hobgoblin on the little shelves where the dead used to be stowed away for ages. I was desperately tired after a few hours of it, and begged the professor to return. But he was bent on exploring certain places, and would not desist. We had but one guide, so I was forced to stay; but Jumal, my man, seeing how weary I was, proposed to us to rest in one of the larger passages, while he went to procure another guide for Niles. We consented, and assuring us that we were perfectly safe, if we did not quit the spot, Jumal left us, promising to return speedily. The professor sat down to take notes of his researches, and stretching my self on the soft sand, I fell asleep.

"I was roused by that indescribable thrill which instinctively warns us of danger, and springing up, I found myself alone. One torch burned faintly where Jumal had struck it, but Niles and the other light were gone. A dreadful sense of loneliness oppressed me for a moment; then I collected myself and looked well about me. A bit of paper was pinned to my hat, which lay near me, and on it, in the professor's writing were these words:

"'I've gone back a little to refresh my memory on certain points. Don't follow me till Jumal comes. I can find my way back to you, for I have a clue. Sleep well, and dream gloriously of the Pharaohs. N N.'

"I laughed at first over the old enthusiast, then felt anxious then restless, and finally resolved to follow him, for I discovered a strong cord fastened to a fallen stone, and knew that this was the clue he spoke of. Leaving a line for Jumal, I took my torch and retraced my steps, following the cord along the winding ways. I often shouted, but received no reply, and pressed on, hoping at each turn to see the old man poring over some musty relic of antiquity. Suddenly the cord ended, and lowering my torch, I saw that the footsteps had gone on.

"'Rash fellow, he'll lose himself, to a certainty,' I thought, really alarmed now.

"As I paused, a faint call reached me, and I answered it, waited, shouted again, and a still fainter echo replied.

"Niles was evidently going on, misled by the reverberations of the low passages. No time was to be lost, and, forgetting myself, I stuck my torch in the deep sand to guide me back to the clue, and ran down the straight path before me, whooping like a madman as I went. I did not mean to lose sight of the light, but in my eagerness to find Niles I turned from the main passage, and, guided by his voice, hastened on. His torch soon gladdened my eyes, and the clutch of his trembling hands told me what agony he had suffered.

"'Let us get out of this horrible place at once,' he said, wiping the great drops off his forehead.

"'Come, we're not far from the clue. I can soon reach it, and then we are safe'; but as I spoke, a chill passed over me, for a perfect labyrinth of narrow paths lay before us.

"Trying to guide myself by such land-marks as I had observed in my hasty passage, I followed the tracks in the sand till I fancied we must be near my light. No glimmer appeared, however, and kneeling down to examine the footprints nearer, I discovered, to my dismay, that I had been following the wrong ones, for among those marked by a deep boot-heel, were prints of bare feet; we had had no guide there, and Jumal wore sandals.

"Rising, I confronted Niles, with the one despairing word, 'Lost!' as I pointed from the treacherous sand to the fast-waning light.

"I thought the old man would be overwhelmed but, to my surprise, he grew quite calm and steady, thought a moment, and then went on, saying, quietly:

"'Other men have passed here before us; let us follow their steps, for, if I do not greatly err, they lead toward great passages, where one's way is easily found.'

"On we went, bravely, till a misstep threw the professor violently to the ground with a broken leg, and nearly extinguished the torch. It was a horrible predicament, and I gave up all hope as I sat beside the poor fellow, who lay exhausted with fatigue, remorse and pain, for I would not leave him.

"'Paul,' he said suddenly, 'if you will not go on, there is one more effort we can make. I remember hearing that a party lost as we are, saved themselves by building a fire. The smoke penetrated further than sound or light, and the guide's quick wit understood the unusual mist; he followed it, and rescued the party. Make a fire and trust to Jumal.'

"'A fire without wood?' I began; but he pointed to a shelf behind me, which had escaped me in the gloom; and on it I saw a slender mummy-case. I understood him, for these dry cases, which lie about in hundreds, are freely used as firewood. Reaching up, I pulled it down, believing it to be empty, but as it fell, it burst open, and out rolled a mummy. Accustomed as I was to such sights, it startled me a little, for danger had unstrung my nerves. Laying the little brown chrysalis aside, I smashed the case, lit the pile with my torch, and soon a light cloud of smoke drifted down the three passages which diverged from the cell-like place where we had paused.

"While busied with the fire, Niles, forgetful of pain and peril, had dragged the mummy nearer, and was examining it with the interest of a man whose ruling passion was strong even in death.

"'Come and help me unroll this. I have always longed to be the first to see and secure the curious treasures put away among the folds of these uncanny winding-sheets. This is a woman, and we may find something rare and precious here,' he said, beginning to unfold the outer coverings, from which a strange aromatic odor came.

"Reluctantly I obeyed, for to me there was something sacred in the bones of this unknown woman. But to beguile the time and amuse the poor fellow, I lent a hand, wondering as I worked, if this dark, ugly thing had ever been a lovely, soft-eyed Egyptian girl.

"From the fibrous folds of the wrappings dropped precious gums and spices, which half intoxicated us with their potent breath, antique coins, and a curious jewel or two, which Niles eagerly examined.

"All the bandages but one were cut off at last, and a small head laid bare, round which still hung great plaits of what had once been luxuriant hair. The shriveled hands were folded on the breast, and clasped in them lay that gold box."

"Ah!" cried Evelyn, dropping it from her rosy palm with a shudder.

"Nay; don't reject the poor little mummy's treasure. I never have quite forgiven myself for stealing it, or for burning her," said Forsyth, painting rapidly, as if the recollection of that experience lent energy to his hand.

"Burning her! Oh, Paul, what do you mean?" asked the girl, sitting up with a face full of excitement.

"I'll tell you. While busied with Madame la Momie, our fire had burned low, for the dry case went like tinder. A faint, far-off sound made our hearts leap, and Niles cried out: 'Pile on the wood; Jumal is tracking us; don't let the smoke fail now or we are lost!'

"'There is no more wood; the case was very small, and is all gone,' I answered, tearing off such of my garments as would burn readily, and piling them upon the embers.

"Niles did the same, but the light fabrics were quickly consumed, and made no smoke.

"'Burn that!' commanded the professor, pointing to the mummy.

"I hesitated a moment. Again came the faint echo of a horn. Life was dear to me. A few dry bones might save us, and I obeyed him in silence.

"A dull blaze sprung up, and a heavy smoke rose from the burning mummy, rolling in volumes through the low passages, and threatening to suffocate us with its fragrant mist. My brain grew dizzy, the light danced before my eyes, strange phantoms seemed to people the air, and, in the act of asking Niles why he gasped and looked so pale, I lost consciousness."

Evelyn drew a long breath, and put away the scented toys from her lap as if their odor oppressed her.

Forsyth's swarthy face was all aglow with the excitement of his story, and his black eyes glittered as he added, with a quick laugh:

"That's all; Jumal found and got us out, and we both forswore pyramids for the rest of our days."

"But the box: how came you to keep it?" asked Evelyn, eyeing it askance as it lay gleaming in a streak of sunshine.

"Oh, I brought it away as a souvenir, and Niles kept the other trinkets."

"But you said harm was foretold to the possessor of those scarlet seeds," persisted the girl, whose fancy was excited by the tale, and who fancied all was not told.

"Among his spoils, Niles found a bit of parchment, which he deciphered, and this inscription said that the mummy we had so ungallantly burned was that of a famous sorceress who bequeathed her curse to whoever should disturb her rest. Of course I don't believe that curse has anything to do with it, but it's a fact that Niles never prospered from that day. He says it's because he has never recovered from the fall and fright and I dare say it is so; but I sometimes wonder if I am to share the curse, for I've a vein of superstition in me, and that poor little mummy haunts my dreams still."

A long silence followed these words. Paul painted mechanically and Evelyn lay regarding him with a thoughtful face. But gloomy fancies were as foreign to her nature as shadows are to noonday, and presently she laughed a cheery laugh, saying as she took up the box again:

"Why don't you plant them, and see what wondrous flower they will bear?"

"I doubt if they would bear anything after lying in a mummy's hand for centuries," replied Forsyth, gravely.

"Let me plant them and try. You know wheat has sprouted and grown that was taken from a mummy's coffin; why should not these pretty seeds? I should so like to watch them grow; may I, Paul?"

"No, I'd rather leave that experiment untried. I have a queer feeling about the matter, and don't want to meddle myself or let anyone I love meddle with these seeds. They may be some horrible poison, or possess some evil power, for the sorceress evidently valued them, since she clutched them fast even in her tomb."

"Now, you are foolishly superstitious, and I laugh at you. Be generous; give me one seed, just to learn if it will grow. See I'll pay for it," and Evelyn, who now stood beside him, dropped a kiss on his forehead as she made her request, with the most engaging air.

But Forsyth would not yield. He smiled and returned the embrace with lover-like warmth, then flung the seeds into the fire, and gave her back the golden box, saying, tenderly:

"My darling, I'll fill it with diamonds or bonbons, if you please, but I will not let you play with that witch's spells. You've enough of your own, so forget the 'pretty seeds' and see what a Light of the Harem I've made of you."

Evelyn frowned, and smiled, and presently the lovers were out in the spring sunshine reveling in their own happy hopes, untroubled by one foreboding fear.

II

"I have a little surprise for you, love," said Forsyth, as he greeted his cousin three months later on the morning of his wedding day.

"And I have one for you," she answered, smiling faintly.

"How pale you are, and how thin you grow! All this bridal bustle is too much for you, Evelyn." he said, with fond anxiety, as he watched the strange pallor of her face, and pressed the wasted little hand in his.

"I am so tired," she said, and leaned her head wearily on her lover's breast. "Neither sleep, food, nor air gives me strength, and a curious mist seems to cloud my mind at times. Mamma says it is the heat, but I shiver even in the sun, while at night I burn with fever. Paul, dear, I'm glad you are going to take me away to lead a quiet, happy life with you, but I'm afraid it will be a very short one."

"My fanciful little wife! You are tired and nervous with all this worry, but a few weeks of rest in the country will give us back our blooming Eve again. Have you no curiosity to learn my surprise?" he asked, to change her thoughts.

The vacant look stealing over the girl's face gave place to one of interest, but as she listened it seemed to require an effort to fix her mind on her lover's words.

"You remember the day we rummaged in the old cabinet?"

"Yes," and a smile touched her lips for a moment.

"And how you wanted to plant those queer red seeds I stole from the mummy?"

"I remember," and her eyes kindled with sudden fire.

"Well, I tossed them into the fire, as I thought, and gave you the box. But when I went back to cover up my picture, and found one of those seeds on the rug, a sudden fancy to gratify your whim led me to send it to Niles and ask him to plant and report on its progress. Today I hear from him for the first time, and he reports that the seed has grown marvelously, has budded, and that he intends to take the first flower, if it blooms in time, to a meeting of famous scientific men, after which he will send me its true name and the plant itself. From his description, it must be very curious, and I'm impatient to see it."

"You need not wait; I can show you the flower in its bloom," and Evelyn beckoned with the *mechanté* smile so long a stranger to her lips.

Much amazed, Forsyth followed her to her own little boudoir, and there, standing in the sunshine, was the unknown plant. Almost rank in their luxuriance were the vivid green leaves on the slender purple stems, and rising from the midst, one ghostly-white flower, shaped like the head of a hooded snake, with scarlet stamens like forked tongues, and on the petals glittered spots like dew.

"A strange, uncanny flower! Has it any odor?" asked Forsyth, bending to examine it, and forgetting, in his interest, to ask how it came there.

"None, and that disappoints me, I am so fond of perfumes," answered the girl, caressing the green leaves which trembled at her touch, while the purple stems deepened their tint.

"Now tell me about it," said Forsyth, after standing silent for several minutes.

"I had been before you, and secured one of the seeds, for two fell on the rug. I planted it under a glass in the richest soil I could find, watered it faithfully, and was amazed at the rapidity with which it grew when once it appeared above the earth. I told no-one, for I meant to surprise you with it; but this bud has been so long in blooming, I have had to wait. It is a good omen that it blossoms today, and as it is nearly white, I mean to wear it, for I've learned to love it, having been my pet for so long."

"I would not wear it, for, in spite of its innocent color, it is an evil-looking plant, with its adder's tongue and unnatural dew. Wait till Niles tells us what it is, then pet it if it is harmless."

"Perhaps my sorceress cherished it for some symbolic beauty—those old Egyptians were full of fancies. It was very sly of you to turn the tables on me in this way. But I forgive you, since in a few hours, I shall chain this mysterious hand forever. How cold it is! Come out into the garden and get some warmth and color for to-night, my love."

But when night came, no-one could reproach the girl with her pallor, for she glowed like a pomegranate-flower, her eyes were full of fire, her lips scarlet, and all her old vivacity seemed to have returned. A more brilliant bride never blushed under a misty veil, and when her lover saw her, he was absolutely startled by the almost unearthly beauty which transformed the pale, languid creature of the morning into this radiant woman.

They were married, and if love, many blessings, and all good gifts lavishly showered upon them could make them happy, then this young pair were truly blest. But even in the rapture of the moment that made her his, Forsyth observed how icy cold was the little hand he held, how feverish the deep color on the soft cheek he kissed, and what a strange fire burned in the tender eyes that looked so wistfully at him.

Blithe and beautiful as a spirit, the smiling bride played her part in all the festivities of that long evening, and when at last light, life and color began to fade, the loving eyes that watched her thought it but the natural weariness of the hour. As the last guest departed, Forsyth was met by a servant, who gave him a letter marked "Haste." Tearing it open, he read these lines, from a friend of the professor's:

"Dear Sir—Poor Niles died suddenly two days ago, while at the Scientific Club, and his last words were: 'Tell Paul Forsyth to beware of the Mummy's Curse, for this fatal flower has killed me.' The circumstances of his death were so peculiar, that I add them as a sequel to this message. For several months, as he told us, he had been watching an unknown plant, and that evening he brought us the flower to examine. Other matters of interest absorbed us till a late hour, and the plant was forgotten. The professor wore it in his buttonhole—a strange white, serpent-headed blossom, with pale glittering spots, which slowly changed to a glittering scarlet, till the leaves looked as if sprinkled with blood. It was observed that instead of the pallor and feebleness which had recently come over him, that the professor was unusually animated, and seemed in an almost unnatural state of high spirits. Near the close of the meeting, in the midst of a lively discussion, he suddenly dropped, as if smitten with apoplexy. He was conveyed home insensible, and after one lucid interval, in which he gave me the message I have recorded above, he died in great agony, raving of mummies, pyramids, serpents, and some fatal curse which had fallen upon him.

"After his death, livid scarlet spots, like those on the flower, appeared upon his skin, and he shriveled like a withered leaf. At my desire, the mysterious plant was examined, and pronounced by the best authority one of the most deadly poisons known to the Egyptian sorceresses. The plant slowly absorbs the vitality of whoever cultivates it, and the blossom, worn for two or three hours, produces either madness or death."

Down dropped the paper from Forsyth's hand; he read no further, but hurried back into the room where he had left his young wife. As if worn out with fatigue, she had thrown herself upon a couch, and lay there motionless, her face half-hidden by the light folds of the veil, which had blown over it.

"Evelyn, my dearest! Wake up and answer me. Did you wear that strange flower today?" whispered Forsyth, putting the misty screen away.

There was no need for her to answer, for there, gleaming spectrally on her bosom, was the evil blossom, its white petals spotted now with flecks of scarlet, vivid as drops of newly spilt blood.

But the unhappy bridegroom scarcely saw it, for the face above it appalled him by its utter vacancy. Drawn and pallid, as if with some wasting malady, the young face, so lovely an hour ago, lay before him aged and blighted by the baleful influence of the plant which had drunk up her life. No recognition in the eyes, no word upon the lips, no motion of the hand—only the faint breath, the fluttering pulse, and wide-opened eyes, betrayed that she was alive.

Alas for the young wife! The superstitious fear at which she had smiled had proved true: the curse that had bided its time for ages was fulfilled at last, and her own hand wrecked her happiness forever. Death in life was her doom, and for years Forsyth secluded himself to tend with pathetic devotion the pale ghost, who never, by word or look, could thank him for the love that outlived even such a fate as this.

THE MAN-EATING TREE*
Anonymous

* Each number we propose to give at least one of the famous stories that have drifted back into the past—and generally into oblivion. Thousands of readers want a copy of the Man-eating Tree. Mr. Edmund Spencer, the author of this story, was for some years a member of the staff of the New York World. See Editorial note.**

** It will be worth the while of those who read this gossip to turn to . . . the wonderful story of The Man-Eating Tree. It was written years ago by Mr. Edmund Spencer for the N. Y. World. While Mr. Spencer was connected with that paper he wrote a number of stories, all being remarkable for their appearance of truth, the extraordinary imagination displayed, and for their somber tone. Mr. Spencer was a master of the horrible, some of his stories approaching closely to those of Poe in this regard. Like many clever men his best work is hidden in the files of the daily press. This particular story of the Crinoida Dajeeana, the Devil Tree of Madagascar, was copied far and wide, and caused many a hunt for the works of Dr. Friedlowsky. It was written as the result of a talk with some friends, during which Mr. Spencer maintained that all that was necessary to produce a sensation of horror in the reader was to greatly exaggerate some well-known and perhaps beautiful thing. He then stated that he would show what could be done with the sensitive plant when this method of treatment was applied to it. The devil-tree is, after all, only a monstrous variety of the "Venus fly trap," so common in North Carolina. Mr. Spencer died about two years ago in Baltimore, Md. (*Current Opinion*, 1888)

In the last number of *Graefe and Walther's Magazine*, published at Carlsruhe, there is a letter in regard to the newly-discovered Crinoida Dajeeana, from the discoverer, Karl Leche, the eminent botanist, prefaced by some notes from Dr. Omelius Friedlowsky, whose deep research in vegetable physiology has had so many important results. Leche's letter, it appears, was originally addressed to Friedlowsky, and they seem to have been pursuing a subject of novel and startling interest, which is likely to give remarkable discoveries to science. Dr. Friedlowsky says:

My special and only motive for publishing prematurely the history of my friend Leche's half-developed discovery is similar to that which influenced Darwin to bring out his book on the origin of species. His theory was not near developed, but his title to priority in discovery was imperiled by the announcement of Mr. Wallace's researches in the Malayan Archipelago. Darwin himself, as well as some American botanists, have lately come so perilously near to the discovery of the problem Leche set himself to investigate, in their studies of drosera and sarracenia, that I think it is due to my friend's credit to make some preliminary announcement of the great progress he has already made towards establishing a point of contact of our organic systems with those of the universe at large through analysis of the constitution of some abnormal plants which have always hitherto puzzled the botanists. The point to which Karl Leche, at my suggestion, has been giving his attention latterly is briefly this: Certain plants, such as drosera (with its outlying species, dionea muscicapa), sarracenia, and some others, departing from the general law, instead of supplying food to animals turn the tables, capture them, and are themselves carnivorous. It has often occurred to me in connection with these insectivorous plants, so abnormal in their constitution, that they might have a widely different origin (or at least an origin widely different in point of time) from the common orders of plants inhabiting our globe, and that if I could establish the nature of this different origin upon reasonable grounds, I might at the same time afford a reasonable explanation at once of the origin and the primordial variations of life. When Leche went to Bombay in response to the call extended to him by the Medical College of that city, he went full of my ideas upon this vastly important subject, and prepared, as I advised him, to make special investigations into the habitats of all such abnormal plants as seem to depart from the characteristic traits of the flora of their respective countries. This I state here, because, while the theory is by no means far advanced, it was while in search of facts to countenance this theory that Leche discovered the remarkable and terrible Crinoida Dajeeana, of which his letter gives such a graphic and forcible description. After quite a long sojourn in India, Leche was induced to go to Madagascar by Dr. Bhawoo Dajee, the liberal-minded, intelligent Parsee physician of Bombay, who, indeed, supplied the means for the expedition, and made so many thoughtful provisions for my colleague's comfort as to win his gratitude and love. Dr. Dajee, it seems, represented to Leche that it was impossible to glean much in a field so carefully worked over by many botanists, and indeed almost exhausted by Hooker. When quite a young man Dr. Dajee had made a voyage to Madagascar in one of Sir Jamsetjee Jeejeebhoy's trading ships, and had been deeply impressed with the remarkably various and beautiful flora of that almost untraveled region. An excellent opportunity offered for going out in one of Cursetjee Jeejeebhoy's traders, which was to stop at Tamatave on her way to the Cape; so Leche embarked, attended by a Madagasy sailor for servant, Dr. Dajee having hired the fellow thinking he would be useful to Leche as guide and interpreter. That was more than two years ago. Since then I have received three letters from Leche— two by way of Bombay, one by way of the Cape—and now last week a fourth, which he had the luck to send by an Arabian trader to Zanzibar, whence it reached me via Aden. After writing of many other things Leche proceeded to say:

But I do not know how soon Seid ben Yalhamah may take a notion to sail, and I want to tell you about the remarkable tree which I have discovered, and which I have named in honor of my benefactor, Crinoida Dajeeana. About two weeks after my last letter to you I went from Tananarivo to a point in the mountains over against Mananzari, to visit a Christianized chief there who had sent me a great many messages. On the way thither my Madagasy servant deserted me, saying he did not want to be killed and eaten by Mkodos, a tribe of inhospitable savages of whom little was known, but who were supposed to dwell in the mountains further to the south, and to be cannibals. In Telliyimat's place I hired (when I reached the chieftain's village) a perfect treasure, in the shape of a Namaqua Caffre, named Henrick, who had fled Graham Town on account of some scrape, and after many wanderings found himself in the chief's retinue. Henrick—he is with me now—is a fearless and intelligent fellow, full of enterprise and spirit, a good hunter, and a most devoted, untiring, and unquestioning follower. I had taken him with me on several botanizing excursions, when he asked me why I did not go to visit the land of the Mkodos, where I would find a great number of curious plants, such as he had never seen elsewhere. I answered that they had the reputation of being inhospitable, cannibals, and all that, but he pooh-poohed the idea. He had been among them twice, he said, and had been well received, and he would guarantee me kind treatment among them. They got their bad name from being continually at war with the other tribes, and from successfully barring their country against all invaders. He then gave me an account of the country, and particularly of the strange plant I have spoken of above, and so excited my curiosity that I resolved to go thither at once, and accordingly, as we were tolerably well equipped, we set out over the mountains without returning to take leave of the chief, my entertainer. The country of Mkodos began about five days' journey from the point whence we started, and was a long valley sloping and descending towards the east and ingirt on three sides by rough, inaccessible mountains; on the fourth separated from the coast by jungles and morass. The approach to it was most arduous, over the crests of several sharp

mountain ridges, frowning with basaltic precipices. No sooner had
we come into the valley, however, than I felt the warm breath of
the Indian Ocean and saw its influence in the vegetation, which
grew rapidly more and more tropical, majestic, and colossal as we
descended. The valley had an average breadth of about thirty miles,
and was about 175 miles long, in the course of which it descended
over 3,000 feet. The Mkodos are a very primitive race, going entirely naked, having only faint vestiges of tribal relations, and no
religion beyond that of the awful reverence which they pay to the
sacred tree. They carry a javelin about six feet long, with which
they conquer the chetah and do not hesitate to encounter the formidable buffalo (bos caffer) that ranges the woody slopes and
savannahs of their country. They are also armed with a short bow
and a quiver of poisoned arrows. They dwell entirely in caves hol-
lowed out of the limestone rocks in their hills, and are one of the
smallest of races, the men seldom exceeding fifty-six inches in
height. Their country must be a very productive one, if I may judge
from the abundance of animal and vegetable life it contains. At
different elevations in the valley, during my short sojourn in it, I
noticed droves of antelopes (the klip-dos of the Cape), the chetah
(felis jubata), hyrax, manis pentadactyla, histrix cristala, and many
other animals, while the lower forests were full of a new species of
gigantic pteropi, which at night flew about as if the land belonged
to them. The variety and richness of the flora of this valley (the
Mkodos have no name for their country, calling it simply Mzemb,
the land,) may be inferred when I tell you that I saw and examined
species of all the palms (including umbraculifera, or tallipot, and
sagus rhumphil), and that among the plants growing commonly I
found acaciae, numerous equisetaceae, mimosae, goseypia, areca,
ricinus, rhamnus lotus, and nymphaea, coerulea, eupatoriae,
diosmata, salices, cassiae, juncus, solandra, aloes, spicata,
balsamodendum myrrha, croton tiglii, cucumis colocynthis,
etc., etc. I attribute this richness and variety to several causes—
the latitude, half tropical, half temperate, the variety of altitude,
and the warm, sultry, vapor-laden winds from the Indian Ocean,
which cause a vast rainfall. At the bottom of the valley (I had no

barometer, but should think it not over 400 feet above the level of the sea), and near its eastern extremity, we came to a deep tarn-like lake, about a mile in diameter, the sluggish oily waters of which overflowed into a tortuous reedy canal, that went unwillingly into the recesses of a black forest, jungle below, palm above. This lake was filled with alligators, and its jungled borders were the home of the chetah and a variety of venomous serpents. Great ferns bent over its margin, and its surface was spotted with leaves and flowers of the lotus. A path, diverging from its southern side, struck boldly for the heart of the forbidding and seemingly impenetrable forest. Henrick led the way along this path, I following closely, and behind me a curious rabble of Mkodos, men, women and children. After we were fairly in the forest, the shade overhead was so dense that the jungle and undergrowth almost disappeared, and instead there was a damp, boggy turf, cold, spongy, and yielding to the tread. The stalks of the tall trees rose like columns, the vines hanging down from them in festoons, and their roots running over the ground in every direction, making walking difficult. Suddenly all the natives began to cry, "Tepe! Tepe!" and Henrick, stopping short, said, "Look!" The sluggish canal-like stream here wound slowly by, and in a bare spot near its bend was the most singular of trees. I have called it crinoida, because when its leaves are in action it bears a striking resemblance to that well-known fossil the crinoid lily-stone, or St. Cuthbert's beads. It was now at rest, however, and I will try to describe it to you. If you can imagine a pineapple eight feet high, and thick in proportion, resting upon its base and denuded of leaves, you will have a good idea of the trunk of the tree, which, however, was not the color of an anana, but a dark, dingy brown, and apparently hard as iron. From the apex of this truncated cone (at least two feet in diameter) eight leaves hung sheer to the ground, like doors swung back on their hinges. These leaves, which were joined to the top of the tree at regular intervals, were about eleven or twelve feet long and shaped very much like the leaves of the American agave, or century plant. They were two feet through in their thickest part and three feet wide, tapering to a sharp point that looked like a cow's horn, very convex on the outer (but now under) surface, and on the inner (now upper) surface slightly concave. This concave face was thickly set with very strong thorny hooks, like those upon the head of the teazle. These leaves, hanging thus limp and lifeless, dead green in color, had in appearance the massive strength of oak fiber. The apex of the cone was a round, white, concave figure, like a smaller plate set within a larger one. This was not a flower but a receptacle, and there exuded into it a clear treacly liquid, honey sweet, and possessed of violent intoxicating and soporific properties. From underneath the rim (so to speak) of the undermost plate a series of long, hairy, green tendrils stretched out in every direction towards the horizon. These were seven or eight feet long each, and tapered from four inches to a half an inch in diameter, yet they stretched out stiffly as iron rods. Above these (from between the upper and under cup) six white, almost transparent palpi reared themselves towards the sky, twirling and twisting with a marvelous incessant motion, yet constantly reaching upwards. Thin as reeds, and frail as quills apparently, they were yet five or six feet tall, and were so constantly and vigorously in motion, with such a subtle, sinuous, silent throbbing against the air, that they made me shudder in spite of myself with their suggestion of serpents flayed, yet dancing on their tails. Here were not corolla, pistil, stamens, a flower, mind you, nor anything like it. For Crinoida, unknown, new species as it is, is nighest akin to the cycadaceae, and perhaps its exact prototype may be found among the fossil cycadae, though I confess I do not remember any one that presents all its peculiar features. The description I am giving you now is partly made up from a subsequent careful inspection of the plant. My observations on this occasion were suddenly interrupted by the natives, who had been shrieking around the tree in their shrill voices, and chanting what Henrick told me were propitiatory hymns to the great tree devil. With still wilder shrieks and chants they now surrounded one of the women, and urged her with the points of their javelins until slowly, and with despairing face, she climbed up the rough stalk of the tree and stood on the summit of the cone, the palpi twirling all about her. "Tsik! tsik!" (drink! drink!) cried the men, and, stooping, she drank of the viscid fluid in the cup, rising instantly again with wild frenzy in her face and convulsive chorea in her limbs. But she did not jump down, as she seemed to intend to do. Oh no! The atrocious cannibal tree that had been so inert and dead came to sudden, savage life. The slender, delicate palpi, with the fury of starved serpents, quivered a moment over her head, then, as if instinct with demoniac intelligence, fastened upon her in sudden coils round and round her neck and arms; then, while her awful screams, and yet more awful laughter, rose wilder to be instantly strangled down again into a gurgled moan, the tendrils, one after another, like great green serpents, with brutal energy and infernal rapidity rose, retracted themselves, and wrapped her about in fold after fold, ever tightening, with the cruel swiftness and savage tenacity of anacondas fastening upon their prey. It was the barbarity of the Laocoon without its beauty—this strange, horrible murder. And now the great leaves rose slowly and stiffly, like the arms of a derrick, erected themselves in the air, approached one another, and closed about the dead and hampered victim with the silent force of a hydraulic press, and the ruthless purpose of a thumbscrew. A moment more, and, while I could see the base of these great levers pressing more tightly towards each other, from their interstices there trickled down the stalk of the tree great steams of the viscid, honey-like fluid, mingled horridly with the blood and oozing viscera of the victim. At sight of this the savage hordes around me, yelling madly, bounded forward, crowded to the tree, clasped it, and with cups, leaves, hands and tongues, got each enough of the liquor to send him mad and frantic. Then ensued a grotesque and indescribably hideous orgie, from which, even while its convulsive madness was turning rapidly into delirium and insensibility, Henrick dragged me hurriedly away into the recesses of the forest, hiding me from the dangerous brutes, and the brutes from me. May I never see such a sight again! Seid ben Yalhamah says he will go aboard his ship in half an hour and sail, so I must be brief. In the course of my stay in the valley of twenty-one days, I saw six other specimens of the Crinoida Dajeeana, but none so large as this which the Mkodos worshipped. I discovered that they are unquestionably carnivorous, in the same sense that dionea and drosera are insectivorous. The retracted leaves of the great tree kept their upright position during ten days, then, when I came again one morning, they were prone again, the tendrils stretched, the palpi floating, and nothing but a white skull at the foot of the tree to remind me of the sacrifice that had taken place there. I climbed into a neighboring tree and saw that all trace of the victim had disappeared, and the cup was again supplied with the viscid fluid. The indescribable rapidity and energy of its movements may be inferred from the fact that I saw a smaller one seize, capture and destroy an active little lemur, which, dropping by accident upon it while watching and grinning at me, in vain endeavored to escape from the fatal toils. With Henrick's assistance and the consent of some of the head men of the Mkodos (who, however, did not dare to stay to witness the act of sacrilege), I cut down one of the minor trees and dissected it carefully. Seid, however, is waiting for me, and I must defer to my next the details of this most interesting examination.

Karl Leche.

In this tantalizing fashion, after some private matters and messages, does Leche's letter end. I have been expecting his next with the utmost impatience, and will communicate its contents to you as soon as received.

Dr. Omelius Friedlowsky.

THE DEVIL TREE

Anonymous

If it were possible for you to go to the lonely and untrodden summit of Mount R—, in the State of New —, you would find there, amid the rude surroundings of rocks and bushes of stunted growth, the black and charred stump of a tree; by its side you would discern a plain marble slab resembling the headstone of a grave on which is carved an inscription: "In memory of Elinor, wife of Herbert Ainslie. Wait."

The explanation for this may be found in the statement of Herbert Ainslie, written by himself and addressed to a friend, with the request accompanying it to give it to the world after a certain number of years should have passed away.

Those who knew Ainslie in life, and whose eyes may fall on these lines, will agree with me that a more gentle and more amiable man by nature than he never lived; and if circumstances developed in him a morbid spirit of vengeance, that possibly may shock those who read of it, let the story of his wrongs, as set forth by him, vindicate his memory.

The statement is also interesting in this—that it throws a flood of light on an event that was an absorbing topic of conversation some forty years ago, and gives a startling answer to a question that was at one time on so many lips—to wit:

"What became of Paul Leonardo?"

And now for the narrative.

I

When I came to live at Mount R—, on the little farm that I had bought as a refuge from the world of society, of which I was heartily weary, no man could have been happier than I.

Elinor, my wife, whom I had just married, seemed contented with our little hermitage, and, although we had but few friends or near neighbors, we managed to find sufficient entertainment and pastime in our respective chosen employments—she in attending to her household duties, her little flower-garden and her stock of pet poultry, and I with my books and in giving free scope to my passion as naturalist.

The chief care of the farm I left to an intelligent hired man. And thus it was that, with a mind absolved from care, I spent the first three years of my residence at Mount R—, living the life of a lover of Nature in her various guises.

It was my delight to roam the woods that covered the slopes of the mountain with verdure, and to wander through the valleys in search of plants that possessed for me the charm of novelty, or of wild-flowers and shining insects. Sometimes, when a bird of peculiarly bright plumage crossed my path, I would shoot it—but, I confess, with many qualms of conscience—for the sake of its brilliant feathery coat.

How often did I spend the whole day in delving into the sequestered nooks of the mountain-side, or loitering on the banks of a rivulet whose clear, limpid waters babbled over yellow sands, now in shadow, now in sunshine, through the odorous and flower-carpeted valley!

How often, returning home with the product of my day's explorations, would I find her sitting on the little veranda of the house, watching for me in pleasant anticipation.

In those days our life was one long honeymoon. Elinor knew little of the excitements of city existence, and her shy, timid nature, which had been molded by village experiences, seemed to have no cravings or aspirations that my love and companionship failed to satisfy. Would to heaven that I could have remained in this delusion until the end of my days, for then— But no matter.

One day, in my expeditions in search of plants, I determined to ascend, if possible, to the extreme summit of the mountain. With my glass I could see from the veranda of the house that this summit consisted of an extensive plateau, somewhat oblong in shape and with lofty perpendicular sides resembling a wall.

The general appearance of the plateau was that of a vast natural fortress. From its centre rose a small solitary tree. I had been told by the people of the vicinity that no human foot, within the memory of living man, ever had trod the summit of Mount R—, for the simple reason that it was inaccessible. This report only increased my ardor, and in my purpose I felt fired with something of the noble inspiration of the discoverer of unknown lands and seas.

Shouldering my gun, and with the basket in which I usually carried my flowers and plants and my spy-glass slung over my shoulder, I set out on my journey.

After an hour's walk, I reached the limit of my previous ascent of the mountain. I found the walls of the plateau fully one hundred feet high. They were composed of grass-grown earth and rock combined, and seemed, indeed, to defy any attempt to scale them.

During the ascent I had caught occasional glimpses through the foliage of the lonely tree that rose above the plateau, but as I went higher and higher it gradually disappeared from my sight.

Wearied out with the endeavor to find some part of the walls that might admit of ascent, I sat down, and casting my gaze around one-half of the horizon, I took in the glorious picture of the world that lay so far beneath me. With my glass I swept the prospect for more than sixty miles. But I turned at last from the inspection of these remote objects to the little cottage that contained Elinor. Once I caught sight of her face at the window—only for a moment. She came like a vision, and like a vision passed away. Her face was turned in the direction of the mountain-top, and I fancied that she was looking for me.

After a while I turned my gaze to the ground at my feet, and then I noticed, for the first time, that near me, and high up along the sides of the plateau was a multitude of tiny flowers with cruciform leaves and of a vivid crimson hue. They grew close to the earth, as if clinging to it, and dotted the space around as with drops of blood.

I gathered a number of them and examined them. Nowhere had I ever seen a specimen of them, nor could I recall any written description of them. I put a few in my basket, and as the hour was growing late I returned home.

I found Elinor in the parlor reading. I told her of the plateau and of the discovery of the rare flower.

"Has it any fragrance?" she asked, taking one from the basket and inhaling its odor. Suddenly her face became as white as the page of the book on her lap, the flower fell from her hand, and her head dropped on her shoulder. She had fainted.

In a few minutes, under my affectionate ministrations, she had recovered her consciousness.

"What ails you, Elinor?" I asked, as she sat with her head resting on my breast.

"That flower!" she exclaimed. "It troubles me!"

"Troubles you? Why, in what way?"

She smiled sadly. "I do not know why, Herbert," she replied. "I can not explain to you how its smell affected me. It seemed to me—"

She shuddered, turned her face aside and motioned with her hand. I understood her, and with a laugh I rose from my seat, kissed her and carried the basket into the next room. When I returned I said to her:

"If these flowers are offensive to you, Elinor, I shall not ask you to assist me in preserving them."

Another shiver passed through her frame and she looked at me mutely, as if imploring me not to be angry with her. I kissed her again and told her to think no more of it, that it was only a fancy of hers in which her imagination had deceived her.

From that day forth I never spoke to her of the mysterious flower that I had found on the mountain. She, I think, rather avoided the subject, and in the course of time, as she never referred to her sickness, the incident of her temporary indisposition passed from my mind. In after years I recalled it vividly; but I must not anticipate.

II

In pursuance of my purpose to discover a means of reaching the plateau if possible, I many times visited the spot. But I soon became convinced that success could be obtained only by means of a long ladder, as climbing the almost vertical walls was out of the question.

After every successive visit I was more impressed with the truth of what the people around me had told me: the summit of Mount R— was inaccessible by any ordinary mode of ascent.

In default of a closer knowledge of the tree that grew there, I spent many hours in looking at it through the glass. In this way I familiarized myself with its appearance. Unlike other trees, it seemed to bear no leaves. I can best describe it as resembling a weeping-willow denuded of its foliage.

Once I noticed a crow flying low over the mountain. It reached a point just above the tree and almost touching it, when suddenly (I was watching it through the glass at the moment), it seemed to drop, as if shot, among the branches. For a few minutes the tree seemed to be in a state of violent agitation. I waited for some sign of the bird, but though I kept my gaze fixed on the tree, I saw it no more.

I have intimated elsewhere in this narrative that my life at Mount R— for three years was one of unalloyed happiness. Yes, just three years!

But the end of this felicity was approaching. How the change came that transformed the paradise of my home into a desert I am now about to relate.

A visitor had come from the city—a schoolmate and friend of Elinor's, who had married and who now resided in town. Naturally enough, during her month's stay with us, she frequently spoke of the pleasures of city-life, with its varieties, its excitements and its daily round of amusements. I saw that Elinor was visibly affected by these recitals, and when, in her artless revelations of her most secret thoughts, she would repeat to me what had been told her, and sigh at the contrast presented by our uneventful existence at Mount R—, I understood only too well that our Eden was an Eden no longer.

What I had anticipated, indeed feared, came to pass.

This was a proposition from the visitor that Elinor should accompany her on her return to her city home and be her guest there as she had been Elinor's. When the plan was broached to me there was no good reason why I should withhold my consent.

"Do as you please," I said to Elinor. "If you desire to accept this invitation, consult your own wishes."

She decided to accompany her friend only for a week or two, she said. I made no opposition, for I was pleased at the thought that she should enjoy herself.

I went with them to the city, and, after a stay of a day, I returned to Mount R— and to my books and my communions with nature.

Elinor's letters to me were full of the new and, to her, intoxicating life that she led in the city. Her friend was a rich and fashionable woman, and the season was at its height, and thus, from the monotonous existence of a secluded farmhouse, she found herself in the feverish whirl of a gayety and license to which she had been unaccustomed.

The two weeks had lengthened into six weeks, and the time approached when Elinor was definitely to return home; but she wrote, saying that her friend insisted that she should remain a month longer.

Always ready to sacrifice my own wishes to secure her happiness, I consented, although I could not refrain from adding to my consent an affectionate reproach for her willingness to postpone the hour of our meeting. She replied in a spirit of vexatiousness and although I smiled at the pique she exhibited, still her letter troubled me, for the tone of it was unlike herself.

Her subsequent letters—which were less regular than of yore—did not serve to lessen my anxiety, for there was a reserve and coldness in them that at times amounted, it seemed to me, to indifference.

Alarmed at this change, but far from suspecting the truth, I wrote to her to prepare for her return, as I should be in the city by a given day.

Before that day came a letter from her reached me which filled my soul with darkness. This was the letter—and when I had read it I fell prone on the floor, lost to life and consciousness:

"Do not come for me, for when you shall read these lines I shall be far away never to see you again. I sometimes think I am mad, for how else could I leave *you* to follow a destiny that drags me along with it—I know not whither! Oh, Herbert, you were so good to me! I do not dare to ask you even to forget me; but if you only could forget me—if I only could feel that henceforth you will cease to remember your unworthy Elinor."

III

I must hurry over this turning-point in my life—this prelude to a new existence in which I ceased to recognize myself.

I repaired at once to the city and went to the house of Elinor's friend. The first question put to me as I entered the parlor satisfied me that Elinor's flight was unsuspected.

"How did you leave Elinor?"

"Well," I answered almost mechanically.

"When your letter came four days ago she packed her things and departed. She said she must return home."

I did not reveal the truth. The duty before me was to obtain, if possible, some clew to the name of the companion of Elinor's flight.

But to do this caution was necessary, for my hope—alas! the only hope left to me in the world—was to keep my misfortune from the knowledge of men.

With feelings that I restrained with difficulty, I listened for an hour to praises of Elinor—praise of her beauty, of her innocence, of the attractive artlessness of her nature.

As her friend prattled on these themes, with scarcely a minute's intermission. I could have seized her by her handsome shoulders and shaken her, and cried, in tones that would, have raised the street: "Enough of this. But what of *him?* Give me his name, or I shall strangle you!"

But, spent as I was with this dreadful mental struggle, I managed to preserve a cool exterior, and by degrees, I came to know all that could be told me of Elinor's special acquaintances and visitors.

Even with this knowledge, however, I was as ignorant as before. There was nothing revealed to clear up the mystery. So far as the world was aware, her conduct had been irreproachable. It was only I who knew. I went away from the house in a blindness of the soul that caused me to stagger and grope through the night like one who walks in darkness.

Artless and innocent! The words chased each other through my brain until they lost all meaning.

The next morning found me calm—yes, calm—for my heart was dead. In those long hours of suffering I passed from life to an apathy as of death. I no longer felt the swelling in the throat that tears, could I have shed them hours before, might have relieved; the pain in the heart had vanished; the fever in my blood had disappeared; the heavy sighs had ceased.

Wonderful transformation, indeed! I had forgotten the memory of my grief. I lived only for vengeance!

Elinor had planned well. Not one of her acquaintances believed but that she had left the city to return to Mount R—. I fancied that her accomplice had been equally prudent. But their caution and secrecy placed an almost insurmountable obstacle in the path in my effort to trace them. Finally, despairing of obtaining any clew through my own exertions. I took into my confidence one of those men whose business it is to follow stealthily suspected or criminal humanity, and opened my heart to him.

Spurred to energy by the promise of a large reward, this worthy man entered with an almost brotherly interest, and in ways that were almost preternatural sought for the pair, but without success.

Then I returned to Mount R—, broke up my establishment there, after writing to my friends in the city that I had removed to a distant State, and started out on a tour of inspection of the different cities of the country.

Months passed, and still no trace of the fugitives. The anniversary of Elinor's disappearance finally came to renew somewhat the recollections of a year before. I had returned to the farm and was living the life of a recluse, shut out from all the world.

When this day of days dawned. I rose early and wandered purposelessly from the house. The night found me still abroad, looking up into the starry skies and dreaming of the hour that should bring with it vengeance. As I gazed into space and weaved the thread of the destiny of that unknown man, I felt exalted above mere humanity. I experienced a strange sense of power for life or for death as I saw him, in a vague vision of retribution, struggling in the toils that I was preparing for him.

I knew that Fate would prove kind to me in my mission, and the thought of how her unerring hand was on my side gave me hope and strength and encouragement.

One day, not long after this, a sudden impulse seized on me to leave my native land. In my hours of solitary musings I often heard a voice that whispered consolation in my ear. It was this voice that had first taught me the meaning of the word "Wait!" that said to me in the stillness of the midnight:

"Cross the ocean; it will be some relief to you. Perhaps you may find them."

I obeyed the injunction. In a week I was on the wide sea, nearing a foreign shore. I visited every country of Europe, peering on the streets into the faces of the passers-by, and scrutinizing the countenances of all handsome women whom I found gathered at hotels and watering-places, and in great public assemblages; but no Elinor.

I left Europe and journeyed into Asia. But do not think that I was weary. Miles were to me but as inches; distance was dwarfed to the dimensions of a mere span. I felt, indeed, as one who held the globe in the grasp of his hand. Time and space diminished into nothingness as I contemplated them through the eyes of vengeance.

I was in Calcutta. In the public mart I stopped to look into a little shop, the contents of which proclaimed its owner, like myself, a lover of nature. The spectacle, in the dingy interior, of a multitude of rare plants, some in bloom, and others dried or embalmed and preserved under glass, awoke in me feelings that long had lain dormant. Mechanically, as it were, I entered the shop and greeted the proprietor—a German, with venerable white beard, and wearing a smoking-cap and a well-worn dressing-gown of figured silk. As I spoke to him, he returned the salutation courteously and asked me to be seated; then, forgetting for a moment my mission in life, I talked of flowers.

Suddenly I remembered that in my pocketbook was one of the blood red flowers I had found growing near the plateau. It was the flower that had dropped from Elinor's hand when its odor had deprived her of consciousness.

"Sir," I said, "you seem to be familiar with every variety of plant. Can you tell me the name of this flower?"

It was still as I had found it—vivid in color, and with its cross-shaped leaves as fresh, apparently, as when I had plucked it from its stem.

He was a very old man, and his hand trembled as he held the flower to the light, the better to inspect it through his spectacles. When he spoke his voice was husky with some bidden emotion.

"The *Sanguis Christi!*" he gasped. "Where did you obtain it?"

"Ten thousand miles from here," I replied. "What of it?"

He seemed lost in thought, as his gaze continued fastened on the tiny flower.

"It is the miracle-flower," he murmured at last. "It is mentioned in the writings of the early Fathers. It is spoken of in the miracle plays and in the mystical chronicles of the Middle Ages. It is the miracle-flower of Merlin, the magician."

"My dear sir," I expostulated, "spare me these musty traditions. Tell me, I pray you, what mysterious virtue lies in it that its odor, simply, should cause a young, beautiful and innocent woman to faint?"

He looked at me in surprise and shook his head.

"I do not understand the meaning of what you say," he replied; then, lowering his voice, he added, "have you never heard, then—"

"I have heard nothing. You call this flower the *Sanguis Christi.* What more?"

"For more than a thousand years it has been sought in vain. Where it grows, and only where it grows, is to be found the *Arbor Diaboli*—the Devil Tree of tradition."

"The Devil Tree!"

He inclined his head reverentially.

"Look," he said, as he drew from a small iron chest at his feet a bag of gold. "This, and as much again, shall be yours if you will but confide to me where this flower grows. To know this is to have greater power than the possession of the philosopher's stone could confer; it is to know all things."

"Pardon, my good sir!" I exclaimed. "I have this knowledge, and yet, to be frank with you, I am only too ignorant on a subject which concerns me nearly. But what of this tree, which is to be found only where this flower grows?"

"The *Sanguis Christi* flower is the guide, as it were, to it. It is the terrible vampire-tree, and its clasp is death to any living thing that may approach it."

"One more question. Is it a small tree, with bare branches which curve downward like the ribs of an open umbrella?"

"Yes; you have seen it, then? It covets solitude and isolation. Only three have been known in the world's history—one on the Himalayas, another on the Atlas Mountains, and the third—"

I rose vehemently. The old man's voice sounded faint and far, and I no longer heard what he said, for I was thinking of the lonely tree on the plateau of Mount R—, of the crow that had dropped into its branches, of the flower which grew near it and which had so powerfully affected Elinor, and of that watchful guidance of kindly Fate which had brought me over so many leagues of land and sea to this man's door.

Before my companion could recover from his astonishment, I bowed hastily to him and departed, leaving him staring at vacancy, with his hand clasping his bag of gold. I had but one thought in my mind, and that was to return to Mount R— at once, and to attain to its summit at all hazards.

IV

The journey was a long one, but the distance was shortened by the thoughts that went with me. I reached Mount R— at last, and the day after my arrival I went for the twentieth time to the top of the mountain. There, as before, I saw springing around me the mysterious flower, with its crimson petals and its cross-shaped leaves, and I knew that the tree of death was not far away. You who read this narrative have already solved my secret and have detected my purpose to make this tree the instrument of my anticipated vengeance. You are right.

I walked slowly around the sides of the plateau, looking carefully for some spot, less steep than the rest, by which to climb to the summit. Then I saw what never had attracted my notice during my frequent investigations—a hole, nearly concealed from view by a bush, and the sides of which seemed well-worn as by the feet of animals. I put my face to it and looked in. Something like a cavern, the floor of which had an upward tendency, met my sight, and I felt a current of fresh air blowing on me, with a dry earthy smell. Evidently there was another opening somewhere; where could it be but at the very summit?

Satisfied that day with my discovery. I returned to the house.

The next morning, provided with a lantern and with half a dozen fowls tied up in a bag, I again ascended the mountain to the mouth of the cave. Digging away enough of the earth from the aperture to enable me to enter the subterranean chamber. I moved forward slowly, holding my lighted lantern in front. As I went on upward the cavern widened, until at last I saw the glimmer of daylight about two hundred feet in advance.

My progress was unimpeded by any obstacle, for the ascent was as gradual as that by a path on the hillside, and a few minutes later I breathed the air of the summit of the mountain, looking out cautiously lest I should emerge within reach of the fatal arms of the Devil Tree. The examination showed me, however, that it was safely on the far end of the summit.

"Ah!" I said, addressing it, as if it possessed life and intelligence; "you are starving! Wait, you shall have rare feasting some day!" It seemed to understand me, for its flexible branches swept the air with a low, hissing sound.

I approached it, but not so closely as not to keep beyond the reach of its arms. It was low in size, not more than twenty feet high, but it covered a great area. Its trunk was of prodigious thickness, knotted with age and covered with a scale-like bark. From the top of this trunk, a few feet from the ground, its slimy branches provided with suckers, and resembling the tentacles of the octopus, curved upward and downward, nearly touching the ground with their tapering tips. Its appearance was that of a gigantic tarantula awaiting its prey.

I looked at its roots. A strange spectacle met my gaze. The ground under it and for twenty feet around it in every direction was dotted with bones and skeletons, bleached to a ghostly whiteness. They were the bones of birds, serpents and quadrupeds. The size of some of the latter seemed to proclaim them the remains of bears and panthers and foxes. Here and there were the skeletons of large birds and rabbits, with tufts of feathers or of fur still clinging to them.

The tree was famishing, as I could plainly see, and I tossed to it the fowls that I had brought with me. In a moment its restless motions changed to a furious agitation. Almost before I could realize the fact, it had twined and twisted its snake-like arms about the fowls until they disappeared in their mazes. I could hear the crushing of bones and the stifled cries of the hapless birds; then all was silent.

In a half-hour the flattened, bloody carcasses dropped one by one to the ground; the gorged branches slowly drooped to their former position, and the tree gave no sign of animation. Its hunger was satisfied, and I knew now that it was harmless.

I made bold to walk up to it, and even take one of its branches in my hand. I saw how the blood of the fowls had been absorbed through the spongy substance of its suckers, leaving crimson stains on the green surface.

Its quiescence encouraged me, and I sat on the ground beneath it for a long time, giving rein to my bitter fancies, and wondering if the day was near when I should see my enemy clasped in its piti-less embrace.

When the shadows began to fall in the dewy valley I rose to go. The stars shone clear and bright as I dragged my reluctant feet across the veranda of my lonely dwelling.

My hand was on the door knob, and I was about to enter the little hall, but a sound of sobbing in the corner of the veranda caused me to pause. For a moment I imagined it was a memory, but quickly turning, I saw Elinor knelt down, her head in her hands. I bent and turned her face so as to look into it.

That face that I had once so loved, and which had been to me the most beautiful in the world, was now pinched and wan and wasted. She spoke in the pauses of her tears, looking at me with appealing eyes.

"I won't trouble you long, Herbert. Pity me and let me die near you."

I have told you that my heart was dead, but can you kill memory altogether? For a moment a torrent of old memories rushed over me, filling my eyes with tears; but I remembered that my revenge was still unaccomplished, and I grew strong again.

"His name?" I exclaimed.

She lifted her clasped hands.

"Oh. Herbert!" she cried, "try to forget your sorrow. When I am dead, forgive me."

"Woman! his name?"

She looked about her for an instant with a stare of insanity. Then she fell senseless at my feet with the cry of "Paul Leonardo!"

I repeated the words mechanically. I had heard of the man—it was enough!

I took her in my arms and carried her to the room that once had been hers. When the light from the lamp fell on her face, I understood the meaning of her declaration that she had come to me to die.

Poor Elinor! I hope that her closing hour was peaceful. She assured me that she died contented because I had forgiven her. Remorse and penitence—these were the words that were ever on her lips. She endeavored to make a general confession, but I would hear nothing. She would have turned in my heart the dagger she had planted there.

I left her for a moment just before she died. When I returned to the room her sightless eyes were fixed on the door. She was looking for me! Her white lips wore a smile, and the kiss that I had refused to the living woman I pressed on the eyes and lips of the dead.

I went so far, indeed, as to cry aloud in my loneliness, "Oh, Elinor!—oh, my darling!" But do not think strangely of me. I addressed only a memory—a something sweet and tender and innocent that had once been.

Her body I conveyed to her native village and surrendered to her family; and under the Devil Tree—the skeletons there having been removed—I placed a marble stone bearing this inscription:

"In memory of Elinor, wife of Herbert Ainslie. Wait."

Within six months of the day on which I placed this memorial in the keeping of the Devil Tree, I had become, under the assumed name of Parker, the boon companion of Paul Leonardo.

It was touching to note our intimacy. He was a talkative fellow in his cups, especially on the subject of his conquests: and you can readily understand how much he annoyed me with his vain-glorious attempts to introduce, among others, the name of Elinor in his graphic conversations.

After one particularly descriptive jest about my wife, I could have murdered him on the spot with more zest; but I did not wish to take his life with my own hand, and so I refrained.

One day (I was on my way to take the train for Mount R—), I said to him:

"You have nothing to do. Come and spend to-morrow with me at my house at Mount R—. We shall wait on ourselves, for I have no servant."

"Mount R—!" he replied, speaking hesitatingly. "Is not that the place where one Herbert Ainslie lives?"

"Ainslie—Ainslie!" I said, as if trying to remember. "Oh, yes! A man of that name—a harmless sort of a fool, whose wife ran away

from him lived near there a couple of years ago, I believe. He removed to the Far West, they say."

His face brightened—I was observing him closely—and, after a
few moments of thought, he answered:

"I suppose I can go up for a day. When shall we start?"

"In half an hour. We are on our way to the train."

"But they will not know at my boarding-house what has become
of me. However, no matter; it is only for a day."

"Only for a day," I repeated.

I thought of the eternity of time that lay between him and the
familiar faces of those who should wait for him and wonder at his
absence.

Before ten hours had passed he was under my roof at Mount R—.

I had not forgotten to bring with me a large hamper, containing all that was necessary to provide us with meals. Especially had
I been careful to include in its contents several bottles of the heady
wine of Burgundy, which I knew from experience Leonardo affected
above all others.

As we entered the house the moon, large and round and sol-
emn, rose above the eastern hills, and shed a flood of rosy light on
Mount R—.

Leonardo stood at the window, as *she* often had stood, and
through the spy-glass inspected the towering form of the mountain. Behind him, in the shadow, was Nemesis.

"Beautiful! Enchanting!" he murmured.

"We will visit the summit to-morrow. We will take luncheon
with us and spend the day there. The ascent is quite romantic, I
assure you. You must pass through a cavern to reach the top."

"Indeed! How strange!"

The hour of noon of the next day found us seated on the top of
the plateau, in the shade of a rock, with our luncheon spread out
before us. For myself, I ate and drank little, pleading a headache
as an excuse. But I plied my dear friend liberally with the Burgundy that I had brought with me in the basket, and as he was
nothing loath to accede to my frequent fillings of his glass, he soon
became merry and hilarious.

I left him with a bottle in one hand and his glass in the other, singing a bacchanal song, while I went to look at the Devil Tree.

I found it as I had anticipated—for it had been starving for a long time—uneasy and tossing its branches eagerly to and fro.

"Patience!" I said to it, in an encouraging tone. "A banquet awaits you!"

Then I returned to Leonardo.

"If you were told," I said to him, almost abruptly, "that a woman lies buried on this lonely mountain top, what would you say?"

He laughed a maudlin laugh.

"What would I say?" he exclaimed. "Why, that she is probably as near to heaven as she'll ever get."

You would have supposed that I was convulsed with the humor of the thing could you have heard the immoderate laughter with which I greeted this sally.

I took him by the arm, partly to steady him, and led him toward the tree. We reached it. Of course his suffused eyes were blind to the weird, swaying motion of its branches.

"Where is this grave?" he said looking vaguely around him.

"There!"

As I spoke I pointed to the slab. He stumbled toward it, and, with a comical start, cried out "Elinor!"

It was then that the tree took him.

I never shall forget the look of drunken amazement and the agony and despair that distorted his countenance as he turned to me and cried, in stifled groans:

"Help! Save me!—save me!"

"Know me as I am, Paul Leonardo!" I shouted, in answer. "I am Herbert Ainslie, the husband of Elinor Ainslie! There is no hope for you, for the embrace of the Devil Tree is death!"

I saw the face of the doomed wretch grow black as a thundercloud; I heard— But why linger over the painful scene? My nature was not naturally cruel, and so I turned aside and walked slowly to the mouth of the cavern on my way down the mountain.

A year later I sought the spot for the first time since the day of sacrifice. Leonardo's bones lay where they had dropped, with the clothing, or what was left of it, grotesquely covering the skeleton, and giving to it a false air of life.

I supplied the tree with food, and then, when it was gorged, I piled wood about it and fired it. Before I left the scene only the charred trunk and a few calcined bones remained. The Devil Tree had accomplished its mission.

Before descending the mountain I closed the lower aperture of the cavern with stones, packing the earth around them so as to conceal it from all detection. I defy any human eye to find the portal that leads to the secret of the plateau!

CARNIVORINE

Lucy H. Hooper

When I, Ellis Graham, being a man of middle age, means, and leisure, determined upon starting, last autumn, for Rome, with a view to studying up the localities for my projected history of the Cenci family, I never expected assuredly that a momentous and important task, regarding other people's affairs and not my own, should be imposed upon me. Yet I could not well refuse the mission. I had known the Lambert family for many years, and had always cherished a warm friendship for Mr. and Mrs. Lambert—a friendship which, after the demise of the former, I had continued to his widow. And Julius, the elder son, had been quite a favorite of mine in his boyish days, though I could not altogether sympathize with his craze for scientific pursuits, and especially for botany. It must be confessed, however, that his researches into the formation and functions of the vegetable kingdom had led to some curious discoveries. But these discoveries had only served to arouse in his mind, as he grew to manhood, a wild ambition for further successes in the same line. I never exactly comprehended what course his investigations had taken, but I knew he was deeply interested in the Darwinian theories, and had set himself, in that connection, some inscrutable problem that he was trying to make out. He lived such a secluded life, shut up with his plants and his theories, that I had wholly lost sight of him for some years, though my visits to Mrs. Lambert were still continued.

I was a good deal surprised, however, on the eve of my departure for Europe, to receive from my old friend a few hurried lines,

73

begging that I would call to see her before I left and fixing the very next evening for my visit. I responded to the appeal, and found the usually serene and dignified lady in a state of unwonted emotion.

"I have sent for you, dear Mr. Graham," she said, "to ask if you will undertake for me a very important mission. It is hardly right, I know, for me to make such a request of you, involving, as your consent will surely do, a good deal of trouble and the loss of a considerable portion of your time. But my peace of mind is at stake, and I do not know what else to do if you are not willing to help me."

"Anything that is in my power to execute, dear Mrs. Lambert, I will gladly undertake," I answered. And, indeed, I was so much moved by her distress and by noticing the traces left upon her still fair features by wearing anxiety, that I was ready to promise anything or to undertake anything in her behalf.

"I want you to find Julius for me."

"Julius? Is he absent from home? I did not even know that he had gone away."

"Yes; he sailed for Europe three years ago. You know, his uncle left him a handsome fortune a little before that time, and he went abroad—to pursue, as he stated, his scientific experiments. I know that he believed himself to be on the verge of a great discovery; but, of what nature that discovery was, he never would reveal, even to me. As you may remember, I have never sympathized with him in his studies, so I suppose he did not consider me worthy of his confidence. Perhaps I did wrong. Maybe, if I had interested myself more in his pursuits, he would not have left me as he has done. He told me, before he went away, that his experiments must be perfected in thorough seclusion, and that he never meant to relinquish them till he had arrived at some great result. We heard from him, afterward, at Paris, and, later on, at Milan; but he has not written to his brothers or to me for months."

"Have you no idea as to his whereabouts at present?"

"I have reason to think that he has taken up his abode somewhere in the neighborhood of Rome. He was seen there, two winters ago, by Alan Spencer, the artist—who had quite a talk with him, but who could find out nothing from him respecting his residence or his pursuits."

"Did he seem well?"

"He looked tired and haggard, Mr. Spencer said, but was otherwise well. The reason for my anxiety is—is—well, I may as well confess it to you at once: I fear that there is some entanglement in the case—a passion for some woman, who may entrap Julius into matrimony."

"And have you any foundation for this dread?"

"Only this: he let fall something to Mr. Spencer about a personage called Carnivorine."

"What an extraordinary name! Did he give his friend any information concerning her?"

"No. He was singularly reticent on the subject, and seemed really distressed at having let even her name slip out unawares. He requested Mr. Spencer never to mention it; but Alan has always been on very intimate terms with Richard and Maude, and, seeing how uneasy we were at Julius's long silence, he did not hesitate, not having made any promise of secrecy, to tell us the little that he knew. So, when you reach Rome, if you will try to find our lost Julius for us, I shall be more indebted to yon than I can well tell you."

I promised to do my best, and Mrs. Lambert, visibly relieved, added some details about her son's banker in Rome and also respecting the few persons that he knew in that city, and who might have learned something concerning him during the last few months. Also, she gave me the name and address of the herbalist before whose door—and, indeed, issuing from it—Alan Spencer had met Julius in such an unexpected fashion.

"You will write to me as soon as you have any news," she said, wistfully, to me, at parting. "And, above all, let me know everything you can find out about Carnivorine. Do not hesitate to tell me the worst—even if Julius has married this creature with the singular name."

I must confess that, when I first arrived in Rome, so many personal interests claimed me that I did not at once begin my search for Julius Lambert, as I had intended to do. There were so many of my old friends and old haunts to revisit, and such numbers of new and interesting statues in the studios of the Roman sculptors, both native and foreign, to go to see, and my negotiations with the artists who were to execute the illustrations for my history of the Cenci family took up so much time, that the weeks insensibly slipped away before I had taken any steps in the matter. I had had the time to receive more than one letter from Mrs. Lambert on the subject before I commenced my investigations. I must acknowledge that I had come to the conclusion that the mystery, on investigation, would prove to be no mystery at all, and that Julius would be discovered in one of the minor hotels in Rome—too busy, or perhaps too much in love, to write. But, when I did finally set out in search of him, I found myself baffled at the very outset by an impenetrable wall of mystery. Nobody had seen him, and nobody knew anything about him. He had drawn all his funds from the banker's on his first arrival in the city. He had been in Rome some two years before, and had bought a collection of the curious insect-eating plants of South America from the old herbalist at whose door Alan Spencer had met him. That was all. If the earth had opened beneath his feet and had swallowed him up, he could not have vanished more utterly from human ken. I sought for him in every direction. I employed the services of a private detective. I offered a reward for any news of him. All was of no use. I succeeded in learning that he had not left Rome—and that was all I could find out.

Some months had elapsed, and I had pretty much abandoned the search in despair, when one day the fancy took me to go on a ride on horseback over the Campagna. I had long cherished the desire to explore the less frequented and scarcely known districts of that vast region, haunted by malaria and tenanted only by a few fever-stricken shepherds, that lies outside the beaten track of tourists and travelers beyond the city walls. As may be imagined, I found my excursion rather dreary. I rode on and on, passing now a flock of sheep watched over by a brigand-looking guardian and a fierce rough dog that looked ready, at a word or a sign from his master, to tear down my horse and throttle its rider, and then some huge arch of a ruined aqueduct that in the days of classic Rome had been musical with laughing water. Sometimes I came upon the shattered fragments of an abandoned hovel, or met with a herd of the gray-coated long-horned oxen of the region, beautiful placid-looking creatures, that gazed at me inquiringly out of their large soft eyes as I rode by, as though saying, What is this stranger doing in this home of solitude and ruin? Still, I was interested by the very novelty of the dreary region, and I rode on and on, till the sun began to sink toward the western horizon. I have always considered myself fever-proof, but, all the same, a ride after sunset over the Campagna is not the healthiest experiment in the world, so I wheeled my horse round and started to return to the city. And, as I did so, I became aware of the existence of a house at a very short distance. I might very well have passed it without noticing it, as it was so embowered in a mass of vegetation, vines, and bushes, as well as trees, that its shape and architecture were barely discernible. As I rode nearer, I saw that it was a modern villa of imposing dimensions, which had been suffered to fall into almost total ruin. Whether the freak of a speculator or the wild idea of some Campagna proprietor had caused the erection, in this lonely unhealthy place, of a costly country residence, there was no evidence to reveal. The grounds, once spacious and well laid out, were overrun with a thick undergrowth of plants and grasses. Here and there, a statue in white marble, streaked with damp and green with mold, showed under the shadow of the trees, and one, a graceful figure of a nymph, overthrown from its pedestal, lay prostrate amongst the rank grass. The facade of the house itself was adorned with moss-grown sculptures, and one of the pillars supporting the doorway had been broken away and its place was supplied by the trunk of a cypress. One-half of the building showed deserted and ruinous with its broken windows and decaying roof. But there were traces elsewhere of human habitation. The roof of the right wing had been mended, the windows were in good condition, and a gleam of firelight from the lower rooms gave a cheery aspect to that part of the edifice. And, oddly enough, in spite of the universal decay and dilapidation, there were traces not only of comfort, but of luxury, in one portion of the premises, which I noticed as I drew near. This was a large conservatory adjoining the inhabited portion of the house. It was in perfect order. Not a pane was missing in its glazed walls, through which I could discern the red glare of the stove-fires within, as well as the dull green of the foliage of the plants.

Both I and my horse were weary, so I decided that I would halt for an hour or so at this singular habitation, and try for a feed of oats for my horse, as well as for a flask of Chianti and a crust of bread for myself. I drew rein at the dilapidated doorway, and, just as I was about to announce my presence by a resounding knock from the butt-end of my riding-whip, the door was suddenly opened and a man came hurriedly forth. He started when he saw me, and was about to retreat into the house; but, by the red light of the waning sunset, I discerned his features and recognized him instantly. It was the man I had so long sought for and in vain—it was Julius Lambert.

"Julius!" I cried, as he was about to vanish through the doorway. "Julius Lambert! Is it thus that you treat an old friend who has come so far to visit you?"

He turned back at the sound of my voice. "So it is really you, Mr. Graham," he said, hesitatingly. "How in the world did you ever find me or the Villa Anzieri? Nobody has come near it or me either, for over two years past. But come in—my man shall take charge of your horse—and you can tell me something about home matters."

I willingly relinquished the charge of my wearied steed to the black-eyed, bronze-complexioned, picturesque-looking young fellow who came in answer to his master's call, and I followed Julius into the house. I could hardly believe my senses, or that I had found my missing friend at last. It had all happened so simply and yet so strangely. Meanwhile Julius, after he had gotten over the first shock of my intrusion, seemed really glad to see me. He piled fresh wood on the fire, and gave orders that dinner should be served as soon as possible, and plied me with questions respecting his mother and his brother and sisters. As for himself, I found him looking far from well. He was never very stout, but he had grown lean and emaciated, and the yellowish pallor of his face gave evidence of the effects that the malaria of the Campagna had on his system. Dinner was served at last—a very palatable stew flavored with red peppers and tomatoes, with the accompaniment of some fine oranges and grapes by way of dessert, and a flask or two of Chianti wine and one of the delicate Civita Lavinia. Throughout the repast, I noticed with pain that Julius talked in a feverish incoherent way, pressing me to eat or to drink, and hurrying questions and remarks about home matters, half the time without waiting for an answer.

At last, pushing my plate aside, I remarked:

"Now, Julius, I have told you everything that you wished to know. It is my turn now to ask for a little information. What have you been doing all this long time in this solitude?"

He moved uneasily in his chair, and his wandering glance avoided mine.

"Nothing," he muttered— "I have done—I am doing—nothing."

"Nonsense! You cannot persuade me of the truth of that assertion, so ardent an experimentalist as you have always been, and so interested in the cause of science. Confess, now—have you not made, or are you not on the verge of perfecting, some great discovery?"

I had touched the right chord. His eyes flashed, and his whole countenance grew bright with animation.

"Yes!" he cried. "I have succeeded at last in my researches. For years I have tried to perfect a demonstration of the link between the vegetable and the animal kingdom. If you have come to scoff at my discoveries, go—go at once! Otherwise, follow me—and be prepared for full conviction as to the truth of what I have said."

He rose as he spoke, and, taking me by the hand, he led me to a door at the extremity of the large room in which we had dined. This door he unlocked with a key which he took from his pocket. Night had closed in, and he completed his preparations by lighting a great torch of pine-branches.

"Wait on the threshold, as you value your life," he said to me, impressively. Then he threw open the door.

It was the entrance to the conservatory. The first thing that struck me was a sort of faint rustling sound like that of a trailing garment or a sweeping bird's-wing. Then, by the light of the torch which Julius held on high, I discerned, in the centre of the room, a vast tub filled with masses of spongy moss, from which rose a strange plant—a hideous shapeless monster: a sort of vegetable hydra—or, rather, octopus—gigantic in size and repulsive in aspect and in coloring. So immense were its proportions, that it filled by itself the whole space of the conservatory. It consisted of a central bladder-shaped trunk or core, from which sprang countless branches—or, rather, arms—thick, leafless, of a livid green, and streaked with blotches of a dull-crimson. Each arm terminated in an oval protuberance which had a resemblance to the human eye. Julius took, from a basket that stood near the door, a great slice of raw meat, and, fastening it to the end of a stick, he advanced it, taking infinite precautions to keep well out of reach within the circle of outstretched branches. Then I saw these great tentacle-like arms fold around their prey, which they transmitted to the central core; and then, closing around it, I saw it no more. It was this slow motion of the branches that had caused the rustling sound which had amazed me on my first entrance.

So repulsive was the aspect of this enormous creature, half plant and half animal, that I was glad to beat a retreat to the dining-room. Julius followed, flushed and elated at the healthful aspect of his monstrous creation.

"The plant you have just seen," he said, "is a Drosera, which, by dint of careful selection and persevering attention, I have developed into this unheard-of size. I have studied the discoveries of Warming and of Darwin concerning those strange plants, the Drosera and the Dionœa—which, though still vegetables, feed on the insects that they kill. It has been my desire for years to perfect the missing link and to develop the animal side of these curious vegetable natures. It has always been my theory that the hydra, the dragon, and other monstrous forms of animal life really did exist, and that, in the evolution of ages and by reason of geological changes on the surface of the earth, these creatures, deprived of their accustomed forms of nourishment, degenerated into trees and plants and took root in the earth. Some of them still preserve their primitive forms, as witness the dragon-tree of Java. It has been my aim and endeavor to resuscitate the animal in the plant. Chance threw in my way a Drosera of great size. I have fed it on animal food for years, and developed it into something that is not yet a dragon or a hydra, but which is surely something more than a plant. Had you ventured within reach of its branches, the grasp of a boa would not have been more swift or more deadly."

"And what further do you propose doing with your dreadful plant?"

"My aim now is to give it locomotion—to see it detach itself from the soil and go forth in search of prey."

"How can you contemplate the possibility of letting loose such a monster on the world?"

"For science, there is no such thing as a monster. Moreover, are there not crocodiles and anacondas and tigers upon earth, to say nothing of the shark and the octopus? Beside these, my creation—my Carnivorine—is a harmless creature."

I started as I heard the name. So this, then, was the object of my poor friend's affections—this ghastly shape, not yet wholly animal, yet scarcely vegetable, with the form of a plant and the appetites of a beast of prey?

Just then, Pietro, the man-servant, came in to announce that my horse was at the door. It was a beautiful moonlight night, promising a pleasant ride to the city. I took my leave of Julius, therefore, with something of the feeling of relief of a man who awakes from sleep after having been oppressed by a terrible nightmare. But I did not depart without leaving my address, and I begged Julius to let me know if his strange discovery took any new developments in the near future.

Weeks passed away, and I had nearly forgotten all about Julius and Carnivorine, when one day I received a letter from him, written in a strain of great exultation and excitement. "Come to me, dear friend," he wrote; "come at once! The hour of the perfecting of my experiment is at hand. Already, amid the masses that surround Carnivorine, I discern the stirring and striving of the roots, that are acquiring powers of independent locomotion. In a few days, the problem will be solved. I want you to be present as a witness of the phenomenon. My ambition is satisfied at last—my name shall be inscribed on the list of the great discoverers of the world of science. Come to me, and be at my side in the moment of my triumph."

It was not without difficulty that I once more made my way to the Villa Anzieri. It was late in the afternoon when I drew rein at the dilapidated doorway that I remembered so well. I knocked loudly at the door, but there was no response to my call. Looking around, I saw that the whole place wore an inexplicable air of desertion. No firelight was visible at the windows, and the red glare of the stove-fire no longer shone behind the dim panes of the hot-house. Finally, in vague alarm, finding that my shouts and knocking produced no response, I tied my horse to one of the door-posts, and, singling out a window of the large room in which we had dined on the occasion of my former visit, I swung myself up to it by the help of a thick stem of ivy, and peered into the room. The sight that I beheld within froze my soul with horror.

At the end of the room, near the entrance to the conservatory, rose the hideous form of Carnivorine, no longer planted in a tub, but supported on what seemed, to me, a pair of paddle-like feet or paws like those of some misshapen antediluvian animal. The powerful branches—or, rather, tentacles—were upraised and closely folded around some central object. And at the summit of these livid green, closely-pressed, serpent-like stems appeared a ghastly object: it was a livid human head—the head of a corpse— and the pallid features were those of Julius Lambert!

With one stroke of my arm, I burst open the casement. I sprang into the room and hastened toward the dreadful object. The long arms quivered and began to unfold themselves. But, before the creature could put itself in motion, a shot from the revolver that I always carried during my Campagna wanderings pierced its central core. The tentacles fell apart, and the hideous plant sank prone upon the ground, bearing with it, in its fall, the crushed and lifeless form of Julius Lambert. A stream of reddish sap that looked like blood flowed from the shattered stem and mingled with the branches, stained as they were with a ruddier crimson—the life-blood of my unhappy friend.

I never discovered how or when the catastrophe took place. From the condition of the body, death must have taken place at least twenty-four hours before my arrival. The servants, brought face-to-face with such a shocking—and, to them, inexplicable—catastrophe, had fled from the house, taking with them whatever money or valuables they could lay their hands upon. I tried to trace them out, but in vain. As to the rest, it was all mere conjecture on my part. The uptorn earth and mosses in the tub in which Carnivorine had originally found an abode seemed to prove that a sudden development of the long-sought-for powers of locomotion in the creature had unexpectedly taken place, and that Julius had been seized either in the act of inspecting its condition or at the moment of offering it food. At all events, the vegetable-animal or animal-vegetable had made a solitary trial of its newly-formed powers, and had found a solitary prey when the bullet from my pistol put an end to its existence.

Among the papers left behind by Julius was a series of memoranda respecting the experiments he had tried and the processes he had used to bring his dread creation to full perfection. These I destroyed without hesitation. It would not have been well to have suffered the race of the vegetable octopus to be extended and propagated by curious scientists in the future. Then, lest a new growth should spring from the stem or branches of the accursed tree, I hewed them to pieces with my own hand and burned the fragments to ashes. The annihilation of my friend's discovery may be a loss to science, but humanity will only have cause to rejoice in the total destruction of Carnivorine.

MY ONE GORILLA
Grant Allen

I looked up from my beetles. The night was warm.

A naked little black girl crossed the dusty main street of the village just in front of my hut, carrying in her hand what seemed to me in the gloaming the largest blossom I had ever observed since my arrival in Africa. That *was* a blossom. It looked like an orchid, pale cream-colour in hue, and very fantastic and bizarre in shape; but what specially attracted my attention at first was its peculiar shining and glistening effect, like luminous paint, which made it glow in the grey dusk with a sort of phosphorescent light such as one observes in tropical seas on calm summer evenings.

To a naturalist, of course, such a vision as that was simply irresistible. "Hullo, there, little girl!" I cried out in Fantee, which I had learned by that time to speak pretty fluently; "let me look at your flower, will you? Where on earth did you get it?"

But instead of answering me civilly, like a Christian child, the scared little savage, alarmed at my white face, set up a wild howl of terror and amazement, and bolted off down the street at the top of her speed, as fast as her small bandy legs would carry her.

Well, science is science. I wasn't to be balked of a unique specimen for my great collection by a trick like that. So, flinging away my cigarette and darting out of my hut, I gave chase incontinently, and rushed, full pelt, down the main street of Tulamba, helter-skelter and devil-take-the-hindmost, in pursuit of my ten-year old.

84

But I reckoned without my host. Children of the Gaboon beat the record for the quarter-mile. I was quite pumped out and panting for breath before I ran that girl to the earth at last, by her mother's door at the far end of the village. A dozen more of the negroes, loitering about on their backs in the dust of the street, had joined the hue and cry with great gusto by that time. They didn't know, to be sure, what the fuss was about; but given a white man—bestower of rum and money—rushing in mad pursuit, and a poor little frightened black girl scampering away for dear life at the top of her speed, in abject bodily terror, and you may confidently reckon on the chivalry of the Gaboon to range itself automatically on the side of the stronger, and to drive the unhappy small child hopelessly into a very bad corner.

When at last I got up with the object of my quest, she was so alarmed and blown with her headlong career that I felt thoroughly ashamed of myself. Even the pursuit of science, I will frankly admit, hardly justified me in so chivvying that frightened little mortal, ten negroes strong, through the street of Tulamba. However, a bright English sixpence, a red silk pocket-handkerchief, and the promise of a box of European sweets from the old half-caste Portuguese trader's shop in the village, soon restored her confidence. Unhappily, it did not restore that broken and draggled, but priceless, orchid. In her headlong flight, the child had crumpled it hopelessly up in her hand, and distorted it almost beyond the possibility of scientific recognition. All I could make out with certainty now was that the orchid belonged to a new and hitherto undescribed species; that it was large and luminous and extremely beautiful; and that if only I could succeed in securing a plant of it, my name was made as a scientific explorer.

The natives crowded round with disinterested advice, and eyed the torn and draggled blossom curiously. "It's a moon-flower," they said in their own dialect. "Very rare. Hard to get. Comes from the deep shades in the great forest."

"How did you come by it, my child?" I asked, coaxingly, of my sobbing little ten-year old.

"My father brought it in," the child answered, with a burst. "He gave it to me a week ago. He was out in the country of the dwarfs, doing trade. He went for ivory, and he brought this back to me."

"Boys," I cried to the negroes who crowded round, looking on, "do you know where it lives? I want to get one. A good English rifle to any man in Tulamba who guides me to the spot where I can pick a live moon-flower!"

The men shook their heads and shrugged their shoulders dubiously.

"Oh, no," they all answered, like supers at the theatre, with one accord. "Too far! Too dangerous!"

"Why dangerous?" I cried, laughing. "The moon-flower won't bite you. Who says danger in picking a flower?"

My head guide and hunter stood out from the crowd, and looked across at me, awe-struck. "Oh, excellency," he said, in a hushed and frightened voice, "the moon-flower is rare; it is very scarce; it grows only in the dark forest of the inner land where the Ngina dwells. No man dare pick it for fear of the Ngina."

"Oho," said I. "Is that so, my friend? Then I'm not astonished." For Ngina, as no doubt you're already aware, is the native West African name for the gorilla.

Well, I took home the poor draggled blossom to my hut, dissected it carefully, and made what scientific study was possible of its unhappy remains in their much tattered condition. But for the next ten days, as you can readily believe, I could think and talk and dream of nothing but moon-flowers. You can't think what a fascination it exerts on a naturalist explorer's mind—a new orchid like that, as big round as a dessert plate, and marked by so extraordinary and hitherto unknown a peculiarity in plants as phosphorescence. For the moon-flower was phosphorescent; of that I had now not the shadow of a doubt. Its petals gave out by night a faint and dreamy luminousness, which must have made it shine like a moon indeed in the dense dark shade of a tropical African forest.

The more I inquired of the natives about this new plant, the more was my curiosity piqued to possess one. I longed to bring a root of the marvellous bloom to Europe. For the natives all spoke of it with a certain hushed awe or superstitious respect: "It is Ngina's flower," they said. "It grows in dark places—the gardens of Ngina. If any man breaks one off, that is very bad luck; the Ngina will surely overtake and destroy him."

This superstitious awe only inflamed my desire to possess a root. The negroes' stories showed the moon-flower to be really a most unique species. I gathered from what they told me that the blossom had a very long spur or sac, containing honey at its base in great quantities; that it was fertilised and rifled by a huge evening moth, whose proboscis was exactly adapted in length to the spur and its nectary; that it was creamy white in order to attract the insect's eyes in the grey shades of dusk; and that, for the self-same reason, its petals were endowed with the strange quality of phosphorescence, till now unknown in the vegetable kingdom; while it exhaled by night a delicious perfume, strong enough to be perceived at some twenty yards' distance. So great a prize to a man of my tastes was simply irresistible. I made up my mind that, come what might, I must, could and would possess a tuber of the moon-flower.

One fortnight sufficed for me to make my final plans. Heavy bribes overcame the scruples of the negroes. The promise of a good rifle induced the first finder of the first specimen to take service with me as a guide. Fully equipped for a week's march, and well attended with followers all armed to the teeth, I made my start at last for the home of the moon-flower.

To cut a long story short, we went for three days into the primeval shade of the great equatorial African forest. Dense roofs of foliage shut out the light of day; underfoot, the ground was encumbered with thick, tropical brushwood. We crept along cautiously, hacking our way at times among the brake with our cutlasses, and crawling at others through the deep tangle of the underbrush on all fours like monkeys. During all those three days we never caught sight of a single moon-flower. They were growing very rare nowadays, my guide explained in most voluble Fantee. When he was a mere boy, his father found dozens of them; but now, why, you must go miles and miles through the depths of the forest and never so much as light on a specimen.

At last, about noon on the fourth day out, we came upon a torrent, rushing with great velocity among huge boulders, and sending up the spray of its boiling rapids into the trees of the neighbourhood. I sat down to rest, meaning to mix the water from the cool, fresh stream with a spoonful or two of cognac from the flask in my pocket. As I drank it, I tossed back my head and looked up. Something on one of the trees hard by attracted my eyes strangely. A parasite stood out boldly from a fork of the branches, bearing a long, lithe spray of huge luminous flowers as big as dessert-plates. My heart gave a bound; the prize was within sight. I pointed my finger in silence to the tree. All the negroes with one voice raised a loud shout of triumph. Their words rent the air: "The moon-flower—the moon-flower!"

I felt myself for a moment a perfect Stanley or Du Chaillu. I had discovered the most marvellous and beautiful orchid known to science.

In a moment I had tossed off my brandy, laid down my rifle, and mounting on the back of one of my negro porters, was swinging myself up to the lowest branch of the tree where my new treasure shone resplendent in its own dim phosphorescence. I couldn't have trusted any hand but my own to pick or egg out that glorious tuber. I meant to cut it bodily from the bark as it stood, and bear it back in triumph in my own arms to Tulamba.

I had climbed the tree cautiously, and was standing almost within grasp of the prize, when a sudden shout among my followers below startled and discomposed me. I looked down and hesitated. My brain reeled and sickened. A strange sight met my eyes. My negroes, one and all, had taken to their feet down the bed of the stream at the very top of their speed, and were making a most unanimous and inexplicable stampede toward the direction of Tulamba.

For a moment I couldn't imagine what had happened to disconcert them; the, casting my glance casually towards the spot where I had flung down my rifle, I became aware at once of the cause of this commotion. Their retreat was well-timed. By the moss-clad boulders which filled the bed of the torrent, somebody with a big, black face and huge grinning teeth, was standing erect, looking up at me and laughing. I had never seen the somebody's awful features before, but I had no need, for all that, to ask myself his name. I paused face to face with a live male gorilla.

For a moment or two, the creature gazed up at me and grinned. Then he raised my rifle in his arms; held it clumsily before him; and, to my intense surprise, taking a very bad aim, or, rather pointing it aimlessly in the air, pulled both triggers with one hand, and discharged the two barrels at me with one pull, simultaneously. The bullets whizzed past me some ten yards off. They knocked off the twigs beyond my precious moon-flower.

Well, I don't deny, as I say, that I was in a state of blue funk at the creature's gigantic and almost supernatural powers. But still, the moon-flower was at stake, and I wouldn't desert it. I was so horribly frightened that I don't believe wife, or child, or fatherland, or freedom would have induced me to stay one moment alone in such dire extremities. But when it comes to orchids! Well, I say no more than that I am above all things a scientific explorer; each of us has his weakness; and mine is a flower. That touches my heart. For that alone can I be wrought up to the utmost pitch of daring conceivable or possible for me.

So I looked at the huge brute, and I looked at the moon-flower. Slowly and cautiously, gazing down all the time as I went to watch the creature's face, I crept along the branch, took my knife from my pocket, and began to loosen the bark all round the spot where the glorious parasite was all a-growing and all a-blowing. The gorilla, from below, stood watching me and roaring. His roar seemed like an invitation to come down and fight. I never in my life heard anything so awfully human in its deep bass roll. It reminded me of the lowest notes of the stage villain in the Italian operas, magnified, so to speak, two hundred diameters.

Presently, as I went on cutting away the bark, as if for dear life, and loosening the precious tuber, my gorilla, who still remained motionless by his moss-clad boulder, left off his roaring, and appeared to grow interested in the process of the operation. A change came o'er the spirit of his dream. He looked up and wondered, with vague brute curiosity, not unmixed with a certain strange air of low cunning and intelligence. It was clear to me as mud that he was saying to himself inwardly, "Why doesn't the fellow cut and run for his life? Does he think I don't know how to climb a tree? Does he imagine that I couldn't be up there in a jiffy if I liked—to choke or scrag him? What the dickens does he go on hacking away at the bark so quietly like that for, when he ought to be all agog to save his own bacon?"

I despaired of explaining to so rude a creature the imperative nature of scientific need. So with one eye on the orchid and one on the brute, at the risk of contracting a permanent squint for life, I continued to egg out that magnificent moon-flower, root and branch and tuber.

The longer I went on, the closer and more attentively did the gorilla take stock of all my acts and movements. "Well, I declare," I could see him say to himself in the gorilla tongue, opening wide his huge eyes and elevating in surprise his shaggy, brown eyebrows, "such an animal as this I never yet did come across. He isn't one bit afraid, apparently of *me*, the redoubtable and redoubted king of the great Gaboon forest."

But I *was*, most consumedly, for all that, though I pretended not to be. Nothing but the presence before my eyes of that magnificent plant would have induced me for one moment to face or confront the unspeakable brute there.

At last I had finished, and held my specimen in my hands entire. The next question now was what to do with it.

I walked slowly and cautiously along the branch of the tree. The gorilla, with his eyes now fixed curiously on the moon-flower, put forth one hairy leg in front of the other, and grinning with a sort of diabolical, brutish good-humour, walked, step for step, on the ground, just as cautiously beneath me.

I came to the end of the bough, and reached the point where interlacing branches enabled me to get on to another tree. I did so somewhat clumsily, for I was handicapped by the moon-flower. The gorilla, still grinning, looked up, and remarked in his own tongue, "I could do that lot, I can tell you, a jolly sight better than you do."

As he smiled those words, I half lost my balance, and, clinging still to my moon-flower in my last chance for life, lowered myself slowly, hand over hand, to the ground in front of him.

With a frightful roar, the creature sprang upon me—and made a wild grab at my precious moon-flower. That was more than human scientific human nature could stand. I turned and fled, carrying my specimen with me. But my pursuer was too quick. He caught me up in a moment. His scowling black face was ghastly to behold; his huge, white teeth gleamed fierce and hideous; his brawny, thick hands could have crushed me to a jelly. I panted and paused. My heart fluttered fast, the stood still within me. There was a second's suspense. At its end, to my infinite horror, he seized—not me—oh no, not me—I might have put up with *that*— but the priceless moon-flower!

I was helpless to defend myself. Helpless to secure or safeguard my treasure. He took it from me with a grin. I could see through those sunken eyes what was passing in the creature's dim and brutal brain. He was saying to himself, like men at his own low grade of cunning, "If that tuber was worth so much pains to *him* to get it, it must be worth just as much to me to keep. So, by your leave, my friend, if you'll excuse me, I'll take it."

I stood appalled and gazed at him. The brute snatched that unique specimen of a dying or almost extinct genus in his swarthy, hairy hands of his—raised it bodily to his mouth, crushing and tearing the beautiful petals in his coarse grasp as he went—ate it slowly through, tuber, stem, spray, blossom—and swallowed it conscientiously, with a hideous grimace, to the very last morsel. I had but one grain of consolation or revenge. It was clear the taste was exceedingly nasty.

Then he looked in my face and burst into a loud, discordant laugh. That laugh was hideous.

"Aha!" it said in effect, "so *that's* all you've got, my fine fellow, after all, for all your pains, and care, and trouble!"

I shut my eyes and waited. *My* turn would come next. He would rend me in his rage for the nastiness of the taste. I stood still and shuddered. But, alas, he meant only to eat the moon-flower.

When I opened my eyes again, the brute had turned his back without one word of apology, and was walking off at a leisurely pace in contemptuous triumph, shrugging his shoulders as he went, and chuckling low to himself in his vulgar dog-in-the-manger joy and malignancy.

It was four days before I straggled alone, half dead, into Tulamba. I never came across another of those orchids. And that is why at Kew they have still no moon-flower.

The Lamparagua

May Crommelin

[When staying lately in Chile, being interested in the superstitions of the lower caste, which is mainly of Indian origin, I heard, among other curious legends, darkly of one which seemed peculiar to this country. Next, chance acquainted me with a gentleman, one of the principal English residents in Chile, who kindly gave me details of the dread lamparagua. This wizard-like creature, of which many persons in the country have never even heard, is strangely enough supposed to inhabit fertile and cultivated districts. And Mr. L— was assured by his labourers that one lamparagua or more infested the marshy edges of a lake, as is its favourite haunt, on his own estate, Culipran.

In the following tale I may have overstated the height of the Thing, concerning which and its mode of progression the details were not exact. Otherwise, its appearance, diet, and the means it employs to secure its victims, are faithfully reproduced, according to the description unwillingly confided to Mr. L— by some of his own peones. And these are men who are declared by Europeans neither to feel pain nor to know fear.]

The two men had held on steadily riding since two hours before dawn, going all day without stopping, save for a brief noontide halt. During the afternoon of yesterday their track had lain across an utterly desolate pampa, therefore they had pushed on to reach cultivated country again, and water before nightfall. Now, towards evening, they found themselves near a long lake, bordered with reeds, the haunt of numberless wildfowl.

A small rocky valley, down which the active Chilian ponies weariedly scrambled, grew greener towards the lake shore, where a stream which the travellers had followed for some time widened into a V-shaped marsh.

"It is near sunset, Pedro. Let us camp here for the night," said Ramsay, shivering slightly; for the fever had taken him two days ago. "Own the truth, man! You have lost your bearings, and don't know whether we are nine miles or nine leagues from the silver mine. Besides, the horses, poor beasts, will be dead beat."

"Of what good is a horse that cannot do his sixty miles when asked?" returned the Chilian guide. "But, truly, the devil seems to have been driving round on these hills, changing their shapes since last I came this way."

He gazed with discontent deepening on his swarthy features at the hills behind, hiding the sandy desert, far beyond which rose the mighty range of the Andes, still veiled in rosy haze this hot December evening. Then, in sudden recollection,—

"There is a rich Englishman who lives near a lake in this neighbourhood. He has smelting works and a large estate. The house may be close at hand."

"Or it may be on the opposite shore," said Ramsay, wearily dismounting. "Hobble the horses, and let us go up to yonder hilly ground jutting into the lake.

"Then if you can see signs of a *hacienda*, we'll make a last push for it. If not, I rest."

"Why not, patron?" said the *huaso*, using the almost invariable courteous Chilian assent to assertions or requests.

Up among rocks and brushwood master and man climbed, till, advancing to the far crest of the hillock, they scanned the lake shores attentively. Northwards, at a mile's distance, a wooded headland arrested their vision; south and west there was no human habitation in sight, though the ground here and there showed signs of cultivation and the pasture was good.

Right across the lake the sun was sinking gloriously red, against a background of the pale olive green and lilac hues seen so often in a Southern Pacific sky. Soothed by the spectacle, Ramsay sat down on a rock to rest and smoke; and with Indian impassibility Pedro did the same. All gringos were mad, he knew; if this one liked staring at nothing, he was more easily pleased than some of the foreign lunatics. But presently Pedro became aware that there was something to be seen among the rocks below. Signing to Ramsay, both men peered stealthily past screening myrtle bushes and witnessed an evening domestic scene in animal life.

The ground rose in two broken ledges from the marsh, and on the upper one a dog-fox and vixen were playing with their cubs near some crannies where was doubtless their home. Presently the mother left the rest, and stretched herself sleepily in the evening sunlight midway on the grass ledge. One cub followed to bite her neck, but, on being repulsed, returned to gambol with his brothers. As he watched them, Ramsay also noticed vaguely a low withered tree, standing in the marsh twenty yards below, alone, and partly submerged, with a hollow cleft in its side.

All at once the peon touched his master's arm and pointed open-mouthed towards the vixen. She had risen as if in terror, both her head and brush curved towards the ledge. Then, while her four paws seemed firmly planted gripping the turf, she was drawn broadside some yards towards the edge by invisible means. The other foxes, old and young, meantime disappeared in the twinkling of an eye into the rock crevices.

As both men eagerly gazed, the vixen's tension relaxed. On the brink she recovered herself and standing still for three or four seconds, as if dazed after deadly effort, she turned tail and darted towards her lair. Two springs only,—on the third she paused in mid-flight! Once more she resisted, but was dragged back towards the edge, this time *tail foremost*. At the same time a rush of wind sounded like a *sh-h* in the stillness. Ramsay knew now he had heard the same sound two minutes before, but had fancied it a light breeze among the leaves. Craning his neck forward, Jock believed he could see an agonised expression in the creature's eyes, as against her will she slid inch by inch—*over!*

The fall was not great. A lower grassy terrace surmounted the marsh. Even as they whispered, the watchers saw the victim rise. A second time—but feebly, like a mouse released from the deadly grip of a cat—the poor she-fox crawled away with drooping brush towards the sheltering rocks. Ramsay searched the marsh with a sportsman's keen glance, to discover whether the creature had been lassoed by some invisible means, and where was the native hunter. Then he bounded to his feet and pointing towards the withered tree, his arm stiffened with amazement, exclaimed, "Look!"

The cleft in the tree-trunk was visibly widening and gaping, till it looked like a hideous bark-lipped mouth that was drawing a long inspiration. Again there came the same sound in the air, and the vixen, curled in a helpless quivering ball, was borne five yards, as on a wind-blast, disappearing right into the hollow of the tree. The withered wooden lips contracted over the creature's living head; two dead branches above stirred slightly, like antennae, the cleft closed, leaving a jagged scar in the tree-trunk. That was all.

The scene was still and peaceful as before. A flight of wild duck circled twice over the lake and then alighted on the surface with distant quacks. Behind in a fuchsia thicket a native thrush was singing. The tree was immovable.

Wondering if he could be dreaming, Ramsay turned to the peon. Pedro's copper skin had taken a pale yellow hue, and he was shivering, though a Chilian peasant is brave to savagery.

"The *lamparagua!* Fly!" he gasped, with a cry of horror, and plunged downwards among the rocks. Jock overtook him just as the *huaso* leaped barebacked on his horse.

"Stay for me, my lad, at the valley head in safety. I'll not leave the saddles and blankets," said the Scotchman coolly. But his own breath fluttered in his throat more than from the run, and while his hands tugged at strap and buckle, his head turned to glance at the tree that remained motionless in the distance.

Rejoining Pedro, who waited half a mile away, the master found the peon on his knees, crossing himself and gabbling over and over every scrap of the Latin prayers he could remember, which the *padres* had taught him in boyhood. They were few, and he mixed them so ludicrously that his listener almost laughed.

"Holy Santa Rosa—miserable sinner!" ended Pedro, rising and saddling up with remarkable haste while throwing off some last ejaculations of this rare access of piety. "It was a witch, *señor*; the country is full of spirits. Holy Saint Peter, I ducked your image last autumn in the sea. Forgive!—but those fishermen are such blasphemers, and rail against you at the first bad weather. I abjure all evil-livers, holy—" An awful oath followed as the pony swerved. Pedro stuck his huge rowels in the beast's flanks and cantered furiously away, his *poncho* filling with air as he worked his arms like a windmill's sails, shouting, "Ride, ride, patron! Leave this God-forsaken country, quick!"

"Aye, if only our horses can travel," muttered the Scotchman.

True enough, the tired beasts soon showed that they could not be roused long beyond an ambling motion, not unlike the gait of a Peruvian pacer; but which, when unbroken all day, may cover a great distance before nightfall. Not till they had gone some miles could Ramsay persuade his terror-stricken guide to talk sensibly.

"What is this beast-tree? *Lamparagua*,* you called it. Does it exist elsewhere in Chili?"

"Who knows, *señor*? I only heard of such rare trees as northern witches from a rough *roto* who came from this country. I remember it was one evening in July, ten years ago, as we sat in a circle on the ground round the brasier. We thought he was improvising a tale, as we had in turn improvised or recited songs and legends—telling lies for fun, as the patron may know is our custom. There was naught more I can call to mind, save that they swallowed animals and lived near marshy places. Saints preserve us! Ride on—on to the mines. *Stop here?* Never!"

---

* Literally, "Lamp of the Water": a kind of will-o'-the-wisp. Though why a light is associated with the tree was not apparent in the account of it given to the writer.

Ramsay dared not lose sight of the man. At least Pedro knew something of the country. He might strike their right track soon. So the soft twilight of the south drew round them, as they rode wearily. And the night came, black and moonless, as they bent in their saddles, more weary yet. The reins lay loose on the horses' necks now, Pedro trusting to the animals' instinct; for "the good land" could not be far where men lived, and there were homesteads and supper and provender.

When midnight was past, Ramsay felt his strength going from him. By the faint starlight they had just plashed through a gravelly stream, in which the horses stopped to drink before reluctantly stumbling up the far bank where their hoofs struck muffled on grass.

"Pedro, I can hold up no longer," called the engineer feebly, reeling in his saddle, as an ague fit shook him like a rigor. "Leave me—if you will. I—must—lie down."

Guessing by his master's voice that the latter must be very ill, the peon hastily came to Ramsay's help in dismounting, then guided him to the shelter of some bushes that were faintly discernible. Here he placed a saddle under the sufferer's head, and laid a blanket over him.

Not far off there was a small grove of shrubs, darker than the surrounding twilight, beside which rose a big tree with a huge bulbous base and exposed roots like those of a cotton tree. Near this Ramsay's horse strayed, cropping the grass; so Pedro, following, tethered him to one of these roots, which he had discovered by stumbling against them in the blackness.

"*Caramba!*" he muttered. "Stay there; animal not to be trusted." His own beast knew him, and never went far from its owner's side.

Then the guide sat down beside his exhausted patron, who slept for fevered snatches, or woke to ramble in delirious talk. So the time passed till the faint light strengthened.

All at once Ramsay fancied he heard Pedro's voice crying out in a tone of desperation—or was it terror?— "*Me voy!* I'm off to bring you help!"

The sick man did not heed, though vaguely conscious he was left alone. It seemed to him that he was in a hospital. The doctor would come round presently; if not, it was peaceful to lie still. Was that his mother, lifting the hair on his fevered brow?

Then he started awake as a horrid cry roused his dulled ears. (It was the scream of a horse!)

What was this well-known valley? Where was he? For, raising himself weakly on one elbow, Ramsay saw a stream running past rocks which were strangely familiar,—and yet *when* had he seen them? The river emptied itself in marshy land. The dawn showed a dark grey surface beyond, like a sea—or lake.

With a cold terror the sick man recognised that he lay not two hundred yards from the marsh of the lamparagua: that headland; the water! All night they must have ridden in a circle.

The horrible scream was already fading from his sick memory like a dream, when a snorting and scuffling noise caused Ramsay to turn slowly his weak head. He saw his horse stamping, pulling back from its halter, and with distended eye-balls staring terrified at a tree, to a root of which it was fastened. What was wrong? The tree had two bare topmost branches like horns, and some lower ones also without leaves, yet this was summer-time; in December. . . . It was withered! And, there above its onion-shaped bole was, surely, a dark scar, a crack! Oh, horror! the top of the tree was that of the lamparagua, in the marsh. And now, as Jock stared with fever-weakened eyes through the dim daybreak, the lower branches moved slowly downwards, clutching the horse's halter with claw-like twigs; the crack in the side of the *Thing* was widening. Again a fearful sound woke the sleeping glen: the horse's cry of terror. Jock tried instinctively to find his revolver, but his senses reeled as the tree aperture gaped, opening upwards. The horse was drawing to-wards it—nearer!—fighting, struggling. Then two shots rang out, and a man fainted, and knew no more.

When Jock Ramsay came to himself, the sun was high in the heavens. He was sheltered by wild myrtle from its heat, and though very weak, his senses had come back. Memory was slower. Ah—he *remembered!* Opening his eyes in a wide stare of apprehension,

Ramsay saw himself lying alone. There was a thicket near, but not the awful tree. Pedro was gone; so were the horses. But perhaps—perhaps—that last vision of the Thing engulfing the poor roan cob had been a nightmare, a fevered frenzy. Feebly reconnoitring the ground, the sick man noticed that he lay on a grassy slope between the stream and the rocks where the foxes lived: a small cape. Behind his head the ground must be open up the valley. There lay safety, away from the horrible marsh and the lamparagua—if there were such a tree indeed. Surely it had all been a hideous dream. Drawing the myrtle leaves aside, as one might a curtain, Jock feebly turned himself to examine the glen. Then his fingers clenched, his breath stopped, and a thrill of horror froze his spine. *The Tree was there!* Out in the open, on the grass, with not a bush near it, right between himself and safety.

Take it quietly! For manhood's sake, think out this business, and don't turn faint like a schoolgirl seeing a snake. First, was the whole affair a dream? Was that withered tree out yonder on the sward the very lamparagua? For if so, there were several, or it could change its situation. It was neither in the marsh, nor by the fuchsia thicket. It . . . . O God!

For, as he peered, Ramsay believed that the tree was moving. It was horribly near, and it was surely creeping forward by inches. He held his breath, and marked a grass tuft at its bulbous base.

Now—now it had passed beyond the tall silvery grass plumes and spear-leaves, and was close by a stone—was stealthily rounding it. Yes, the Thing was approaching him; doubtless it had stayed quiet till now, gorged with its morning meal, but it was slowly nearing its next victim. With eyes fascinated by fear, Ramsay saw its roots moving forward like giant knotty suckers that gripped and held fast in the herbage, noiselessly moving with the motion of a tortoise.

The hair of the young man's flesh stood up, an icy coldness numbed his blood. Then with a strong effort he gathered his senses to think out escape. The rocks ahead were his only chance. There among the crannies, where the foxes had their dens and hid in safety, he could hide. But he could not rise! His head was dizzy with fever; his strength was as running water: his legs and feet seemed not his own, mere useless weights to be dragged on by sheer pluck. For he had already started—

Grasping the myrtle stems to give himself an impetus, Ramsay was crawling away towards the rocks, foot by foot. He lay outspread like a lizard, for his only strength remained in his arms and chest. Inch by inch, he crept onward as fast as he could go, clutching at the grass tufts, at the sage-bushes, drops of perspiration running down his face.

Faster, faster, if it could only be done! The man had covered some yards; surely the tree moved more slowly. *Ah!*

A blast blew backwards over Ramsay's head, raising his hair. By instinct he dug his nails into the ground, flattening his body as much as he possibly could. The indraught was as if air had rushed by into a deep cavity, while a sound like that of an escape pipe hissed in the air. Then it was over.

As drowning men are said to see a thousand past scenes in a few moments, so in an agonisingly lucid flash, Jock Ramsay reviewed his life. Then he recalled yester-evening, how the wretched fox had gotten breathing-time twice, as once he had now. How long would this horrible game last? The beast-tree was paralysing the human being: he thought of a snake fascinating a rabbit.

Slowly, more feebly, the victim still crawled. Why did that second blast not follow? Could the lamparagua be so near, it needed no aid beyond that of its cruel hooked branches? *He must see!*

Turning his head, as he still dragged himself onward, the fever-stricken wretch beheld a strange sight. He had left his blanket behind upon the ground when first making his escape, and it was now wrapped round the tree-bole, as if the lamparagua had failed to suck it in, and was wrestling with this unknown prey, both branches holding it fast outspread on claw-like twigs. It was a respite! A few seconds more of air, light, life!

Yes, the beast-tree was standing still; yet it had covered more ground than its hunted prey, during the time both had moved. Ramsay felt for the revolver in his pocket. There was one bullet left, he knew, and if escape were hopeless, then—

At last! The rocks were near. The man began scrambling painfully up a steep incline of loose earth and rounded stones which resembled a moraine, and that gave no hold to his desperate grasp. Looking up, he saw with hopeless eyes that there had been a slight landslip lately, which had left the bank projecting overhead, so that he could not reach the top; looking down, that the lamparagua was slowly but steadily approaching once more over the grass, foot-root following foot-root. There was a torn piece of crimson blanket hanging on one bough.

He must struggle across the face of this treacherous slide to where a clump of yuccas were smouldering, their stems blackened as one often sees them, whether from spontaneous combustion or sun-fired in some inexplicable manner, no man knows.

Fire! The smoking plants suggested a thought to the man. He stayed still, holding on half-way up the scree. He felt for his match-box; there were two matches left.

Then Ramsay, instead of longer seeking escape upwards, flung himself in still more desperate eagerness down the steep slope again towards his enemy. He was at bay.

Where the grass began, the man stopped and stooped, plucking dry blades and twigs with the haste of one who has but a few moments to live should this plan fail of success. Not a drop of rain had fallen since last October; the scorching summer heat had burnt the grass to tinder. There came the spurt of a match.

Two moments: five—!

The fire-spark, kindling, seemed about to spread, when a roaring wind-gust through the valley's stillness blew it out, and the man felt himself sucked irresistibly towards a clump of prickly pear, to which he clung palpitating, with his face pressed against the thorny broad discs that tore the skin to bleeding. Ah!—*that was over!*

For the last time one chance was left,—one match! Again Ramsay snatched what dry fuel lay within his grasp, as he sheltered beneath the bushes. His papers, cheque-book, all were in a small valise he had instinctively thrust overnight under his saddle-pillow. There was one letter left in his breast pocket, which he had carried there two years—the last one ever written by his mother. He tore it out.

With shaking fingers, and blinded by blood-drops he dared not wait to wipe from his eyes—knowing the while that the lamparagua was stalking a yard nearer at each motion—its victim carefully struck the match. Sheltering the tiny flame with one hand, he turned the wax-stem gently till it lit. Next the letter; and the fire licked the words "My dearest Son," then blazed and crackled in the funeral pyre of broken bramble and dried myrtle leaves that burnt a dead woman's last token of love to her youngest born. Gladly would she have known it sacrificed on the slight chance to save his life! Ramsay thrust both hands deep into the burning mass, and recovering strength in the excitement of hope, he staggered towards some clumps of tall grass of the pampas a few feet away. The sparks fell, making a trail as he went that caught the dry herbage. Hurrah! How the giant grass-stems took fire, blazing high in a glorious bonfire!

A hasty glance over his shoulder. The lamparagua was not twelve yards distant; its jaws were widening. But the fire-wall was between them.

There came a rush of wind ending in a sound more fierce than a wounded lion's roar. The man was caught by the blast as he stood upright, weak yet defiant, matching his puny being against the strength of the brute-tree with the help of the mind within him controlling the fiery element as a weapon. Sucked forward, blinded by smoke, scorched, Ramsay fell on his face and lay still with a last conscious effort to save his life. Beyond his body the myrtles and fuchsias were crackling, the tall *chajual* blossoms blazed like high torches, the fire was spreading, leaping up to the *boldo* branches in yonder thicket, running over the open ground in a low sheet that burnt the lamparagua roots.

For half a minute the Thing stayed, trying to stand its ground. Now it was in full flight! The great sucker-feet were travelling over the burning herbage, dragging its tree-trunk with agonised efforts, yard upon yard, towards the stream.

Five minutes later, there came a galloping of horses down the valley; men's shouts. But Ramsay did not hear them. He seemed to lie prone at death's door, too weak to enter unless spirit hands lifted him over its threshold and brought him within to be at peace and rest.

But they were earthly hands that were now trying to pour some brandy down Ramsay's throat. When his eyes opened, Pedro was supporting his master's head, while a group of men around were watching the stranger curiously, foremost among whom was an English gentleman.

"Coming to all right?" said the latter. "A near shave that. You began to smoke, I take it, finding yourself pretty nearly lost and famished, so the valley got fired. We have been out searching for you since morning, when your man rode up to my hacienda, worn out and demented. We passed the head of the valley at ten o'clock, but could see no sign of your horse, which Pedro said he had tied to a tree. What's the matter?"

For Ramsay struggled up, and was staring round.

"*The tree!* It was out there before the fire: Pedro, you know—where is it gone?"

Pedro only shivered and stared. Some of the other peones, muttering, and giving sidelong glances at each other, crossed the burnt ground looking about them. One saw a partly submerged tree at some distance down stream, floating slowly into the marsh. His attention was caught by a gleam of something scarlet tangled in the topmost withered bough.

A few days later, Ramsay was stretched at ease in a cane deck-chair, with a tall glass of iced drink in the wicker socket by his arm. Overhead a verandah was shaded with masses of roses, stephanotis and bignonia. Sunshine flooded the garden stretching beyond like a dream of enchantment, where tall palms shot above high flowering trees, and oranges and lemons were mingled lower with gardenias and poinsettias.

Jock had just finished after talking during some twenty minutes, so felt thirsty, exhausted, and excited.

"That's the whole story," he ended. "Now, do you believe me, Mr. Campbell? Till now, I fancy you thought me mad."

"No, but possibly a bit delirious in your fever, so that you imagined some tale Pedro told you of the lamparagua had really happened to yourself. That was all," said the kindly host.

"Man alive! There is Pedro to witness also. And where is my horse? And your own lad saw the torn red blanket in the marsh!" cried Ramsay.

"True, quite true," nodded Campbell, coolly reflecting. "Well, my dear fellow, if it is any satisfaction to you, I do believe you are one of the few living human beings who have seen the lamparagua. What is more, for some years back I have heard rumours of such a thing, and that it haunted this lake and another adjoining it, both on my estate. But, to confess the truth, I fancied the story was a convenient legend of my cattle-herds to account for missing beasts. Yes, I believe. But hardly any one else will, even in Chile, among our own wise educated class. Of course the peones know. They are nearer Nature than we."

THE FLOWER OF DEATH

Flavel Scott Mines

"I should have been surprised if you had not come," said Margaret, smiling, as she welcomed him, "for we regard you as the chief support of our days at home. This is the second Wednesday you have saved from being a hollow mockery—for if there is anything that makes you feel absolutely foolish it is to be ready and waiting to receive people who never come."

Selden bowed, and blushed like a boy. "Thank you," he murmured. "It is doubly delightful to be praised for what you do as a pleasure."

"We have been packing all day," began Margaret, watching the doorway, "and day after tomorrow we close the house and take flight. It will be quite a relief to get away, and I am longing for the country. We are going to be very quiet this summer, staying most of the time with mamma's brother in Pennsylvania, and the change will be delightful."

"Yes," assented Selden, slowly. "I'm going away myself. I feel like taking a long, long journey. I've finished the picture that I've been working on all the spring and I want some rest. I—I suppose I won't see you until the fall?"

He said this somewhat wistfully, but Margaret thought best to pass it over.

"I am so glad your picture is done," she returned. "Now the next thing, I presume, will be a purchaser."

Selden shook his head and shrugged his shoulders. "Oh, probably," he answered, carelessly. "I've been thinking of other things.

Other thoughts—other dreams have engrossed me. Margaret," he said, growing suddenly earnest and bending forward, "I have been thinking and dreaming of you."

The girl started. A frightened look came into her eyes for a moment and her face paled, but Selden did not notice it. "Of you," he repeated; "and the world holds nothing else to me. I must tell you now—I cannot wait until the fall without seeing you. I had not expected to say this when I came this afternoon; but all the sunshine of my life is gone if you—if you—"

Margaret made an involuntary movement as the young man hesitated. Her deep brown eyes had grown deeper and more serious. There was a womanly grace and sweetness in her face that Selden had never seen before, and she spoke so tenderly, so sweetly.

"Please say no more, Mr. Selden. I had not thought of this. We have been such good friends that—"

"Don't, don't!" cried Selden, vehemently, interrupting her; "don't, I pray you! Wait—wait—until the fall, and then tell me—not now."

"That would be unfair to you," she rejoined, gently. "My regard is too strong to allow you to labor under any deception. You have misunderstood me—you do not know me—and it would be wrong to let you believe otherwise. I am very, very sorry if I pain you. Unintentionally, I know, you have saddened me—because I never dreamed of this. You can forget me before long."

They had risen to their feet, and Selden had grown stern. "Good-by," he said, holding out his hand. "I ask your pardon."

"It is for me to crave forgiveness of you," answered Margaret, taking his hand, and looking at him with a frank, open glance. "I have been blind."

For a moment Selden hesitated, as if about to speak; then he bent and kissed her hand and walked hurriedly away.

"Good-by," he repeated, turning at the door; "I trust your summer—your life—may be happy." He was too far away to see the tears which filled the woman's eyes as she inclined her head, and then, after a brief look, he went out.

Henry Selden came down the steps of the house slowly and carefully, as a man walks in his sleep. To him the street was changed.
The sun shone through a haze. Shadow of black was merged into
the gray stone on which it fell. At the corner of the street he halted
mechanically to allow a cab to pass; and then he wondered why he
had not gone on and let the cab run over him if the driver so fancied. For what was life to him any longer; what cared he for living?

He walked down the street without thought of where he was
going; he did not care for the present. But unconsciously, as he
went along, he turned his steps toward his club, where so many of
his friends usually gathered at the dinner hour. He found himself
at the door before he quite realized it; and as he glanced at the
little park opposite, watching the warm sunshine of the dying day
gild and play among the fresh green leaves, the beauty of all life
had so passed from him that he felt apart from all his surroundings. Could he have screamed outright like a petulant child, he
knew that he would have felt better.

Once inside the familiar building he grew more composed, and
smiled and nodded at his friends, feeling proud that some familiar
faces still crossed his path at whom he could smile and nod. It was
a strange feeling. Three men whom he knew well were at a table
on the rear balcony, awaiting their dinner, and Selden joined them.
Two were lawyers, possessing larger incomes than practices, while
the other was Bartow, an enthusiastic lover of nature, whose wanderings took him to all parts of the world. He had returned, in fact,
only a short time before from the little-known South American
countries.

"Selden in his new role as understudy to Melancholy," laughed
Jackson, as Selden stepped through the open window which led to
the veranda.

"He's probably sold a picture," suggested Gardner, "and seeks
to conceal his joy."

But Bartow only laughed, and pointed to the vacant chair at
the table. "Dinner is ordered," he said. "Sit down; summon the
minion, and you can quench your thought in drink."

"Just the thing," returned Selden, with a forced laugh; "a draught of Lethe is exactly what I want."

During the meal that followed Selden was almost fierce in his mood at times, laughing loudly at all jests and indulging in wild, wayward humors. His friends remarked only upon his high spirits, for he kept them amused with the wildest fancies and turns of thought. He tried hard to forget himself. With the advent of the coffee and cigars, Bartow was pressed to tell something of his adventures and experiences in his late travels.

"Which reminds me," he said. "Come round to my house now, and I'll show you something you never saw before;" and the four men went out.

Bartow lived immediately around the corner, and entering the house, he led his friends to a conservatory in the rear, just off his study. He stopped before a small box resting upon a shelf, covered with a sash which was bolted down securely at both ends. Under the glass were two plants in blossom, one bearing a red and the other a yellow flower, oval in shape. The blooms were not alike in any respect, nor did the leaves of the plants resemble each other, and both were unfamiliar to the visitors.

"Here," said Bartow, pointing to the box, "is my prize curiosity. One of these is an ordinary wild flower of the Andes, the other is what the Indians call the 'Flower of Death,' but I don't know which the other is. A seed of the Flower of Death was given to me by an old chief, a remnant of the tribes whom Pizarro conquered. In some way I got the seed of the ordinary plant mixed with it, and now of those two I cannot tell which is which. So, in order to avoid possible trouble, I have planted and kept them together in this box. One is perfectly harmless; and one, according to the tales of the Indians, is deadly. It is said that a man who inhales its perfume is surely doomed. The effects are pleasant and slow, but none the less fatal. Now, of course I do not know that this is really so," added Bartow, as he saw the others smile, "but I have seen so many strange things in nature that I want to be on the safe side. I'm not going to fool with any such growths to determine the truth, and in keeping these two together I believe the noxious one will kill the other eventually."

"Pretty good story," laughed Gardner. "Easy way to commit suicide. A friend of mine has a pet parrot I'd like to bring around for experimental purposes."

"Don't be too sceptical," advised Bartow, leading the way back to the library and setting out a bottle and cigars; "you can't afford to jest with dreadful uncertainties. I heard the story of this fatal flower from a number of persons at different times, and I believe it; but I wish that in my chuckle-headed asininity I hadn't mixed them up."

"A disappointed lover might be willing to find out the truth for you," suggested Jackson, holding a glass up to the light to determine the quality of the stock.

Selden threw himself on a lounge and laughed harshly. "Disappointed lovers are not so unselfish," he said, in a rough way. "It is seldom that a man is willing to give up life for a mere crossing of his affections—the memory of a girl."

"Right you are," cried Gardner; "one girl doesn't make the world."

"She does to the true lover," interposed Bartow; "and she unmakes it as well. True love—"

"True nonsense!" retorted Selden, rather more fiercely than the occasion seemed to warrant. "Are we a lot of callow boys trying to solve the problem of love? Bah!"

"All right, bah," said Bartow, quietly; "but wait until you are taken, old man, and there will be a reversal of ideas."

"Bartow knows," put in Jackson, "for I am acquainted personally with three girls—"

Selden rose from his seat hurriedly. "I'd like to make a sketch of those blossoms," he said, turning to Bartow; "they interest me, and when I get back I hope we can discuss some intelligent subject."

Bartow nodded. "Go ahead," he answered; "you won't see many such flowers; they're genuine curiosities."

Selden went alone into the conservatory, lighted by a single lamp. He was angry and pained. It seemed almost as though his friends had been making sport of him. He stood before the glass for several moments, not looking at the flowers beneath, but thinking, thinking; then, almost unconsciously, he tried one of the bolts. It slipped easily in its place, and Selden turned to see if he could be observed from the other room, and found that he was hidden. Suppose he should leave all to Fortune—to chance—and risk one smell? If one flower really was deadly and he should inhale it, what difference would it make to him? But if Margaret did love him, or would learn to love him, then Fate would lead him to the harmless blossom. By all the laws of nature, he reasoned, he would not be sacrificed to a moment's caprice when a certainty of bliss was assured. So thinking, he released the other bolt, and bending over the flower nearest to him, drew in one long breath of its fragrance. It exhaled a sickish-sweet odor, different from any he knew of. Then he lowered the glass, bolted it, and hurriedly made a sketch of the flowers to satisfy his friends. As he turned away he smiled at the childishness of his act in thus accepting an old Indian legend, and then pretending to play at a game with Fate. It was a piece of foolishness, and laughing at it, he also blushed. Then he joined his friends.

They were discussing modern society; and Selden, feeling no interest in the subject, sat silently smoking and looking at his sketches. He wanted to have company about him, for he wished to forget the horror of the day—it was to him as the memory of something terrible. All might be different on the morrow, and as he held the sketches before him, he tried to think which flower he had smelt, the red or the yellow. Then he blushed again at his nonsense, and broke into the conversation with some wholly absurd and irrelevant remark. For an hour or two they chatted, examined the sketches, and then the three visitors went out together, Selden leaving his friends at the corner of the street.

He walked slowly to his studio, thinking over his lost love, but feeling somewhat more hopeful than in the afternoon. He knew nothing more, but grasping at any idea which brought peace of

mind, he did not stop to reason. As he opened his door he noticed
an envelope lying just inside, and picking it up, found it to be a
telegram. With trembling fingers, after lighting the gas, he opened
it and read:

> "I was mistaken this afternoon, and spoke with-
> out thinking. Come to me.
>
> Margaret."

A sense of perfect happiness, of supreme peace, entered into
Henry Selden's soul at the moment. He would obey her injunction
the first thing in the morning, and meanwhile would send a telegram in answer. Sitting down at once, he wrote the address and
the words, "Your message received," and then stopped. It was not
necessary for him to send it, for she knew he would come at the
very first opportunity, and it was too late that night for telegram
or call. He looked around for the message he had received, and
failed to find it. Then high and low he searched, going through
drawers and boxes not disturbed or opened for days, until another
thing caught his eye and gave him a new thought. The telegram
was all forgotten. Before him on the easel rested a landscape of
May, the picture which he had just finished. It was his best work,
he believed, and as he looked at the light green of the trees and
grass, the pink and white of the orchard blossoms, the face of
Margaret rose before his eyes. What a beautiful background it
would make for her portrait! and as the thought came, he sat down
before the easel and began the outline. He needed no model, no
guide; the sweet face was too deeply imprinted on his soul for him
ever to forget it. Nervously he worked, taking no note of the passage of time until it was complete. He dashed on the color with a
sweep and a swing entirely different from his usually slow, pains-
taking method of painting; but, urged on by happiness and excitement, he was able to work fast. The labor of weeks was destroyed
in a few hurried minutes; but to his mind the world held a single
joy, one figure, which he vainly sought to reproduce on canvas. . . .
Yet, after all, it was well done, he thought, as he laid aside his

palette and drew up his easy-chair before the easel. The sweet, proud face looked serenely at him from out the mass of blossoms— eyes so tender, so pleading, invested with all the strength of love. Selden gazed longingly, ardently, on the work of his midnight frenzy, praying that the morrow might hasten, when he would see her. Suppose he had smelt the wrong flower—the Flower of Death? Then he laughed heartily at the idea of ever having been so down-hearted or sceptical as to believe or seek to prove the Indian fable. He started to rise for his pipe, but the loving face that for him was gazing out from the canvas caught his eye again, and he lay back entranced. He seemed to be in a dream—music came to his ears. . . .

His three friends alone guessed at the truth. In the box by the two flowers were scattered the ashes which fell from Henry Selden's cigar.

"There are three things which can never be explained," remarked Bartow, gravely, a day later: "Why did he cover that picture with daubs of paint picked at random from the palette and having no outline? Why did he address a message to Miss Winthrop, when she stated positively that she had sent him no telegram? The poor girl is completely prostrated to-day, for she really truly loved Hal. And thirdly," continued Bartow, after a moment's pause, "which flower is the Flower of Death?"

The Man-Killing Tree of Ceylon

Anonymous

"It was something more than the love of sport and adventure that took me back to Ceylon for a second visit," said Major Carter of her majesty's service. "I had resolved to solve the mystery of Lieutenant Gordan's most unaccountable disappearance on that wild island five years before. Gordan was a fine fellow, young, daring and enthusiastic, with a promising future before him, and the uncertainty of his fate preyed upon my mind.

"I had often heard weird stories of the man killing tree of Ceylon, but I did not believe there was the least foundation for them. To my mind the story was a myth, for I had found a man might rest in security beneath the so called deadly upas, and yet the story of the upas was never so improbable as that of the fiendish tree said to live on flesh and blood.

"Lieutenant Gordan had shared my skepticism to a certain extent, and yet he was inclined to search for the demon tree in dark depths of the wildest jungles. He had a daring and dangerous way of rambling far into the forests, his only companions being a native guide and his dark skinned servant. More than once I told him he would provide a square meal for a tiger or some other wild animal, but he only laughed at my fears.

"One night he did not return. The guide and the servant came back, both frightened nearly to death, and they told a story that aroused our party to a high pitch of excitement. They declared Lieutenant Gordan had fallen a victim to the man-eating tree, saying it was near mid-afternoon when they came to the mouth of a deep and dark valley, into which the venturesome young man insisted on penetrating. At the mouth of the valley the natives found a small stone idol, before which were scattered human skulls and bones. This served to warn them against entering the forbidding place, and they refused to accompany the lieutenant.

"Gordan was not daunted, and he bade them await his return, after which he boldly went down into the gloom of the place, leaving the natives mumbling and prostrating themselves before the idol.

"In about 20 minutes the guide and the servant heard a terrible shriek of fear and agony that came up from the mysterious and dismal valley. The cry was that of a human being in the greatest agony, and so frightened were the natives that they instantly took to their heels and fled from the spot.

"We rebuked them for their cowardice, and all of us believed Gordan had been attacked by a wild animal or a serpent. We even entertained hope that he might put in an appearance, but the night passed and morning came without any sign of him. Then nearly the entire party set out to find the dismal valley and solve the mystery of our comrade's fate.

"The guide was very reluctant about leading us, but we forced him to do so. For hours we tramped about in the jungle without finding the valley, and the guide finally declared he did not know how to lead us to it. This made us very angry, and we nearly scared the fellow to death, asserting we would flay him alive if he did not take us to the place. He started on again, and we followed, but night found us unrewarded for our pains. In returning to the camp, both the guide and Gordan's servant slipped away and disappeared in the forest, and neither was seen afterward.

"This mysterious affair threw a damper on our spirits, and the hunt was far from a success. The most of the party were inclined to believe the lieutenant had been murdered by the two natives, and I thought it not improbable.

"During the five years that elapsed before I again visited Ceylon, I often thought of Jack Gordan and longed to know the truth concerning his fate. When I found myself once more in the vicinity of our former adventures, I resolved to search for the fatal valley. Captain Starbuck, a loyal friend and a man with plenty of courage. agreed to accompany me, poor fellow! I was glad to have a white man as a companion, although I protested against taking him from his elephant shooting, but he professed some faith in the story of the man eating tree and expressed a desire to look upon the monster of the vegetable kingdom.

"Taking our servants along, we made a party of four, although we knew we could not depend on the blackskins in case of emergency. It was near midday of our first and final search that we came to the mouth of a valley that seemed to me like the one described by the native guide and Gordan's servant. All at once both our dusky aids flung themselves face downward on the ground and began chanting something in the most doleful tones and then we saw they were bowed before a hideous stone image, around which were scattered bones and human skulls!

"'We have found the fatal valley!' I cried.

"It was useless to attempt to persuade the blackskins to accompany us into the gloom of the place, and they entreated us not to go there, saying we would never come forth if we ventured. Telling them to await our return and looking to make sure our weapons were ready for instant use, we entered the valley.

"A deep gloom hung over the place, which was disturbed by no sound save our footfalls, and they did not seem to make an echo. As we moved slowly onward a feeling of horror gradually and surely crept over me, although I tried to throw it off. It seemed that there was something uncanny about the valley—something weird and deadly. I looked at the captain and saw his fact was pale, although his jaws were set and determination was written on his features.

"In vain we looked about for sign of living creature in that dismal vale. No bird nor animal greeted our vision; not even a snake squirmed across our path. For all of the gloom, the vegetation was luxurious and rank, but the air seemed laden with perfumes that were sweet to the point of nauseation.

"In a short time we came to a wall of barren stone. A cry broke from my lips, and stooping: I picked up a rusty rifle that lay at the foot of the wall. After a minute examination I asserted:

"'This was Lieutenant Gordan's gun. His initials are carved on the stock.'

"My voice sounded hollow and strange. I looked up at the rugged wall and made a motion to ascend. Captain Starbuck nodded, and we were soon climbing side by side.

"As we mounted upward a singular sound came to our ears. It was a sort of swishing or hissing, like the sound of a strong wind in rank reeds, and yet unlike it. This grew more distinct as we neared the top of the wall, and there was something blood chilling in the sound.

"The top was soon reached, and we looked over into a circular basin, in the very center of which rose a tree that was of a vividly green hue from its roots to its highest point. And such a tree! There were no leaves upon it, and its bare branches were round and supple, like so many serpents. From its body to its upper limit the tree was in motion. The slender limbs were whipping and cutting through the air like things of life, making the hissing sound we heard.

"A cry of amazement broke from Starbuck's lips. In an instant the tree was still, and every branch pointed straight at us. At that moment I lost my footing and slipped back a bit, falling below the level of the wall's highest point. I felt something knock my hat from my bead, and then I heard a terrible shriek from my companion. My horrified eyes beheld a hundred twining, twisting things encircle him and snatch him from view in a twinkling. For a moment others played and squirmed over the wall as if feeling for me, and then they vanished.

"A short time I clung there, paralyzed with such horror as never possessed me before, and then I drew myself up to the top of the wall again. I can never forget the horrible sight that greeted my eyes. Captain Starbuck was in the grasp of that demon tree, the limbs of which were twined about him like serpents. Some had twisted themselves about his neck, and I saw he was already dead, having been strangled. And over the body the snaky arms of the accursed tree fought and squirmed.

"Sick and fainting with terror, I slid down to the foot of the wall and ran from that infernal spot as fast as my legs could carry me. I did not stop when I reached the mouth of the deadly valley, and the two natives, reading the truth on my face, kept me company.

"When I told the story at camp, it was received with mingled doubt and credulity. Some of the men could not bring themselves to believe such a thing possible, while others, knowing me better, did not doubt my word.

"We spent three days searching for that valley, and, singular as it may seem, it could not be found again. I do not know that it has been found to this day. But were I able to go direct to it," concluded Major Carter, "the wealth of England would not tempt me into its horrid confines!"

The Death Plant of South Africa*

H. B. M. Buchanan

The full African sun, from a sky of the hardest blue, poured down its fierce rays on the sandy plains beneath, which, already overcharged with heat, reflected them back from its yellowish surface, till the air felt like solid iron bands of heat. From the horizon came bounding along a herd of the jetel or hartebeest antelope, with their beautiful red chestnut skins glistening in the declining sun like the coats of well-groomed English hunters. Rapidly approaching, they stopped by a patch of nabbuk bushes to eat of the small fruit, which, like miniature apples about the size of nutmegs, had fallen in large quantities to the ground. The leader of the herd mounted a white-ant hill to keep faithful watch over his flock against any approaching danger.

Amidst some tall grasses, that lay between the forest and the nabbuk bushes, a lion awoke from his midday sleep; he stretched himself lazily, first with one paw, then with the other, and, with

---

* The grapple plant (*Harpagophytum*) is a prostrate herb growing in South Africa. Its flowers are purple, and in shape like the English foxglove. Its fruit has very formidable hooks, which, by clinging to any passer-by, is conveyed to situations where its seeds may find suitable conditions for growth. The principle is illustrated by the burrs of the English burdock. Sir John Lubbock says it has been known to kill lions.

eyes dull from sleep, surveyed leisurely the plain before him. Suddenly he spied the herd of antelopes feeding on the fruit of the nabbuk bushes. At once the loosened muscles became firm, and drawn out like whipcord, the head rigid and attentive, the body crouched close to the ground, the eyes fixed, bright and cruel; the tufted tail, quivering with emotion, moved slowly from side to side. Softly and slowly he began to move amidst the grass that lay between him and the nabbuk bushes; one clumsy shake of the grasses above him, or the slightest exposure of his body would have given the alarm to the watchful leader of the antelope herd, and a few moments would have seen them disappear on the clear-cut horizon. Moving forward a few paces, with every step considered; then pausing, as if resting from the tension that this cautious approach caused him, the great beast crept on.

The lion at last came to the edge of grass, a long space separating him from the nearest antelope. Could he spring the distance, or would he fall short, and slink away, ashamed of his failure? He paused for a few seconds to collect together all his strength for the final leap; the body crouched close to the ground, and bent backwards well over the hind hocks, the head firm and raised, the claws sent into the ground for a better grip, the body oscillating backwards and forwards a few times, and then with a great roar the tawny lion sprang. He had measured his strength rightly; one great paw came down with sledgehammer violence on the beautiful head of the nearest antelope. With growls and kind purrings the great beast began his work of destruction. Every now and then, as the lion lay across the mangled body of his victim, he would pause and look around, but with no fear in his look. And so he fed without dread.

As the sun was about to set, a refreshing breeze came whispering from the forest over the sandy plain towards this strange mystery of life and death. Gaining in strength, it drove slowly on the fruit of the grapple plant, whose formidable-looking hooks were awaiting to attach themselves to any passer-by, so that it might be conveyed to some spot where the seed contained within the array of hooks might find suitable lodgment for growth. Rounding themselves into balls, sometimes travelling faster, sometimes slower, sometimes stopping altogether, according to the varying strength of the soothing, refreshing breeze, on they came, dry, roundish balls, innocent-looking enough, and apparently not likely to do harm to anything. At last one lazily rolled under the hind-quarters of the lion as he lay occupied with his victim, and unrolling itself, the hooks very slowly got hold of his tawny quarters, at first so gently that the lion fed on unheeding. As the hooks got a firmer hold, they began to curl and creep into the flesh, until a sudden grip revealed to the lion that something unusual was upon his quarters. With a deep growl he lifted himself off the carcass of the deer to examine the source of his annoyance. At first he tried to brush off the fruit with a front paw, but the hooks had now got firm hold, and were not to be easily moved. After repeated efforts he desisted, and smelt it with his nose, not understanding what it was, or why it was there.

The hooks gradually tightening their hold were now giving the lion considerable pain, which caused him to lose his composure somewhat, and with deep, angry growls he worked all the harder with his front paws to remove the tenacious fruit. But the more he did so, the firmer it clung, and the worse grew the pain, till, driven to desperation, he seized the fruit in his mouth and tried to tear it away from its lodgment. But the fruit remained firm. Agonized with pain, he now lost his majestic self-control, and with savage mutterings tore away with all his strength. At last the tenacious fruit gave way into the lion's mouth, but, still obedient to its nature, it wound its sharp prongs into the tongue, roof, and throat of the distracted and maddened beast. Then the dreadful death agony began. Growling, moaning, blinded with pain, the noble head jerking rapidly from side to side, the mane flying about in utter confusion, the mouth wide open. Rolling on the ground, standing up, rolling again, running round and round, standing still, lifting his head high up in the air, burying it in the sands; tearing at his mouth with his claws, the weary death struggle went on.

At last the fight against fate gradually ceased, the convulsions and twitchings grew less and less violent, till perfect stillness stole over that habitation of strength and endurance. The pale light of the African moon shone forth from a clear sky, dotted with innumerable stars. Its gentle beams fell upon the strange tragedy, embracing with its calm light the mangled antelope, the choked lion, the buried seed.

THE GUARDIAN OF MYSTERY ISLAND

Dr. Edmond Nolcini

On the white slope of the sandy beach at Orr, a company of fishermen, just in from the night's catch, were variously employed in loading, disposing of their traps, or mending their nets. There were two quiet figures in the picture outlined in the clear summer atmosphere between the shore and the sea. A young man, who marked three points ahead in the line of intellectual development, was standing beside an overturned boat, upon which was seated an old fisherman, engaged in mending his net, and conveying to the attentive ear of his companion some interesting bits of information concerning the surrounding islands of the bay. There were relative values an artist would have appreciated, afforded by the contrast in dress and person of the two men. The fair, sensitive face of the young man, with his lithe and elegant figure coolly clad in white flannel, was a complement to the burly form of the sailor, roughly clothed, and with weather-stained features composing a simple but kindly countenance, well shaded under an oilskin hat.

"No land twixt her en Spain, sir."

"A period between continents," interrupted the young man jocosely.

"En I wouldn't go anighst her fur all the gold en the mint. Thar's plenty of land twixt her en us, thank God! Ye ken see she's the furtherest out nor all the islands."

"Yes, I see, Tom," replied the young man, directing a quizzical glance toward a small dark spot between the two spaces of blue. "She must be ten miles out."

"Nigh onter it."

"Well, what is out there to prevent a man from visiting your 'Mystery Island,' if he wants to?"

"Fur one thing, sir, Kidd's gold ez buried out thar, but thar hain't a feller on this yer coast dar's to go anighst it. Cauz the cove, what's only a narrer cut twixt two cliffs thet crawls inter sarpent ledges under the warter, makes it a damned nasty place ter git inter, even ef it warn't guarded—"

"Guarded? Guarded by whom?"

"A dorg, a confounded sperret dorg, with eyes like lighthouse lanterns, thet kin be seed ten miles out, whenever anything is goin' ter harpen. Whoever sees thet ar dorg might just's well make peace with God, fer he hain't likely ter stay round much longer 'mong men."

The young man, whose name was Lenartson,—Sam Lenartson,— laughed outright. It seemed the most ridiculous story he had ever heard credited by otherwise sensible men.

He determined at once to administer a rebuke to their foolish superstitions.

"Tom," he said, wheeling about impulsively, "give me a dory and a pair of oars, and I will go out there to-day and explode all your thrilling romance about the island."

"My God, sir!" Tom dropped his horny hands helplessly, an ashy pallor creeping over his face.

"Yer don't know, sir. Twenty years ago, sir, there was a party of young chaps from the city, who wouldn't hear to nuthin', went out there en never come back. Ye hain't lived round these parts en watched the signs. Thar's the awfullest rocket strikes this yer coast en a hurricane every time thet unarthly beast ez seed. 'Twould be like a helpin' ye to commit suicide; et's damned folly ter think uv et."

"Tom, you might just as well let me have your boat as to put me to the trouble of getting another, as I shall certainly go out to Mystery Island, and I should like to go this morning. I vow solemnly to break the awful spell which has power over you only from your belief in it. And when I have entered the cove, braved the dog, and upset the kingdom of the devil supposed to be established there, not one of you fellows will dispute my right to Kidd's gold."

Tom's revolutions of thought were too slow to frame a new objection. Hypnotized by the spirit and energy of his companion, he rose from his seat, pointing doggedly at the boat.

"Ef ye will, ye will, I spoze; take her en go; ye don't go unwarned.

"Ye ken look out fur a squall," he shouted after the departing youth, who flung up his hat like a person taking leave of a party of particular friends, as he paddled out.

Sam was not by nature over-cautious, so that the admonition regarding the weather gave him no concern of mind as he floated past the beautiful islands of Casco Bay. One after another they disappeared behind him, as the island for which his oars were bent loomed up more definitely before him. Suddenly, conscious of a chill penetrating the atmosphere, he looked up, to remark a marshaling force of clouds that, unperceived by him, had been marching up the heavenly plain for the last half hour, and were now rapidly darkening with a summer shower.

An ominous lash of the wind struck the bosom of the great deep. With a startled throb, it lifted the boat sharply. Sam looked around him with critical and troubled eyes.

He was not far from the little cove, which presented itself as a sharply inclined sand-bar displayed between the cliffs that rose precipitously upon either side of it.

But the ledges upon either side of the passage rendered it so narrow and dangerous that they were called the Black Snakes. Around them the seething tide boiled like a witch's pot, flinging the white foam of the angry billows high against the cliffs, that returned it with such force that a boat carried in this direction must have been doomed to certain destruction.

Just as Lenartson was about to breast the wave which should have carried him safely into the little harbor, a fierce gust of wind from an unexpected quarter seized upon his light craft, and before he could make an effort to resist it, he was whirled about broadside upon one of the rising breakers. In this position, half capsized and water logged, blinded by the falling rain, his face wet by the salt spray, he must have been borne to certain death had not the capricious wind, playing with the frail craft like a paper toy, suddenly reversed it. Thus it was set upon the crest of a falling breaker in such a direction as to be flung into the cove, landing with a sharp collision some twenty feet up the beach.

The shock threw Lenartson face forward, where he lay for a moment half stunned. Then, as a flash of light and crash of thunder aroused him to a sense of danger, he sprang out of the boat, dragging it up the incline just in time to save it from the returning wave. After finding a broken stake, to which he secured his boat, he fled to the trees, seeking shelter from the rain among the tall and serried columns of pine and fir, whose thick mat of interlaced branches made the darkness almost impenetrable.

When, the shower ended, light through the breaking clouds penetrated the internal fastness, Lenartson discovered a rank growth of foliage not common to these islands nor the latitude in which they were located. Everywhere flowers and plants of variegated hues were massed in such rich profusion as to suggest the land of the deadly cobra, while even the more familiar trees had reached a height and breadth that seemed wholly foreign.

As he began to work his way through the thick undergrowth toward the interior, he came to the conclusion not only that the island was uninhabited, but that the place had not been marked by human footsteps for many years, as the small animals, and the birds that flew from cover, seemed quite fearless.

He had but just arrived at this conclusion when there rose upon the air the distinct bay of a dog, apparently not many feet away.

Evidently some one else had chosen the same day to pay a visit to the island.

Led by the sound of the animal's voice, he soon emerged upon what had been a small clearing, but at the present time was entirely covered with the second growth of trees, shooting up over an area of a hundred square feet. Here, amidst a medley of decayed stumps and underbrush, he saw a rude board hut, before which, with his nose in the air, sat the dog who had led him to question and investigation.

But, far from being the formidable creature of the fisherman's yarn, this noble wreck of the mastiff breed was ill fitted to hold midnight revels with hurricanes and to conjure with infernal powers, since every fiber of his poor old body seemed to call for a blanket and a kennel.

His eyes, instead of appearing the baleful globes of fire that fishermen's fancies had made visible ten miles out at sea, were rather dim and piteous in their appeal for friendly recognition.

The poor creature had somehow missed his master—or such was Sam's conclusions—and in dog anguish thus lamented his misfortune.

"Hullo, old boy! have you lost him? Well, never mind, we'll set that straight directly."

Having convinced himself by a glance into the interior of the cabin, which was filled with spiders' webs and their crafty weavers, that it had not been used for many years, Lenartson turned once more to the dog.

"Come, Jack," he said, "let us go after your master."

With one of those peremptory barks that is interpreted as dog consent, the great lion-like creature bounded into the thicket.

This action served to reveal what had at one time been a path, but now, like every other effort of man here, indicated a contention with, and partial subjection to, the native wildness of the woodland.

Through bramble and brier they pushed along the overgrown path, the dog still ahead, until a space of light suddenly penetrated the open branches of the trees. A moment later, they emerged upon a plot of ground, where was revealed to Lenartson's astonished gaze a stately old mansion, built of stone, and enclosed by neglected terraces and overgrown gardens, upon which, at some time, had been bestowed much expense and care.

Now, however, the sharp tooth of time had gnawed into the vitals of the old place, from the broken chimneys and sunken flags of the walks to the defaced and fallen fence, rotting away beneath the mold of the drifting leaves.

The deserted house conveyed an air of melancholy to all of its surroundings.

It seemed a little singular to the young man, as he came upon this scene, that no person at Orr had ever mentioned its builders and occupants to him.

"Why not?" he wondered.

The dog left him no time to consider this point at length. He bounded up the steps, ran across the stone veranda, and leaped through the wide door into the hall, at the entrance of which rose a flight of winding stone stairs.

As Lenartson made haste to follow him, he had time to notice that the curtains at the lower windows were rendered almost invisible from the outside by the thick veil of dust encrusting the glass panes. He further felt the chill of a damp and moldy house while ascending the stairs.

The upper hall presented a tableau in still life of open doors, dusty floor, and cobwebbed corners. His steps seemed to evoke a ghostly ring of answering echoes through the vacant halls. As the dog passed through one of the open doors leading off at the right of the staircase, Lenartson paused upon the threshold to listen to the labored breathing of a sick or dying person.

Another moment, and his singular quest had brought him to the bedside of an old woman, lying beneath a heap of worn silk quilts and battered blankets, tossed about her emaciated figure in utmost confusion. The lips, thin, seamed, and crossed by yellow wrinkles, were parted above toothless gums in an almost vain struggle for breath. The talon-like fingers clutched nervously at the worn coverlid, as the great creature at Lenartson's side leaped upon the bed, lapping the withered cheek of his mistress; then settled down, with his head upon his paws, and his eyes fixed in appeal upon the stranger.

In bewilderment Lenartson glanced about the room, to observe, here as elsewhere, the absence of care denoted in the carpet of dust upon the oak floor, the array of cobwebs festooning the ceiling or woven across the brocade shades depending in sags from the four large windows of the room.

Here was a mystery of Mystery Island that made his blood boil with indignation. An old woman! Abandoned, it was evident, and dying thus, unattended except by a dog, her last earthly friend!

As he entered, she regarded him with no apparent recognition of a human presence, but turned the wandering glance of her wild, dark eyes toward a crucifix placed upon a table near the head of the bed. This crucifix was the only thing within reach of her vision to suggest solace to the dying, as there was neither bread upon the table to sustain her perishing frame, nor water to cool her parched lips.

"You are sick," affirmed the young man, with great pity vibrating in his voice; "what can I do for you?"

At the sound she sprang up in bed, and glared angrily upon him from dark and cavernous eyes. She stretched forth her long, lean arms, away from whose unlovely bones fell the tattered lace of her night-robe.

"Pierre! Pierre!" she almost shrieked, as Lenartson shrank repulsed from the uninviting embrace. "At last! at last! Oh, my God, why did you leave me alone in this strange deserted land?"

She spoke in French, and Lenartson, understanding it well, thus discovered her lineage.

Then she had been deserted, this poor old creature,—a refugee from a sunny land, abandoned to a life of wretchedness on this forsaken isle.

"Madame," he interrupted in reverent sympathy, "I am not Pierre; I am a stranger, providentially brought to you in this hour of need. What can I give you, food or drink, and where can either be found?"

With a supreme effort she pulled herself forward, a movement that called his attention to the glittering rings that hung upon her yellow, shrivelled hands.

"Ah! you would deceive me, and to what purpose, I ask?"

She pointed in his face her old, skinny forefinger, an index of scorn shaken by wrath.

"Sir, I command you to leave me. If alone, well, so be it. If the King's head has fallen, it is a pretty piece of business these dogs have done. Never fear, the end will find France restored to reason. We shall make another King. No, sir! I decline your assistance in this matter. We are not a race of cowards."

As these scenes unshadowed themselves, she used first this tone of haughty complacency, and then, when the full horror of some fearful situation made itself felt, she threw up her arms with a cry of terror.

"What are they doing, these brutes in the street? It is she, my dear lady. Quick, give my cloak—this way—we must not be seen. The Bastille has fallen! It is the Conciergerie where they would carry our innocent, woe-white queen! It is dark, my dear,—give me your hand,—we are suspected, but we are also protected. Let us fly! The nobles are in the winepress, the people are on top— blood flows, curses darken the air. This is not France, it is a pan- demonium; it is a mad-house; it is hell!"

Through this hurried, breathless speech of terror, Lenartson stood as if rooted to the spot. At the close of it Madame sank, white with exhaustion, among the pillows. Then, as the dying candle fire flickered into a blaze, the old lips muttered:—

"Have mercy, my lord! Do not leave me with these rough fellows even for so short a time. Do you believe the weak hand of a woman can protect such immense treasure? The earth where it lies buried is but an open storehouse, when, by your absence, the lock is removed from silence, and that devil, cupidity, which I see in each man's eye is free to manifest itself.

"Ah! the weed—the devil-weed! I had not thought about it. Plant it to-morrow upon yonder ledge that will lift it to the sun and air. Superstition will stay their greedy clutch for your gold, sir count. It will live,—like the evil in men's hearts, it is too viperous to die."

She tossed herself uneasily. Great drops of perspiration stood upon her forehead.

"Pierre! Pierre!" she moaned, "it is not a devil-weed, it is a soul bound and restless; it is my soul shrieking silent maledictions to heaven.

"Ah, sir count, it was an awkward slip to take a woman from palaces and thrones to a hut in the woods; from association with princes to a company of thieves. But the gold tempted you, my poor count. For the promise of a title under the new regime we plot-ted—a pirate sold to you the secret of hidden treasure. He had sailed with the great captain; he knew it was here. We were an odd assemblage, I vow, but the house was built by stealth, of material brought in the ship,—the treasure concealed. It was thought to be a secret, but when two have a secret it becomes public matter. Your devil-weed was planted to secure the gold. Your devil-weed—only a little evil, like the incipient causes of a revolution; the hand that cozened it into unholy life and nurtured its growth grew weak as the evil grew strong, to encompass the land. So, with the count's devil-plant, the treasure was no longer protected; it was buried and consumed by that thing which he brought from India,—a little curling, crawling weed, concealed in a golden box, a cousin to the breathing plant, but an apostate, a wretched outcast from the world of flowers, embodying all their passion of growth and reproduc-tion, yet endowed with the cruel instincts and power of a viper."

What was she talking about? There seemed so little coherency in what she said.

From what he could patch together of this ragged information, it led him to suppose she was a refugee from the French Revolu-tion, who had sought these shores in company with her son, or whoever Pierre or the count might have been; that in their flight they had fallen in with a company of buccaneers, who had piloted them to this spot, where now lay concealed beneath some mon-strous growth their hidden treasure. But, hark! she spoke again, placing her hand on the dog's head.

"Ah, Rollin, is it you? You are more faithful than men. They left me alone here to die,—for I am dying,— but in death I will not lie in quiet amidst this savagery of nature.

"Would it be possible, if my body were bound to this accursed soil, that my spirit could abandon the scene of its torture? No! no! I should traverse the earth until the resurrection of the dead. Like yonder devil-plant, to which my feet have worn a path through the wilderness, I should writhe and creep and live, forever.

"Back to France! O souls of the dead! if ye have ears for mortal complaint,—if ye bear in your spirits a kinship and sympathy for human woe, I call upon you to witness the last cry of my embodied spirit for the land of its nativity: Bear me back to France!"

With a shriek of agony that made Lenartson's blood curdle, she threw her face, in the last desperate action of despair, forward upon her knees. Lay thus, with her features concealed, her arms stretched forth, and her hair straying loosely about her thin, white figure like a scant and shredded veil.

Lenartson, shocked and awakened from his trance, hastened to lift her so as to give her air. Too late! The candle had nickered out. She was dead.

Gravely he composed the old limbs and worn features of the Grand Madame. What a sad romance. How singular that he should have witnessed the closing scenes of such a tragedy!

Having done what was possible, he determined to return to Orr, to give information of what had happened. And if it was true that treasure was concealed on this island, the final cry of the departed soul should be answered. She should be carried back to France. First, however, he must solve the final mystery of the gold and the devil-plant.

After a short search he discovered what appeared to be an over-grown path, which led out of the garden toward the interior, directly opposite to the one by which he had entered, and began at once to make his way through it.

At length he arrived at an open space where, for half a mile, the trees were dwarfed at every point of the circle where they approached it. In the center of this enclosure of green earth, thus denuded of shrubs and trees, there was situated a long ledge, rising in some places to a height of thirty or forty feet. All about it the tall grass pliantly bent to the light touch of the wind. Covering the entire cliff, and often dripping to the ground along the face of it, was a peculiar mass, whose narrow, spiked leaves presented a living sea of green. The entire plant seemed to be endowed with voluntary motion, as without apparent cause it rose and fell like the jerky hunch of an inchworm, or the ceaseless motion of the waves of the sea.

Some of the limbs of the plant dropping over the head of the boulder were as large as the body of an anaconda. They were clothed in smooth, mottled bark somewhat resembling the skin of that reptile in color. The limbs and stems were set about with a glossy corolla of leaves, about four inches between each cluster. From their centers depended a bunch of tendril and a cluster of flame-like, star-shaped blossoms. Long, and dank, and dark, this beautiful devil-plant swung to and fro. At an interval of about ten seconds the limbs and tendrils contracted in such a manner as to bring all of the leaves together so as to entirely conceal the branches upon which they grew, then stretched forth again.

It was this singular motion, somewhat like that of the breathing plant, which caused the heaving, crawling motion of the whole mass above and the tremulous vibration of the limbs below.

Curiously fascinated, Lenartson crept somewhat nearer, hoping to determine something of the character of the plant's malign influence without perilous adventure.

As he approached nearer and nearer, fixing his eyes upon the plant with the suspicion of watching for an enemy in ambush, he kept pushing his foot cautiously through the long grass. "Was it here?" he speculated, "or over yonder, directly beneath that restless sea of leaves, the great treasure was buried?"

Suddenly he struck something concealed in the grass that leaped upon him, coiling with such a sharp, unexpected pressure about his feet and ankles, that, thus entangled, he was jerked from his feet, falling backward upon the earth. In this position, before he had time to struggle to his knees, he felt himself being rapidly drawn toward the cliff, upon which grew the great mass of the devil-plant, a limb of which, serpent-like, coiled and concealed in the grass, had caught his wary feet and was now rapidly coiling up his body, to bear him with angry jerks toward the great monster plant that, to Lenartson's horrified eyes, appeared to rise and approach him, full of malignant life. At that moment he remembered a fish knife which he happened to have in his pocket, and, seizing it, he commenced a desperate attack upon the vine as he struggled to his knees.

It was a short, sharply contested battle, in which the man realized that, once within the grasp of the great mass of deadly limbs and viperous tendrils of the great plant, there would be no more to-morrows for him upon the earth.

He succeeded none too soon in freeing himself from the obnoxious embrace of the fearful thing, whose wounded part continued by jerky hunches to retire toward the main body, trembling to receive it into its umbrageous bosom; while the severed portion about his legs, with a faint quiver as of departing life, uncoiled itself and dropped, with the soft thud of dead material, lengthwise upon the grass.

Filled with a great sense of gratitude and relief, not unmixed with horror, he made haste to beat a retreat toward the woodland, moving backward with his white face set suspiciously toward the enemy. When once assured that safe distance had been placed between them, he stood for some minutes watching the heaving body of green with its serpent arms flung over the cliff. He was deeply impressed by Madame's characterization.

"It is not a plant! It is my soul shrieking maledictions to heaven."

What was it? He could not classify it as other than a rare specimen from a prehistoric period—a monstrous growth and prophecy in plant life of the mighty powers of intelligence destined to inherit and subdue the earth, significantly saved to this age for the study and wonder of man. In the unreckoned ages of its existence it had survived the sweep of universal conflagration; it had beheld the God-abandoned race perishing in the carburetted atmosphere, smothered in subterranean caverns, plunged in boiling oceans, or buried beneath mounds of burning cinders that followed the trail of the red serpent of the air. It had witnessed the age of darkness and cold, and now, a living chronicle of disaster, it had been captured by the daring hand of man and transplanted to a foreign shore.

It was five o'clock when Lenartson set out on his homeward journey. The sky was clear, the sea was calm, so that nothing occurred to withdraw his mind from meditating deeply upon ways and means by which the devil-plant might be overcome, the gold secured, and Madame's body returned to France.

He concluded that he would not speak to the people at Orr about the later portion of his adventure, as it would be likely to open inquiries that would lead to the discovery of the gold,—a secret that he did not wish at present to reveal to them.

Late as he arrived, for it was after sunset, he found Bill Maynard awaiting him. The old fisherman greeted him with surprise and emotion, and on hearing a portion of the story, hastened to bear the tidings from house to house. In consequence, Lenartson found himself an hour later besieged at the hotel by a crowd of curious people, to whom he rehearsed the tale of the finding of the dog, his pursuit to the deserted house, and the impressive death-bed scene of the Grand Madame.

The kerosene lamp upon the clerk's desk made a narrow circle of light around the room. In the center of it Lenartson occupied a wooden chair. He frequently changed his position as he talked.

Each strong-featured lad or bearded and weather-stained man kept his face attentively set toward the narrator. Each sharply silhouetted ghost upon the white-plastered wall showed scarcely a tremor of the immobile figures that surrounded him. Lenartson represented all the action of the company at the center.

The young man being unpleasantly conscious of the profound impression made upon his own high-wrought sensibilities, attempted to assume an air of carelessness.

To cover a slight tremor of his limbs, which he could not wholly repress, he would push himself up on the back legs of his chair, and sit thus, with his hands in his pockets, talking almost waggishly. Then, almost irresistibly overcome by the intensity of his feelings, he would drop suddenly forward, with a tragic earnestness that made itself felt in every heart.

They comprehended at once how cruel superstition had made them to this poor old creature, the harrowing scenes of whose death-bed lost nothing by Lenartson's tragic recital, excepting her connection with the concealed gold, and the devil-plant.

Finally, they agreed that a company of twenty men should accompany Lenartson in the morning to Mystery Island, for the purpose of bringing Madame's body to Orr, where for a time, at least, it should remain, peacefully interred.

They did not separate until about one o'clock, and then, few of them who had listened to the story slept much for the night. As for Lenartson, he threw himself dressed upon the bed, from which he frequently started up to pace the floor.

All night he was haunted by the cry of Madame's departed spirit for the land of its nativity.

It lay upon him, a fearful injunction he could but obey. The devil-plant must in some way be overcome, the vast treasure unearthed, and Madame's embalmed body returned to the dear, sunny land of her birth.

As the yacht was launched, he moved among them, a strangely silent figure, with set lips and pallid cheek, his hat pulled low over his brow, his gaze abstracted from present scenes, his soul filled in all its chambers of sense with that piteous cry.

When they arrived at Mystery Island the mid-day sun had plowed his passage to the zenith without a cloud to vex his progress. They made haste to secure their boats, then dropped into Indian file, twenty men behind their leader, pushing and breaking their way through the overgrown path toward the old house in the woods.

The sharp clink of their stout heels sprang up behind them in startling echoes along the wide hall and stone stairway.

Upon the threshold of the room Lenartson had left yesterday, so full of tragic pictures memory would ever recall, he stopped a moment, looking over his shoulder into the pale and kindly faces behind him.

"Poor old Madame! It was here, boys, I left her yesterday after all was over."

Thus remarking, he turned his face inward and approached the bed. He stood before it aghast; the bed was empty! There was the yellow, crumpled linen, there were the soiled blankets and tattered coverlid which the long, thin, bejeweled fingers had plucked at yesterday. But she and the dog were gone!

For the space of ten seconds each man stood staring in help-less silence. Then one of them ventured to suggest that he had made a mistake in the room. No one thought of doubting him. His face was too plain an index of his astonishment.

"That's it," concluded Bill Maynard. "You gut addled. Let's try another room."

Lenartson, continuing to gaze in a bewildered way at the bed, shook his head. "No, it was right here, and no other place, that I passed through the experience I have related to you. There must be some other person on the premises, and all that talk about being deserted was Madame's lunacy. Let's look about."

As they commenced their investigation, the noise of their approach and departure startled the bats from their corners in the empty rooms. Everything was covered with dust and mold; even the chairs and floors were thickly encrusted. Through the holes in the roof the rain had beaten unchecked and the resulting fungus life consumed, as it grew, the wooden sills and doorways. Cobwebs hung in festoons from the ceiling, and cut in elaborate patterns of gray lace the corners of the rooms, in one of which a rabbit had made her nest and was rearing her young. Across the threshold of another a serpent slipped into the golden shimmer of the outer sunshine.

In a cupboard was found a china service, and a silver or pewter pot so black with long exposure to the air and moisture, its true metal could not at once be determined. And everywhere was, the all-recording dust, covering the entire house like a pall cloth upon the face of the dead. There was no food, nor evidence of recent occupancy in the entire house.

Once again they looked at each other, and then to Lenartson, the question trembling upon each man's lips he feared to utter.

Superstition repossessed them. Lenartson, dazed and dis-tressed, placed his hand against his forehead, struggling to think.

Ah! the devil-weed and the treasure! If those things existed in reality, it would establish the fact of his having spoken with a dying woman yesterday.

"Boys, I must leave you for half an hour. Will you wait for me here?"

"Out there," they consented gruffly, pointing to the garden. No man cared to remain within.

In feverish impatience he darted away from them, tearing his way along the gloomy woodland path toward the spot where that terrible thing grew.

At the point where the opening would reveal the cliff, he stopped short, struck by a chill of horror. Great drops of perspiration rolled over his face. His heart heat with stifling throbs in his bosom, while his hands clenched themselves unconsciously.

In this mood, appalled by awful doubt, he dashed out into the open space,—then stopped short, an exclamation of joy bursting from his fevered lips. Thank God, it was there, and she had been!

Steeped in the still sunshine of the upper air, that monster plant still crawled over the gray head of the great boulder, emitting fiery sparks from its bosom, as with each lift of its huge body the round rings of its red blossoms flashed into view. The long, gray, snake-like limbs, bristling with their gay corolla of spiked leaves, swung, contracted, and lengthened, exactly as he had seen them yesterday.

Cautiously he crept forward, his nervous fingers clutching the handle of his knife, treading carefully through the long grass which appeared to grow here like some dangerous accomplice of the enemy.

Now he understood why no shrub or tree grew near the boulder. The devil-plant had, as it grew, grasped, one after another, every living thing which could afford resistance to its malignant clutch. It had made itself a supreme evil in the garden of God, annihilating all living beauty excepting the long, pliant grass, through which it might creep and glide towards the object to be destroyed. Not a wonder Madame, who knew its nature, moaned, "It will encompass the land." And the treasure beneath it—Ugh! the whole thing grew uncanny. He commenced to feel that any attempt to recover a treasure upon which rested the curse of Madame's passion-withered lips would prove fatal. He could almost see the ghastly glistening of dead men's bones impaled in the meshes of that fearful thing. An accursed root had sprung out of the practical Maine soil, engrafted upon it from some kingdom of the damned.

A shadow crossed the sun, followed by another and still another in quick succession, like the swift lifting of gigantic wings.

The trees shivered. The air leaped at once into strong currents, gathering velocity and darkness as they traveled. The sky lowered with a blaze of fury, followed by deafening thunder and accompanied by the roar of the sea.

Lenartson felt himself raised bodily by the wind and dashed down again like chaff. In terror, lest the mighty breath of the tempest make him the plaything of yonder devil-weed, now tossing forward and flinging up its long, crawling arms into the sulphurous air, he grasped the trunk of a tree with his arms, and flung himself face down upon the ground.

Ships went down everywhere along the coast that day. Their own boat dragged her anchor and was driven upon the rocks. Houses were unroofed and blown about like paper toys. It was a day of doom. It was like the passionate protest of the dead in league with the elements.

"I would haunt the land forever. I will not lie on this accursed soil. Bear me back to France!"

Pale, and shaken, and drenched by the pitying floods of the sky, Lenartson crept back, when the tempest was past, to the old house, where he met a company of stern, white faces.

"Boys," he said brokenly, "I cannot talk of what has happened on this mysterious island. I only ask to be taken away. Bill Maynard, give me your hand, old boy. I am no longer able to jeer at your superstitions."

None seemed inclined to talk.

When at last they swung out upon the broad, blue breast of the ocean, under a sunny sky, every man thanked God he had left the place forever.

And although at times some bold lad dares to steer his skiff beneath the haunted cliff, where he declares the dog Rollin may still be seen on watch at the cove, there has been none other ambitious to investigate the mystery of Mystery Island.

The old house in the woods remains untenanted and unvisited. Dank and dark the devil-weed swings in the undisturbed silence of its green oasis.

The treasure buried upon the island is to many but a vague speculation. To Lenartson there appears no doubt as to the reality of the concealed treasure, and the Grand Madame is to him one of the most marvelous mysteries of life. Who was the Grand Madame? What was it that he saw at the old house? What did he hear? He had not slept and dreamed. Was it a visitation from the other world? A disturbed and earthbound soul enacting the closing scene of its mortality? If not, what? Where did the Grand Madame and the dog Rollin disappear?

THE MAN-TRAP CACTUS: A STORY OF THE ORINOCO

Anonymous

Let me tell you how I lost my comrade, Dan Blind, in the Orinoco forest. If you don't believe it, I reckon it won't shock me much, for I've told the tale often; and it I've been rated as a gospeller once, I've been told I'm a liar a hundred times. A man gets used to that sort of thing, though, when he yarns about the Brazilian forest. First time I got into the "ete" (that part of the wooded interior above the inundation line) I could hardly believe my eyes. It was spring and all the flowering tress of the forest were blazing away in blossoms—purple, saffron, blood red, bright blue, gold and every color you can think of was about. The cassiae and silk-cotton tree just made me gasp. It wasn't Nature as I had known the old lady up to then. It was so like a great big lie, that it was a while before I felt sure I was myself and it was itself.

That was two years or so before I met Dan, and we west off hunting and all the rest of it together. The "hunting" was an excuse; Dan was more after flowers, and I was more after excitement and exploring than game of any kind.

What made Dan most eager to come was a love affair. He had proposed to a girl and she said, "No, thank you." I can't understand a fellow taking those affairs so seriously; they never troubled me overmuch. Asking a girl to marry me, and getting refused, isn't much worse than asking the price of a diamond ring in a Paris jeweller's window and being told it was 5000 francs or so above my figure. I guess it's a matter of constitution. My constitution runs short in romance, I've been told before now.

141

"Well, then, you come right along with me, Blind," I said to Dan, when I ran against him in Cayenne, where he was seeing if he couldn't make things even hotter for himself than this girl had done.

We had played poker and billiards together, and smoked each other's weeds. Fellows soon thicken outside Europe, especially when the supply of suitable pals is uncommonly short. It was in New York that Dan had had his disappointment. He took a cruise down South after it, and we knocked together at Cayenne.

"Stay long here?" I asked him as soon as we had nodded.

"Till I'm dead, I expect," said he.

That raised a laugh in me; and when I had slapped him on the back, and told him not to be a fool, and we had drunk a squash or two, David and Jonathan weren't in it with us.

All the same, from first to last, I never knew where he hailed from. There was nothing among his boxes to give me a clue. He was just "Daniel Blind, a jilted man"; and he was that and no more when I had him on the ground in front of me with all his blood sucked out of him, and the color of rather mellow ivory. His mouth was open, as if he had cried "Oh!" when I buried him, poor chap; and I missed him fine in working my way back through the forests.

Said Dan to me before we started (I had had a pretty job to recover his spirits for him; but I had done it, and was proud of the deed):—

"There's a certain love of a plant I'm bound to come back with if it's in our beat; that is, if we can carry it. It kind o' reminds me of Mary—"

"Mary" was the girl that had said "No, thank you."

He pulled up when he had said "Mary." If he had gone one better, I might have had a chance of letting her know what happened to him. As it was, I put "Dan Blind's" name in the New York papers as dead; but, of course, I don't knew for sure if she saw it there.

"It's a sort of a kind of a cactus," Dan went on to say; "and I met a man at Trinidad who told me things about it that show it to be a demon of the first water. For one thing, it's a man-killer."

"Poison?" said I.

"Yes, and more, by the looks of them," said Dan. "But the man didn't know the particulars. He'd seen it in flower, and smelt it, and there was no smell in all the perfume shops of Europe (let alone its flowers) to come nigh it for its ravishing sweetness. His idea was that it just made fellows drunk with joy—if you can imagine such a silly state—and then they died, poisoned, but happy, though, from all accounts, *looking* anything but happy."

In fact, according to Dan's precious acquaintance, this flower really did kill folks. He had seen a couple of German botanists lying toes-up by it, and no wound on them—alive and in spectacles in the morning, and in the afternoon white and stiff on the ground, with their spectacles inside the flower of the cactus, which, he reckoned, stank the sweeter for the spectacles, or something. He said the red spider-bee kind of flourished on the flowers; the petals shook backwards and forwards, and rubbed each other up and down, and seemed to lick and fondle each other; and it was all he could do to keep his nose out of the scent pot. The sight gave him more than one turn, and he was convinced that the flower was as humanly alive, and full of a sort of wicked intelligence, as the couple of dismal German orchard-hunters about its stalk were dead 'uns. That's the lovely creature of a plant poor Dan Blind was set on capturing. If "Mary" was like that she was a treasure for some man.

As for me, I laughed at Dan's tale. I knew well enough that there are rum plants in the 'Selvas,' but I had never come across a brute like that, and I didn't believe in it.

"Nor do I," said Dan; "but I mean to *see* if it's true."

Well, I believe it now, and so does Dan himself, if folks keep their wits going into the next world. But I'll be surprised if you don't rate me as a high-class liar, as I said before.

Well, we started, Dan and I, and a numbskull of an Indian called Pedro, and for days we enjoyed all the sweets of sublime laziness as Pedro paddled upstream. Now and then we popped at a bird or beast, but mostly we saved powder and shot until we were right in the wilds. We didn't know what might happen, you know. They not all civilised folk, the denizens the Selvas; and they tip their arrow heads, some of them, with that nice stuff "curara," which belies its name in being far from easy to cure when it gets into a wound.

We had a guitar, and we started the monkeys with it—at least I did. Dan wasn't in the mood for love songs, nor yet comic songs, which was more in my line. I *used* to be a very funny fellow then. That coffee-colored thick-head, Pedro, would often drop his paddle and grin, though of course he didn't catch the tit-bits of humor in the words of the songs. As for Dan, he just lay on his back in the shade, and smoked and yawned and thought of that jade Mary. I taxed him with wasting his mind over her; but it wasn't any use.

"Can't help it," he would say. "You'd say 'ditto' if you'd seen her."

Would I, though? I'd a deal sooner have boxed her pretty ears. I guess I'm far from being a lady's man, and I can't abide crooked-ness in a man, woman, or child.

And so we got plump into the forest after awhile—all among passion flowers and orchids and snakes and humming birds, Botocudos, and females who thick it a neat trick to wear the coral snake for a living necklace. It was before the time when every chap who goes out of temperate latitudes takes a kodak and a notebook, and returns home to spout lectures with limelight illustrations at the Lord-knows-how-many pounds apiece, else I might have made good business of that expedition, and especially where Dan came to grief. All the same, though, cold-blooded coon that I am, I don't believe I have had cheek enough to turn to pressing buttons just when Dan was saying "How d'ye do?" to Death. There are fellows who could do it, I've been told, but they're not my sort.

We had a rattling fortnight with our guns, and I bagged a lot of thing worth skinning and keeping. Dan too, was nigh off his head with excitement about the plants. The orchid he got would have excited Mr. Chamberlain to turn Home Ruler, or anything, to have the fingering of them.

Towards the end of the fortnight however, poor Dan got some-thing else—a bad go of fever. It made him mighty weak, and didn't—along with his ravings about Mary—tend to improve his wits. But I stuck well to the poor chap, and, between nursing and quinine, we managed to bring him back to something like his old self.

I make bold to say that from the time he told me that tale about the man-eating cactus to the time he was through the fever neither of us thought one bit about this ghoul of a plant. I know I didn't, for I put it all down to the credit of high falutin'; and I'm sure Dan didn't, just because he was so taken up with the other real wonders that tickled his ears in every blessed direction.

But the time was at hand, as they say in the play, when the villain's turn for checkmate is about due.

It was the very first day, indeed, after Dan's first toddle after lying up. He found himself in better fettle that both expected. Cassava suited him fine.

I think I can see him now, as he said to me that morning:—

"You know where we were yesterday, boss?"

He called me "boss," not because he reckoned me his better half, but because I "bossed" the show, and kicked Pedro when it was needed.

"Why, cert," I answered, "and a nice thick mess of tangle we got on to the off-side of."

"Right," said he, "that's just the place; I mean to get ahead there. There was a melastoma" (I think that's the word he used) "up in a tree there, just the color of a woman's eye, and I know you'll swarm up and nick it for me."

I chaffed him a bit about the thing being "the color of a woman's eye." As if women's eyes were all like that vixen Mary's!

"Go it, boss," poor Dan said, kind of wearily, when I had laid on to that unknown young woman pretty smart. "I'm not up to cudgelling for her yet. Next week you'll see what I'll give you."

"Done with you, Blind," said I. "If you can throw me with leg, arm or wing by this time next week, I'd like nothing better. It'll show you're in trim for pushing on West at double quick."

We didn't have any more words together after that. We shouldered out guns, had another look at our jack-boots (useful things, those, in that land o' snakes), gave Pedro a merciful clout or two by way of teaching him to do his best with the dinner, and started slick off.

Once, Dan opened his mouth to say quietly, "There's a fortune in that flower, boss," And I threw him back the words, "Don't you think it. The odds it rots are five-and-twenty to one. Besides, we haven't sniffed it yet."

I reckon it was about half an hour after saying this that I was sitting straddled across a big bough of a tree, with my toes in the top of a huge tree fern, doing my best to bag the melastoma, or whatever it was, with the flower "the color of a woman's eyes."

Dan had encouraged me up that tree, and when I was safe on the bough, I shouted to him that the thing was as good as his.

"Thanks so very much, old fellow!" he shouted back to me, and I never heard him speak again.

Well, I had got the flower, root and all, right enough, and could look about for the return journey.

"Where are you, Dan?" I called. He didn't answer, so I cried out to him to take care how he wandered and tell him that I would be with him in a minute. Then I took to the ropes of the creepers like a monkey.

But I hadn't got more than half-way down when I saw a sight that touched me queer. On the far side of my tree, rising ten or twelve feet into the air, were the spiked palisades of a cactus, and between the spikes were three flame-colored basins (so they looked like), standing on stalks about five high. There were really four of these beastly basins, but the fourth was hidden, because poor Dan had got his head screwed fast in it. I had wondered whet made the forest smell stronger than usual. Now I guessed all in a minute, for it flashed home to me that the tale about the man-eating cactus was true, and no yarn.

Dan was fighting with hands and feet, but the filthy flower was also fighting. You can believe me or not, when I tell you that I was so staggered by what I saw that I hadn't the sense for many moments to drop down quickly. And this is what I saw: that red hole closed about Dan's neck tighter and tighter; and, as if to clinch matters, one at those murderous great spiked poles of green curvetted forwards, and wound itself round the poor fellow just like a boa constrictor. It didn't waste any time either.

I breathed forth two or three strong swear words, and slid down the ropes. It took me, perhaps, fifteen seconds, and another half-minute to wrestle my way to Dan's neighborhood.

But I was too late, for there, on the ground, lay the poor chap, dead as an Egyptian mummy. I could see that his face was bad to look at: blue with suffocation, yet pricked all over with blood spots.

Then I turned to the fiend of a cactus. Man! it was something devilish to see. The flower that had done Dan was quivering; and its pink, pear-shaped bits of furniture seemed to be licking each other as if they enjoyed Dan's blood amazingly. And the filthy palisade that had curled over to finish strangling Dan was brandishing about like the skirts of a dancing girl when she twirls. I expect there could be nothing more graceful than the way it moved, but to me it seemed to be preening itself on its cleverness in having parted a human soul from its body. The other three flowers, mind you, and all the other palisades were still as death.

I didn't hesitate what to do very long, when I had examined Dan and found him good for nothing on this earth. Lord! how strong he smelt of the flower! There was a good little axe in my belt, and I plied it against that assassin of a cactus till there wasn't three inches of it standing above ground.

Then I ran to the tent, and, between us, Pedro and myself got poor Dan away. We were almost knocked over by his perfume, the like of which, for diabolical sweetness, I guess I'll never smell again on this earth.

There! that's my tale, If you doubt its truth, go into the Selvas, by the Orinoco, yourself, and, unless I've hacked down the last of these murdering plants (which I hope), you may come upon one of them. If you do, cart it home, and invite me to be present while it is tortured a bit, Indian fashion, before getting the *coup de grace*.

A FLESH-EATING PLANT

Anonymous

The desultory talk of a little group of travellers in one of the hotel corridors the other evening had drifted to natural curiosities, and, as usual on such occasions, the stories had grown slightly taller as the ball went around the circle. Finally it was "passed up" to a sallow-faced man who had registered from San Jose, Costa Rica, and who had listened to the narratives of the others in thoughtful silence. "I scarcely know what I can add to you symposium," he said, in response to some pressing, "for I have really seen very little that was out of the ordinary in my life, and nothing at all that compares with the extraordinary things that have just been described. If you are willing to risk being bored, however, I'll tell you briefly about a rather curious carnivorous plant I found a couple of years ago in Southern Nicaragua.

"I was on a prospecting expedition at the time," he continued, "and had penetrated a practically unknown region southwest of the lower lakes. One day while I was pushing my way through an almost tropical stretch of forest, I noticed a very strange-looking plant at the foot of on immense cabbage palmetto. It consisted of a single green stalk nearly as big around as my wrist, but only about two feet high, with a few thick, lumpy leaves, and a large, cup-shaped, purple blossom perched at the extreme tip. The Central American jungles are full of all sorts of fantastic flowers, but this was so widely different from anything I had over seen that I sat down to study it in detail. While I was scrutinising the queer growth, a bumblebee, fully as large as the end of my thumb, came

148

sailing down, and after a few preliminary pirouettes, dived into the purple cup. Instantly the ends of the petals curled inward, and in less time than it takes to tell it the blossom had assumed the appearance of a globe, imprisoning the insect inside. I saw then that I had encountered a new and singular specimen of the carnivorous or flesh-eating plant." "Oh, yes! they are well known to botanists," said a gentleman from California, who had told a story about a double-headed bullfrog; "I've seen several varieties myself." "Exactly," replied the Central American, with a courteous gesture, "but I warned you in advance I had nothing remarkable to relate. Compared to your frog, my plant was a mere weed." "That's all right," replied the Californian, indulgently; "go on and tell us about it."

"When I recognised the true character of the plant," continued the sallow stranger, "I become very much interested. All the carnivorous floral varieties of which I have knowledge confine themselves to tiny gnats and such small game, but here was a growth hardy and voracious enough to take in a huge bumblebee at a single mouthful. In less than five minutes the petals slowly unfolded and the insect had disappeared. Upon that I determined to take the plant with me for further study, and digging it up with a machete, I carefully planted it in a large earthen water-jar and turned it over to one of my Indian guides. About two weeks later I returned to the town of Elarno, on the river, where I was then living, and one of the first things I did was to put the plant on the centre-table at my house. During the journey the Indian had fed it faithfully on flies, and it was apparently in an excellent condition.

"The thing was so human in the way it opened and shut its mouth that I named it William Henry, after on old friend of mine who had rather a remarkable appetite, and, as flies were somewhat bothersome to secure, it occurred to me to try it on meat. I gave it a small piece of beefsteak to begin with, and it was really pathetic to see the evident relish with which it gobbled it down. The poor thing had never tasted civilised food before, and as soon as it disposed of the fragment of steak it opened its petals so wide that I was actually afraid they would split apart. It was its dumb way of pleading for more. I am fond of good living myself," the Central American went on, "and my house as well stocked with all sorts of delicacies in tin and glass. After the experiment with the steak I had William Henry placed on the table whenever I ate, and would feed him exactly as one might feed a pet animal He seemed to take naturally to foreign luxuries, and his appetite was something incredible.

Whenever I looked up from my plate I would see that yawning purple mouth staring me in the face like a young bird begging for a worm, and it was hard to resist the appeal. I always gave him any special dainty that happened to be hand, I will never forget the first time William Henry tasted *pate de foie gras*. He absorbed it slowly, the petals squeezing together to half their natural size, and a sort of delightful shudder ran through all his fat green leaves. Then the flower flew open so suddenly that the top petal was dislocated for a week. Another great favorite of his was devilled kidney with Madeira sauce, and he had a pronounced weakness for soft-shelled crab, broiled. One evening, merely as an experiment, I gave him a few drops out of a cocktail I was drinking before dinner, and presently I noticed with surprise that his petals were no longer firm and outspread, but were wobbling strangely on their stem. He ate little or nothing that night, and next day was curiously languid. It is my positive conviction that William Henry was drunk.

"But I fear I am tiring you and will hasten to a conclusion. Several months went by and all this high living began to have a marked effect on my singular pet. The thick green stalk had swollen in the centre until it resembled a gigantic mango, and the side leaves were mere sacks of pulp. In fact, the whole plant was strongly suggestive of some fat, dissipated old clubman. Moreover, I notice unmistakable signs of had health, especially after heavy meals, and I was greatly distressed, for foolish as it may seem, I had grown deeply attached to the strange creature. I tried to put him back on a simple diet of flies, but his luxurious tastes had become confirmed, and he refused positively to receive them. Meanwhile he was continually growing larger but it was a morbid vegetable obesity, and I was profoundly grieved but no particularly surprised when I awoke one morning to find the stalk collapsed and the purple blossom melted and dead. Strange to say, the earthen jar was cracked in a dozen pieces, and on examination I found that the tips of roots had swollen to enormous proportions. From that and other evidence I am convinced that William Henry died of gout, brought on by over-eating. Good-night, gentlemen. I shall remember that double-headed bullfrog with much pleasure."

THE GRAY WEED

Owen Oliver

Owing to the lamented death of Professor Newton, to whose wisdom and courage the world owes its deliverance, I have been asked to contribute to the first newspaper issued in the new era some account of the terrible weed which overran the earth, and threatened to stifle out mankind.

The professor had intended dealing with the origin of the weed, its relations to ordinary plants, the nature of its growth, so far as this proceeded, and the forms which it would ultimately have assumed. Unfortunately his notes upon these points are so abbreviated and technical as to be unintelligible to me; and personally I possess no qualifications for dealing with the scientific aspects of the case. So I must confine myself to a plain narrative of the occurrences which I witnessed.

It was nine o'clock in the evening of November 10, 1908, when I left my office in Norfolk Street, letting myself out with a duplicate key which the hall-porter had intrusted to me. I thought at first that it was snowing; but when I put out my hand and caught a few of the particles, I found that they were flimsy white seeds, something like those of melons, only less substantial. Where they lay in heaps—as I thought—in the road, their color appeared to be gray. At the Embankment end of the street the "heaps" were larger; and when I came to them I discovered that they were not seeds, but a growth of gray weed, which fastened round my shoes as I tried to walk over it.

152

I stooped and took hold of a piece to examine it; but, when I attempted to pluck it, it stretched like elastic, without breaking off. The tendrils were round, and about one-fourth of an inch in diameter when not stretched. They had, at intervals, spherical bulges which, at a distance, bore the appearance of small berries. These appeared to be of the same substance as the tendrils. The latter began twining round my fingers, and I had some difficulty in releasing them. The road and the Embankment were deserted by people, but three or four horses at the cab stand were plunging with fright as the weed wound round their legs. It had grown perceptibly in the few minutes that I had been observing it, and, feeling somewhat alarmed, I made my way back along Norfolk Street.

The weed had spread a good deal there also; and I noticed that wherever a white seed fell a fresh plant sprang up, and grew with marvelous rapidity. In the Strand the weed was nearly a yard high. The 'bus drivers were whipping their frightened horses in a vain attempt to drive over it. The foot-passengers were unable to move, except a big man, who, with a small axe, hacked a passage through the growth for himself, his wife and his daughter—a pretty girl of about nineteen.

They were making their way down to the Embankment, but I warned them that the weed was thick there. The young lady then suggested that they should try to get into one of the houses, and I invited them to come to my offices. The tendrils were seizing people and pulling them down and binding them like flies in a spider's web. We could hear cries and screams all along the Strand, and a cab was upset by the struggles of the horse. The weed had spread over Norfolk Street, while we were talking, and it clung to our feet as we ran. The lady tripped and fell. The tendrils seized her immediately, and we had great difficulty in freeing her. When we had entered the door of the house we could not close it until we had chopped away the tendrils that followed us.

I turned on the electric light in the halls, and took my new friends to my rooms, which were on the fifth floor. The elder lady was faint, and I gave her some brandy and soda and biscuits. I had a good stock of these fortunately.

The gentleman's name was George Baker, his wife was Marian Baker, and the girl was Viva. They had been buying curiosities in the Strand, and the axe—a roughly engraved Moorish instrument— was fortunately among their purchases. Some people whom they met in the streets had told them that the weed was growing all over London, and that the Guards had been ordered out to cut it away. A learned old gentleman had conjectured that the seeds were the atoms of some dissipated planet, or the elements of some world that was to be, and that they contained the raw elements of life, which set them growing when they came into contact with suitable matter.

"It's diabolical!" Mr. Baker said furiously. "The vestries ought to send round water-carts with weed-killer, or—or something. I don't know what they ought to do; but they ought to do something." He wiped his face excitedly with his handkerchief. "Diabolical!" he repeated. "It grows through the flagstones, the wood paving, everything. It—it seizes people!"

"Seizes people!" his wife repeated, wringing her hands. "We saw it."

"It clings to you," the girl added tremulously. "*Clings* to you. If it goes on growing—!"

Her mother gave a sharp scream, and her father groaned.

"If it goes on growing—!" they said together.

"It won't," I assured them, with an indifferent appearance of confidence. "Those things that grow like—like fungi—never do. It will shrivel up suddenly, and let people go again. I don't suppose they're really hurt, only frightened. In an hour or so you'll be on your way home, and laughing about it; and I shall be thanking the— the fungus—for some pleasant acquaintances. I look upon this as a little surprise party."

The girl wiped her eyes and forced a smile.

"A little surprise party," she agreed. "What are you going to do for our entertainment, Mr. Adamson?—I saw the name on the door-plate."

"Henry Adamson," I said, "and very much at your service, Miss Viva— I have some cards, but—"

I paused doubtfully. Her mother held up a trembling hand, and her father shook his head.

"We won't have any fool's games," he said. "Let's talk."

Viva and I talked in broken sentences, and her mother and father in monosyllables. We kept glancing at the window, but no one had the courage to draw up the blind for nearly an hour. Then we opened the window and looked out. The weed was fully six feet high in the street, and higher in the Strand. It had overrun the 'bus that stood at the opening. If there were people on the 'bus, it had overrun them, too.

"It doesn't seem to hurt," I said. "There's no screaming now." I shuddered as soon as I had said it.

"There is no screaming now," Viva repeated. "I suppose they— they are all—"

Her voice broke. Her father shut the window sharply and drew her away.

"It will be gone in the morning," he asserted, "as—as our friend said. We shall have to impose on your hospitality for the night, I am afraid, Mr. Adamson."

"There is no question of imposing," I assured him. "I cannot say how glad I am to have your company."

We made a couch for the ladies by putting several hearth-rugs on the table in the clerks' room, and laying two rugs of mine to cover them. Mr. Baker and I dozed in front of the fire in my room in chairs. Toward the morning I fell into a sounder sleep. When I woke he had pulled up the blind.

"It's fifteen feet high at least," he told me. "Halfway up the second windows. God help us!"

I joined him and saw the roadway filled with a sea of gray weeds. They looked like india-rubber reeds. The largest were as thick as my little finger, and the bulges were the size of damsons. We opened the window and listened. Presently a caretaker opened a window nearly opposite and called to his wife.

"Here's a rum go, Mary," he shouted, with a laugh. "Bulrushes growing to the street! We sha'n't have any clerks pestering us to-day."

The woman joined him, and they laughed together because they would have a holiday. They treated the matter as a joke, and evidently disbelieved us when we told them of the terrible events of the preceding night. So we closed the window and called the ladies. I made some tea on my ring-burner, and we breakfasted on that and biscuits. The ladies avoided the window, and so did I, but Mr. Baker went to it every few minutes. After each visit he whispered to me that it was still growing. Mrs. Baker seemed in a stupor, but Viva tried hard to cheer us. She sang little snatches of song under her breath as she washed the tea-cups; and once she said that it was great "fun." Her mouth trembled when I looked reproachfully at her.

"Mother is so nervous," she whispered. "I have to pretend, to cheer her. Do you think it will—grow?"

"Heaven knows!" I said. "But you are very brave."

After this she and I sat at the window, watching the tendrils growing and growing, and clutching incessantly at the air. I thought, at first, that they were swaying in the wind, but there was no breeze. Also there was an indescribable air of purpose about their movement. A number of long branches spread themselves over a window opposite. Their swaying ceased, and they pressed on it steadily, till at last it broke with a dull crash. Mrs. Baker fainted, and her husband lifted her on to the sofa. Viva clung to my arm. The malicious tendrils broke down the window-frame, piece by piece, and spread slowly into the room, winding themselves round the tables and chairs.

"If anyone had been there," Viva cried hoarsely. "If—if—" She looked at me. Her eyes were big with fright.

"They must be doing something to stop it," I said— "the—the authorities. If we could find out! I'll try the telephone."

After several calls I obtained an answer. It was a girl's voice. Six of them had stayed all night in the exchange, she said. They were in communication with the police and the Government Offices. The soldiers had been out since the previous evening, and had cut their passage from Chelsea Barracks to Victoria Street, and along this almost to Westminster Bridge. They had intended

coming on to Whitehall and the Strand; but the stuff grew almost
as quickly as it was cut down, and had overpowered many of them.
Over a hundred had been crushed to death by it, and they had sent
for gun-cotton to try and blow it up, as a last resort. It was known,
through the telegraph, that the weed had appeared all over England and on the Continent. It was also growing out of the sea.
The English Channel was choked in places, and several vessels had
been bound by the weed in sight of the coast. "It's alive!" she wailed;
"alive! Its eyes are watching us through the windows!" (The bulges
had the appearance of eyes.)

I was unable to obtain any further answers, although I tried
the telephone several times. By one o'clock the third-story
windows were covered. The thickest tendrils were then nearly the
diameter of a florin, with the bulges the size and shape of exceedingly large plums. The stems and bulges seemed to be of one
homogeneous material. There were no leaves or fruit or flowers at
this time, but branches were beginning to sprout from the main
stems. There did not appear to be any communication between one
stem and another; but, according to Professor Newton's notes, this
undoubtedly took place at the roots, which interlaced so as to form
a gigantic nervous system or brain.

We made another meal of tea and biscuits. Mrs. Baker seemed
stupefied with horror, and her husband was evidently overcome
by his anxiety for her, and scarcely spoke. Viva and I tried to talk,
but our voices broke off in the middle of words. We listened vainly
for any explosions, and concluded that the attempt at rescue had
failed. By four o'clock the weed was up to the window-sill. Mrs.
Baker was in a prolonged faint. Her husband sat beside her, with
his head on his hand. He did not look up when I suggested carrying her out on the roof.

"The cold would rouse her," he said. "It is best as it is. You're a
good chap, I think. Do what you can for my little girl."

I put on my overcoat, crammed the pockets with biscuits and a
flask, and persuaded Viva to accompany me to the roof to look for
a way of escape, for us and for her parents. We never saw them
again.

Some people from neighboring houses were on the adjoining roofs already, two old caretakers, a man and a lad. We saw about twenty more on the roofs in other streets. Some of them were raving and singing. The caretakers who had spoken to us in the morning flung their window open. They were laughing as if they had been drinking. They brought two pailfuls of boiling water and emptied it upon the weed. There was a soft hissing sound. Then two—four—six quivering tendrils reached slowly toward them. The man and woman seemed fascinated. They did not attempt to move, only screamed. The tendrils seized them; bound them round and round. Viva buried her head on my shoulder, and I shut my eyes. It was about half a minute, I think, before the screams ceased. Then there was crash after crash as windows were broken in. The weed had its passions, it seemed.

"Take me back to my mother and father," Viva begged. "We can all die together—if you would rather die with us?"

"Yes. I would rather die with you, Viva," I said. "I should have liked you very much if we had lived."

We returned to the trap-door, but the staircase was choked with the weed. As we looked down it seemed to be a pit of twirling gray snakes. We called to her mother and father, but there was no answer. Viva would have flung herself among the weed, but I held her and carried her back to the roof. The weed was beginning to crawl over the gutters. Long ropelike filaments were surrounding the other people who were on the roofs. They huddled together and did not attempt to escape. The tendrils overran, them and bound them round and round. I think they had mostly fainted. There was only one cry.

The tendrils lashed one another and fought over their prey. Their struggles made a repulsive, "scrooping" noise—a noise like the sound of stroking silk, only louder. There was also a sound of crunching bones.

I did not notice the weed closing round us till Viva clutched my arm.

"Hold me," she begged. "Hold me tight! I thought life had only just begun—"

I supported her on one arm, and backed toward the Strand end of the roof, where the weed had encroached less. We stumbled against a skylight. The attic below was empty. I opened the frame, lowered Viva and jumped down after her. We crouched in a corner watching the window. One—two minutes passed. Then the gray weed, with the bulges that simulated eyes, pressed upon it. The glass shivered upon the floor. I lifted Viva in my arms—she was too faint to walk—and carried her out on the landing.

The light was bad, and I saw no weed till we reached the next landing. Then it stretched toward us from the broken window-frame. A dozen gray ropes crept toward us from the stairs when we approached them. The lift was standing open. I pushed Viva in, jumped after her, slid the steel railing to and lowered us. A tendril caught at the lift as we started. I heard it snap.

In my excitement I lowered the lift too fast. We were thrown against the sides and almost stunned when it stopped. There was barely a glimmer of light, and we did not know if we had reached the bottom of the shaft or had been stopped by the weed. We listened for a long while and heard nothing. Then we let ourselves out and advanced a few inches at a time, feeling round us with our hands. We seemed to be in the hall of the basement. We came upon a table and found a tray on it with biscuits and milk. We drank the milk and Viva stuffed the biscuits in her pockets, as mine were full. There was a dim, barely perceptible light from an area window. We peered up through the grating into the forest of huge weeds. The trunks, which had grown to the size of young elms, only swayed a little; but the branches above twisted and twined incessantly. Viva shuddered when she saw them, and I took her away.

"We are safe down here," I assured her; but she pressed her hand over my mouth.

"Hush!" she whispered. "Hush! It may hear."

We wandered about in the darkness till we found a caretaker's room. We sat there on a sofa, holding hands. We never lost touch of each other all the time. I do not know how long it was. It seemed years. The basement was very quiet, but the sound of the india-rubbery motion came down to us. Once or twice we thought we heard a human cry. Once a mouse squeaked, and a spider dropped on the couch beside us with a thud. We were always listening.

After an unknown time we groped our way into the scullery to get water. We had just drunk when we heard the sound of india-rubbery tentacles dragging themselves over the walls. Something clung to my hand. Something held her skirt. It tore as I pulled her from it. Something was in the way when we tried to close the door. It followed us across the room and into the passage. We felt along the walls for the door that we thought led to the cellars—found it—fastened it after us—groped down the stairs. It was darker than the darkness of the basement above—darkness that could be felt. We stumbled over some coals—and a rough, hoarse voice came out of the darkness.

"Give us your hand, guv'nor," it said, "just a touch of your hand. I've been alone here for—for a thousand years!"

Something staggered toward us—stumbled against us; and a huge rough hand gripped my arm.

I put myself between him and Viva and pressed her arm for silence. The voice and grip were not reassuring, and I hoped he did not know she was there. "Here is my hand," I said.

"And mine," said Viva eagerly. "You are a friend—of course you are a friend. God bless you."

"God bless you, lady." The rough voice softened strangely. "I—I'm sorry to intrude."

He drew back a little way from us and sat down. I could not see him, but I could hear him breathe. Another unknown time passed. Then Viva whispered that she was thirsty.

"There's a pail of water," the man said, "if I can find it." He moved about in the darkness till he kicked it. Then he brought it to us. We drank from the pail and ate a few biscuits. I offered him some, but he said that he had a crust left. Viva and I explored the cellar and found a shovel and a pick. I suggested that we should try to break through into the next cellar, on the chance of finding food; but Viva and the man feared that the weed might hear us.

She and I sat on an empty packing-case, and she laid her head on my shoulder and slept. After a time I slept too. The man woke us.

"There's something moving, guv'nor," he said hoarsely. "I think it's growing out of the floor. Strike a match, and give me the shovel."

We found forty or fifty weed plants growing. He beat some down with the shovel, but others clutched him round the legs. He was a strong, rough-looking man and he fought furiously, but they pulled him down. I gave Viva the matches and went to his rescue with the pick. The weeds seized me too, but he cut us both free with a clasp-knife, and at length we destroyed them all.

We saw by the match-light that the wall was cracking in one place. So we resolved to try to get through it. The man dislodged a few bricks with the pick, and we pulled others away till our fingers bled and the last match gave out. At length he managed to crawl through.

"You come next, sir," he proposed. "The lady would be frightened of me."

"Dear friend," Viva said, "I am not in the least afraid of you."

So he helped her through, and I followed. We discovered a passage, and along the passage another doorway—and people. I do not remember our words when we found one another in the dark—only the gladness of it.

There were about twenty of them—men, women and children. They had food and drink which they had collected before they fled to the cellar. Professor Newton was among them. He seemed acknowledged as their leader, and he proposed me as his second. He wanted the aid of an intelligent and educated man, he whispered, in fighting the weed.

"We *must* fight it," he declared, tapping me on the arm with his finger, "but I don't know how. I—don't— know—how!—I can't even guess what it is; still less what it is going to be. It may be mere vegetable life—a man-eating plant. It may be brute animal life—a *carnivorous* animal! It may be intelligent—diabolical intelligence. Whatever it is, it will develop as it grows, develop new organs and new powers, new strength and new weaknesses. We must strike *there*. What weaknesses? Ah-h! I don't know! It may outgrow itself and wither. It may perish from the little microbes of

the earth, like the Martians in Wells's romance. We thought that
an idle fancy *then*. It may grow into an intelligent—devil! It may
be one now and merely lack the organs to carry out fully its evil
will. On the other hand, its malevolence may be purposeless—a
blind restlessness that it will outgrow—after we have stifled in the
darkness at its feet. We must fight it anyhow. To fight it we must
understand it. To understand it we must study it. Will you risk your
life with me?"

"Yes," I said.

Viva cried softly when I told her I must go; but she did not try
to keep me from my duty. The professor and I crawled up the stairs
into the basement, and finding nothing there went up in the lift in
the dark. We heard the weed moving about on the second landing.
I jumped out, turned on the electric light, and jumped in again.
The tendrils followed me and clutched at the steel curtain, but
could not break it. We hacked with our penknives at those that
crept through. The juice which ran out from them had an oily smell.
They beat furiously on the curtain. The professor studied them
calmly with a microscope. The bulges were the beginning of eyes,
he thought. He pronounced some feathery sprays sprouting from
them to be the rudiments of organs like hands. I do not know
whether he was right, but he always maintained that they would
develop organs of sense. Anyhow the character of the weed was
clearly changing. It had grown harder and drier, but without
losing its flexibility or strength.

After a time the professor decided that I should return to the
others. He went up again in the lift when he had lowered me. Viva
was waiting for me in the dark just inside the door.

I had obtained some candles. We lit one and stuck it in a bottle.
I shall never forget the group in the low, wide cellar, huddled together on boxes or on the floor. The man we met first was nursing
an ailing child. Lady Evelyn Angell had gathered a young flower-
girl under her opera cloak. A policeman was binding up a wounded
hand with his handkerchief. A shivering old match-seller wore his
cape. Viva took a little boy on her lap and told him about Jack and
the Beanstalk. Steel—a card sharper, I learned afterward—who had

been indefatigable in helping everyone, was chatting to Lady Evelyn. Some ill-clad youths had draped themselves in sacking. A rouged and gaudily dressed woman was mothering some younger ones. She had comforted Viva while I was away, I heard, and had offered to accompany her in a search for me, but the others had persuaded them that they would only be a hindrance to us.

After a couple of hours—I had wound my watch again—the professor reappeared. His clothes were torn and his face and hands were bleeding.

"They broke the steel curtain at last," he explained, "but I got away. Good heavens, how it grows! I can't make up my mind about it."

After a time, when most of us were dozing, a portion of the roof and the wall fell in. The growth of the roots under the street had pressed the earth upon it, the professor conjectured. A faint light streamed down the tall weeds and through the opening. The branches overhead were still moving, but the lower stems seemed inert. The professor decided to venture among them in search of knowledge. I went with him. There was just room enough between the weeds for us to pass.

The houses upon the other side of the street were all down. So were many in the Strand. In Fleet Street we saw the way it was done. The huge weeds leaned upon them, till they fell with a crash. The Law Courts went so. We found the clock among the weeds. Sometimes the branches pushed themselves through the windows and walls of houses which were still standing. Once or twice we heard human cries. We found a woman, with a baby and a dog, walking among the weed-trees, and took them with us.

The light which straggled down through the waving branches overhead was feeble and patchy, and we lost our way for a time. At length we found Norfolk Street; but as we were entering it, some of the tendrils, which seemed to be fighting one another viciously overhead, broke off and dropped at our feet. They writhed upon the ground like huge gray snakes, and wound themselves round the weed-trees and lashed out blindly. One of them caught the woman and dashed her against a trunk. We pulled her away from the tendril as its violence lessened, but she was dead. The baby was not hurt and still slept. I carried it in my arms.

A moment later a broken tendril dropped right upon the dog. He howled loudly, and in his fright bit at an unbroken tendril hanging down among the trees. (There were a good many such, but we had succeeded in avoiding them hitherto.) It shook as if with rage and pain, wrapped its extremity round the dog, and bore him aloft, still howling. Hundreds of tendrils stretched toward it, and fought with it for the dog. They still fought after his cries ceased; and other tendrils began reaching downward, in every direction round us, as if searching for further prey. The professor watched them intently, oblivious of danger.

"They make a different sound now," he remarked abstractedly. "It is no longer the scroop-scroop of clammy india-rubber—they *rustle*. It doesn't seem like decay. They are stronger—stronger. There is always weakness in excess of anything—even strength. Let me think!"

"Quick!" I cried. "Quick! They are falling upon us. Run!"

We dodged rapidly among the weed-trunks. He was slow and I pushed him. Tendril after tendril rustled downward, and the trunks themselves swayed. Two almost fixed the professor between them—he was a stout man—but I dragged him through. The light from above was entirely shut out by the descending tendrils, and we must have been lost but for an electric lamp burning in one of the houses. As it was, the descending tendrils must have caught us but for their struggles among themselves. Broken pieces dropped and wriggled madly all round us, and we had to dodge them. One caught at my foot, and dragged my shoe off as I pulled myself away. Several touched us as we slid down the debris into the cellar. They followed us there.

A few of the people screamed. A few fainted. The rest backed in a huddled, wide-eyed crowd toward the farthest wall. Lady Evelyn stood in front of the children, holding out her arms as if to shelter them. Steel came and stood in front of her.

"Dear lady," he said, "these have been the best days of my life—since we met. I should have been a better man if I had met you before." She smiled very sweetly at him.

"I like you greatly, Mr. Steel," she said.

The rouged woman came and took the baby from me, and I tried to pull the professor back; but he would not come. Viva ran out from the crowd and put her arms round me. The tendrils drew nearer and nearer. Some came along the ceiling, hanging their heads like snakes. Others crawled along the floor, raising themselves as if to dart at us. I do not know whether they saw us, heard us or smelt us, or how they knew where we were; but they *knew*.

They were within a yard of the professor, and still he did not move; only took the burning candle from the bottle, and railed at them as if they could hear. I thought that he had gone mad.

"Do you think man has learned nothing in his thousand generations?" he shouted. "That you can crush him with the brute strength of a few days? Come and see! Come and see!"

The foremost tentacle wound round him; began to lift him. He felt it carefully with his hands. "It is dry," he shouted— "*dry!*"

Then he put the candle to it!

There was a wilderness of white light. Then a purple darkness. I heard the professor fall. When our eyes recovered from their dazed blindness the weed was utterly gone. The daylight was streaming into the hole in the wall, and the professor was picking himself up from the floor. His hair and beard were badly singed, and his eyebrows were gone.

"It dried too fast," he told us, with a queer angry chuckle. "That was its weakness. It dried—dried—"

He kept on repeating the word in a dull, aimless tone. The rest repeated it vacantly after him. Viva was the first to speak coherently—a faint whisper in my ear.

"My dear!" she said. "My *dear!*"

Lady Evelyn spoke next—to ex-card sharper Steel.

"The world begins afresh," she said; "and—you *have* met me, Mr. Steel."

The tears rolled down her cheek and his, and they stood smiling at each other.

"The world begins afresh," the professor called in a loud voice. "Come with me and make it a better world." He strode toward the light, but some held back.

"The weed!" they cried timorously.

"The weed has gone—burned in an instant, from the end of the world to the end of the world!" he assured them. "Follow me."

We followed him out of the darkness into the sunlight. It was a mild, bright day for November, and a pleasant air.

The weed had disappeared entirely, as the professor predicted; and, speaking generally, the conflagration had been too sudden to do much harm; but most of the buildings had subsided upon the sudden destruction of the weed-roots which had undermined them. Here and there houses, stones and timber had caught fire; and in many districts the fire spread, and lasted for days.

The statistics, which are being prepared in the New Department for the Service of the People, over which I have the honor to preside, are not yet quite complete; but I may mention that seventeen per cent. of the buildings on the north of the Thames are found to have been destroyed, and ninety-three per cent. on the south— the wind having blown mainly in that direction; and that the destruction of property in Great Britain and Ireland generally is roughly estimated at fifty-five per cent.

The adventures of our little band, after we came out from our hiding-place, scarcely belong to this story; but I must set down a few events which stand out in red letters in our calendar of the world after the Gray Weed.

Upon the first afternoon we learned that there were other survivors—which we had not dared to hope—by finding a man, woman and child nearly dead with hunger and fright, hiding in a basement. We formed ourselves at once into small parties to go round London, wherever houses yet stood, and rang the church bells, and blew trumpets, and beat drums, and shouted to all those who remained to come out. Here and there frightened groups of white-faced, famished, disheveled people answered the call. As our numbers increased we sent parties to search the cellars and other hiding-places, and rescued many at their last gasp. The total number of survivors in London, where the percentage of deaths was highest, amounts to some 35,000.

Upon the second day we obtained several replies to our calls by telegraph to the provinces; and the next day we were in telegraphic communication with most parts of the United Kingdom and even the Continent. In almost all towns at least one or two persons had escaped. In some parts the Gray Weed had left open spaces, or a few houses, to which people could flee, and only a portion of those who reached them had died from starvation. In a few instances it was alleged to have refrained from injuring those with whom it came in contact. Also it failed to crush many of the ships which it seized at sea—the sea-growths generally being less virulent than those on land. So far as our statistics go at present, we hope that nearly one-eighth of the population of Europe has survived.

On the fourth day the first train from the provinces to London was run; and several ships, which the weed had overgrown without injuring, came into port. After this, traffic was rapidly re-established.

A fortnight later our present government was provisionally established. The professor, whom all hailed as their deliverer, refused office himself; but upon his nomination I was appointed to my present position. Several of our little band were assigned important posts, including Steel—now known by another name, and married to Lady Evelyn—and Viva, who is presiding over the London Homes for Orphans, until our marriage. The day after tomorrow a newspaper appears.

We have toiled unremittingly to reconstruct the social and commercial life of the country, and not without success. We have few luxuries, but no wants; fewer workers, but no drones; fewer to love—but we love more—I think the world will go well, now, because we love one another so much.

"The Gray Weed has solved the problems of poverty, envy, crime and strife, which have puzzled mankind for ages," the professor said, just before he died. "Don't cry, little Viva. Ah! But I felt a tear on my hand! There is nothing to cry about, my child. *They* have gone; and *I* am going; but *you* have learned to love. It is all for the best!"

"All—for—the—best," he repeated at the last, and smiled. That is his message to you to whom I write, dear friends.

The Tale of the Scarlet Butterflies

Beatrice Grimshaw

I

"Takee-Me some those small-fellow yam 'long cabin belong me pretty (adjective) quick!" said the Kapitani.

The Solomon Island crew gave Vaiti the brevet title of Captain, much as the Eastern Islanders had done in her father's day. Vaiti could not inhabit any ship without making her presence vividly felt on board. It was Tempest, her husband, the ex-naval officer, who commanded the *Sybil* in these days, but his command was, as the white mate expressed it, a very William-and-Mary sort of affair. There was trouble on this head some times, but not near so often as might have been supposed. Vaiti and Tempest were a pair of fine sailors, and they seldom disagreed about anything that concerned the actual running of the ship.

To-day, the schooner being almost ready for sea, and about to quit little Iorana, Vaiti and Tempest's "very own" island, for the Motua group, the Kapitani was overseeing the stowing of the cargo, while the Captain was working out the course in his cabin. He did not know the Motua group, and neither did Vaiti, but a new steamship service had lately been put on there, and it was the best and nearest market for the copra which the Solomon "boys" had been busy cutting and drying, on Iorana, during the last few weeks.

The two adventurers were going through a stage of extreme respectability at present, induced by the high price of copra. There was nothing in sight so paying as the simple disposal of the cocoanuts produced by Iorana. Therefore, they were mere copra merchants, beyond the touch of island gossip or slander, and they were

169

going right off to Motua, a British-owned group with a Resident
Commissioner who kept as much state as many full-blown Gover-
nors, and a native police and even—what Tempest detested and
avoided as much as possible—a regular run of man-of-war visits.
He would not have set his course for Motua at all, under these circumstances, had it not been the hurricane season, when His
Majesty's ships stay safe down South about Auckland or Sydney,
and leave the chances of the hurricane belt to simple little traders
who have to face the winds of heaven as they come.

Vaiti was very warm, and the thermometer of her temper had
risen in sympathy with her bodily condition. The Solomon Islanders were stupid about stowing the cargo, and the mate did not know
enough "beach-de-mar" English to direct them. She had caught
them leaving behind two of her own camphor-wood boxes in the
palm-leaf house on the shore, when the luggage for the hold was
being brought down, and they had all but dropped her basket of
little "chief" yams into the sea. They were a stupid lot of bush-pigs
and cannibals, in her opinion, and so she told them freely, at the
same time throwing one of the little yams at the biggest man with
such accuracy that he staggered, struck under the ear, and sat down
forcibly on deck. Before he had done growling over the injury to
his constitution, and the insult to his tribe (you can not annoy a
man-eater more effectually than by hinting at the nature of his
food) the other men had picked up the yam and carried it off to the
cook-house. They did not know what kind it was, it being evidently
something that did not grow in their own country, but it was meat
for their masters, and therefore worth taking.

Vaiti, annoyed with the delay caused by her own piece of discipline, snatched at the basket of yams, and slammed them into the
upper berth of an unused cabin so carelessly that the palm-leaves
burst, and the roots were scattered all over the floor below. She
turned the key in the door, and went off to argue violently with
Tempest about the course he was setting.

He need not suppose, she said, that, because he had once been
a man-of-war's officer, he knew everything about navigation in
the Pacific. There were as many lies about the trade winds in the

Admiralty Sailing Directions (said Vaiti) as there were cockroaches in her cabin. And as for great circle sailing—the Kapitani could not find words strong enough to express her contempt for it. Pressed to explain, she declared that the sea, in the Pacific, sometimes sloped uphill and sometimes down—all sailors knew it did, except the fool Englis'men on the warships, who never would believe anything you could not see the reason for. As the two commanding officers, however, agreed on the vital point of the course to give the helmsman, the rest of the discussion was postponed while the *Sybil* was making sail.

They got away with a fair wind, and Vaiti's temper recovered itself magically when the log showed the schooner to be doing eleven knots an hour, once clear of the land. For some days the pleasant weather continued, and there was peace and harmony from main-mast truck to keel of the flying, leaning ship.

Ten days out, the weather changed, and they came into a belt of squalls and calms, where the heavens dropped roaring lakes of warm water upon the decks punctually at meal-times, just as Carter was struggling aft from the galley with his dishes, and the winds alternated staggering smacks with flat oily stillness. And on the steamiest, gustiest day of all, when they should have been within sight of the Motua group, had the weather been clear enough to see the horizon, word came aft that the best of the Solomon A. B.'s was taken sick.

"What's the matter with him?" asked Tempest, looking up from his lazy lounge on the cabin sofa. He was beginning to develop a touch of the prevailing malady of the Pacific—mat fever—in these days. Mat fever is the first step down that the white man takes on his way to the "beach"—that lowest hell of the broken man. Drink is the next, wearing native clothes is the next, and after that the steps are lost in one long plunge, down which a man goes quicker than the pretty girls of Samoa fly down the Sliding Rock to the deep, dark pool below. If any further elucidation is necessary, let it be remarked that the mat is the sleeping place, and lounging place, and idling place, all over the South Seas.

Tempest had his dark hours, too, in these days, even as Saxon, Vaiti's father, whose history no man knew, had had in his time—as hundreds more of the lost legion that wanders forever about the waste corners of the earth have their dark hours, their moments of desperation, their days of a loneliness of soul that is all the worse because it is unaccompanied by solitude of body. The man had cut the throat of his own career by a certain "absence-without-leave" (with a woman at the bottom of it, be sure) that had unluckily synchronised with a time when gunpowder was in the air. Dismissal, with a strong flavor of disgrace, followed; the white feather was fixed in the cap of one who, whatever his faults might be, had not a grain of cowardice in his composition—and one more was added to the ranks of the broken men. His marriage with a half-caste, who had the reputation of being half a pirate as well, and who had almost caused his dismissal from the navy some years before, was the final cutting of the last link that bound him to all he had known, desired, or cared for. At the present moment, the wild adventurous life had its compensations. But the future was beginning to loom ahead, and not even Vaiti's beauty and curious, half-evil charm could keep away the Furies—sometimes. The worst of the Furies was tearing at his heart to-night, and its name was "Forever."

Forever—this. Forever men like Smith and Carter, at best, as his associates, palms and coral shores and burning, hurricane-haunted seas for country, an ill-smelling copra schooner for home. Never, as long as life endured, the cool gray gloaming of England, the country houses among the ancient oaks and elms, the rose-cheeked English girls, the clean, well-bred, quiet-eyed men, who knew things, and understood things. Never the jolly life of the wardroom again, with its comradeship and its common ambitions; its easy assumption of good things in the future, good things all the way—its vivid interludes of fighting, the one thing in the world worth living for—its sweets of flattery and consideration from folks ashore—the folks who didn't matter, or, at least, not as they of the Service did. He was one of the people who did not matter now, forever.

It was quite in Vaiti's experience of the natural order of things that white men should have gloomy fits from time to time, much as people in the Western Isles had fever. Most of them drank, at such times. Tempest didn't. She almost wished he did; he would have been so much easier to manage.

To-day, for instance, when she went down into the cabin to tell him that Jacky Guadalcanar was sick, and to get the medicine chest out, Tempest had nothing at all to say except that, if Jacky pegged out now, he'd be saved trouble to come, and it would be a good thing for some of us if we had never been let grow up—which had nothing whatever to do with the matter in hand.

Vaiti, shooting out her underlip scornfully, made a rough selection from the chest, and went on deck again. Presently, she came back, silent, and stretched herself out on the settee opposite Tempest.

The latter guessed that something out of the ordinary had occurred, by the curious brightening of the Kapitani's eyes. She looked a trifle excited, and a trifle thoughtful. But Vaiti never volunteered news, and Tempest was out of humor with the world. So neither of the odd pair spoke, and the matter passed out of Tempest's mind, for that day at least.

On the morrow it was recalled. The squally weather had cleared off, and Motua was close at hand, sticking up tall and green and purple into the pale, hot sky, quite like the South Sea Island of a boy's story-book And Carter, the cook, his labors over until tea-time, came out of the galley, and stood near Tempest on deck, enjoying the afternoon breeze, and watching secretly for a word or a look from his captain. Carter was a broken gentleman, a remittance man picked up in Sydney. He was big and sandy and red-faced, very young, and absurdly devoted to Tempest. Off the ship, they were equals, but, on it, the captain kept up something very like man-of-war discipline.

"Well?" said Tempest curtly, by and by. The breeze was off the land, and they were making slow progress. There was no need to trouble about barrier reefs yet a while.

Carter turned his rosy, foolish face toward the captain and stood at attention, which was his way of expressing respect.

"Jacky is better, sir," he observed.

"I know he is; I saw him about his work this morning," replied Tempest, his eye on the coast ahead.

"Did you see him when he was ill, sir?"

"No."

"Mrs. Tempest would no doubt tell you about him, sir. It was a very odd sort of illness. The men say it came from eating a bit of a yam he—he—picked up on deck. I hope you don't mean to eat the rest, sir."

"Of course, not, if there's anything bad about them. We found them on Iorana, in the bush. They were the only ones on the island, worse luck. Pity the ordinary wild yam doesn't grow there; it would come in very useful."

"Well, sir, it was a queer effect it had on Jacky. Seemed to me when I saw him he was sort of hypnotized. I—I used to take an interest in that sort of thing at—at Cambridge—" apologetically—"and Jacky seemed hypnotized right enough. He couldn't move or speak, and his eyes stared as if he was unconscious. But, when Mrs. Tempest spoke to him—or me, sir, or even one of the other boys—he'd go and do just what we told him to, though he went on, just as if he was asleep. Like that for hours he was. Mrs. Tempest gave him brandy, but it didn't have any effect. It seemed to wear off, by and by. The boys said some awfully funny things about it, sir."

"Yes," said Tempest, who thought his cook had done quite enough talking. "You needn't be afraid any more of them will be eaten, Carter. Probably, they were not yams after all; it's easy to be mistaken, if you are no botanist. You might get another keg of that beef up before six o'clock."

"Yes, sir," said Carter, hurrying off to the lazarette, the interview over.

"What were the boys saying about Jacky Guadalcanar?" Tempest asked Vaiti, by and by.

Vaiti was swinging up and down the deck with the air of a rear-admiral at the very least. She was got up for shore-going, in a white dress with gilt anchor buttons, and a cap with a gold band. All the nautical frippery worn on board the *Sybil* was worn by her. Tempest would sooner have dressed himself in a whale-tooth necklace and a red-edged bath-towel, Samoa fashion, than have worn anything that in the faintest degree recalled a uniform.

The gay figure in white and gold answered promptly.

"They saying spilit belong Jacky he clear out, go for walk. When some people speaking Jacky, that people's spilit getting inside him, doing all the blooming thing it like. By-an'-by, spilit belong Jacky he come back, then he all same other people. That yam he make spilit go 'way for little, Solomon boy say he one devil yam."

"They aren't yams at all, I should think; we won't eat any of 'em," said her partner. "Where are the rest?"

"I look, by-'n-by; now I go get with swell dress belonging me. I think Governor he give blow-out tonight," said Vaiti. She had met the amiable, elderly soldier administrator of Motua in the days when she was Queen of Liali, and she felt sure of an invitation to dinner.

Tempest was busy getting the ship safe into port after that, and did not see anything of his partner until they were within a few cables' length of the inner reef. At this critical point, the Kapitani reappeared, but not as she had gone down into the cabin. She exploded up the companion like a shell, and once on deck, instantly burst, so to speak. For the next minute the air was full of "beach-de-mar" English of the most vivid description. Smith, the gentleman mate, who was up in the cross-trees looking for coral horseheads, breathed a short but fervent prayer of thanksgiving, in that he was safe out of the way. Carter shut and bolted the galley door, and sat down, in a hot, greasy gloom, upon an upturned saucepan, murmuring, "Gad, what a woman!"

Tempest, the legal owner of the human firecracker, was the only man who faced the music with anything like coolness, and even he lost his equanimity when he saw Vaiti hurl herself across the deck, seize a mallet that had been left on the top of the skylight by the carpenter, and pitch it at the head of the helmsman with an accuracy of aim that knocked that luckless A. B. flat on his back. There he lay, his eyes stupidly open, his cut scalp oozing red across the stainless planks, while the *Sybil*, released from control, yawed alarmingly and threatened to swing broadside on to the reef.

Whatever Vaiti was, she was first of all, and last of all, a sailor. Seeing what she had done, she dropped her rage like a garment, took three steps over to the wheel, and began handling it like a mistress of the art. Tempest, exceedingly angry, on his own side, was fully occupied for a minute or two getting the ship back into the channel, and keeping her off the ugly ruffle of foam that sank and swelled dangerously close to her stately bow. Into the green calm of the inner lagoon they swept: the sails came rattling down, the anchor chains roared home to their sandy bed and the ship lay safe and still before the little white tin-roofed town of Motua.

The injured A.B., who was not much hurt, now gathered himself up and disappeared. The island canoes came skimming out toward the ship like long-legged brown waterflies. The doctor's white boat put off.

"Vaiti, what in the name of all that's infernal did you mean by doing that? Don't you know you might have lost the ship?" demanded Tempest, a good deal softened, however, by the fine exhibition of steering he had just seen.

"You know jolly well. Know so much you knowing, any day," replied the irrepressible. "I plenty mad with that crab-face, shark-liver pig, Jacky."

"What's happened?"

"Happen? He leave my camphor-trunk one thousan' mile away, stop Iorana, after all I say I do! One trunk got my swell thing in him—what they calling you 'glad rags', 'long Frisco. He leave that! Kovana (Governor) give blow-out, I not got nothing to wear. What you think that?"

"Oh, you'll look all right," replied Tempest with conjugal coolness. "You'll beat them all, Vi, you always do."

"Fool man!" was his partner's comment. "Men they liking me, no matter what close I got, no matter got very little! Those women, I thinking about. I like make them feel plenty dam sick, time they seeing me. How you think they feel sick, see me in one clean white muslin, that all?"

"Very sorry, my dear girl, but I can't cry. Here's the local Sawbones coming off; I must interview him, if you want us to get pratique to-night. Go and see the men stow that jib a bit neater, will you? I want the ship to do us credit here."

"You liking make all the sailor man he feel sick, when he look at *Sybil*, only got mud-cow boat himself," observed Vaiti, moving off to the congenial task. "You all same me, what?"

II

"Hope your wife's coming, Mr. Tempest. Shouldn't like to miss her: you know I've met her in the old days," said the Chief Magistrate.

He was an elderly, white-moustached gentleman with a twinkling eye and a comfortable figure. He wore white drill, with a little round white jacket, and a neat black cummerbund—the evening dress of the Tropics. He stood upon the steps of his own wide green-shaded veranda, and welcomed in the visitors as they came.

They were a wondrous crew. The *Sybil* had been lucky enough to hit upon no ordinary guest-night, but the birthday party annually given by the British Government to Kalavai, the former Queen of the group. It is by graceful acts such as these that British diplomacy plants the flag of Empire firmly in the remotest of her possessions. Circumstances beyond its control had reluctantly compelled Great Britain to take away her kingdom from Kalavai, but they gave her a salute from visiting warships, three hundred a year, and an annual birthday party instead—which, as everyone admitted, was doing the thing handsomely.

The Resident Commissioner's house was almost all veranda, with an unimportant inner kernel of two or three bedrooms and a sitting-room. It did not appear that these latter were much used, for the great supper-tables were laid out on the side veranda, the guests were collecting on the front veranda, and upon the back veranda, when one or two curious guests wandered round to inspect, were to be seen a bed with a dim shrouding of mosquito curtain, and a tin bath, propped up against the door of an open shed. This was, however, the custom of the country, most island bachelors living in the same way. An Irish trader had been heard to say that what a man really wanted in the Motua climate was a good four-sided veranda without any house at all, but architectural difficulties had been found to lie in the way of realizing this ingenious ideal.

It was certainly hot to-night. The moon was invisible, and the stars winked languidly out of a thunderous purple gloom. Every now and then, a flash of sheet lightning spurted up behind the huge black flags of the bananas, and showed that they stood motionless as marble against the sky. The cool sound of the surf on the reef, and the white glimmer of its restless foam, only added, by the force of contrast, to the heaviness of the overheated, overweighted, overscented dusk inland. But the hotter it grew, the more the Chief Magistrate's guests seemed to enjoy themselves.

By the time Tempest made his appearance, the early shyness had worn off. At first, the native guests—men in white shirts worn loose and flowing outside their other garments, duck trousers, and bare feet, women in the swelling loose-gown of the Pacific, with flowers wreathed round neck and head—sat uncomfortably on chairs, looked at the white traders and planters and their wives, and seemed to wish the entertainment well over, and themselves safe at home on their sleeping mats. By and by, a white woman sang a coon song, accompanying herself on a banjo, and this delighted the Motuans so much that certain of the women ran across the room and thumped the performer on the back by way of applause—after which it seemed possible to subside on the floor cross-legged and comfortable, and the stiffness wore off.

Dancing was not part of the official entertainment, as it was known that the good manners of the Motuan, painfully acquired and carefully rooted throughout two generations of missionary enterprise, were not to be depended on for more than two minutes after the merry dance got under way. They would, and did, dance, in spite of the remonstrances of the Church, at funerals and other private gatherings, but the Resident Magistrate barred the island can-can in any of its variations at the official entertainment. So there was nothing to do but look at each other's dresses, hear the white people sing, and eat.

This last, the real business of the evening, was beginning. Kalavai, the former Queen, had just arrived—very tall, very fat, and suffering agonies of heat in a waistless gown of red furniture velvet, decked with several ponderous cables of strong-scented flowers—and had at once led the way to the supper veranda, whither all her subjects had followed her joyously. The white people had a table to themselves.

It is native etiquette to clear away everything in the way of food that may be provided by the most generous of hosts, and the Motuans were working nobly to keep up local tradition. Seated in ranks on the floor, their plates on their laps, fingers openly taking the place of forks, they assaulted the good things with a will. Whole flocks of fowls disappeared as fast as if they had spread their featherless wings and flown out of the window; tarts and pies melted away like dew on a banana leaf at sunrise; warm lemonade (there were no ice machines in Motua) flowed like a river. Kalavai, one of the few who sat at table, was making the best of her time in her own way. The laws of Motua allow liquor to the chiefs, and only the chiefs, so Kalavai, by way of emphasizing her ex-royal status, had poured sherry, port, champagne, lemonade, raspberry vinegar, and a dash of whisky, into a "long peg" tumbler, adding at the last a flavoring from most of the sauce bottles in the cruet, and was drinking the horrible brew with an expression of perfect content.

"You'll have an awful head to-morrow, Queen," warned the Chief Magistrate, hurrying round the table to see that everyone was supplied.

"To-morrow is the fish that never was spawned," replied Kalavai, with royal dignity, filling up her bumper with French claret, which she had forgotten to sample.

And still Vaiti did not come.

It grew later; the feasting was almost over; the chorus singing had commenced. Most of the guests were now sitting cross-legged on the veranda, singing an interminable part-song, accompanied with pantomimic action, descriptive of the good time they had had that evening. The leader of the chorus, who sat in the middle, and improvised every verse and every pose, was covered with ribbons flung to him by admiring women, and the girls beside him had each her tribute in the shape of a gay handkerchief, a chunk of plug tobacco, a bottle of sixpenny scent, tossed in her lap by the delighted native audience. The chorus was slacking a little, when a sudden revival put fresh spirit into every voice and limb, and caused the white people, who were getting decidedly bored, to come out on the veranda, and look about them.

Most of them did not know Motuan, but the Chief Magistrate, who did, translated the song for the benefit of his European guests. It was a chant in praise of Mrs. Tempest, he said; there she was, just coming in, and the Motuans were singing appreciation of her toilette.

Her toilette! They might well sing its praises. Nothing like that had ever crossed the steps of the Chief Magistrate's veranda in all the thirty years that had elapsed since first Great Britain "protected" Motua. Nothing like it, indeed, as events proved, had ever been seen anywhere.

Vaiti was wearing a white dress, full, soft and floating, on which a swarm of marvelous scarlet butterflies seemed to have settled. They quivered on the round of the shoulder like crimson epaulets, they perched upon the hem, they fluttered up the skirt in long, loose trails, they gathered on the bosom in splendid knots, they lay like red light of sunset among the massy black waves of her hair. No such butterflies were known in Motua, nor indeed, as far as the amazed partner of Vaiti could recollect, in any other part of the world. What, and whence, were these strange, lovely insects? Were they alive or dead? And where, in the name of all the probabilities, had she contrived to get them?

There were more than Tempest who asked that question. Vaiti was surrounded in an instant by a curious and admiring crowd. She had never looked half as handsome in her life. Not even the famous Paris dress, about which so many adventures had circled in her early days, had become her like this snowy robe set off with the quivering, dancing, flame-like creatures that hovered about breast and foot and hair. Each butterfly was as big as a sparrow; all had shining dark eye-spots on their brilliant wings, setting off the pure scarlet of their hue, and somewhere about the head of every one trembled long, spiral, hornlike antenna; of a crimson as bright as the wings.

The murmur from the native women was not unmixed with little bitter laughs of spite, which Vaiti garnered in as so much honey. They meant what she wanted—a real triumph. The white women stared also, with emotions not very far removed from those of their dark sisters. She was so unnecessarily handsome, this lawless Sea-Queen, and so audaciously conscious of her beauty and her power, that she made everyone else feel like a farthing rushlight beside a blazing jet of gas. Not for a fortune would the missionaries' and traders' wives have gone closer to her, to examine that wonderful trimming.

But the Resident Magistrate, being troubled by no jealousies, and being moreover very curious to know what the decoration was, went over at once to Vaiti, as she stood in the full light of the hanging lamp on the front veranda, and asked her point blank what on earth she had got hold of.

"There aren't any butterflies of that sort in the whole Pacific, that ever I—" he was beginning, when he stopped—having now come quite close to Vaiti—and put out one hand to touch the wonderful insects.

"Orchids!" he fairly yelled.

There are two men in the Pacific who know everything about orchids. One is the Governor of the most important English group of islands in the South Seas. The other is the Resident Magistrate of Motua. At this moment, the latter official felt much as Keat's

watcher of the skies.
When some new planet swims into his ken

—only perhaps rather more excited than the over-quoted astronomer may have been. For no one has ever had occasion to observe that the discovery of a new planet brings fortune as well as fame to its lucky finder—while the silliest schoolgirl who ever munched chocolates through a general information lesson knows that a new orchid may be worth its weight, not in gold, but in diamonds. And this was newest of the new. There are orchids that imitate birds, reptiles, insects in plenty, but there is no orchid, save the one discovered thus accidentally by the Sea-Queen, that you simply can not tell from a living scarlet butterfly of huge size, until you touch it. Perhaps, the English bee orchid, known to not very many, is the nearest parallel.

"My dear Mrs. Tempest, where did that come from?" gasped the Magistrate, his hands quivering over the flowers with eagerness to handle them.

Vaiti courteously detached one or two, and gave them to him, before explaining that they were the flowers of something she had taken for a small yam, that grew in one spot of Iorana, and in one only. She had had all the roots dug up and put in one of the cabins, she said, and they had flowered during the voyage, unexpectedly, as she had found out when she opened the cabin to look for something, while she was dressing. So she had picked all the flowers, and put them on because, as she phrased it, she wanted to look "very dam nice."

"Well, my dear lady," said the Magistrate, drawing a long breath, "allow me to remark that you are wearing the most expensive costume ever worn by mortal woman. I should say that you are worth, as you stand, some ten thousand pounds. What a find! Lucky people, what a find!"

It is perhaps a measure of Vaiti's vanity that she smiled and glowed first of all with appreciation of the sartorial triumph she had achieved, and secondly over the golden profits that the Resident Magistrate seemed to suggest. Tempest was not so divided in his mind. He entered at once into a discussion with his fellow countryman as to the best means of selling the roots, the price likely to be obtained, and other practical details. It was agreed that the Magistrate should come down to the ship the first thing in the morning, to see the roots and talk about their disposal. Meantime, the three moved into one of the inner rooms of the house, to have a "yarn" and a drink before parting company.

All this time, the guests—native—were melting away, the party being over. They did not come to say good-bye, but simply slipped off down odd corners of the veranda, their dresses stuffed out with cake, cold ham, pigeons, puddings, and anything else that came handy. This custom is native etiquette, but it is never carried out in an ostentatious manner. Nothing must be left, but your host must be allowed to suppose, if he likes, that everything has been eaten at the table.

The evening was well over when Vaiti and Tempest started to walk back to their ship. Even Kalavai, the former Queen of Motua, had departed, simply and unostentatiously, through a back window, with half a turkey stuffed into the bosom of her dress and an unopened bottle of claret up one voluminous sleeve. The white people were gone long ago, and the night was far spent.

Perhaps, Vaiti and her partner were a little exalted, though not with wine, as they walked side by side through the scented purple gloom under the huge dark flags of the banana groves. The fortune that had thus suddenly dropped into their hands made their blood run quicker, and set even Vaiti's tongue going fast. There was no end to the things they were going to do, and be, and have, all through the roots that had borne those wonderful scarlet butterflies.

The cabin ports of the *Sybil* shone out in unwonted light as the owners of that errant beauty came in sight of the harbor.

"What the deuce have they got in there?" asked Tempest angrily. "I didn't give leave for a party, confound them."

A party there was, however—that was clear. As they neared the harbor, sounds of loud talking, even shouting, became audible. Someone was distressed about something. Someone seemed drunk. Some people were evidently near fighting.

It may have been second sight, or not, that started Vaiti running like a deer when she heard the disturbance. It was certainly knowledge of his wife's character, and nothing else, that made Tempest keep step for step beside her and hold himself ready to look out for squalls. After events proved that both the pair had made intelligent anticipation of coming events.

Vaiti took the gang plank with one spring and the break of the poop with another. Two more landed her down the companion and into the cabin. Tempest, close on her heels, no sooner caught sight of the scene within than he snatched the knife out of Vaiti's belt and hid it under his coat.

He was not an instant too soon. The slender brown hand leaped to the hip like a tiger springing on its prey, and, missing the well-known hilt, snatched at Tempest's arm.

"Give me that knife belong me!" hissed Vaiti, with burning eyes and grinding teeth.

"Not much; you keep your hair on," was her husband's reply. "You're in no state to handle knives, Vi. Keep cool, can't you? I see what's happened as well as you, but knifing people isn't going to help us any."

The blood of those many English ancestors of hers, who had belonged to the class that suppresses feeling as rigidly as crime, came to the aid of the half-caste girl and she pulled herself together. But the fire was still in her eyes as she looked on the scene before her.

The cabin was full of chiefs—Motua chiefs whom she had seen at the party an hour or two before. Men and women, in their gaudy, semi-European clothes, were leaning stupid and half-senseless the narrow table. There was brandy there, and Carter, the cook, who had evidently had his share, was snoring on the settee in the corner. Smith, the mate, was standing in the midst of the group, looking scared. He had been trying to arouse them by screams and blows, and he had apparently met with small success.

On the table were the remains, in two or three plates, of the roots from the cabin—the roots that were worth their weight in diamonds—that were to have opened the gates of fortune and freedom to Vaiti and Tempest—the roots that had come from far Iorana, and that were nowhere else in the known world to be obtained. Not even on Iorana could they be had now, for every one had been taken away. And the chiefs of Motua had—eaten them.

That was perfectly clear. The roots had been boiled in the galley, and devoured in the cabin. There was scarce a scrap left. Vaiti, knowing the customs of her own class, understood how the thing had happened, without inquiring particulars from the trembling Smith, who had been left in charge of the ship and had too evidently gone ashore. The chiefs, coming on board the schooner to look over her, had found the roots stripped of their flowers and had—like Vaiti herself—taken them for the small "chief" yam, sacred to the use of the upper classes. As an act of defiance against Vaiti and a protest against the "airs" she was supposed to assume, the chiefs had solemnly cooked and eaten the tabu'd food they supposed her to be reserving for herself—and now, one and all, they were suffering from the results. It was very simple, as simple as the fire that catches a drapery in a bedroom and burns down a mansion worth a quarter of a million in two brief hours. It was equally complete.

In pregnant silence, Vaiti gazed for a full minute at the ruin of her new bright hopes, and then turned to her husband. Tempest noticed a light in her eye that he did not fully understand, nor did he catch at once the meaning of her remark:

"We make 'um sail."

"Make what?" demanded the Englishman.

"Make 'um sail. Now. Quick. I tell you by-'n-by. You b'lieve me, Tempest; no time for talk. You get Smith, get Solomon boy, get out of harbor."

"With all those chiefs?"

"Eo! we see, by-'n-by. You go quick."

Tempest knew his wife well enough to be sure that there was some profitable scheme working inside her dusky head, and he made no more delay, but went on deck, routed out the Solomon crew, and got the ship under way at once. A fine light breeze was blowing, and they cleared the harbor inside of twenty minutes.

Once away from the land, Vaiti came on deck, sat down by her husband on the hatch, even as they had sat on that wild night in the New Hebrides, years ago, when they two had first met, and told him what her plan was. It was so simple that Tempest wondered he had not thought of it himself. It was good enough, too, to put him more in heart with fortune than he had felt since discovering the scurvy trick that the fickle goddess had played that eventful night.

The ship ran smoothly through the windy dark, and on the next morning, when the chiefs of Motua awoke to the full consciousness of their surroundings, they found themselves over a hundred miles away from their homes. Indignation loud and deep, and freely expressed, seized upon every one of the proud band. They demanded that the ship should instantly be turned back, and that they should be brought home as fast as sails would take them. What had happened to them the night before, seeing that the white pig of a cook had drunk all the spirits before they got on board, they could not say, but they did not like a ship where such things occurred, and they would thank the owners to let them out of her as soon as might be.

Then it was that Vaiti produced a document that struck not only dismay but superstitious horror to the hearts of the Motuans. It was a paper drawn up in the veritable handwriting of the principal chief, who was something of a scholar, and signed by every one of the party, engaging themselves to go to Queensland as laborers in the sugar plantations for the space of four years.

"This is witchcraft!" gasped the high chief, staring at the traces of his own hand, for which his own brain could offer no account.

"Witchcraft indeed," chimed in the rest, staring, open-eyed, at the indisputable signatures that ended the page. They had all been taught reading and writing at the mission school, and none had any doubt as to his own handwriting.

"Whatever it is," said Vaiti, speaking in their own tongue, "you have signed the agreement and are bound to go to Queensland as common laborers—"

She was interrupted by a wail of dismay and horror from the Motuans.

"—Unless," she concluded, "you will pay to have the agreement destroyed and yourselves brought home. Did we ask you to come?

Did we make you sign the paper? You are not children, but grown men and women. You signed it of yourselves, last night."

Which was perfectly true—only the Motuans did not know the hypnotic properties of the strange root on which they had supped, nor did they remember the low, persistent voice that had dictated the paper written by the high chief, and directed the placing of the signatures at the foot.

Not knowing, they were equally frightened and mystified, and spoke once more of witchcraft.

"Witchcraft or none," said Vaiti, who did not by any means object to the imputation of supernatural power, "you will have to pay much money, if we tear up the agreement, and bring you back."

It is well to know when you are beaten. The chiefs of Motua knew, and they gave in gracefully.

When the obnoxious agreement had been torn up, and another, relating to the payment of certain moneys, had been made out and signed, Vaiti and Tempest were four figures richer—in prospect— than they had been before the discovery of the orchids. That golden dream was indeed past, but it had left a lump of solid consolation behind it, such as dreams seldom leave in this unromantic world. Under every stitch of sail, the *Sybil*, put about, ran deviously for Motua. And Vaiti, leaning over the rail, remarked with some regret:

"That finish Motua for you, for me, Tempest. Go back this one time, never go back no more. I think better."

THE BLACK ORCHID

Marjorie L. C. Pickthall

"O Rosario, is not this the place?"

"Not yet, señor. In a little while, if the saints are kind."

Muller rested on his paddle, and watched the oily gray stream as it ran past the dugout.

"My own fault," he growled to Warwick. "Ach, yes! There is nothing romantig about orgids! I have heard you say it. But there is heat and evil smells and jaguars and aye-ayes and aboriginals of a golossal stupidity. Nothing romantig! I belief you!"

"You would come," suggested the other young man mildly. "I told you you wouldn't get much stuff for your paper unless we found it; and then it wouldn't interest your public."

"I do not belief there is anything to find."

"O Rosario! Tell the señor again!"

"There is nothing to tell, señores. I have seen the flowers, but I have not touched. My father also. The old god looks out across the river and the stones and the graves of devils. And the flowers are in his arms, so! They are black—black as the mud on the shoal, black as the night under the mangroves. They have been there—he has been there—how long? *Quien sabe?*"

"I do not for a moment belief they are black. They will be burble."

"Well, we shall soon see!"

Warwick's eyes snapped with excitement. "A black orchid," he murmured to himself dreamily. "So possible! The dream of so many!"

Through the fever-reek above the oily river he saw the high banks in flashes of color,—rose, coral, canary, amethyst,—where the orchids bloomed on the strangled trees, and the lianas fell to the middle like ropes of jewels. But the flower of his dream was black.

"Burble," grunted Muller; but he swung again to the paddle, and the dugout surged heavily against the current.

The forest reeled past like wide ribbons. Rosario's muscles rippled under his drenched cotton. Muller set his teeth against the overwhelming lassitude of the place, and planted his blade deep. So, for an hour or more, through the choking growth, the reek and steam of life decaying, of living decay.

"I do not belief," said Muller at last, faintly.— "Bob, the quinine!—How many days since we left the Essequibo? How many days since we buried poor Fernando? It is—it is—"

"We will turn when you like," said young Warwick quietly.

They looked long into each other's lean, fever-drawn faces.

"No," said Muller at last. "I am an amadeur only. But we will find him; we will not turn back. But it is not romantig."

"I knew you wouldn't turn back, Otto."

Rosario turned in his place, a little glint of triumph in his melancholy face. "Look, señores."

At first they could see nothing but the forest, as they had seen it for days. Then, through the quiver of wet heat, the outline of other things appeared amid that terrible vegetation. Very little was left; but the bank of the river showed fitted stones. There was the wreckage of the causeway, which once must have been of royal size, down which, perhaps, dark, imperial processions had passed—in what dim ages of the world?

"*Quien sabe?*"

A little hillock rose where the larger trees fell away.

"The usual truncated byramid," murmured Muller, shaking his shock of fair hair discontentedly. "After last year in Yucatan, Bob, this is trifial."

But they were hushed as the little dugout swung slowly to the landing-place; for what feet had trodden it last, and when?

"Doesn't look much of a place to camp, Otto. Is that tinned beef safe?"

But their hands shook a little, and their eyes looked everywhere in the gloom of the leaves. They had seen many such ruins of the mysterious races, but few as sinister. As they landed, there was a slimy rush and haste in the growth, and the vines clung about their knees as if with horrible soft hands.

Rosario slashed a path with his great knife.

"A very evil place," he whispered, as they stumbled up the stones of the king's causeway, "full of ghosts of the dead whom no man remembers."

The two white men did not contradict him.

"Señores, there is the god. I have fulfilled my bargain. Now look, and let us go."

They looked at what they had thought some great tree or stump—a shadow, a blur of ruin. And features began to grow out of the blur, features and a dreadful face. There the old god sat, gazing out across the river under his tall head-dress of ranged plumes; his shoulders were nothing but a mossy block of stone; between his grotesque, outstretched arms was a platform of stone some six feet long; from it a flight of steps descended, all heaved apart with green growing things. The god was nothing but impossible arms and a face.

"Let us hope," said Bob Warwick, a little breathlessly, "that face is impossible, too."

"Look!" said his friend.

Within the god's hold, upon the stone platform, was a little tuft of green leaves and dark blossoms—three-petaled, with long, blackish stamens like a spider's legs. Warwick and Muller hesitated a moment, fearing to look further. Then they sprang forward together.

Rosario flung his long brown arms round Warwick; his black eyes were alight with fear.

"It is destruction!" he cried. "For the love of heaven, señores, let us go. Take nothing from the god, for fear he takes all from us! He is the Life-taker—"

Rosario's soft Spanish slid into a jumble of gutturals, perhaps the tongue his fathers had spoken when they built the causeway and shaped the god. Warwick put him aside and followed Muller.

Muller was scrambling up the broken steps that led, as it were, into the arms of the god.

"It will be burble," he grunted to himself obstinately, but his heart beat hard.

The strange dark flowers floated just above him as he heaved himself at last from the wreckage and stood upon the platform. He shouted triumphantly, and something in the forest cried harshly in answer.

The carved face above him now had the curious effect of gazing down upon the platform. What terrors of evil seemed to be in those long eyes and cruel lips! Muller checked himself in an involuntary shudder, and reached out to grasp the orchid.

The platform tilted under his feet. Startled, he caught at the stone, but found no hold. There was one quick moment of fear, in which he heard Rosario's cry, saw Warwick's astonished face below—saw, also, the stone face above him with its carven sneer. Then the stone yielded still more, and shot him down into darkness, swinging back into place above his head.

He came to himself, sick with fear, and clinging desperately with hands and feet to long, slime-covered roots of trees. All about was black darkness, except for a phosphorescent gleam of dead wood and decay. The air was dead, heavy and reeking with moisture, but not poisonous. He could see the old roots to which he clung only by their ghastly gray radiance. They were all dead, and formed a network which yielded to his very breathing. When he moved, his hands slipped and slid upon their slime. He could not tell how far he had fallen, nor what dreadful depths lay below him.

"Bob—O Bob! Rosario!"

They could not hear him, but call he must. In that place he was losing even his iron young nerve. How that old stone face up there in the sunlight must be sneering! He seemed to see it, patterned with fine carving, marked with evil older than the white races of men. It seemed to float in the dark, watching, mocking.

"O Rosario! Rosario!"

How many poor fellows, in the old days, had been shot from that stone of sacrifice?

"*Du Lieber Gott!* It is as if I with these eyes saw. They would fall down, down—into what? What lies hereunder?

"The dark and the old dead! The dark and the old dead! O thou dear God, deliver me! Bob, Bob!"

They would lie there, bound and rotting in the slime, until there was nothing. Nothing! No cry would penetrate the walls of that pit, no prayer soften the hearts of those who had carved the face of the god. Not yet was the Life-taker satiated.

"I go to join their company if Bob is not quick. The roots slip. They are like old dead serpents. Everything here is dead, dead!

"Rosario! O Rosario!"

How long had he been clinging there? An hour? His hands grew cramped, and the heavy beating of his heart ran to the ends of his fingers in little shocks of pain. His strained eyes grew used to the dark. Where the phosphorescence glimmered, he saw ghostly shapes of stones dripping with slime. He was in a pit walled with well-fitted stones, which had resisted time and climate. What was it floored with? Stone, that would kill kindly and quickly? Or mud—the horrible, crawling mud of river shallows? His brain seemed to quiver and shrink at the thought, and wheels of whirling color rolled before his eyes. In the midst of them was the old god's face, battered, grotesque, but alive with evil as old as the earth. Would they never come? Were they going to leave him there till he fell and joined the forgotten dead below?

The white roots were sliding slowly, slowly through his desperate grip. He dared not shift his hold. The hot, wet darkness seemed to surge against his ears with the shock of hammers, but it was only the throbbing of veins in his head. Somewhere, too, there was a small, faint tapping, so faint that it could come from nothing larger than a lizard. Was there life in that pit? No, nothing but the face of the Life-taker was alive.

It seemed to float in the darkness wherever he looked. He shut his eyes, but it was still there. Wet—not the wet of that reeking pit—rolled down his face. He groaned, and shivered from head to foot. Time, reason, everything was effaced. Only fear was left, fear old as the world—fear of the dark and the thing that waited in it.

Would they never come? "How long, O thou kind God, how long!"

He sobbed with fear like a child, and the roots slipped in his wet hands. For a second all the blackness of the pit seemed to surge up to meet him, and he screamed, too, like a child.

And then—why, then fear was not. For there was light—daylight, a glaring shaft glowing suddenly on the wet stones, on the bleached roots; light, on his straining hands, shining on his desperate face. Light! And the Life-taker was only an ugly old idol carved long ago. He dared not look down; but he could look up, up to a square of heavenly light, and Rosario's terrified head.

"Señor, O señor!"

"Safe, Rosario. O Bob! Be quick, my friendt. How much longer do you leave me here suspended?"

And there was Rosario coming down on a long rope of flexible liana, like a monkey.

"I will make it fast under your arms, señor. So—and so! Holy Virgin! it would bear the weight of that old stone devil himself. I will meddle no more with the cities of the old people. They can stay in peace, they and their dead and their devils. A fruit-stall in Santa Maria Corona—"

There was Rosario ascending the taut rope, more monkey-wise than ever. There was the quick jerk, the slow withdrawal of the pit and the dead roots and the unplumbed dark. There was the bright square growing larger and nearer. And at last there were Bob's strong arms, and Rosario weeping on the steps.

"Otto, Otto! my dear old boy! I was so scared I was just sick. Sure you're all right? Yes, the stone swung on a sort of central pivot—never saw anything like it. Here, drink some of this. It took us ten minutes to get the beastly thing prized open again. How d'you feel?"

"Ten minutes! Ten minutes! *Du Lieber Gott!* I was dying, my friendt, for ten hours—all alone with the powers of darkness." He sat up weakly. "And the orgid?"

Warwick laughed shakily. "The orchid was crushed to pulp, Otto," he said, "by the upswing of the stone. There is nothing of it left. And it was the only one."

"It would haf been burble," said Otto faintly. "But that settles it. We will go home. I do not like this business; it is not romantig."

The Adventure of the Devil's Foot

Arthur Conan Doyle

In recording from time to time some of the curious experiences and interesting recollections which I associate with my long and intimate friendship with Mr. Sherlock Holmes, I have continually been faced by difficulties caused by his own aversion to publicity. To his sombre and cynical spirit all popular applause was always abhorrent, and nothing amused him more at the end of a successful case than to hand over the actual exposure to some orthodox official, and to listen with a mocking smile to the general chorus of misplaced congratulation. It was indeed this attitude upon the part of my friend and certainly not any lack of interesting material which has caused me of late years to lay very few of my records before the public. My participation in some if his adventures was always a privilege which entailed discretion and reticence upon me.

It was, then, with considerable surprise that I received a telegram from Holmes last Tuesday—he has never been known to write where a telegram would serve—in the following terms:

Why not tell them of the Cornish horror—strangest case I have handled.

I have no idea what backward sweep of memory had brought the matter fresh to his mind, or what freak had caused him to desire that I should recount it; but I hasten, before another cancelling telegram may arrive, to hunt out the notes which give me the exact details of the case and to lay the narrative before my readers.

It was, then, in the spring of the year 1897 that Holmes's iron constitution showed some symptoms of giving way in the face of constant hard work of a most exacting kind, aggravated, perhaps, by occasional indiscretions of his own. In March of that year Dr. Moore Agar, of Harley Street, whose dramatic introduction to Holmes I may some day recount, gave positive injunctions that the famous private agent lay aside all his cases and surrender himself to complete rest if he wished to avert an absolute breakdown. The state of his health was not a matter in which he himself took the faintest interest, for his mental detachment was absolute, but he was induced at last, on the threat of being permanently disqualified from work, to give himself a complete change of scene and air. Thus it was that in the early spring of that year we found ourselves together in a small cottage near Poldhu Bay, at the further extremity of the Cornish peninsula.

It was a singular spot, and one peculiarly well suited to the grim humour of my patient. From the windows of our little whitewashed house, which stood high upon a grassy headland, we looked down upon the whole sinister semicircle of Mounts Bay, that old death trap of sailing vessels, with its fringe of black cliffs and surge-swept reefs on which innumerable seamen have met their end. With a northerly breeze it lies placid and sheltered, inviting the storm-tossed craft to tack into it for rest and protection.

Then come the sudden swirl round of the wind, the blistering gale from the south-west, the dragging anchor, the lee shore, and the last battle in the creaming breakers. The wise mariner stands far out from that evil place.

On the land side our surroundings were as sombre as on the sea. It was a country of rolling moors, lonely and dun-colored, with an occasional church tower to mark the site of some old-world village. In every direction upon these moors there were traces of some vanished race which had passed utterly away, and left as its sole record strange monuments of stone, irregular mounds which contained the burned ashes of the dead, and curious earthworks which hinted at prehistoric strife. The glamour and mystery of the place, with its sinister atmosphere of forgotten nations, appealed to the imagination of my friend, and he spent much of his time in long walks and solitary meditations upon the moor. The ancient Cornish language had also arrested his attention, and he had, I remember, conceived the idea that it was akin to the Chaldean, and had been largely derived from the Phoenician traders in tin. He had received a consignment of books upon philology and was settling down to develop this thesis when suddenly, to my sorrow and to his unfeigned delight, we found ourselves, even in that land of dreams, plunged into a problem at our very doors which was more intense, more engrossing, and infinitely more mysterious than any of those which had driven us from London. Our simple life and peaceful, healthy routine were violently interrupted, and we were precipitated into the midst of a series of events which caused the utmost excitement not only in Cornwall but through-out the whole west of England. Many of my readers may retain some recollection of what was called at the time "The Cornish Horror," though a most imperfect account of the matter reached the London press. Now, after thirteen years, I will give the true details of this inconceivable affair to the public.

I have said that scattered towers marked the villages which dotted this part of Cornwall. The nearest of these was the hamlet of Tredannick Wollas, where the cottages of a couple of hundred inhabitants clustered round an ancient, moss-grown church. The vicar of the parish, Mr. Roundhay, was something of an archae-ologist, and as such Holmes had made his acquaintance. He was a middle-aged man, portly and affable, with a considerable fund of local lore. At his invitation we had taken tea at the vicarage and had come to know, also, Mr. Mortimer Tregennis, an independent gentleman, who increased the clergyman's scanty resources by taking rooms in his large, straggling house. The vicar, being a bachelor, was glad to come to such an arrangement, though he had little in common with his lodger, who was a thin, dark, spectacled man, with a stoop which gave the impression of actual, physical deformity. I remember that during our short visit we found the vicar garrulous, but his lodger strangely reticent, a sad-faced, intro-spective man, sitting with averted eyes, brooding apparently upon his own affairs.

These were the two men who entered abruptly into our little sitting-room on Tuesday, March the 16th, shortly after our breakfast hour, as we were smoking together, preparatory to our daily excursion upon the moors.

"Mr. Holmes," said the vicar in an agitated voice, "the most extraordinary and tragic affair has occurred during the night. It is the most unheard-of business. We can only regard it as a special Providence that you should chance to be here at the time, for in all England you are the one man we need."

I glared at the intrusive vicar with no very friendly eyes; but Holmes took his pipe from his lips and sat up in his chair like an old hound who hears the view-halloa. He waved his hand to the sofa, and our palpitating visitor with his agitated companion sat side by side upon it. Mr. Mortimer Tregennis was more self-contained than the clergyman, but the twitching of his thin hands and the brightness of his dark eyes showed that they shared a common emotion.

"Shall I speak or you?" he asked of the vicar.

"Well, as you seem to have made the discovery, whatever it may be, and the vicar to have had it second-hand, perhaps you had better do the speaking," said Holmes.

I glanced at the hastily clad clergyman, with the formally dressed lodger seated beside him, and was amused at the surprise which Holmes's simple deduction had brought to their faces.

"Perhaps I had best say a few words first," said the vicar, "and then you can judge if you will listen to the details from Mr. Tregennis, or whether we should not hasten at once to the scene of this mysterious affair. I may explain, then, that our friend here spent last evening in the company of his two brothers, Owen and George, and of his sister Brenda, at their house of Tredannick Wartha, which is near the old stone cross upon the moor. He left them shortly after ten o'clock, playing cards round the dining-room table, in excellent health and spirits. This morning, being an early riser, he walked in that direction before breakfast and was overtaken by the carriage of Dr. Richards, who explained that he had just been sent for on a most urgent call to Tredannick Wartha. Mr.

Mortimer Tregennis naturally went with him. When he arrived at Tredannick Wartha he found an extraordinary state of things. His two brothers and his sister were seated round the table exactly as he had left them, the cards still spread in front of them and the candles burned down to their sockets. The sister lay back stone-dead in her chair, while the two brothers sat on each side of her laughing, shouting, and singing, the senses stricken clean out of them. All three of them, the dead woman and the two demented men, retained upon their faces an expression of the utmost horror—a convulsion of terror which was dreadful to look upon. There was no sign of the presence of anyone in the house, except Mrs. Porter, the old cook and housekeeper, who declared that she had slept deeply and heard no sound during the night. Nothing had been stolen or disarranged, and there is absolutely no explanation of what the horror can be which has frightened a woman to death and two strong men out of their senses. There is the situation, Mr. Holmes, in a nutshell, and if you can help us to clear it up you will have done a great work."

I had hoped that in some way I could coax my companion back into the quiet which had been the object of our journey; but one glance at his intense face and contracted eyebrows told me how vain was now the expectation. He sat for some little time in silence, absorbed in the strange drama which had broken in upon our peace.

"I will look into this matter," he said at last. "On the face of it, it would appear to be a case of a very exceptional nature. Have you been there yourself, Mr. Roundhay?"

"No, Mr. Holmes. Mr. Tregennis brought back the account to the vicarage, and I at once hurried over with him to consult you."

"How far is it to the house where this singular tragedy occurred?"

"About a mile inland."

"Then we shall walk over together. But before we start I must ask you a few questions, Mr. Mortimer Tregennis."

The other had been silent all this time, but I had observed that his more controlled excitement was even greater than the obtrusive emotion of the clergyman. He sat with a pale, drawn face, his anxious gaze fixed upon Holmes, and his thin hands clasped convulsively together. His pale lips quivered as he listened to the dreadful experience which had befallen his family, and his dark eyes seemed to reflect something of the horror of the scene.

"Ask what you like, Mr. Holmes," said he eagerly. "It is a bad thing to speak of, but I will answer you the truth."

"Tell me about last night."

"Well, Mr. Holmes, I supped there, as the vicar has said, and my elder brother George proposed a game of whist afterwards. We sat down about nine o'clock. It was a quarter-past ten when I moved to go. I left them all round the table, as merry as could be."

"Who let you out?"

"Mrs. Porter had gone to bed, so I let myself out. I shut the hall door behind me. The window of the room in which they sat was closed, but the blind was not drawn down. There was no change in door or window this morning, or any reason to think that any stranger had been to the house. Yet there they sat, driven clean mad with terror, and Brenda lying dead of fright, with her head hanging over the arm of the chair. I'll never get the sight of that room out of my mind so long as I live."

"The facts, as you state them, are certainly most remarkable," said Holmes. "I take it that you have no theory yourself which can in any way account for them?"

"It's devilish, Mr. Holmes, devilish!" cried Mortimer Tregennis. "It is not of this world. Something has come into that room which has dashed the light of reason from their minds. What human contrivance could do that?"

"I fear," said Holmes, "that if the matter is beyond humanity it is certainly beyond me. Yet we must exhaust all natural explanations before we fall back upon such a theory as this. As to yourself, Mr. Tregennis, I take it you were divided in some way from your family, since they lived together and you had rooms apart?"

"That is so, Mr. Holmes, though the matter is past and done with. We were a family of tin-miners at Redruth, but we sold our venture to a company, and so retired with enough to keep us. I won't deny that there was some feeling about the division of the money and it stood between us for a time, but it was all forgiven and forgotten, and we were the best of friends together."

"Looking back at the evening which you spent together, does anything stand out in your memory as throwing any possible light upon the tragedy? Think carefully, Mr. Tregennis, for any clue which can help me."

"There is nothing at all, sir."

"Your people were in their usual spirits?"

"Never better."

"Were they nervous people? Did they ever show any apprehension of coming danger?"

"Nothing of the kind."

"You have nothing to add then, which could assist me?"

Mortimer Tregennis considered earnestly for a moment.

"There is one thing occurs to me," said he at last. "As we sat at the table my back was to the window, and my brother George, he being my partner at cards, was facing it. I saw him once look hard over my shoulder, so I turned round and looked also. The blind was up and the window shut, but I could just make out the bushes on the lawn, and it seemed to me for a moment that I saw something moving among them. I couldn't even say if it was man or animal, but I just thought there was something there. When I asked him what he was looking at, he told me that he had the same feeling. That is all that I can say."

"Did you not investigate?"

"No; the matter passed as unimportant."

"You left them, then, without any premonition of evil?"

"None at all."

"I am not clear how you came to hear the news so early this morning."

"I am an early riser and generally take a walk before breakfast. This morning I had hardly started when the doctor in his carriage overtook me. He told me that old Mrs. Porter had sent a boy down with an urgent message. I sprang in beside him and we drove on. When we got there we looked into that dreadful room. The candles and the fire must have burned out hours before, and they had been sitting there in the dark until dawn had broken. The doctor said Brenda must have been dead at least six hours. There were no signs of violence. She just lay across the arm of the chair with that look on her face. George and Owen were singing snatches of songs and gibbering like two great apes. Oh, it was awful to see! I couldn't stand it, and the doctor was as white as a sheet. Indeed, he fell into a chair in a sort of faint, and we nearly had him on our hands as well."

"Remarkable—most remarkable!" said Holmes, rising and taking his hat. "I think, perhaps, we had better go down to Tredannick Wartha without further delay. I confess that I have seldom known a case which at first sight presented a more singular problem."

Our proceedings of that first morning did little to advance the investigation. It was marked, however, at the outset by an incident which left the most sinister impression upon my mind. The approach to the spot at which the tragedy occurred is down a narrow, winding, country lane. While we made our way along it we heard the rattle of a carriage coming towards us and stood aside to let it pass. As it drove by us I caught a glimpse through the closed window of a horribly contorted, grinning face glaring out at us. Those staring eyes and gnashing teeth flashed past us like a dreadful vision.

"My brothers!" cried Mortimer Tregennis, white to his lips. "They are taking them to Helston."

We looked with horror after the black carriage, lumbering upon its way. Then we turned our steps towards this ill-omened house in which they had met their strange fate.

It was a large and bright dwelling, rather a villa than a cottage, with a considerable garden which was already, in that Cornish air, well filled with spring flowers. Towards this garden the window of the sitting-room fronted, and from it, according to Mortimer Tregennis, must have come that thing of evil which had by sheer horror in a single instant blasted their minds. Holmes walked slowly and thoughtfully among the flower-plots and along the path before we entered the porch. So absorbed was he in his thoughts, I remember, that he stumbled over the watering-pot, upset its contents, and deluged both our feet and the garden path. Inside the house we were met by the elderly Cornish housekeeper, Mrs. Porter, who, with the aid of a young girl, looked after the wants of the family. She readily answered all Holmes's questions. She had heard nothing in the night. Her employers had all been in excellent spirits lately, and she had never known them more cheerful and prosperous. She had fainted with horror upon entering the room in the morning and seeing that dreadful company round the table. She had, when she recovered, thrown open the window to let the morning air in, and had run down to the lane, whence she sent a farm-lad for the doctor. The lady was on her bed upstairs if we cared to see her. It took four strong men to get the brothers into the asylum carriage. She would not herself stay in the house another day and was starting that very afternoon to rejoin her family at St. Ives.

We ascended the stairs and viewed the body. Miss Brenda Tregennis had been a very beautiful girl, though now verging upon middle age. Her dark, clear-cut face was handsome, even in death, but there still lingered upon it something of that convulsion of horror which had been her last human emotion. From her bedroom we descended to the sitting-room, where this strange tragedy had actually occurred. The charred ashes of the overnight fire lay in the grate. On the table were the four guttered and burned-out candles, with the cards scattered over its surface. The chairs had been moved back against the walls, but all else was as it had been the night before. Holmes paced with light, swift steps about the room; he sat in the various chairs, drawing them up and reconstructing their positions. He tested how much of the garden was visible; he examined the floor, the ceiling, and the fireplace; but never once did I see that sudden brightening of his eyes and tightening of his lips which would have told me that he saw some gleam of light in this utter darkness.

"Why a fire?" he asked once. "Had they always a fire in this small room on a spring evening?"

Mortimer Tregennis explained that the night was cold and damp. For that reason, after his arrival, the fire was lit. "What are you going to do now, Mr. Holmes?" he asked.

My friend smiled and laid his hand upon my arm. "I think, Watson, that I shall resume that course of tobacco-poisoning which you have so often and so justly condemned," said he. "With your permission, gentlemen, we will now return to our cottage, for I am not aware that any new factor is likely to come to our notice here. I will turn the facts over in my mind, Mr, Tregennis, and should anything occur to me I will certainly communicate with you and the vicar. In the meantime I wish you both good-morning."

It was not until long after we were back in Poldhu Cottage that Holmes broke his complete and absorbed silence. He sat coiled in his armchair, his haggard and ascetic face hardly visible amid the blue swirl of his tobacco smoke, his black brows drawn down, his forehead contracted, his eyes vacant and far away. Finally he laid down his pipe and sprang to his feet.

"It won't do, Watson!" said he with a laugh. "Let us walk along the cliffs together and search for flint arrows. We are more likely to find them than clues to this problem. To let the brain work without sufficient material is like racing an engine. It racks itself to pieces. The sea air, sunshine, and patience, Watson—all else will come.

"Now, let us calmly define our position, Watson," he continued as we skirted the cliffs together. "Let us get a firm grip of the very little which we *do* know, so that when fresh facts arise we may be ready to fit them into their places. I take it, in the first place, that neither of us is prepared to admit diabolical intrusions into the affairs of men. Let us begin by ruling that entirely out of our minds. Very good. There remain three persons who have been grievously stricken by some conscious or unconscious human agency. That is firm ground. Now, when did this occur? Evidently, assuming his narrative to be true, it was immediately after Mr. Mortimer Tregennis had left the room. That is a very important point. The presumption is that it was within a few minutes afterwards. The cards still lay upon the table. It was already past their usual hour for bed. Yet they had not changed their position or pushed back their chairs. I repeat, then, that the occurrence was immediately after his departure, and not later than eleven o'clock last night.

"Our next obvious step is to check, so far as we can, the movements of Mortimer Tregennis after he left the room. In this there is no difficulty, and they seem to be above suspicion. Knowing my methods as you do, you were, of course, conscious of the somewhat clumsy water-pot expedient by which I obtained a clearer impress of his foot than might otherwise have been possible. The wet, sandy path took it admirably. Last night was also wet, you will remember, and it was not difficult—having obtained a sample print—to pick out his track among others and to follow his movements. He appears to have walked away swiftly in the direction of the vicarage.

"If, then, Mortimer Tregennis disappeared from the scene, and yet some outside person affected the card-players, how can we reconstruct that person, and how was such an impression of horror conveyed? Mrs. Porter may be eliminated. She is evidently harmless. Is there any evidence that someone crept up to the garden window and in some manner produced so terrific an effect that he drove those who saw it out of their senses? The only suggestion in this direction comes from Mortimer Tregennis himself, who says that his brother spoke about some movement in the garden. That is certainly remarkable, as the night was rainy, cloudy, and dark. Anyone who had the design to alarm these people would be compelled to place his very face against the glass before he could be seen. There is a three-foot flower-border outside this window, but no indication of a footmark. It is difficult to imagine, then, how an outsider could have made so terrible an impression upon the company, nor have we found any possible motive for so strange and elaborate an attempt. You perceive our difficulties, Watson?"

"They are only too clear," I answered with conviction.

"And yet, with a little more material, we may prove that they are not insurmountable," said Holmes. "I fancy that among your extensive archives, Watson, you may find some which were nearly as obscure. Meanwhile, we shall put the case aside until more accurate data are available, and devote the rest of our morning to the pursuit of neolithic man."

I may have commented upon my friend's power of mental detachment, but never have I wondered at it more than upon that spring morning in Cornwall when for two hours he discoursed upon celts, arrowheads, and shards, as lightly as if no sinister mystery were waiting for his solution. It was not until we had returned in the afternoon to our cottage that we found a visitor awaiting us, who soon brought our minds back to the matter in hand. Neither of us needed to be told who that visitor was. The huge body, the craggy and deeply seamed face with the fierce eyes and hawk-like nose, the grizzled hair which nearly brushed our cottage ceiling, the beard—golden at the fringes and white near the lips, save for the nicotine stain from his perpetual cigar—all these were as well known in London as in Africa, and could only be associated with the tremendous personality of Dr. Leon Sterndale, the great lion-hunter and explorer.

We had heard of his presence in the district and had once or twice caught sight of his tall figure upon the moorland paths. He made no advances to us, however, nor would we have dreamed of doing so to him, as it was well known that it was his love of seclusion which caused him to spend the greater part of the intervals between his journeys in a small bungalow buried in the lonely wood of Beauchamp Arriance. Here, amid his books and his maps, he lived an absolutely lonely life, attending to his own simple wants and paying little apparent heed to the affairs of his neighbours. It was a surprise to me, therefore, to hear him asking Holmes in an eager voice whether he had made any advance in his reconstruction of this mysterious episode. "The county police are utterly at fault," said he, "but perhaps your wider experience has suggested some conceivable explanation. My only claim to being taken into your confidence is that during my many residences here I have come to know this family of Tregennis very well—indeed, upon my Cornish mother's side I could call them cousins—and their strange fate has naturally been a great shock to me. I may tell you that I had got as far as Plymouth upon my way to Africa, but the news reached me this morning, and I came straight back again to help in the inquiry."

Holmes raised his eyebrows.

"Did you lose your boat through it?"

"I will take the next."

"Dear me! that is friendship indeed."

"I tell you they were relatives."

"Quite so—cousins of your mother. Was your baggage aboard the ship?"

"Some of it, but the main part at the hotel."

"I see. But surely this event could not have found its way into the Plymouth morning papers."

"No, sir; I had a telegram."

"Might I ask from whom?"

A shadow passed over the gaunt face of the explorer.

"You are very inquisitive, Mr. Holmes."

"It is my business."

With an effort Dr. Sterndale recovered his ruffled composure.

"I have no objection to telling you," he said. "It was Mr. Roundhay, the vicar, who sent me the telegram which recalled me."

"Thank you," said Holmes. "I may say in answer to your original question that I have not cleared my mind entirely on the subject of this case, but that I have every hope of reaching some conclusion. It would be premature to say more."

"Perhaps you would not mind telling me if your suspicions point in any particular direction?"

"No, I can hardly answer that."

"Then I have wasted my time and need not prolong my visit." The famous doctor strode out of our cottage in considerable ill-humour, and within five minutes Holmes had followed him. I saw him no more until the evening, when he returned with a slow step and haggard face which assured me that he had made no great progress with his investigation. He glanced at a telegram which awaited him and threw it into the grate.

"From the Plymouth hotel, Watson," he said. "I learned the name of it from the vicar, and I wired to make certain that Dr. Leon Sterndale's account was true. It appears that he did indeed spend last night there, and that he has actually allowed some of his baggage to go on to Africa, while he returned to be present at this investigation. What do you make of that, Watson?"

"He is deeply interested."

"Deeply interested—yes. There is a thread here which we had not yet grasped and which might lead us through the tangle. Cheer up, Watson, for I am very sure that our material has not yet all come to hand. When it does we may soon leave our difficulties behind us."

Little did I think how soon the words of Holmes would be realized, or how strange and sinister would be that new development which opened up an entirely fresh line of investigation. I was shaving at my window in the morning when I heard the rattle of hoofs and, looking up, saw a dog-cart coming at a gallop down the road. It pulled up at our door, and our friend, the vicar, sprang from it and rushed up our garden path. Holmes was already dressed, and we hastened down to meet him.

Our visitor was so excited that he could hardly articulate, but at last in gasps and bursts his tragic story came out of him.

"We are devil-ridden, Mr. Holmes! My poor parish is devil-ridden!" he cried. "Satan himself is loose in it! We are given over into his hands!" He danced about in his agitation, a ludicrous object if it were not for his ashy face and startled eyes. Finally he shot out his terrible news.

"Mr. Mortimer Tregennis died during the night, and with exactly the same symptoms as the rest of his family."

Holmes sprang to his feet, all energy in an instant.

"Can you fit us both into your dog-cart?"

"Yes, I can."

"Then, Watson, we will postpone our breakfast. Mr. Roundhay, we are entirely at your disposal. Hurry—hurry, before things get disarranged."

The lodger occupied two rooms at the vicarage, which were in an angle by themselves, the one above the other. Below was a large sitting-room; above, his bedroom. They looked out upon a croquet lawn which came up to the windows. We had arrived before the doctor or the police, so that everything was absolutely undisturbed. Let me describe exactly the scene as we saw it upon that misty March morning. It has left an impression which can never be effaced from my mind.

The atmosphere of the room was of a horrible and depressing stuffiness. The servant had first entered had thrown up the window, or it would have been even more intolerable. This might partly be due to the fact that a lamp stood flaring and smoking on the centre table. Beside it sat the dead man, leaning back in his chair, his thin beard projecting, his spectacles pushed up on to his forehead, and his lean dark face turned towards the window and twisted into the same distortion of terror which had marked the features of his dead sister. His limbs were convulsed and his fingers contorted as though he had died in a very paroxysm of fear. He was fully clothed, though there were signs that his dressing had been done in a hurry. We had already learned that his bed had been slept in, and that the tragic end had come to him in the early morning.

One realized the red-hot energy which underlay Holmes's phlegmatic exterior when one saw the sudden change which came over him from the moment that he entered the fatal apartment. In an instant he was tense and alert, his eyes shining, his face set, his limbs quivering with eager activity. He was out on the lawn, in through the window, round the room, and up into the bedroom, for all the world like a dashing foxhound drawing a cover. In the bedroom he made a rapid cast around and ended by throwing open the window, which appeared to give him some fresh cause for excitement, for he leaned out of it with loud ejaculations of interest and delight. Then he rushed down the stair, out through the open window, threw himself upon his face on the lawn, sprang up and into the room once more, all with the energy of the hunter who is at the very heels of his quarry. The lamp, which was an ordinary standard, he examined with minute care, making certain measurements upon its bowl. He carefully scrutinized with his lens the talc shield which covered the top of the chimney and scraped off some ashes which adhered to its upper surface, putting some of them into an envelope, which he placed in his pocketbook. Finally, just as the doctor and the official police put in an appearance, he beckoned to the vicar and we all three went out upon the lawn.

"I am glad to say that my investigation has not been entirely barren," he remarked. "I cannot remain to discuss the matter with the police, but I should be exceedingly obliged, Mr. Roundhay, if you would give the inspector my compliments and direct his attention to the bedroom window and to the sitting-room lamp. Each is suggestive, and together they are almost conclusive. If the police would desire further information I shall be happy to see any of them at the cottage. And now, Watson, I think that, perhaps, we shall be better employed elsewhere."

It may be that the police resented the intrusion of an amateur, or that they imagined themselves to be upon some hopeful line of investigation; but it is certain that we heard nothing from them for the next two days. During this time Holmes spent some of his time smoking and dreaming in the cottage; but a greater portion in country walks which he undertook alone, returning after many hours without remark as to where he had been. One experiment served to show me the line of his investigation. He had bought a lamp which was the duplicate of the one which had burned in the room of Mortimer Tregennis on the morning of the tragedy. This he filled with the same oil as that used at the vicarage, and he carefully timed the period which it would take to be exhausted. Another experiment which he made was of a more unpleasant nature, and one which I am not likely ever to forget.

"You will remember, Watson," he remarked one afternoon, "that there is a single common point of resemblance in the varying reports which have reached us. This concerns the effect of the atmosphere of the room in each case upon those who had first entered it. You will recollect that Mortimer Tregennis, in describing the episode of his last visit to his brother's house, remarked that the doctor on entering the room fell into a chair? You had forgotten? Well I can answer for it that it was so. Now, you will remember also that Mrs. Porter, the housekeeper, told us that she herself fainted upon entering the room and had afterwards opened the window. In the second case—that of Mortimer Tregennis himself—you cannot have forgotten the horrible stuffiness of the room when we arrived, though the servant had thrown open the window. That servant, I found upon inquiry, was so ill that she had gone to her bed. You will admit, Watson, that these facts are very suggestive. In each case there is evidence of a poisonous atmosphere. In each case, also, there is combustion going on in the room—in the one case a fire, in the other a lamp. The fire was needed, but the lamp was lit—as a comparison of the oil consumed will show—long after it was broad daylight. Why? Surely because there is some connection between three things—the burning, the stuffy atmosphere, and, finally, the madness or death of those unfortunate people. That is clear, is it not?"

"It would appear so."

"At least we may accept it as a working hypothesis. We will suppose, then, that something was burned in each case which produced an atmosphere causing strange toxic effects. Very good. In the first instance—that of the Tregennis family—this substance was placed in the fire. Now the window was shut, but the fire would naturally carry fumes to some extent up the chimney. Hence one would expect the effects of the poison to be less than in the second case, where there was less escape for the vapour. The result seems to indicate that it was so, since in the first case only the woman, who had presumably the more sensitive organism, was killed, the others exhibiting that temporary or permanent lunacy which is evidently the first effect of the drug. In the second case the result was complete. The facts, therefore, seem to bear out the theory of a poison which worked by combustion.

"With this train of reasoning in my head I naturally looked about in Mortimer Tregennis's room to find some remains of this substance. The obvious place to look was the talc shelf or smoke-guard of the lamp. There, sure enough, I perceived a number of flaky ashes, and round the edges a fringe of brownish powder, which had not yet been consumed. Half of this I took, as you saw, and I placed it in an envelope."

"Why half, Holmes?"

"It is not for me, my dear Watson, to stand in the way of the official police force. I leave them all the evidence which I found. The poison still remained upon the talc had they the wit to find it. Now, Watson, we will light our lamp; we will, however, take the precaution to open our window to avoid the premature decease of two deserving members of society, and you will seat yourself near that open window in an armchair unless, like a sensible man, you determine to have nothing to do with the affair. Oh, you will see it out, will you? I thought I knew my Watson. This chair I will place opposite yours, so that we may be the same distance from the poison and face to face. The door we will leave ajar. Each is now in a position to watch the other and to bring the experiment to an end should the symptoms seem alarming. Is that all clear? Well, then, I take our powder—or what remains of it—from the envelope, and I lay it above the burning lamp. So! Now, Watson, let us sit down and await developments."

They were not long in coming. I had hardly settled in my chair before I was conscious of a thick, musky odour, subtle and nauseous. At the very first whiff of it my brain and my imagination were beyond all control. A thick, black cloud swirled before my eyes, and my mind told me that in this cloud, unseen as yet, but about to spring out upon my appalled senses, lurked all that was vaguely horrible, all that was monstrous and inconceivably wicked in the universe. Vague shapes swirled and swam amid the dark cloud-bank, each a menace and a warning of something coming, the advent of some unspeakable dweller upon the threshold, whose very shadow would blast my soul. A freezing horror took possession of me. I felt that my hair was rising, that my eyes were protruding, that my mouth was opened, and my tongue like leather. The turmoil within my brain was such that something must surely snap. I tried to scream and was vaguely aware of some hoarse croak which was my own voice, but distant and detached from myself At the same moment, in some effort of escape, I broke through that cloud of despair and had a glimpse of Holmes's face, white, rigid, and drawn with horror—the very look which I had seen upon the features of the dead. It was that vision which gave me an instant of sanity and of strength. I dashed from my chair, threw my arms round Holmes, and together we lurched through the door, and an instant afterwards had thrown ourselves down upon the grass plot and were lying side by side, conscious only of the glorious sunshine which was bursting its way through the hellish cloud of terror which had girt us in. Slowly it rose from our souls like the mists from a landscape until peace and reason had returned, and we were sitting upon the grass, wiping our clammy foreheads, and looking with apprehension at each other to mark the last traces of that terrific experience which we had undergone.

"Upon my word, Watson!" said Holmes at last with an unsteady voice, "I owe you both my thanks and an apology. It was an unjustifiable experiment even for one's self, and doubly so for a friend. I am really very sorry."

"You know," I answered with some emotion, for I have never seen so much of Holmes's heart before, "that it is my greatest joy and privilege to help you."

He relapsed at once into the half-humorous, half-cynical vein which was his habitual attitude to those about him. "It would be superfluous to drive us mad, my dear Watson," said he. "A candid observer would certainly declare that we were so already before we embarked upon so wild an experiment. I confess that I never imagined that the effect could be so sudden and so severe." He dashed into the cottage, and, reappearing with the burning lamp held at full arm's length, he threw it among a bank of brambles. "We must give the room a little time to clear. I take it, Watson, that you have no longer a shadow of a doubt as to how these tragedies were produced?"

"None whatever."

"But the cause remains as obscure as before. Come into the arbour here and let us discuss it together. That villainous stuff seems still to linger round my throat. I think we must admit that all the evidence points to this man, Mortimer Tregennis, having been the criminal in the first tragedy, though he was the victim in the second one. We must remember, in the first place, that there is some story of a family quarrel, followed by a reconciliation. How bitter that quarrel may have been, or how hollow the reconciliation we cannot tell. When I think of Mortimer Tregennis, with the foxy face and the small shrewd, beady eyes behind the spectacles, he is not a man whom I should judge to be of a particularly forgiving disposition. Well, in the next place, you will remember that this idea of someone moving in the garden, which took our attention for a moment from the real cause of the tragedy, emanated from him. He had a motive in misleading us. Finally, if he did not throw the substance into the fire at the moment of leaving the room, who did do so? The affair happened immediately after his departure. Had anyone else come in, the family would certainly have risen from the table. Besides, in peaceful Cornwall, visitors did not arrive after ten o'clock at night. We may take it, then, that all the evidence points to Mortimer Tregennis as the culprit."

"Then his own death was suicide!"

"Well, Watson, it is on the face of it a not impossible supposition. The man who had the guilt upon his soul of having brought such a fate upon his own family might well be driven by remorse to inflict it upon himself. There are, however, some cogent reasons against it. Fortunately, there is one man in England who knows all about it, and I have made arrangements by which we shall hear the facts this afternoon from his own lips. Ah! he is a little before his time. Perhaps you would kindly step this way, Dr. Leon Sterndale. We have been conducing a chemical experiment indoors which has left our little room hardly fit for the reception of so distinguished a visitor."

I had heard the click of the garden gate, and now the majestic figure of the great African explorer appeared upon the path. He turned in some surprise towards the rustic arbour in which we sat.

"You sent for me, Mr. Holmes. I had your note about an hour ago, and I have come, though I really do not know why I should obey your summons."

"Perhaps we can clear the point up before we separate," said Holmes. "Meanwhile, I am much obliged to you for your courteous acquiescence. You will excuse this informal reception in the open air, but my friend Watson and I have nearly furnished an additional chapter to what the papers call the Cornish Horror, and we prefer a clear atmosphere for the present. Perhaps, since the matters which we have to discuss will affect you personally in a very intimate fashion, it is as well that we should talk where there can be no eavesdropping."

The explorer took his cigar from his lips and gazed sternly at my companion.

"I am at a loss to know, sir," he said, "what you can have to speak about which affects me personally in a very intimate fashion."

"The killing of Mortimer Tregennis," said Holmes.

For a moment I wished that I were armed. Sterndale's fierce face turned to a dusky red, his eyes glared, and the knotted, passionate veins started out in his forehead, while he sprang forward with clenched hands towards my companion. Then he stopped, and with a violent effort he resumed a cold, rigid calmness, which was, perhaps, more suggestive of danger than his hot-headed outburst.

"I have lived so long among savages and beyond the law," said he, "that I have got into the way of being a law to myself. You would do well, Mr. Holmes, not to forget it, for I have no desire to do you an injury."

"Nor have I any desire to do you an injury, Dr. Sterndale. Surely the clearest proof of it is that, knowing what I know, I have sent for you and not for the police."

Sterndale sat down with a gasp, overawed for, perhaps, the first time in his adventurous life. There was a calm assurance of power in Holmes's manner which could not be withstood. Our visitor stammered for a moment, his great hands opening and shutting in his agitation.

"What do you mean?" he asked at last. "If this is bluff upon your part, Mr. Holmes, you have chosen a bad man for your experiment. Let us have no more beating about the bush. What *do* you mean?"

"I will tell you," said Holmes, "and the reason why I tell you is that I hope frankness may beget frankness. What my next step may be will depend entirely upon the nature of your own defence."

"My defence?"

"Yes, sir."

"My defence against what?"

"Against the charge of killing Mortimer Tregennis."

Sterndale mopped his forehead with his handkerchief. "Upon my word, you are getting on," said he. "Do all your successes depend upon this prodigious power of bluff?"

"The bluff," said Holmes sternly, "is upon your side, Dr. Leon Sterndale, and not upon mine. As a proof I will tell you some of the facts upon which my conclusions are based. Of your return from Plymouth, allowing much of your property to go on to Africa, I will say nothing save that it first informed me that you were one of the factors which had to be taken into account in reconstructing this drama—"

"I came back—"

"I have heard your reasons and regard them as unconvincing and inadequate. We will pass that. You came down here to ask me whom I suspected. I refused to answer you. You then went to the vicarage, waited outside it for some time, and finally returned to your cottage."

"How do you know that?"

"I followed you."

"I saw no one."

"That is what you may expect to see when I follow you. You spent a restless night at your cottage, and you formed certain plans, which in the early morning you proceeded to put into execution. Leaving your door just as day was breaking, you filled your pocket with some reddish gravel that was lying heaped beside your gate."

Sterndale gave a violent start and looked at Holmes in amazement.

"You then walked swiftly for the mile which separated you from the vicarage. You were wearing, I may remark, the same pair of ribbed tennis shoes which are at the present moment upon your feet. At the vicarage you passed through the orchard and the side hedge, coming out under the window of the lodger Tregennis. It was now daylight, but the household was not yet stirring. You drew some of the gravel from your pocket, and you threw it up at the window above you."

Sterndale sprang to his feet.

"I believe that you are the devil himself!" he cried.

Holmes smiled at the compliment. "It took two, or possibly three, handfuls before the lodger came to the window. You beckoned him to come down. He dressed hurriedly and descended to his sitting-room. You entered by the window. There was an interview—a short one—during which you walked up and down the room. Then you passed out and closed the window, standing on the lawn outside smoking a cigar and watching what occurred. Finally, after the death of Tregennis, you withdrew as you had come. Now, Dr. Sterndale, how do you justify such conduct, and what were the motives for your actions? If you prevaricate or trifle with me, I give you my assurance that the matter will pass out of my hands forever."

Our visitor's face had turned ashen gray as he listened to the words of his accuser. Now he sat for some time in thought with his face sunk in his hands. Then with a sudden impulsive gesture he plucked a photograph from his breast-pocket and threw it on the rustic table before us.

"That is why I have done it," said he.

It showed the bust and face of a very beautiful woman. Holmes stooped over it.

"Brenda Tregennis," said he.

"Yes, Brenda Tregennis," repeated our visitor. "For years I have loved her. For years she has loved me. There is the secret of that Cornish seclusion which people have marvelled at. It has brought me close to the one thing on earth that was dear to me. I could not marry her, for I have a wife who has left me for years and yet whom, by the deplorable laws of England, I could not divorce. For years Brenda waited. For years I waited. And this is what we have waited for." A terrible sob shook his great frame, and he clutched his throat under his brindled beard. Then with an effort he mastered himself and spoke on:

"The vicar knew. He was in our confidence. He would tell you that she was an angel upon earth. That was why he telegraphed to me and I returned. What was my baggage or Africa to me when I learned that such a fate had come upon my darling? There you have the missing clue to my action, Mr. Holmes."

"Proceed," said my friend.

Dr. Sterndale drew from his pocket a paper packet and laid it upon the table. On the outside was written "*Radix pedis diaboli*" with a red poison label beneath it. He pushed it towards me. "I understand that you are a doctor, sir. Have you ever heard of this preparation?"

"Devil's-foot root! No, I have never heard of it."

"It is no reflection upon your professional knowledge," said he, "for I believe that, save for one sample in a laboratory at Buda, there is no other specimen in Europe. It has not yet found its way either into the pharmacopoeia or into the literature of toxicology. The root is shaped like a foot, half human, half goatlike; hence the fanciful name given by a botanical missionary. It is used as an ordeal poison by the medicine-men in certain districts of West Africa and is kept as a secret among them. This particular specimen I obtained under very extraordinary circumstances in the Ubangi country." He opened the paper as he spoke and disclosed a heap of reddish-brown, snuff-like powder.

"Well, sir?" asked Holmes sternly.

"I am about to tell you, Mr. Holmes, all that actually occurred, for you already know so much that it is clearly to my interest that you should know all. I have already explained the relationship in which I stood to the Tregennis family. For the sake of the sister I was friendly with the brothers. There was a family quarrel about money which estranged this man Mortimer, but it was supposed to be made up, and I afterwards met him as I did the others. He was a sly, subtle, scheming man, and several things arose which gave me a suspicion of him, but I had no cause for any positive quarrel.

"One day, only a couple of weeks ago, he came down to my cottage and I showed him some of my African curiosities. Among other things I exhibited this powder, and I told him of its strange properties, how it stimulates those brain centres which control the emotion of fear, and how either madness or death is the fate of the unhappy native who is subjected to the ordeal by the priest of his tribe. I told him also how powerless European science would be to detect it. How he took it I cannot say, for I never left the room, but there is no doubt that it was then, while I was opening cabinets and stooping to boxes, that he managed to abstract some of the devil's-foot root. I well remember how he plied me with questions as to the amount and the time that was needed for its effect, but I little dreamed that he could have a personal reason for asking.

"I thought no more of the matter until the vicar's telegram reached me at Plymouth. This villain had thought that I would be at sea before the news could reach me, and that I should be lost for years in Africa. But I returned at once. Of course, I could not listen to the details without feeling assured that my poison had been used. I came round to see you on the chance that some other explanation had suggested itself to you. But there could be none. I was convinced that Mortimer Tregennis was the murderer; that for the sake of money, and with the idea, perhaps, that if the other members of his family were all insane he would be the sole guardian of their joint property, he had used the devil's-foot powder upon them, driven two of them out of their senses, and killed his sister Brenda, the one human being whom I have ever loved or who has ever loved me. There was his crime; what was to be his punishment?

"Should I appeal to the law? Where were my proofs? I knew that the facts were true, but could I help to make a jury of countrymen believe so fantastic a story? I might or I might not. But I could not afford to fail. My soul cried out for revenge. I have said to you once before, Mr. Holmes, that I have spent much of my life outside the law, and that I have come at last to be a law to myself. So it was even now. I determined that the fate which he had given to others should be shared by himself. Either that or I would do justice upon him with my own hand. In all England there can be no man who sets less value upon his own life than I do at the present moment.

"Now I have told you all. You have yourself supplied the rest. I did, as you say, after a restless night, set off early from my cottage. I foresaw the difficulty of arousing him, so I gathered some gravel from the pile which you have mentioned, and I used it to throw up to his window. He came down and admitted me through the window of the sitting-room. I laid his offence before him. I told him that I had come both as judge and executioner. The wretch sank into a chair, paralyzed at the sight of my revolver. I lit the lamp, put the powder above it, and stood outside the window, ready to carry out my threat to shoot him should he try to leave the room. In five minutes he died. My God! how he died! But my heart was flint, for he endured nothing which my innocent darling had not felt before him. There is my story, Mr. Holmes. Perhaps, if you loved a woman, you would have done as much yourself. At any rate, I am in your hands. You can take what steps you like. As I have already said, there is no man living who can fear death less than I do."

Holmes sat for some little time in silence.

"What were your plans?" he asked at last.

"I had intended to bury myself in central Africa. My work there is but half finished."

"Go and do the other half," said Holmes. "I, at least, am not prepared to prevent you."

Dr. Sterndale raised his giant figure, bowed gravely, and walked from the arbour. Holmes lit his pipe and handed me his pouch.

"Some fumes which are not poisonous would be a welcome change," said he. "I think you must agree, Watson, that it is not a case in which we are called upon to interfere. Our investigation has been independent, and our action shall be so also. You would not denounce the man?"

"Certainly not," I answered.

"I have never loved, Watson, but if I did and if the woman I loved had met such an end, I might act even as our lawless lion-hunter has done. Who knows? Well, Watson, I will not offend your intelligence by explaining what is obvious. The gravel upon the window-sill was, of course, the starting-point of my research. It was unlike anything in the vicarage garden. Only when my attention had been drawn to Dr. Sterndale and his cottage did I find its counterpart. The lamp shining in broad daylight and the remains of powder upon the shield were successive links in a fairly obvious chain. And now, my dear Watson, I think we may dismiss the matter from our mind and go back with a clear conscience to the study of those Chaldean roots which are surely to be traced in the Cornish branch of the great Celtic speech."

Spores of Death

Sax Rohmer

I have been asked many times since the days with which these records deal: Who *was* Dr. Fu-Manchu and where did he hide during the time that he pursued his operations in London?

The first of these questions I have, thus far, found myself unable satisfactorily to answer; the second is more susceptible to explanation. For a time, my friend Nayland Smith supposed, as I did myself, that the opium den adjacent to the old Ratcliffe highway was the Chinaman's base of operations: later, we came to believe that a certain mansion near Windsor was his hiding place, and later still, a hulk lying off the downstream flats. But I think I can state with confidence that the spot which he had chosen for his home was neither of these, but one hard by the site of the opium shop, an East End riverside building which I was the first to enter. Of this I am all but sure, for the reason that it not only was the home of Fu-Manchu, of the slave girl, Karamaneh, and her brother, Aziz, but the home of something else—of something of which I shall speak later.

The dreadful tragedy (or series of tragedies) which attended the raid upon the place will always mark in my memory the supreme horror of a horrible case. Let me endeavor to explain what occurred.

By the aid of the girl, Karamaneh, who at last had become our ally, we had located the whilom warehouse, which, from the exterior, was so drab and dreary, but which within was a place of wondrous luxury. At the moment selected by our beautiful accomplice,

Inspector Weymouth and a body of detectives entirely surrounded it; a river police launch lay off the wharf which opened from it on the river-side; and this upon a singularly black night, than which a better could not have been chosen.

"You will fulfill your promise to me?" said Karamaneh, and looked up into my face.

She was enveloped in a big, loose cloak, and from the shadow of the hood her wonderful eyes gleamed out like stars.

"What do you wish us to do?" asked Nayland Smith.

"You—and Dr. Petrie," she replied swiftly, "must enter first, and bring out Aziz. Until he is safe—until he is out of that place—you are to make no attempt upon—"

"Upon Dr. Fu-Manchu?" interrupted Weymouth; for Karamaneh hesitated to pronounce the dreaded name, as she always did. "But how can we be sure that there is no trap laid for us?"

The Scotland Yard man did not entirely share my confidence in the integrity of this Eastern girl whom he knew to have been a creature of the Chinaman's.

"Aziz lies in the private room," she explained eagerly, her old accent more noticeable than usual. "There is only one of the Burmese men in the house, and he—he dare not enter without orders!"

"But Fu-Manchu?"

"We have nothing to fear from him. He will be your prisoner within ten minutes from now! I have no time for words—you must believe!" She stamped her foot impatiently.

"And the dacoits?" snapped Smith.

"They also."

"I think perhaps I'd better come in, too," said Weymouth slowly.

Karamaneh shrugged her shoulders with quick impatience, and unlocked the door in the high brick wall which divided the gloomy, evil-smelling court from the luxurious apartments of Dr. Fu-Manchu.

"Make no noise," she warned. And Smith and myself followed her along the uncarpeted passage beyond.

Inspector Weymouth, with a final word of instruction to his second in command, brought up the rear. The door was reclosed, and a few paces farther on a second was unlocked. Passing through a small room, unfurnished, a farther passage led us to a balcony. The transition was startling.

Darkness was about us now, and silence: a perfumed, slumberous darkness—a silence full of mystery. For, beyond the walls of the apartment whereon we looked down waged the unceasing battle of sounds that is the hymn of the great industrial river. About the scented confines which bounded us now floated the smoke-laden vapors of the Lower Thames.

From the metallic but infinitely human clangor of dock-side life, from the unpleasant but homely odors which prevail where ships swallow in and belch out the concrete evidences of commercial prosperity, we had come into this incensed stillness, where one shaded lamp painted dim enlargements of its Chinese silk upon the nearer walls, and left the greater part of the room the darker for its contrast.

Nothing of the Thames-side activity—of the riveting and scraping, the bumping of bales, the bawling of orders, the hiss of steam—penetrated to this perfumed place. In the pool of tinted light lay the deathlike figure of a dark-haired boy, Karamaneh's muffled form bending over him.

"At last I stand in the house of Dr. Fu-Manchu!" whispered Smith.

Despite the girl's assurance, we knew that proximity to the sinister Chinaman must be fraught with danger. We stood, not in the lion's den, but in the serpent's lair.

From the time when Nayland Smith had come from Burma in pursuit of this advance-guard of a cogent yellow peril, the face of Dr. Fu-Manchu rarely had been absent from my dreams day or night. The millions might sleep in peace—the millions in whose cause we labored, but we who knew the reality of the danger knew that a veritable octopus had fastened upon England—a yellow octopus whose head was that of Dr. Fu-Manchu, whose tentacles were dacoity, thuggee, modes of death, secret and swift, which in the darkness plucked men from life and left no clue behind.

"Karamaneh!" I called softly.

The muffled form beneath the lamp turned so that the soft light fell upon the lovely face of the slave girl. She who had been a pliant instrument in the hands of Fu-Manchu now was to be the means whereby society should be rid of him.

She raised her finger warningly; then beckoned me to approach.

My feet sinking in the rich pile of the carpet, I came through the gloom of the great apartment in to the patch of light, and, Karamaneh beside me, stood looking down upon the boy. It was Aziz, her brother; dead so far as Western lore had power to judge, but kept alive in that deathlike trance by the uncanny power of the Chinese doctor.

This secret—the hold which Fu-Manchu had upon Karamaneh—for long had eluded us: but, the mystery solved, in a flash we had perceived why the beautiful oriental girl had acted as the Chinaman's emissary in so many of his black deeds.

We who had thought her an accomplice of the arch murderer had realized that she was in truth his victim.

"Be quick," she said; "be quick! Awaken him! I am afraid."

From the case which I carried I took out a needle-syringe and a phial containing a small quantity of amber-hued liquid. It was a drug not to be found in the British Pharmacopoeia. Of its constitution I knew nothing. Although I had had the phial in my possession for some days I had not dared to devote any of its precious contents to analytical purposes. The amber drops spelled life for the boy Aziz, spelled success for the mission of Nayland Smith, spelled ruin for the fiendish Chinaman.

I raised the white coverlet. The boy, fully dressed, lay with his arms crossed upon his breast. I discerned the marks of previous injections as, charging the syringe from the phial, I made what I hoped would be the last of such experiments upon him. I would have given half of my small worldly possessions to have known the real nature of the drug which was now coursing through the veins of Aziz—which was tinting the grayed face with the olive tone of life; which, so far as my medical training bore me, was restoring the dead to life.

But such was not the purpose of my visit. I was come to remove from the house of Dr. Fu-Manchu the living chain which bound Karamaneh to him. The boy alive and free, the Doctor's hold upon the slave girl would be broken.

My lovely companion, her hands convulsively clasped, knelt and devoured with her eyes the face of the boy who was passing through the most amazing physiological change in the history of therapeutics. The peculiar perfume which she wore, which seemed to be a part of her—which always I associated with her—was faintly perceptible. Karamaneh was breathing rapidly.

"You have nothing to fear," I whispered; "see, he is reviving. In a few moments all will be well with him."

The hanging lamp with its garishly colored shade swung gently above us, wafted, it seemed, by some draught which passed through the apartment. The boy's heavy lids began to quiver, and Karamaneh nervously clutched my arm, and held me so whilst we watched for the long-lashed eyes to open. The stillness of the place was positively unnatural; it seemed inconceivable that all about us was the discordant activity of the commercial East End. Indeed, this eerie silence was becoming oppressive; it began positively to appall me.

Inspector Weymouth's wondering face peeped over my shoulder.

"Where is Dr. Fu-Manchu?" I whispered, as Nayland Smith in turn appeared beside me. "I cannot understand the silence of the house—"

"Look about," replied Karamaneh, never taking her eyes from the face of Aziz.

I peered around the shadowy walls. Tall glass cases there were, shelves and niches: where once, from the gallery above, I had seen the tubes and retorts, the jars of unfamiliar organisms, the books of unfamiliar lore, the impedimenta of the occult student and man of science—the visible evidences of Fu-Manchu's presence. Shelves, cases, niches were bare.

Of the complicated appliances unknown to civilized laboratories, wherewith he pursued his strange experiments, of the tubes wherein he isolated the bacilli of unclassified diseases, of the yellow-bound volumes for a glimpse at which (had they known of their contents) the great men of Harley Street would have given a fortune—no trace remained. The silken cushions, the inlaid tables, all were gone.

The room was stripped, dismantled. Had Fu-Manchu fled? The silence assumed a new significance. His dacoits and kindred ministers of death all must have fled, too.

"You have let him escape us!" I said rapidly. "You promised to aid us to capture him—to send us a message—and you have delayed until—"

"No," she said; "no!" and clutched at my arm again. "Oh! is he not reviving slowly? Are you sure you have made no mistake?"

Her thoughts were all for the boy; and her solicitude touched me. I again examined Aziz, the most remarkable patient of my busy professional career.

As I counted the strengthening pulse, he opened his dark eyes— which were so like the eyes of Karamaneh—and, with the girl's eager arms tightly about him, sat up, looking wonderingly around.

Karamaneh pressed her cheek to his, whispering loving words in that softly spoken Arabic which had first betrayed her nationality to Nayland Smith. I handed her my flask, which I had filled with wine.

"My promise is fulfilled!" I said. "You are free! Now for Fu-Manchu! But first let us admit the police to this house; there is something uncanny in its stillness."

"No," she replied. "First let my brother be taken out and placed in safety. Will you carry him?"

She raised her face to that of Inspector Weymouth, upon which was written awe and wonder.

The burly detective lifted the boy as tenderly as a woman, passed through the shadows to the stairway, ascended, and was swallowed up in the gloom. Nayland Smith's eyes gleamed feverishly. He turned to Karamaneh.

"You are not playing with us?" he said harshly. "We have done our part; it remains for you to do yours."

"Do not speak so loudly," the girl begged. "*He* is near us—and, oh, God, I fear him so!"

"Where is he?" persisted my friend.

Karamaneh's eyes were glassy with fear now.

"You must not touch him until the police are here," she said—but from the direction of her quick, agitated glances I knew that, her brother safe now, she feared for me, and for me alone. Those glances sent my blood dancing; for Karamaneh was an Eastern jewel which any man of flesh and blood must have coveted had he known it to lie within his reach. Her eyes were twin lakes of mystery which, more than once, I had known the desire to explore.

"Look—beyond that curtain"—her voice was barely audible—"but do not enter. Even as he is, I fear him."

Her voice, her palpable agitation, prepared us for something extraordinary. Tragedy and Fu-Manchu were never far apart. Though we were two, and help was so near, we were in the abode of the most cunning murderer who ever came out of the East.

It was with strangely mingled emotions that I crossed the thick carpet, Nayland Smith beside me, and drew aside the draperies concealing a door, to which Karamaneh had pointed. Then, upon looking into the dim place beyond, all else save what it held was forgotten.

We looked upon a small, square room, the walls draped with fantastic Chinese tapestry, the floor strewn with cushions; and re-clining in a corner, where the faint, blue light from a lamp, placed upon a low table, painted grotesque shadows about the cavernous face—was Dr. Fu-Manchu!

At sight of him my heart leaped—and seemed to suspend its functions, so intense was the horror which this man's presence inspired in me. My hand clutching the curtain, I stood watching him. The lids veiled the malignant green eyes, but the thin lips seemed to smile. Then Smith silently pointed to the hand which held a little pipe. A sickly perfume assailed my nostrils, and the explanation of the hushed silence, and the ease with which we had thus far executed our plan, came to me. The cunning mind was torpid—lost in a brutish world of dreams.

Fu-Manchu was in an opium sleep.

The dim light traced out a network of tiny lines, which covered the yellow face from the pointed chin to the top of the great domed brow, and formed deep shadow pools in the hollows beneath his eyes. At last we had triumphed. The man's ruling vice had wrought his fall!

I could not determine the depth of his obscene trance; and mastering some of my repugnance, and forgetful of Karamaneh's warning, I was about to step forward into the room, loaded with its nauseating opium fumes, when a soft breath fanned my cheek.

"Do not go in!" came Karamaneh's warning voice—hushed, trembling.

Her little hand grasped my arm. She drew Smith and myself back from the door.

"There is danger there!" she whispered. "Do not enter that room! The police must reach him in some way—and drag him out! Do not enter that room!"

The girl's voice quivered hysterically; her eyes blazed into savage flame. The fierce resentment born of dreadful wrongs was consuming her now; but fear of Fu-Manchu held her yet. Inspector Weymouth came down the stairs and joined us.

"I have sent the boy to Ryman's room at the station," he said. "The divisional surgeon will look after him until you arrive, Dr. Petrie. All is ready now. The launch is just off the wharf and every side of the place under observation. Where's our man?"

He drew a pair of handcuffs from his pocket and raised his eyebrows interrogatively. The absence of sound—of any demonstration from the uncanny Chinaman whom he was there to arrest—puzzled him.

Nayland Smith jerked his thumb toward the curtain.

At that, and before we could utter a word, Weymouth stepped to the draped door. He was a man who drove straight at his goal and saved reflections for subsequent leisure. I think, moreover, that the atmosphere of the place (stripped as it was it retained its heavy, voluptuous perfume) had begun to get a hold upon him. He was anxious to shake it off; to be up and doing.

He pulled the curtain aside and stepped into the room. Smith and I perforce followed him. Just within the door the three of us stood looking across at the limp thing which had spread terror throughout the Eastern and Western world. Helpless as Fu-Manchu was, he inspired terror now, though the giant intellect was inert—stupefied.

In the dimly lit apartment we had quitted I heard Karamaneh utter a stifled scream. But it came too late.

As though cast up by a volcano, the silken cushions, the inlaid table with its blue-shaded lamp, the garish walls, the sprawling figure with the ghastly light playing upon its features, quivered, and shot upward.

So it seemed to me; though, in the ensuing instant I remembered, too late, a previous experience of the floors of Fu-Manchu's private apartments; I knew what had indeed befallen us. A trap had been released beneath our feet.

I recall falling, but have no recollection of the end of my fall, of the shock marking the drop. I only remember fighting for my life against a stifling something which had me by the throat. I knew that I was being suffocated, but my hands met only the deathly emptiness.

Into a poisonous well of darkness I sank. I could not cry out. I was helpless. Of the fate of my companions I knew nothing—could surmise nothing.

Then—all consciousness ended.

I was being carried along a dimly lighted, tunnel-like place, slung, sackwise, across the shoulder of a Burman. He was not a big man, but he supported my considerable weight with apparent ease. A deadly nausea held me, but the rough handling had served to restore me to consciousness. My hands and feet were closely lashed. I hung limply as a wet towel: I felt that this spark of tortured life which had flickered up in me must ere long finally become extinguished.

A fancy possessed me, in these the first moments of my restoration to the world of realities, that I had been smuggled into China;

and as I swung head downward I told myself that the huge, puffy things which strewed the path were a species of giant toadstool, unfamiliar to me and possibly peculiar to whatever district of China I now was in.

The air was hot, steamy, and loaded with a smell as of rotting vegetation. I wondered why my bearer so scrupulously avoided touching any of the unwholesome-looking growths in passing through what seemed a succession of cellars, but steered a tortuous course among the bloated, unnatural shapes, lifting his bare brown feet with a catlike delicacy.

He passed under a low arch, dropped me roughly to the ground and ran back. Half stunned, I lay watching the agile brown body melt into the distances of the cellars. Their walls and roof seemed to emit a faint, phosphorescent light.

"Petrie!" came a weak voice from somewhere near. "Is that you, Petrie?"

It was Nayland Smith.

"Smith!" I said, and strove to sit up. But the intense nausea overcame me, so that I all but swooned.

I heard his voice again, but could attach no meaning to the words which he uttered. A sound of terrific blows reached my ears, too.

The Burman reappeared, bending under the heavy load which he bore. For, as he picked his way through the bloated things which grew upon the floors of the cellars, I realized that he was carrying the inert body of Inspector Weymouth. And I found time to compare the strength of the little brown man with that of a Nile beetle, which can raise many times its own weight.

Then, behind him, appeared a second figure, which immediately claimed the whole of my errant attention.

"Fu-Manchu!" hissed my friend, from the darkness which concealed him.

It was indeed none other than Fu-Manchu—the Fu-Manchu whom we had thought to be helpless. The depths of the Chinaman's cunning—the fine quality of his courage, were forced upon me as amazing facts.

He had assumed the appearance of a drugged opium-smoker so well as to dupe me—a medical man; so well as to dupe Karamaneh—whose experience of the noxious habit probably was greater than my own. And, with the gallows dangling before him, he had waited—played the part of a lure—whilst a body of police actually surrounded the place!

I have since thought that the room probably was one which he actually used for opium debauches, and the device of the trap was intended to protect him during the comatose period.

Now, holding a lantern above his head, the deviser of the trap whereinto we, mouselike, had blindly entered, came through the cellars, following the brown man who carried Weymouth. The faint rays of the lantern (it apparently contained a candle) revealed a veritable forest of the gigantic fungi—poisonously colored—hideously swollen—climbing from the floor up the slimy walls—climbing like horrid parasites to such part of the arched roof as was visible to me.

Fu-Manchu picked his way through the fungi ranks as daintily as though the distorted, tumid things had been viper-headed. The resounding blows which I had noted before, and which had never ceased, culminated in a splintering crash. Dr. Fu-Manchu and his servant, who carried the apparently insensible detective, passed in under the arch, Fu-Manchu glancing back once along the passages. The lantern he extinguished, or concealed; and whilst I waited, my mind dully surveying memories of all the threats which this uncanny being had uttered, a distant clamor came to my ears.

Then, abruptly, it ceased. Dr. Fu-Manchu had closed a heavy door; and to my surprise I perceived that the greater part of it was of glass. The will-o'-the-wisp glow which played around the fungi rendered the vista of the cellars faintly luminous, and visible to me from where I lay. Fu-Manchu spoke softly. His voice, its guttural note alternating with a sibilance on certain words, betrayed no traces of agitation. The man's unbroken calm had in it something inhuman. For he had just perpetrated an act of daring unparalleled in my experience, and, in the clamor now shut out by the glass door I tardily recognized the entrance of the police into some barricaded part of the house—the coming of those who would save us—who would hold the Chinese doctor for the hangman!

"I have decided," he said deliberately, "that you are more worthy of my attention than I had formerly supposed. A man who can solve the secret of the Golden Elixir" (I had not solved it; I had merely stolen some) "should be a valuable acquisition to my Council. The extent of the plans of Mr. Commissioner Nayland Smith and of the English Scotland Yard it is incumbent upon me to learn. Therefore, gentlemen, you live—for the present!"

"And you'll swing," came Weymouth's hoarse voice, "in the near future! You and all your yellow gang!"

"I trust not," was the placid reply. "Most of my people are safe: some are shipped as lascars upon the liners; others have departed by different means. Ah!"

That last word was the only one indicative of excitement which had yet escaped him. A disk of light danced among the brilliant poison hues of the passages—but no sound reached us; by which I knew that the glass door must fit almost hermetically. It was much cooler here than in the place through which we had passed, and the nausea began to leave me, my brain to grow more clear. Had I known what was to follow I should have cursed the lucidity of mind which now came to me; I should have prayed for oblivion—to be spared the sight of that which ensued.

"It's Logan!" cried Inspector Weymouth; and I could tell that he was struggling to free himself of his bonds. From his voice it was evident that he, too, was recovering from the effects of the narcotic which had been administered to us all.

"Logan!" he cried. "Logan! This way—*help*!"

But the cry beat back upon us in that enclosed space and seemed to carry no farther than the invisible walls of our prison.

"The door fits well," came Fu-Manchu's mocking voice. "It is fortunate for us all that it is so. This is my observation window, Dr. Petrie, and you are about to enjoy an unique opportunity of studying fungology. I have already drawn your attention to the anaesthetic properties of the *Lycoperdon*, or common puff-ball. You may have recognized the fumes? The chamber into which you rashly precipitated yourselves was charged with them. By a process of my own I have greatly enhanced the value of the puff-ball in this respect. Your friend, Mr. Weymouth, proved the most obstinate subject; but he succumbed in fifteen seconds."

"Logan! Help! *Help!* This way, man!"

Something very like fear sounded in Weymouth's voice now. Indeed, the situation was so uncanny that it almost seemed unreal. A group of men had entered the farthermost cellars, led by one who bore an electric pocket-lamp. The hard, white ray danced from bloated gray fungi to others of nightmare shape, of dazzling, venomous brilliance. The mocking, lecture-room voice continued:

"Note the snowy growth upon the roof, Doctor. Do not be deceived by its size. It is a giant variety of my own culture and is of the order *Empusa.* You, in England, are familiar with the death of the common house-fly—that is found attached to the window-pane by a coating of white mold. I have developed the spores of this mold and have produced a giant species. Observe the interesting effect of the strong light upon my orange and blue *Amanita* fungus!"

Hard beside me I heard Nayland Smith groan, Weymouth had become suddenly silent. For my own part, I could have shrieked in pure horror. *For I knew what was coming.* I realized in one agonized instant the significance of the dim lantern, of the careful progress through the subterranean fungi grove, of the care with which Fu-Manchu and his servant had avoided touching any of the growths. I knew, now, that Dr. Fu-Manchu was the greatest fungologist the world had ever known; was a poisoner to whom the Borgias were as children—and I knew that the detectives blindly were walking into a valley of death.

Then it began—the unnatural scene—the saturnalia of murder.

Like so many bombs the brilliantly colored caps of the huge toadstool-like things alluded to by the Chinaman exploded, as the white ray sought them out in the darkness which alone preserved their existence. A brownish cloud—I could not determine whether liquid or powdery—arose in the cellar.

I tried to close my eyes—or to turn them away from the reeling forms of the men who were trapped in that poison-hole. It was useless: I must look.

The bearer of the lamp had dropped it, but the dim, eerily illu-minated gloom endured scarce a second. A bright light sprang up—doubtless at the touch of the fiendish being who now resumed speech:

"Observe the symptoms of delirium, Doctor!"

Out there, beyond the glass door, the unhappy victims were laughing—tearing their garments from their bodies—leaping—waving their arms—were become *maniacs!*

"We will now release the ripe spores of giant *Empusa*," contin-ued the wicked voice. "The air of the second cellar being super-charged with oxygen, they immediately germinate. Ah! it is a tri-umph! That process is the scientific triumph of my life!"

Like powdered snow the white spores fell from the roof, frost-ing the writhing shapes of the already poisoned men. Before my horrified gaze *the fungus grew;* it spread from the head to the feet of those it touched; it enveloped them as in glittering shrouds. . . .

"They die like flies!" screamed Fu-Manchu, with a sudden fe-brile excitement; and I felt assured of something I had long sus-pected: that that magnificent, perverted brain was the brain of a homicidal maniac—though Smith would never accept the theory.

"It is my fly-trap!" shrieked the Chinaman. "And I am the God of Destruction!"

The clammy touch of the mist revived me. The culmination of the scene in the poison cellars, together with the effects of the fumes which I had inhaled again, had overcome me. Now I knew that I was afloat on the river. I still was bound: furthermore, a cloth was wrapped tightly about my mouth, and I was secured to a ring in the deck.

By moving my aching head to the left I could look down into the oily water; by moving it to the right I could catch a glimpse of the empurpled face of Inspector Weymouth, who, similarly bound and gagged, lay beside me, but only of the feet and legs of Nayland Smith. For I could not turn my head sufficiently far to see more.

We were aboard an electric launch. I heard the hated guttural voice of Fu-Manchu, subdued now to its habitual calm, and my heart leaped to hear the voice that answered him. It was that of Karamaneh. His triumph was complete. Clearly his plans for departure were complete; his slaughter of the police in the underground passages had been a final reckless demonstration of which the Chinaman's subtle cunning would have been incapable had he not known his escape from the country to be assured.

What fate was in store for us? How would he avenge himself upon the girl who had betrayed him to his enemies? What portion awaited those enemies? He seemed to have formed the singular determination to smuggle me into China—but what did he purpose in the case of Weymouth, and in the case of Nayland Smith?

All but silently we were feeling our way through the mist. Astern died the clangor of dock and wharf into a remote discord. Ahead hung the foggy curtain veiling the traffic of the great waterway; but through it broke the calling of sirens, the tinkling of bells.

The gentle movement of the screw ceased altogether. The launch lay heaving slightly upon the swells.

A distant throbbing grew louder—and something advanced upon us through the haze.

A bell rang and muffled by the fog a voice proclaimed itself—a voice which I knew. I felt Weymouth writhing impotently beside me; heard him mumbling incoherently; and I knew that he, too, had recognized the voice.

It was that of Inspector Ryman of the river police; and their launch was within biscuit-throw of that upon which we lay.

"'Hoy! 'Hoy!"

I trembled. A feverish excitement claimed me. They were hailing us. We carried no lights; but now—and ignoring the pain which shot from my spine to my skull I craned my neck to the left—the port light of the police launch glowed angrily through the mist.

I was unable to utter any save mumbling sounds, and my companions were equally helpless. It was a desperate position. Had the police seen us or had they hailed at random? The light drew nearer.

"Launch, 'hoy!"

They had seen us! Fu-Manchu's guttural voice spoke shortly—and our screw began to revolve again; we leaped ahead into the bank of darkness. Faint grew the light of the police launch—and was gone. But I heard Ryman's voice shouting.

"Full speed!" came faintly through the darkness. "Port! Port!"

Then the murk closed down, and with our friends far astern of us we were racing deeper into the fog banks—speeding seaward; though of this I was unable to judge at the time.

On we raced, and on, sweeping over growing swells. Once, a black, towering shape dropped down upon us. Far above, lights blazed, bells rang, vague cries pierced the fog. The launch pitched and rolled perilously, but weathered the wash of the liner which so nearly had concluded this episode. It was such a journey as I had taken once before, early in our pursuit of the genius of the Yellow Peril; but this was infinitely more terrible; for now we were utterly in Fu-Manchu's power.

A voice mumbled in my ear. I turned my bound-up face; and Inspector Weymouth raised his hands in the dimness and partly slipped the bandage from his mouth.

"I've been working at the cords since we left those filthy cellars," he whispered. "My wrists are all cut, but when I've got out a knife and freed my ankles—"

Smith had kicked him with his bound feet. The detective slipped the bandage back to position and placed his hands behind him again. Dr. Fu-Manchu, wearing a heavy overcoat but no hat, came aft. He was dragging Karamaneh by the wrists. He seated himself on the cushions near to us, pulling the girl down beside him. Now, I could see her face—and the expression in her beautiful eyes made me writhe.

Fu-Manchu was watching us, his discolored teeth faintly visible in the dim light, to which my eyes were becoming accustomed.

"Dr. Petrie," he said, "you shall be my honored guest at my home in China. You shall assist me to revolutionize chemistry. Mr. Smith, I fear you know more of my plans than I had deemed it possible for you to have learned, and I am anxious to know if you have a confidant. Where your memory fails you, and my files and wire jackets prove ineffectual, Inspector Weymouth's recollections may prove more accurate."

He turned to the cowering girl—who shrank away from him in pitiful, abject terror.

"In my hands, Doctor," he continued, "I hold a needle charged with a rare culture. It is the link between the bacilli and the fungi. You have seemed to display an undue interest in the peach and pearl which render my Karamaneh so delightful, in the supple grace of her movements and the sparkle of her eyes. You can never devote your whole mind to those studies which I have planned for you whilst such distractions exist. A touch of this keen point, and the laughing Karamaneh becomes the shrieking hag—the maniacal, mowing—"

Then, with an ox-like rush, Weymouth was upon him!

Karamaneh, wrought upon past endurance, with a sobbing cry, sank to the deck—and lay still. I managed to writhe into a half-sitting posture, and Smith rolled aside as the detective and the Chinaman crashed down together.

Weymouth had one big hand at the Doctor's yellow throat; with his left he grasped the Chinaman's right. It held the needle.

Now, I could look along the length of the little craft, and, so far as it was possible to make out in the fog, only one other was aboard—the half-clad brown man who navigated her—and who had carried us through the cellars. The murk had grown denser and now shut us in like a box. The throb of the motor—the hissing breath of the two who fought—with so much at issue—these sounds and the wash of the water alone broke the eerie stillness.

By slow degrees, and with a reptilian agility horrible to watch, Fu-Manchu was neutralizing the advantage gained by Weymouth. His clawish fingers were fast in the big man's throat; the right hand with its deadly needle was forcing down the left of his opponent. He had been underneath, but now he was gaining the upper place. His powers of physical endurance must have been truly marvelous. His breath was whistling through his nostrils significantly, but Weymouth was palpably tiring.

The latter suddenly changed his tactics. By a supreme effort, to which he was spurred, I think, by the growing proximity of the needle, he raised Fu-Manchu—by the throat and arm—and pitched him sideways.

The Chinaman's grip did not relax, and the two wrestlers dropped, a writhing mass, upon the port cushions. The launch heeled over, and my cry of horror was crushed back into my throat by the bandage. For, as Fu-Manchu sought to extricate himself, he overbalanced, fell back, and, bearing Weymouth with him, slid into the river.

The mist swallowed them up.

There are moments of which no man can recall his mental impressions, moments so acutely horrible that, mercifully, our memory retains nothing of the emotions they occasioned. This was one of them. A chaos ruled in my mind. I had a vague belief that the Burman, forward, glanced back. Then the course of the launch was changed.

How long intervened between the tragic end of that Gargantuan struggle and the time when a black wall leaped suddenly up before us I cannot pretend to state.

With a sickening jerk we ran aground. A loud explosion ensued, and I clearly remember seeing the brown man leap out into the fog—which was the last I saw of him. Water began to wash aboard.

Fully alive to our imminent peril, I fought with the cords that bound me; but I lacked poor Weymouth's strength of wrist, and I began to accept as a horrible and imminent possibility, a death from drowning, within six feet of the bank.

Beside me, Nayland Smith was straining and twisting. I think his object was to touch Karamaneh, in the hope of arousing her. Where he failed in his project, the inflowing water succeeded. A silent prayer of thankfulness came from my very soul when I saw her stir—when I saw her raise her hands to her head—and saw the big, horror-bright eyes gleam through the mist veil.

We quitted the wrecked launch but a few seconds before her stern settled down into the river. Where the mud-bank upon which we found ourselves was situated we had no idea. But at least it was terra firma and we were free from Dr. Fu-Manchu.

Smith stood looking out towards the river. "My God!" he groaned. "My God!"

He was thinking, as I was, of Weymouth.

And when, an hour later, the police boat located us (on the mud-flats below Greenwich) and we heard that the toll of the poison cellars was fourteen men, we also heard news of our brave companion.

"Back there in the fog, sir," reported Inspector Ryman, who was in charge, and his voice was under poor command, "there was an uncanny howling, and peals of laughter that I'm going to dream about for weeks. Somehow the voice reminded me of Weymouth's—"

Karamaneh, who nestled beside me like a frightened child, shivered, and I knew that the needle had done its work, despite Weymouth's giant strength.

Smith swallowed noisily.

"Pray God the river has that yellow Satan," he said. "I would sacrifice a year of my life to see his rat's body on the end of a grappling-iron!"

Thunder Beast
Joseph B. Ames

I

Ted Graham thrust two forked sticks firmly into the ground on either side of the small fire, placed across them a slender length of ironwood, and deftly slung from this a battered kettle half full of water from the nearby stream. Then he settled back on his heels and his gaze wandered across the little clearing hacked out of the jungle to where, about another fire, a score of blacks squatted silently.

For a moment or two he watched them thoughtfully, a puzzled pucker crinkling his smooth forehead. This was the second day that he had missed their constant shrill chatter and frequent bursts of carefree laughter. And there was something now in their huddled closeness which stirred in the boy a vague, indefinite uneasiness. Brushing one flannel sleeve across his flushed, moist face, he glanced over to where Ford Patterson sat, busily wiring neat tags upon the specimens they had collected the day before.

"Say, Pat," he asked abruptly, "what the dickens is the matter with the men?"

The young man looked up quickly. "The men?" he repeated. He glanced swiftly over one shoulder. "Oh! You mean— Why, they— er—don't like this part of the country."

"They don't? What's the matter with it? I think it's pretty slick."

Patterson laughed at the boy's tone of enthusiasm. "It's not bad—for Africa," he agreed. "As a matter of fact it's been a simply wonderful locality for specimens. Why, in the past week we've found three new varieties of orchids and two—"

"Oh, I know all about that," interrupted Ted, removing his hat to fan himself. He did not share his cousin's botanical enthusiasm. "But what have the men got against it. I should think one place would be as good as another as long as they're being paid."

"I can't make out exactly what it is," shrugged Patterson. "They're close-mouthed beggars sometimes. Ever since day before yesterday Imboza's been hinting in all sorts of ways that this isn't a healthy place to be in and trying to persuade us to move south. To-day he's turned grouchy and I've got to have it out with him as soon as I finish these labels."

"You want to give it to him good and plenty," advised Ted, with the severity of sixteen years. "He's nutty. There's nothing to kick about here, with—"

He broke off with a loud yell and leaping to his feet clapped both hands to the back of his neck. Something soft, brown, shapeless, fell to the ground and was instantly crushed under foot to the accompaniment of furious exclamations.

"You didn't think it was so funny when one dropped on you last week," sputtered the boy, surprising on the other's face a stifled grin.

He tenderly caressed his neck on which had leaped up an angry red welt like the rash which comes from the poisoned fur of browntail caterpillars, but multiplied ten-fold. Patterson twisted on a final label and stood up.

"I've always told you not to sit under those elephant-eared plants," he reminded the boy. "Tiger slugs seem to love them. Well, I guess I'll tackle Imboza and see if I can't drag something definite out of him. Better get out the iodine bottle, old man."

He strolled off toward the other fire and Ted, taking his advice, sought the medicine chest and anointed his burning neck with antiseptic. The pain somewhat relieved, he rummaged amongst the supplies for tea and biscuits and was annoyed to find that a horde of red ants had invaded one tin through an imperfectly closed cover. It took him ten minutes to clear them out and when he returned to the fire, flushed and triumphant, he found Ford there, his face serious and puzzled.

"I can't make head or tail of it all," he said in answer to Ted's question. "They're in earnest all right and pretty well frightened over something. But the whole business sounds like a fairy tale or a nightmare."

"What is it? What are they scared of?"

Ford looked at him quizzically.

"The—Thunder Beast," he returned briefly.

Ted's eyes widened. "What are you trying to do?" he demanded. "Kid me?"

Ford shook his head. "Nope. I'm simply telling you what I finally extracted from Imboza."

He dropped down cross-legged on the ground. Ted set down the rescued tin of biscuits and two cups, mechanically poured some tea into the boiling water and removed the kettle from the fire. Then he settled back on his haunches, his eyes having scarcely once left his cousin's face.

"Well?" he prodded impatiently.

Patterson drew a long breath. "Imagine," he began slowly, "a creature covered with scales, whose body would reach from here to—to that wild mango tree across the stream—roughly a hundred feet. Imagine a thing with a neck like an enormous python, a long snout with a horn on it, a thick, flat tail like a kangaroo."

He paused. Ted shook his head emphatically.

"I can't, Pat," he said briefly. "I really can't."

Ford shrugged his shoulders. "I don't know that I blame you, Ted, but there it is. That's the kind of a beast Imboza describes and which he says inhabits the jungle hereabouts and to the south and east. The natives call it the Thunder Beast because of a sort of thunderous, whistling roar it makes while rushing through the forest. Imboza swears he's heard it; and once, when he was a young man, he got a glimpse of the creature near a lake some distance south."

Ted's jaws gaped. "But surely Pat," he stammered, "you—you don't believe—"

The young man hesitated, his face thoughtful, pondering. "I— don't know," he answered slowly at length. "I've seen and heard of strange things in this vast, unknown part of Central Africa. You remember when I was down in Rhodesia two years ago? I ran up against one of the mounted police, an awfully decent chap named Jennings. We got talking one night about queer experiences and he told me of one which had happened to him over a year before while he was patrolling in Barotseland. He was lost for several days and while following the edge of a vast swamp he came upon an enormous monster, half beast, half lizard, lying asleep in the open. He was so dazed and frightened by the size and horrible look of the creature, that he took refuge in a clump of brush. Before he got back his nerve he said that the thing woke up and glided into the swamp, traveling at a great speed. His description was practically identical with Imboza's."

"But why didn't we hear about it?" asked Ted quickly. "I should think a thing like that would raise the dickens of a stir and be in all the papers."

"Jennings never told anyone. He was afraid of being laughed at. And that's the very reason I haven't opened my head about it until now. People would say he was off his nut. You know yourself you don't believe it even after what Imboza's told us."

"But how can I believe it, Pat?" protested the boy. "It's so—so awfully wild and improbable. Why, there never was such a crea- ture on earth, so how—"

"Oh, yes there was," interrupted Patterson quickly. "Haven't you ever read about the mammoth and the dinosaurus and all the rest of those weird prehistoric beasts? Ages and ages ago the earth was full of all kinds of monstrous horrors, and in a climate like this and a country where hundreds of thousands of square miles are unexplored, I suppose it's not entirely impossible that some of them may have survived. I'm not up on the details, but Sten— By the way, where the deuce *is* Sten?"

"Oh, he went off exploring a couple of hours ago," shrugged Ted. "Looking for that everlasting Death Plant, I suppose."

Ford merely raised his eyebrows a trifle and made no answer. But his heart stirred a little as it always did at the though of this mysterious plant which was the main cause of their presence in the unexplored depths of the African jungle.

Nelson had heard of it at Benguela on the coast from a Lunda porter just returned from the interior. He described it as a monstrous purple bloom, the petals splashed with gold, which gave forth a scent so sweetly powerful that it "stole away the senses." To breathe in that perfume was death, said old Losaka, adding vaguely that it "turned red blood white."

Nelson and Patterson paid little heed to these cryptic remarks and to later warnings, setting them down to native superstition. Losaka's description of the amazing flower remained unshaken by much cross examination, and it really seemed as if he must actually have beheld this extraordinary plant. The two Americans, who had come to Africa for botanical specimens for an American Arboratorium, thrilled at the possibility of finding an entirely unknown species and lost no time in organizing an expedition into central Congo.

Ted Graham was not a botanist, nor had he any official connection with the search. He was simply a big, wholesome fellow of sixteen, unusually well-developed, mentally and physically, who lived with his father in the African coast town where Mr. Graham, agent for a big New York importing house, made his headquarters. He and Ford Patterson were cousins, and about the time the expedition was organizing, Mr. Graham was forced to make a business trip to New York. He was not particularly anxious either for the boy to go with him or to stay behind alone, and Ford's suggestion that he make one of their party came as a welcome way out of a difficult situation.

So far Ted had had the time of his life. He enjoyed every moment of the long river trip and the even longer forest journey that followed it. He was able to make himself useful in a score of different ways and this trait, combined with his cheerful disposition and almost abnormal sense of humor, made him popular with every member of the party.

It is true that he had very little interest in the specimens which aroused so much enthusiasm in the two white men. To him one plant was very like another, and he even poked fun at "Death Plant," in whose existence he had no belief whatever. But though Sten Nelson was a rather serious person to whom botany was almost a religion, he did not seem to mind these occasional slighting references and they had become great friends.

"We may as well have our tea," remarked Patterson presently, breaking a rather prolonged silence, "and then I think we'll take a look for him. I'm afraid the situation is serious and we'll have to decide pretty quickly what we mean to do."

Ted poured out a cup of tea and passed it over, his eyes questioning.

"I mean about the men," explained Patterson. "They absolutely refuse to go on, and they're so dead scared they may bolt at any time."

"Gee-whiz!" exclaimed the boy. "We'd be in a beastly mess if they did that."

Almost in silence they hurried through the simple meal and then sought the corner of the clearing where Ted had last seen Nelson. Once in the forest his trail was easy to follow, for it had been literally hacked out of the mass of living green by one of those long, machete-like knives they all carried. Patterson led the way and Ted followed close behind, his usually cheery chatter conspicuously lacking.

He was thinking of Imboza's thunder beast. Back there in the cheerful brightness of the clearing the tale had seemed too utterly incredible to consider seriously, but here in the weird, perpetual jungle twilight it was curiously different.

Living as he did in the more open country near the coast, Ted had never grown used to the somber, ghostly panorama of the forest. Those countless gray columns, strung together by myriads of slender, pendant threads, loops and festoons of silvered parasites, were not to him like real trees. There was a touch of mystery in the profound spaces of shadow out of which strange vegetable shapes thrust themselves, assuming weird semblances of humanity.

The very sunshine—stray, feeble glints, perpetually changing and shifting—was like a magic dust of softened light. Against a gray filigree of vine stems, the crimson dots of phyrnia berries or the red knots of the amoma fruit, stood out like unknown jewels. Here and there a monstrous mushroom stared whitely from a loose sheaf of delicate fern, bearing a horrid likeness to some leprous, decaying skull. Distorted, tumorous lumps on trees exuded gum like tears. The long, whiplike calamus, the squirming, twisting lianes writhing from tree to tree might easily have been living serpents. The luxuriant growth on every hand was amazing, but to Ted, though he had not reached the point of putting his feeling into words, it was the unwholesome, bloated luxuriance of the sort which feeds on decay and rotting death.

In such a place as this, he thought, nothing was too wild to fancy. As he followed Patterson rapidly along the tunnel-like path Nelson had hacked out of the undergrowth, he found himself trying to form a mental picture of the dread, prehistoric Thunder Beast. Its great body would reach easily from that giant teak clear to the copal-wood tree whose glossy, burnished foliage he could just glimpse away off to the right. The snakelike neck, with its horn-crowned, hideous head, might rise—

"Ugh!" he muttered with a shiver of disgust. "I'm getting dotty. Say, Pat," he added aloud, "doesn't it seem as if Sten had chewed out quite a path for not much more than two hours work?"

"He's made progress, all right," returned Ford absently. He paused. Then: "Do you—smell anything, Ted?"

"Smell anything? Sure. The place is full of smells. What do you mean?"

"This isn't like—the others." Ford's voice held an odd note in it. "It's sort of—sweet and rather— Well, I can't seem to describe it exactly."

Ted sniffed the air vigorously and for the first time was conscious of an alien scent which he also found difficult to describe. It was sweet—cloyingly sweet, and yet underneath that sweetness there was a faint touch of something that repelled him. And as he moved forward along the path it grew stronger, more gripping.

His interest in trying to place the odor, which was like nothing he had ever smelled before, made him forget to reply to Patterson. But the latter did not seem to notice that omission. His pace quickened; his head was thrust slightly forward; his eyes, staring intently along the curving path, were filled with a strange mingling of hope, incredulity and growing dread.

Ahead the jungle brightened. Suddenly over one of Patterson's bent shoulders, Ted saw across the tunnel a narrow strip of mottled sunshine. A moment later they emerged into a tiny glade through which there flowed a narrow, sullen forest stream. And there with one accord they stopped abruptly.

To Ted it seemed as if that wave of sickening perfume drifting across his face was like a tangible presence. A spasm of nausea came over him and he saw Ford reel slightly. Then he stumbled forward to his cousin's side and an instant later a sharp cry burst from his lips.

At their feet, half hidden in the jungle growth, lay the body of Sten Nelson, face down, motionless!

For a single stricken second the boy stared at that still, silent length of gray flannel and khaki. Than his eyes traveled swiftly upward from the outthrust hands and something seemed to grip his throat chokingly.

Before him and above the fallen man, a monstrous bloom of purple splashed with gold seemed to hover in the air. It was huge—incredibly, unbelievably huge. Indeed, a foot rule would scarcely have spanned that open trumpet mouth. The calyx and the hole cuplike interior shone like dull, molten gold, and below it was a luxuriant mass of thick, fleshy, dark-green leaves covered with spots of full crimson.

"The—Death—Plant!" gasped Patterson in a strange voice.

He took a stumbling step forward, but Ted caught his arm and dragged him back. His brain was swimming and it was almost pure instinct that warned him of their danger. Before him the purple flower seemed to sway and move like something alive and venomous and through his dazed brain floated the words of the old Lunda porter "it steals away the senses."

Then all at once one hand brushed against the hilt of the long knife hanging at his side and his fingers closed spasmodically around it. With an effort he drew it forth and bending forward, he slashed through the thick green stalk that held the flower. As this fell at his feet the boy snatched it up and hurled it furiously from him. There was a faint, wavering cry of protest from Ford as the purple thing whirled through the air, gleaming gorgeously for an instant in a ray of sunlight, and then fell with a splash into the black stream and vanished out of sight.

"Oh, Ted! You've—you've—"

"What ja—want me—to do?" mumbled the boy. "In about two seconds—we'd both have—been down and out."

He drew a long, relieved breath. Already his head was clearing as the fumes of that sickening perfume grew less and less. Then he glanced anxiously at the body on the ground and of a sudden he saw something which brought a gleam of horror into his eyes and made him wonder whether the beastly poison scent still lingered to distort his vision.

Nelson's head was turned slightly to one side, his face not more than a foot away from the base of the Death Plant. The collar of his flannel shirt was opened, and fastened to his throat in a tight bunch were a number of slender, pale green curving things that writhed out from under the red splashed leaves like so many actual serpents.

The fact that they were not, seemed worse to Ted than if they had been living reptiles. Forgetting the knife dangling from his fingers, he stood paralyzed with bewildered horror until he was roused by a cry from Ford, who dropped on his knees and began tearing at the green things with his hands. These seemed to resist as if they were made of some tough, rubberlike substance. Then one broke suddenly and from the severed end some drops of blood began to drip.

"Your knife!" cried Patterson sharply. "Quick!"

Ted passed it swiftly to him and with a slash he severed the other tubes, and together they dragged the unconscious man away from the plant. Even now the cut ends of those green tubes clung to his neck like suckers and were removed with difficulty. When they finally came away they left a series of small round punctures on the skin from which the blood oozed slowly.

A bandage was speedily improvised, water dashed in Nelson's face, and presently his eyes opened. For a space he lay there dazedly. Then he lifted one hand inquiringly to his throat.

"You'll be all right in a minute," reassured Ford.

"What—happened?"

Patterson hesitated a moment. "It was the—Death Plant," he explained slowly at length. "It's a hateful thing, Sten—a regular plant vampire. The perfume overpowers one evidently, and then those beastly tubers fasten on the flesh—and suck the blood."

Nelson was silent for a moment. "I remember the scent," he murmured reflectively, "and seeing that gorgeous blossom. Then everything began to whirl around and—and I went out." He struggled up on one elbow and stared eagerly across the glade. "But where—"

"Ted cut it off and threw it away," explained Ford. "Good thing, too! We were both of us about done for."

The look of disappointment which came into Nelson's face made Ted stare at him in amazement.

"I suppose it couldn't be helped," murmured the botanist with a touch of regret. "Fortunately the root is still uninjured and we can take that back with us."

But this was too much for even Ford. "We can't now at any rate," he said hastily. "We're in a rotten fix, Sten, and we'll have to get back to camp as quickly as possible. The men are scared to death and likely to bolt at any minute."

In a few words he explained the situation and Nelson's attention was effectually diverted. With an effort he got on his feet and after a little experimenting decided that by going slowly he could manage the walk back to camp. But before they started he insisted on inspecting the Death Plant.

They approached it cautiously. The slender pale green tubes were still visible thrusting forth from beneath the broad, red-splashed fleshy leaves. It was plain now that these were part of the plant itself, growing out of the main stem just above the ground. Investigating with a branch, Ted happened to touch one of the severed ends and the thing stirred feebly, curving upward slightly and stretching out.

"Ugh!" grunted the boy with disgust. "Let's get away from the beastly thing."

Then his foot crunched something on the ground which proved to be the skeleton of some small jungle beast. There were several lying around the base of the plant and one larger skull which might have been that of a half-grown chimpanzee.

"You're right, Ford," said Nelson thoughtfully as they turned away. "The perfume stupefies and those suckers do the rest. There's never been anything like it ever heard of, unless you except that legend of the devil tree of the South American jungles. It's harmless now, and if we can only dig up the root to-morrow and get it back to civilization it may live."

Ted sniffed scornfully. "You'd have to grow it in an air-tight glass house, water it with a hose and feed it on live rats or guinea pigs," he remarked in a ribald tone.

Nelson paid no attention to his scoffing. In fact his interest in the plant quickly gave place to the graver difficulty which confronted them. When they finally reached camp they found the natives in a state of unrest bordering on panic. They were determined not to advance a step and no arguments either of the men could bring up moved them in the slightest. It was only by promising to turn westward the first thing in the morning that they could even be induced to spend the night here, and Nelson was not certain they could count on that much.

"They are like a herd of Cape Buffalo before a storm—ready to stampede at anything," he remarked as they sat eating a belated supper around the fire. "I wish—"

He paused, his forehead wrinkled thoughtfully. The swift, tropic darkness had fallen and all about them lay impenetrable blackness, broken only by the cheerful flicker of the two fires and the luminous starlight glow overhead. Patterson moved restlessly.

"What do you think of it all, Sten?"

Nelson looked at him steadily for a moment.

"I do not know just what to think," he answered presently in his low, pleasant voice which held just the faintest touch of foreign intonation. "You know your Latin, perhaps? Wasn't it Herodotus who wrote '*Ex Africa semper aliquid novi?*' How true that is. Out of Africa comes always something new. We have found it so to-day, eh? Whoever could imagine a thing in nature like that purple vampire? And I've had other strange experiences in the past. It is practically an unknown country, brushed merely by the fringe of civilization. Almost anything might lie hidden in its vast depths— even a survival of prehistoric—"

"Ah!" interrupted Patterson, straightening suddenly. "You thought of that, too?"

"Naturally. Imboza's description, even lacking as it was in detail, quite fits the Brontosaurus, one of those monsters that flourished in the Eocene age. Why, the very name translated means—"

The words clipped off and Nelson stiffened suddenly, his head turned, listening. From somewhere in the jungle depths there came a strange, uncanny, awful sound, shattering the stillness of the night. It started low, an eerie whistle rising crescendo, gathering strength and volume till it became a thunderous, bellowing roar that chilled the blood and lifted the hair of the three who sat as if paralyzed around the fire. Then it ceased abruptly and for a single, awesome second deathly, terror-stricken silence lay over the encampment like a pall.

It was broken by a series of piercing shrieks and smitten wailings from the blacks. In an instant a score of wild figures came leaping, crashing across the clearing, silhouetted against the glow of the further fire. In the lead was the headman, Imboza, his air of native dignity gone, his face distorted with fear. Close at his heels raced old Losaka, eyes popping, and mop of grizzled hair standing out from his head like a mass of gray twisted wires.

"The Thunder Beast!" cried Imboza, without pausing. "He comes! Baas fly quickly!"

In a thrice the whole mad throng had padded past and vanished leaving the leaders to stare white-faced, irresolute at one another. For an instant no one spoke. Then Nelson moistened his lips.

"The guns!" he whispered, whirling toward their tent.

The others darted after him and all three fumbled frantically in the darkness for their weapons. As they emerged, Nelson and Patterson with high-power Mausers and Ted carrying a ten gauge shot gun and his revolver, they were aware of an ominous crashing in the forest to the east of camp.

Two of them, at least, knew the sound made by a bull elephant plunging through the jungle and carrying everything before him. It was this sound, but multiplied tenfold, which smote now on their dazed senses. And it was coming rapidly nearer. Already they could hear the distinct crash of falling trees and the spongy earth seemed curiously to vibrate as beneath some gigantic tread. Nelson's glittering eyes swept the clearing.

"Which way?" he muttered. "We might run straight under his feet. Besides, we can't make any sort of speed through that tangle—"

Ted gave a sharp, suppressed cry. "The path! The one you made this afternoon! That leads north."

"Good boy," murmured the Dane. "It's no good trying to shoot it in the dark; we've got to run."

He darted toward the lower side of the clearing, the others at his heels. Ted came last, and he had scarcely left the circle of firelight when again that awful, whistling roar smote suddenly on his senses with a deadly, deafening volume that was like an actual physical shock. A cry of sheer terror rose to his lips, but he choked it back and fled after the others. He had almost reached the beginning of the jungle path when one foot caught and he fell headlong.

The roaring ceased, but back of him the crashing undergrowth sounded horribly near. Scrambling to his feet, he cast a terror stricken glance over one shoulder, and of a sudden his blood seemed turned to ice.

"The fire kindled by the blacks gleamed brightly across the clearing, illumining the trees and undergrowth just beyond their little camp. But as Ted looked, that screen of jungle growth was torn suddenly aside. Trees fell, bushes vanished and a towering, shadowy shape—immense, black, horrible—plunged into sight. Vague outlines he caught of something incredibly huge—something that seemed to hover smotheringly over the little clearing like an enormous, collapsing balloon of black rubber.

An instant later the fire was blotted out.

II

The blotting out of the camp fire beneath that monstrous advancing body seemed to release Ted Graham from the spell of horrified fascination which had held him momentarily paralyzed. With a gasping cry he fled blindly through the darkness, plunged into a thorny bush, which tore his outstretched hands, stumbled out of that and in another moment was gripped by a muscular hand which dragged him irresistibly sideways.

For perhaps a dozen paces he kept his feet. Then, tripping, he lost his balance and was dragged on a few yards further by Ford Patterson's sheer strength before the older fellow struck some hidden obstacle and they both crashed down together.

As he lay there panting, his face pressed close against the foul jungle mould, Ted felt certain that his last hour had come. Beneath his shrinking body the earth shook and quivered with the pressure of that enormous living weight. To his right there came a crashing in the undergrowth and a tree, covered with clinging vines and creepers, was flung suddenly across his legs. He heard plainly the squelching sound of a huge foot in the soft ooze and at almost the same instant he was conscious of a foul animal odor—loathsome, stifling, indescribably nauseating, which turned him sick and made his head swim. And then—and then. . . . How long it was before his tense muscles began to relax, Ted had no idea. He only knew that little by little they did relax; that presently he found himself beginning to breathe again with some approach to freedom, to move his legs gingerly under the weight of the fallen tree. Then, all at once, he was blinking up at the white dazzling circle of an electric torch and listening vaguely to Sten Nelson's voice, pitched in a cautious undertone.

"Are you all right, Ford?"

There was a rustle beside Ted, a long-drawn sigh, and Ford Patterson's face emerged from the green tangle which quite covered him.

"I guess so," he murmured. His face was pale and drawn and plastered down one side with mud. "My legs are stuck under this blooming tree and a bunch of ants are exploring down my neck, but nothing matters—now. . . . It's gone, hasn't it?"

"Yes; straight away to the eastward. It was a mighty close shave, that."

"I'll say so!" With an effort Ford pulled himself a little further into view. "Too close for comfort. I tell you, Sten, I could *feel* the thing's beastly foot squashing down right alongside of me. Ugh!"

He shivered at the recollection; then his glance sought Ted's face.

"How about you, kid?"

"Oh, I—I'm all right," answered the boy a bit unsteadily. "Do—do you think it's gone for good, Pat?"

"You've got me. I certainly hope so."

The man wriggled out from under the mass of foliage and stood up. Ted followed his example. He felt decidedly shaky and for the first time he began to be aware of a number of cuts and bruises on his limbs and body which throbbed and ached painfully. But even that consciousness was something vague in the back of his mind, and was completely dominated by an overpowering sense of strained listening.

Far off to the eastward he could barely distinguish the last faint crashings of the Thunder Beast. Presently even these died away in the distance and silence fell—a silence so utter and so unnatural that it attracted the instant attention of all three.

The harsh, rasping cry of the lemur, which usually made night hideous, was strangely absent. So was the almost as common noise of a playful chimpanzee beating against the trees. The varied cries, roars and wailings of the beasts of prey were conspicuous by their absence. Even the monotonous piping of the cicadæ and the perpetual booming of the frogs seemed to have ceased entirely. It was as if all nature, frightened by the gigantic horror which had just passed, held its breath in momentary panic.

But even panic is seldom long endured when its cause has been removed. Before they reached the end of the narrow jungle path which had proved such a haven of refuge the nocturnal chorus was in full swing again. It all sounded so commonplace and natural that Ted became oppressed by a sudden sense of unreality, as if that whole awful business hadn't actually happened at all. It was so weird, so monstrous, so much the type of thing that comes only in nightmare visions, that he felt almost as if he would presently wake up and find that it had been nothing but a beastly dream.

But when they came out into the clearing and felt their way blindly over to the site of their camp, the substantial nature of that visitation was only too apparent. Of the two fires not so much as a single glowing coal remained. They had both been crushed out to the last smoking ember as if the Thunder Beast regarded them as something living, menacing, to be stamped deliberately into powder. The rough shelters of the blacks, thatched with broad phrynia leaves, were mere heaps of wreckage ground into the dirt. Their own tent lay flat, but when a fire had been kindled and they could see more clearly they found that it had been merely flung down as if the creature had brushed against it in passing. Their stores, specimens and belongings were scattered about in great confusion but most of them had escaped trampling on and complete ruination.

Nevertheless the situation was serious and disheartening. They were alone in one of the wildest and least explored portions of Central Africa, a region to whose perilous possibilities another greater than all the rest had just been added. There was little hope of Imboza and the porters returning, and without their aid most of the stores and equipment, much of the ammunition, and—worst of all—the entire collection of rare plants they had spent over two months in gathering must be abandoned.

"There's not a chance of our getting them out alone," said Nelson, regretfully yet quite decidedly. "The weight would be more than we could manage if we carried nothing else. It is heart breaking to leave so much that is almost priceless, but we have more than one reason for traveling light."

Patterson raised his eyebrows. "You think it might—come back?" he asked.

"I've not the least idea," shrugged Nelson, "but frankly I do not wish to take a chance. I suppose there are scientists in the world who would give years of their lives—or say they would—for such a glimpse as we have had of a living survival from prehistoric ages. For me one encounter is enough. Another might end—differently."

The other two entirely agreed with him. They had not the slightest desire ever to see the amazing Thunder Beast again. In fact all three were oppressed with a subtle horror lest it should return before they could escape from this place which they had come to loathe. Without a moment's loss of time they set to work sorting their belongings, weighing, considering, rejecting, and finally packing the little they felt they could not possibly do without into three equal portions. That little consisted almost entirely of ammunition and food, but when the first pink flush of dawn pierced blurring through the thick jungle haze, Nelson produced a short spade and quietly announced that he meant to dig up the death plant.

"It's worth all that other stuff put together," he said, his blue eyes glowing with the fire of an enthusiast. "It's our last chance of getting it, too, for after what's happened here you won't get a Congo native to come within a hundred miles of this place—ever. I'm willing to carry it in addition to my own pack."

"Shucks!" growled Patterson, ashamed of the momentary feeling of protest that had welled up within him. "You'll do nothing of the kind. We'll all take turns. I'll go and help dig it up while Ted keeps an eye on the breakfast."

But after they had gone Ted did not pay half so much attention to the pots and pans hanging over the fire as he did to that wide swath of torn, trampled undergrowth and shattered, riven trees which marked the passage of the Thunder Beast through the forest to the eastward. He, too, was ashamed of the swift panic that had assailed him at the thought of delaying here for a single instant longer than was absolutely necessary, but the panic remained with him, keen and vivid. While he mechanically stirred the stew his eyes roved anxiously over the treetops, and his ears were strained for the slightest unnatural sound in the surrounding forest. He was a perfectly normal boy, with rather more than the average amount of courage. But before the men had been gone ten minutes, he began to wonder what had happened to delay them; by the time half an hour had passed he had worked himself into a state of nerves as unpleasant as it was unusual.

Nelson and Patterson appeared at last, having made uncommonly good time, for the plant had to be wrapped in soft moss and sewed up in a protecting bag of stout burlap. Even nearly stripped of earth, the roots were cumbersome and bulky and would add not a little weight to backs already loaded to the breaking point. Ted eyed the thing with fervent but unexpressed dislike.

"It's hoodoed the whole trip," he thought. "I wish to thunder we'd never seen it."

Breakfast was hurriedly eaten and, shouldering their packs, the three lost no time in setting out along their back trail. At the edge of the clearing the two men glanced back regretfully at the patch of canvas which covered the bales of precious roots and bulbs, but Ted Graham was only too thankful when the cool shade of the jungle closed about them. The mere fact that the clearing, with all its disquieting signs of devastation had vanished out of sight was soothing to the boy's nerves, and before many hours he had quite recovered his usually cheery good temper.

But as the time passed it was not so easy to be cheerful and carefree, even on the surface. It is one thing to travel through the jungle with merely a machete dangling from the belt and perhaps a rifle over one shoulder or crooked beneath an elbow, and quite another to labor along under a dead weight of fifty or sixty pounds with periodically the added burden of a clumsy burlap package of roots and stems. At the end of the day's march there was no longer any pleasant pottering around while the natives made the clearing, put up the tents and gathered wood for fires. The tents had been abandoned with the other things and they were forced to make their own rude shelters or go without. They could not go without fires because of the protection these gave them from all sorts of roving jungle beasts, and the mere collecting of enough wood to last through the night sometimes took hours. Often, the swift, purple darkness caught them before they had even begun to cook their meal. And after that meal had been gulped down with little appetite, they crawled into their shelter and fell into a sleep of utter exhaustion from which not even the clouds of stinging insects had the power to rouse them.

Naturally as the days passed and they grew more hardened to the incessant toil, things weren't always quite so bad. Also the fact that they were following their own recently made trail and did not have to laboriously hack their way through the almost impenetrable growth, made the going easier than it would otherwise have been. But it was nevertheless quite difficult enough, and though Ted never complained he was conscious of a slowly forming hatred of the jungle.

Plodding along that narrow, shut-in path for hours in silence, his imagination had full play. And gradually, almost impercepti-bly, he came to feel that the vast surrounding stretches of shad-owy unknown was not a mere trackless wilderness of swamp and endless forest, hiding in its depths fierce beasts and even fiercer men, but an actual, concrete presence—a vast, relentless, evil thing, sleepless, alert, waiting with a calm, eternal, horrible kind of patience for the moment when it could clutch them smotheringly to its bosom and engulf them body and soul forever.

Of course it was morbid; such fancies always are. Ted realized this quite well and did his best to stifle the feeling. But frequently in those long hours of silent tramping it returned and at length he found himself wishing desperately for something to happen that would break the appalling monotony. He did not much care what it was so long as it served to take his mind from those unpleasant fancies. Afterwards, he had a curious, illogical sense of guilt, as if his constant, fervent mental longings had helped in some cryptic manner to bring about the catastrophe.

This came, as such things often do, quite suddenly and unexpect-edly. The morning had been like any other of the eleven mornings since their departure from the ruined camp. They had set out with a certain sort of briskness and enlivened the way for a space with desultory conversation. But since all hope had now been abandoned of encountering any of the deserting blacks, there was little to discuss and the talk soon languished, giving place to the usual silence.

Ted happened to be walking in the lead and to keep his mind from other things, he occupied himself with an elaborate mental calculation as to how long it would take them to reach the distant river where they had left their boats. This was, to be sure, somewhat futile, for on the way in they sometimes spent several days in one locality searching for specimens. But it proved sufficiently absorbing to Ted and at least a couple of hours passed without his once reverting to those morbid notions about the jungle.

What made him lift his eyes at that precise moment he never knew. It might have been mere chance, or possibly those drifting crimson flower-petals drew his glance upward automatically. A dozen feet above his head a great limb, covered with masses of broad shining leaves, reached out across the path. Festoons of vines, brilliant with the blood-red flowers, hung down from it, but Ted's startled glance sought something above the vines—something small, round, yellow, like the weazened face of a child, grown incredibly old and evil—which hung there motionless in the frame of shiny leaves.

For a bewildered moment Ted stared blankly at that little, beastly face with its vicious eyes and snarling mouth. Then a sharp exclamation from Patterson seemed to break the spell. Without sound or apparent motion the face seemed to melt into the leaves. There was a slight tremor of the hanging vines and a few more crimson petals floated down through the hot, still air; but that was all.

"What was it?" cried Ted, turning swiftly.

Patterson's face had grown suddenly strained and anxious. "I—I'm not sure." He glanced at Nelson. "You think—"

"I'm afraid so. I saw one once back in the Ashango country. I don't in the least understand what they're doing around here, but unless this was just a solitary, roving specimen we're likely to be in for trouble."

"But what are they?" demanded Ted impatiently. "I wish you'd tell me—"

"Pygmies," explained Patterson absently, his eyes searching the undergrowth to the left of the path. "Dwarf Negroes. The natives call them the Poison Ones." He half turned and stared into the jungle on the other side. "They're more afraid of them than—"

The words ended in a sharp, hissing intake and Nelson cried out warningly. Something flashed past Ted's face, a slim, short, stick-like object which stuck into his cousin's pack and hung there quiveringly. It was like a child's arrow, and the boy reached out to pluck it forth when Nelson's sharp command halted him.

"Don't touch it! It's poisoned. The least prick— It didn't cut you, Ford?"

"No," answered Patterson, his face white and ghastly. "But if I hadn't turned just then— Give 'em the buckshot, Sten—quick!"

But already the Dane had crammed two shells into his gun and jerking the weapon to his shoulders, he fired both barrels into the forest to their left. The explosions roared through the silent jungle and simultaneously there came a thin, wailing screech that turned Ted's blood cold. It was followed by a sudden pattering like rain falling on the leaves and five or six more of the deadly little arrows slithered through the undergrowth upon them.

Four of these stuck into the packs, for instinctively all three had turned their backs upon the danger quarter. But one, deflected perhaps by an intervening branch, fell at Ted's feet and he saw that the point was smeared with a thick, dark, gummy substance. Then Nelson's heavy charges plowed again into the undergrowth and a moment later Patterson spoke sharply.

"It's up to us to beat it, fellows. Step on the gas, son. We've got to get out of here, quick."

The boy obeyed instantly, only too thankful for a chance to move, and in single file they darted down the trail with all the speed their cumbersome packs permitted. For over a mile they ran and then slowed down merely because their breath was gone. No more arrows had reached them. There was not a sign of their pursuers in the surrounding tangles, and yet each one of the three was

BotanicaDelira

oppressed by the feeling that the dwarf folk were all about them, hiding in the shadows, swinging along through the trees like monkeys, watching, waiting for a chance to send one of those deadly poison missiles home.

"We—can't—stop," panted Nelson. "They'll never give up—so soon. The only hope is to keep—straight on."

His words were punctuated by the appearance of two more arrows. Their flight was spent, showing that the pygmies were afraid to come up very close. But as a symbol of dogged, persistent, tireless pursuit they were entirely effective. Nelson paused long enough to fire his gun again and they were off.

Two hours later they were still moving in alternate bursts of speed and intervals of slower jogging. Inevitably the former lessened and the latter were prolonged. Burdened as they were it was a sheer impossibility to keep up that first rapid pace for very long. They might have thrown away their packs, but to face the African jungle without food or ammunition would have meant as sure a death as the venom from a poisoned arrow.

Slowly but surely they were being worn out, and the bitter thing was that though they knew it, there was nothing else for them to do. They could not make a stand because their enemies were invisible. It was like trying to fight a horde of stinging insects in the dark. They might shoot a few by accident as they had done that first one, but the bulk of the vicious, savage creatures would hang upon their flanks by day and night until they dropped from sheer exhaustion and became an easy prey.

Panting and dizzy with fatigue, Ted thought of this and wondered despairingly how long they could keep it up. Already it seemed as if their enemies were venturing closer. What was going to happen when darkness fell? He shuddered and choked back a dry sob. What was going to happen to them *anyway?* Ahead of them was nothing—nothing save this endless, barren path. There was no goal, no haven, no native village, even, where they might take refuge.

"We'll just run on and on until we drop," thought the boy hopelessly. "And then—"

Out of the thick tangle on his right a naked black arm thrust him by the wrist. The boy jerked back instinctively and gave a sharp cry—a cry which, in its very crescendo of nervous panic, changed abruptly to amazed, bewildered recognition.

"Imboza!" he gasped incredulously.

The Lunda headman nodded, his glance sweeping to Patterson, who was close behind.

"Baas come quick," he said hurriedly. "Woods full of Poison Ones. Trail no good. This only way."

His tone was curt and agitated and his black face wrinkled and slightly gray in hue. Plainly he was laboring under the stress of great anxiety or even fear, and when he drew aside and showed the beginnings of a narrow, trodden path leading away from the trail, the others paused to ask no questions but made haste to follow him in silence.

The path was just wide enough for them to move in single file, but it was hard packed as if from constant use. They thread the jungle everywhere, forming the only means the natives have, save water, of going from place to place.

For a mile and more Imboza swung along it with an easy, swinging stride which Ted, weary and sweating, envied intensely. He envied the other's nakedness, too, and that smooth ripple of muscles beneath the dark skin. If only he could have flung off his clothes and that hateful pack, which seemed to weigh about a thousand pounds, it would be like having a new lease of life.

Suddenly the headman paused and stood listening intently. Then he glanced back over one shoulder.

"Poison Ones come," he whispered. "Must make haste."

There followed a period of stress—how long or short it was he never knew—the remembrance of which Ted felt would never leave him. It was one long horror of panting breath, of tortured muscles, of weariness so dead and dragging that it seemed quite certain each step would be his last. But in spite of everything he did not pause— he dared not. For Fear, scourging as a whiplash, trod close upon his heels and drove him on.

There came a time at last when his stumbling running had grown quite mechanical, when the changing panorama of jungle growth on either side swam in a dizzy mist. Mouth open, parched lips glued against his teeth, hot, staring eyes set straight ahead, he saw nothing save the black, moving figure of the Lunda headman. Even the slithery, snaky sound of arrows piercing the heavy undergrowth had no longer power to make his heart leap. The roar of Nelson's shotgun came to him vaguely as if from a great distance, but it did not make him pause. Imboza kept on and he followed doggedly, quite unaware that ahead the jungle had begun to lighten.

He was thus unprepared for the great glare of light that smote suddenly on him like a physical blow. On either hand the dark shadows seemed to hide smoothly black as if on rollers; the hot sun blazed into his eyes painfully. He staggered forward a few steps and then realized that they were on a river bank. . . . Imboza bent over a heavy log canoe lifting something. . . . It was the body of a Negro, limp, sprawling, curiously swollen. . . . A moment later Ted saw that another lay close to the water's edge. . . . The limbs were twisted, the face hideously contorted, and in the bloated body there were stuck—two frail, short shafts!

At almost the next minute, it seemed, the boy was crouching in the bow of the canoe and they were out in the middle of the narrow river. Behind him Imboza bent low over his paddle; further back Pat wielded another, the sweat streaming down his flushed face. In the stern lay Nelson, gun in hand, his eyes riveted on the wooded banks where presently appeared vague, shadowy figures, dwarfed, stunted, which ran along on either side, keeping for the most part safe in the shelter of the jungle.

For a time no one had breath to waste in talk, but after a while, in scraps and snatches, the headman explained what at first had seemed a miracle. The flight of the panic-stricken porters had lasted, it appeared, for several days. Even then none of them would listen to Imboza's suggestion that they await the appearance of the white men, whom he felt sure would follow if they escaped the Thunder Beast. They were determined to make their way back to the coast at once and in the end Imboza, dominated by a combination of loyalty and unwillingness to sacrifice his pay, was left alone. He was afraid to go back to meet them, and it was while lingering in the neighborhood of the trail that the forest was suddenly invaded by the Poison Ones.

Whence they came or whither they were going the headman had no idea. He only knew that suddenly one morning they seemed to be all about him and in a panic he hid himself near the river, determined when night fell to swim across and escape that way. While there he witnessed the ambush of the two blacks in the canoe, and at the same time discovered that there were pygmies on the other side of the stream as well.

This had happened that very morning. Within an hour there was a sudden bustle and scurrying about among the little people, and presently most of those on this side of the stream vanished to the south.

Imboza's first impulse was to fly in the canoe, even though the river flowed in quite the opposite direction from the coast. Then he realized the canoe was too heavy for one paddle; alone he could not make speed enough to escape the pygmies on the other shore, which might easily have boats in which to pursue. Apparently he had no recourse save to stay in hiding until the swarm of invaders passed on, as they were sure to do before very long. Having spent an hour or two getting a meal of wild fruit in the jungle, he lay down to sleep and was awakened by a distant gunshot. In a flash the explanation of that sudden departure southward of the Poison Ones came to him. He spent a few moments in worried cogitation and then decided to slip along the jungle trail and reconnoiter.

What followed they all knew, and it now appeared that they were by no means out of danger. For the moment they were safe. By keeping to the middle of the river, they were just out of range of arrows from either side. But they did not dare to land and at any time a narrowing of the stream by even a score of feet would bring them into peril.

There seemed nothing for it but to keep on as they were, trusting to luck that the river would not decrease in width until such a time as the pygmies wearied of their fruitless chase. They were a nomadic people of very low intelligence, and Nelson was hopeful of their growing soon discouraged.

Unfortunately he quite underestimated their persistence. Dominated by Heaven only knows what impulse of greed or desire for vengeance, the Poison Ones hung on their flank like a horde of vicious, angry hornets. Morning after morning found them slinking along through the jungle on either side, rarely showing themselves, sparing now even of the deadly arrows, but always there—waiting in the background for some lucky chance which would deliver the beleaguered party into their hands.

The plight of the latter may easily be imagined. With no means of making fire, their food was eaten raw from tins; for drink they had only the warm, brackish river water. Penned up by day and night in the narrow confines of the canoe, it was possible for only one at a time to relax his cramped limbs. All day long the fierce tropical sun beat down out of a cloudless sky; at night, poisonous mists surrounded them and clouds of stinging insects tortured their broken rest. And through it all, growing hourly graver and more disquieting, there loomed a possibility beside which even such discomforts became as nothing.

The river flowed sluggishly, but almost undeviatingly, in a southeasterly direction. They were, as a matter of fact, being carried, not only back into the region from which they had just fled, but, what was worse, even further into that vast, mysterious, central part of Africa which is almost entirely unknown to civilization. What lay before them even Imboza had no idea. Patterson had once skirted the southern border of this wilderness; both men were familiar with countless legends of its secrets. But none of them really knew anything definite about the country save one disturbing fact—it was precisely this direction that the monstrous Thunder Beast had taken that night two weeks ago when he plowed through their camp and vanished into blackness.

For a time no one ventured to speak of what was on his mind. After all, in these thousands of square miles of wilderness the chances of a second meeting with the nightmare horror were remote. But as they penetrated further and further into the unknown, an increasing sense of nervous apprehension became apparent in all four. And finally it developed that what each one supposed was confined solely to his own thoughts, had been as prominent all this time in the minds of the other three.

A serious consultation took place that night as they drifted slowly along through the purple darkness. All day the river had been widening, until at dusk it was over twice its former breadth. No faintest outline of either shore came to them through the mist. They might have been floating on the bosom of an inland sea, miles from land, and the situation suggested to Ford Patterson's fertile brain a possible, though hazardous, means of escaping the Poison People.

"They can't see us any more than we can see them," he explained. "Now, suppose tomorrow we keep straight ahead all day as usual. They'll trail us, of course, and when night comes they'll keep on going as they've done every night so as to be up with us in the morning. But what will happen if the minute it's full dark we turn about and paddle up-stream?"

"By Jove!" murmured Nelson, a note of enthusiasm in his tired voice. "That might work, Ford. We'll pass them in the dark and with both going in opposite directions we'd be miles apart by morning."

"What's more, they wouldn't know whether we were ahead or behind," added Pat; "and they'd waste a lot more time deciding which. Of course, we'd be paddling against the current—"

"But that hasn't been strong any part of the way," cut in Ted. "Here you can hardly feel it. Gee, Pat! I move we try it. I—I don't like what may be ahead of us."

Imboza added his approval to the scheme. He was not sure of its success, but he, too, was in a state bordering panic as to what might lie ahead. After all, a certain danger was better than the unknown, and before settling down for the night, they had perfected every detail of their plan.

Ted Graham was particularly delighted at the outcome of it all. He had the first watch that night and as he reclined in the stern, one hand resting on the steering paddle, now almost useless, he was conscious of a relaxation and relief from mental strain such as he had not known for many days.

The feeling made him drowsy and once or twice he dozed briefly, to awake with a start and a sense of chagrin. But each time he found the canoe floating placidly along through the mist exactly as it would drift, he told himself, without a single quiver of the loosely lashed paddle. The result was inevitable. Presently his eyes closed again and this time did not open. Before very long he was sleeping heavily.

He awoke with a start and a queer, instinctive sense of something strange. A gentle breeze had sprung up and was blowing away the mist. The moon had not yet risen but there was a luminous quality to the darkness which made him glance guiltily at Pat's radiolite watch to find that it was past midnight. Then his glance shifted to the right and to his dismay he saw that they had drifted close to shore. In fact the jungle loomed up darkly apparently not more than twenty yards away, and with a stifled exclamation he thrust the steering paddle hard to one side.

It was a swift, instinctive movement made before his eyes had time to take in the amazing quality of that growth which lines the bank. They were not trees at all, but reeds growing straight out of the water. Immensely tall, incredibly large of girth, they towered up straight and branchless in endless ranks, the slender tops moving gently in the night breeze. Ted had never seen anything in the least like them before, and in a panic he poked Patterson in the back with one foot.

"I went to sleep, Pat," he confessed hurriedly as the man sat up sleepily. "I don't know what's happened to us, but—but just look around."

Wide awake in an instant, Ford stared about him in astonishment.

"Gosh!" he muttered. "What do you know about this!"

Nelson and Imboza were hastily aroused and without delay they paddled the canoe further out into the stream. Here by the aid of the increasing brightness they saw that it was no longer a stream at all. They lay in the middle of what seemed like a small lake, irregular in shape, with the tall reeds surrounding them on ever side, though the shore near which they had first drifted did have a slightly more solid look, like a mound or island rising out of a morass.

"It's a swamp," said Patterson presently. "That stuff looks like papyrus and canebrake, though it's far bigger than any I've ever seen." He paused a moment. "I—I don't like it," he confessed in a slightly uneasy tone. "It reminds me too much of that swamp I saw down in Barotseland two years ago. A chap named Jennings showed it to me. You remember the one who told me about—"

He broke off with an odd catch in his breath. From somewhere beyond that impenetrable screen of reeds there came the sound of a mighty splash.

For a space the four occupants of the boat might have been turned to stone. It was as if they scarcely dared even to breathe. Then Imboza's teeth began to chatter and Ted gave a queer, strangled sort of gasp.

Even then no one spoke. In the growing brightness of the rising moon their figures were plainly visible. Nelson sat like a statue, staring intently into the shadowy wastes ahead. Imboza crouched in a stricken heap, his shoulders visibly shaking. Patterson's head moved swiftly from side to side like a hunted thing seeking cover. He was the first to break that ghastly silence.

"The moon!" he whispered hoarsely. "We can't stay here. . . . The reeds might—hide us."

"Right," muttered the Dane.

He plucked a paddle from Imboza's nerveless fingers; Ford already had the other in his hands. In a moment they had turned the canoe and were moving noiselessly across the stagnant water toward the spot where they had first drifted.

They reached the outer growth of reeds and the boat nosed through them with a soft, slithering scrape that seemed horribly loud to their strained nerves. Ted bent forward from the bow and helped by parting the flexible canes with both hands. Part of the canoe was still out in the open water when that appalling splash came again, this time distinctly nearer.

Pushing, pulling, prodding with the paddles, they managed to thrust the boat forward a score of yards and then it scraped across some mud flats and bumped into something solid. It was land, soft and oozy to be sure, but still firm enough to bear their weight. In feverish haste they disembarked, and carrying only the weapons, felt their way up a mucky, gradual slope. They gave no though to the Poison Ones. Insensibly they felt that even if these dared venture into the swamp, which was more than doubtful, they would rather take a chance of meeting them than of an encounter with the terrifying Thunder Beast.

The low mound up which they pushed was covered with a frail, lush sort of growth which broke to the touch and made them feel that in the rainy season the whole mound was probably under water. There were no trees or any other solid vegetation, and as they came above the level of the reeds they stopped abruptly.

Huge, round and yellow, the full moon was just rising over the swamp, which stretched away on every side to far, far horizons, dusky and mysterious. An atmosphere of incredible desolation lay over that strange, flat expanse. It was as if they had been transported to another sphere, or to another age of this one. Water, swamp and mammoth reeds! It was like one of those weird pictures of the world before the deluge. And in another moment the final touch of horror was added to the ghastly likeness.

A mammoth splash, a monstrous crashing in the reeds suddenly shattered the stillness. Like a riven curtain, the growth edging that wide lagoon below was torn away and into the open there surged a nightmare shape. Dimensions quite failed the numbed brains of the cowering watchers. They only knew that the thing was huge beyond all possible comparison. The massive body covered with a glistening black skin like polished leather reached nearly to the top of the tallest reeds—reeds that had towered up thirty or forty feet above their own heads. The lapping water came barely to its belly.

For a moment or two it stood there motionless, long neck thrust out before it. Then all at once that neck swung swiftly upward and became erect, silhouetting against the yellow moon a head of incredible hideousness. It was broad and flat, with wide, protruding snout, and crowned by two round knobs like stunted horns. The eyes were large and heavy lidded, and seemed to stare with a horrid fixed intentness straight at the little mound where the four men crouched paralyzed.

The creature had appeared so suddenly that at first they dared not stir; now it seemed almost as if motion had become impossible. There was a dreadful sort of fascination in that steady, fixed glare, like the fascination of snake for fluttering bird. With tongue cleaving to the roof of his mouth and eyes fairly starting from his head, Ted had a weird conviction that presently he would be drawn straight down into the monster's clutch. At least when it came after them, as he felt sure it would, he did not believe he could stir a muscle. Then all at once a faint whisper from Patterson penetrated to his brain.

"The brute sees us, Sten. . . . There's only one thing left to do. . . . The Mausers will carry. . . . You take the right eye. . . . Tell me when you're ready."

Slowly, cautiously the two men stretched themselves at length and drew the high-power rifles into position. Something of that dead-helpless feeling seemed to pass away from Ted and his heart began pounding until he felt as if his head would burst. Though he knew both men to be really marvelous shots it scarcely seemed as if mere bullets could make the least impression against that living mountain. And yet—

"Ready," breathed Nelson presently.

"When I say three," murmured Patterson, sighting with the greatest care. "One . . . two . . . *three!*"

Like a single shot the roar of the two Mausers broke the death-like stillness. The sound seemed caught up, prolonged, made infinitely horrible by a thunderous, appalling scream from the Thunder Beast. For one single moment the creature stood motionless. Then it plunged forward a dozen steps, stopped short, whirled about and lurched blindly the other way. The long neck squirmed snakewise, straightened, lashed the reeds with a sweeping motion that cut through them as a scythe mows down a stand of wheat.

Again it screamed that awful, infernal scream, and threshed the water with a monstrous tail. Then, with a sort of surging, staggering gait, it tore through the further reeds and vanished, roaring as it went.

Gradually the volume of sound lessened. . . . Once, in the distance, that dreadful head writhed up for an instant against the glowing moon. . . . The roaring grew thinner, and mingled with it was a sort of wheezing whistle. . . . At length even that ceased.

The unknown had swallowed up again that amazing survival of another age. Whether it will ever reappear to human eyes is a question which time alone can answer. One thing is quite certain. If it does, not one of the four men huddled on the little mound and just beginning to breathe with some approach to freedom, will be there to see it.

ORCHID DEATH

James Hanson

"Riley Heslop, I am going to kill you!"

"That's a good bluff, Grayson," laughed Heslop, "but it won't work."

"It's no bluff," came the ironical rejoinder. "I mean exactly what I said."

Heslop half-started from his seat, then sank back.

During the cryptic silence that followed, Grayson's eyes, through narrowed lids, focused on the florid face opposite him at the table.

Heslop realized that it was no bluff. He knew that the happenings of the last half-hour was the result of a carefully pre-arranged plot. Grayson, in his own limousine, had accosted him on Van Ness Avenue and had requested to be accompanied home. Upon arriving at Grayson's residence he had been overpowered by four rowdies whom he recognized as members of the notorious Forty Strong Gang. He knew, when it was too late, that he had carried his nefarious work too far. He resolved to bluff.

"Have a care, Grayson," he insinuated.

Grayson leisurely selected a cigar from the humidor at his elbow and calmly bit off its end.

"Heslop," he began at length, "there is only one thing on earth that is lower than a snake, and that thing is you—a blackmailer. For the past year you have been clinging to my side like a loathsome leach, always with your freckled paw outstretched for blood-money. It was the old, old game—the badger game. A blind fool and a clever trap! You had your witnesses; you knew that the police could not act without publicity, and you had me powerless."

"Yes," broke in Heslop uneasily, "I'll admit that I went a little too far. I—"

"Don't interrupt," snapped Grayson. "You went a little too far, all right. You would expose me with your false evidence if I did not pay. I paid, all right—until I was on the verge of financial ruin, so that my domestic harmony might not be broken, for I could not hope to convince anyone of my innocence."

"For God's sake, don't say any more," pleaded Heslop, cringing wretchedly in his chair. "I'll promise not to bother you again."

Grayson laughed sardonically.

"Promise! Hump! Your promises are worthless." Grayson was half-speaking to himself. "A little too far, Heslop, when you fixed your greedy eyes on my girl. Did you have mercy on me when I pleaded with you not to exact this terrible toll from me? No! So you must pay, and in your own words: 'I've got it on you.'"

Heslop sprang from his chair, assuming the air of a bully, his arms upraised above the other.

"By God!" he roared. "You can't intimidate me, Grayson. You can't get away with it."

Grayson touched a bell.

"As well as blackmail," was his cool answer.

Heslop was seized by the gangsters and held fast.

"You see?" said Grayson, with a wave of his hand. "Nobody knows you are here; nobody saw you come; and nobody will see you go. As for these men; they are well-paid, which has its significance."

Heslop looked around the room anxiously. He resolved to bide his time and perhaps some avenue of escape might offer itself through which he might flee; yet as he saw the fixed gaze in the other's eyes he knew there was no hope.

Grayson threw open the door. A musty smell came from the pitch-dark interior. He switched on a light.

"I fixed up this little room for you, Heslop," he said, "while my family is away. It's noise-proof, and I want you to get acquainted with some of its inhabitants. You can take your choice. And to-night my yacht, the *Vagabond*, sets sail for a short cruise up the coast. Your remains will be on board—until we pass the red bell-buoy off the Farallone Islands, then you'll disappear forever." Then to the gangsters: "In with him!"

The door snapped shut.

Heslop ventured to a table. He shrank back from a small oval object. He knew it. It was a poisonous puff-ball from the New Hebrides. A pin puncture, and one sniff of its brown dust would make a gibbering maniac of a strong man for the rest of his life. The words of Grayson came to him: "You can take your choice."

He sickened.

He stood before a glass of ants. He well knew that the Filipinos buried their victims in the ground with the exception of the head—the ants did the rest.

He recoiled, wide-eyed with fear from a coverless box. It contained a pair of swamp-denizens from India.

He caught a glimpse of the orange-and-black beaded body of a Gila Monster. Then the lights went out—then silence.

He was horror-stricken, and he dared not move for he knew not what the other boxes contained. Perhaps there were trap-doors through which he might fall, or perhaps poisoned nails were protruding from the walls. He had heard of people being trapped in places where the ceiling came down and crushed them.

The darkness was oppressive!

A tiny stream of light filtered through a nail-hole. He advanced toward it cautiously, inch by inch, and applied his eye. He could see some greenery through the hole, and the odor of warm loam came to him. The hole was in a door. And the door was unlocked! Ah! He would make Grayson pay dearly—more dearly than ever!

He stumbled through a knee-deep tangle of vines and blooms to the end of the hot-house and attacked a window pane. It was frosted iron! Perspiration broke out on his forehead, and an oath was emitted from his thick lips at the discovery of artificial light.

He would try another place. The vines held him fast! His arm became entangled in them when he stooped to slash them away.

He cursed and struggled to free himself from the snake-like arm which came creeping across his back.

A mauve-and-pink blossom was within a foot of his face. Like an orchid, it was, delicately frail and deathly beautiful. Ugh! Its odor was nauseating!

And the leaves. The underside was rough, as a cat's tongue; dark velvety-green on the upper side, with red veins as though filled with blood. Heslop almost fainted with horror. Blood! His own blood! The orchid death!

Up reached a creeper that was gnarled and slimy-cupped as the tentacle of an octopus. Slowly it came. Now a foot from his throat. Three inches! One! It tightened! And just before his murky soul passed on he saw visions —visions of cold green water closing over his weighted bulk, and of sinking, twisting, sinking—slowly sinking by the red bell-buoy, in the Pacific, off the Farallones.

Drosera Cannibalis

René Morot

I do not know why anyone should try to cast doubt on the death of Professor Hartenstatter, the celebrated botanist, for I am myself perfectly qualified to prove that it actually took place. The great botanist has not merely disappeared; he is really dead. I saw him while he was dying, and again when he was dead; and I was one of the two witnesses who signed his death certificate in November 1918, while I was still in the army.

Nobody need doubt that he has disappeared for good. It is necessary to say "for good" when one talks about the death of a queer scientific enthusiast, who has been reported dead many times when he had simply disappeared; for it was his custom to vanish mysteriously for two or three years at a time, in the virgin forests of Africa or South America, searching for the unknown plants whose discovery and classification had made him the greatest botanist of his day.

You probably remember that Hartenstatter was passionately devoted to the study of carnivorous plants and that he had succeeded in giving some of them a truly monstrous development. In the great greenhouse, forty or fifty feet high, which he had erected near his villa at Rothmunster and into which no one, not even his servant, was allowed to go, his growing specimen of *Drosera longifolia* attained a height of almost thirty feet, and the distinguished professor insisted that he could produce a growth half again as great in less than two years.

In the notebook in which Hartenstatter summed up his daily observations, I have found jottings that seem like the wildest fantasy, calmly written down with the unconsciousness of the research student whose whole mind is intent on his scalpel's point. Without any considerations of pity, humanity, or morals, Hartenstatter was wholly bent on wresting one more secret from nature; a master executioner torturing his victim in order to extract a confession. He had made all kinds of observations on the growth and movement of the genus *Drosera*, plants which, as everyone knows, have the ability to capture the flies and other insects that alight on their leaves, closing over the victims immediately and in a few hours, thanks to the secretion of a very active pepsin, absorbing them wholly without leaving the slightest trace.

For a long time Hartenstatter had devoted himself to stimulating and developing the appetite of one particular giant *Drosera* which grew into a tree with enormous branches, and had slowly become capable of absorbing first grasshoppers, then guinea-pigs, then mice, then rabbits, and finally lambs.

In Hartenstatter's notebook there are descriptions, written with an almost fiendish joy, of the slow and complete absorption of animals by these monstrous vegetables; for the botanist notes that the plants have more appetite—it is his own term—for living beings than for dead.

What a triumph when the scientist finally achieved definite proof that these plants are gifted with the power to *see!* Yes, he proved it. The plants do see. It is true that death did not give him time to make out where the organs of vision are located and how they function, but he relates an experiment which he conducted many times, placing a mouse or a guinea-pig under a bell glass behind a screen. The *Drosera* never moved. No instinct, no divination, revealed to it the meal within reach of its tentacles. But they stirred and stretched slowly toward it when the screen was taken away and the mysterious organs of vision received their stimulus.

Everyone knows that plants are sensitive to light, that they stretch their branches toward it, appreciate it, love it, but

Hartenstatter demonstrated that his *Drosera* actually looked around them and, still more, that they did not see in the dark; for the same experiments carried out at night did not cause them to move at all.

"I have proved," he writes in his notebook, "that plants look around and see, and I have proved it—as exactly as Sir Jagadish Chandra Bose proved it in his Calcutta laboratory with his ingenious crescograph, which multiplies the least movement thousands of times—that a plant is a small impressionable person, vibrating with various and constant movements. With the needle of his apparatus, Sir Jagadish proved that plants are not the same by day and night, that they have various positions, that they have a special position for sleep. I confirm his discovery when I say that the plants see by day but do not see by night. Plants have senses. We knew long ago that they have sex. This general activity shows how close is the link that unites the vegetable and animal kingdoms, and confirms the kindly thesis of Claude Bernard, who proclaims the common life of all things."

In noting that his *Drosera* seems to prefer to devour living rather than dead animals, Hartenstatter adds that, up to the very minute of their death, the victims feel no pain. They do not seem to understand their situation, even when they have already begun to be absorbed by the plant; and each meal of the monster, which seems insatiable, leads within two or three days to an increase in the circumference of the trunk and the length and strength of the boughs and leaves.

One day Hartenstatter, deciding to give a new turn to his researches, brought back from the military hospital, where he went each morning to serve as a surgeon, the hand of a wounded man which had been amputated and which he had cleverly extracted from a heap of surgical debris destined for destruction. The notebook says that his *Drosera gigantis* absorbed the hand completely in five hours and forty-eight minutes, and although three times the same weight of food from a rabbit the week before had increased the trunk of the *Drosera* only half a millimetre, the human flesh in this experiment increased it about two thirds of a millimetre. Dr.

Hartenstatter was triumphant. He had discovered a man-eating plant, *Drosera cannibalis*!

From that day on, the horrible doctor used all his astuteness in procuring human flesh, which his official duties made it all too easy for him to obtain. In a few weeks, a question appears in one of his notes. Since the *Drosera* prefer living animals to dead ones, might it not be the same with living human flesh? Horrible to relate, on the second of January 1917, Dr. Hartenstatter brought home a baby two months old, which he had stolen in the country, and the notebook adds that the *Drosera* absorbed its "nourishment" even more rapidly than usual. Hartenstatter did not dare to write "the child," though he describes the gag that he put on the mouth of his victim who does not seem to have suffered.

Hartenstatter, pen in hand, took notes of all the phases of that infernal meal, and there they stand in his notebook to this day. Unfortunately, many pages were lacking when I found the book, preserved by chance amid the ruins of his dwelling, which had been sacked and burned by a furious mob when his horrible experiments were discovered. But the pages that remain are frightful, although full of daring, almost mad guesses, which may later be confirmed and then declared strokes of genius. Can one read without trembling such a cynical confession as this: "May 12, 1918. These imbeciles who object to vivisection! What does the disappearance of nine youngsters amount to [for it was now six months after his first crime] when one is wresting such a secret as this from nature! Is she not pitiless herself, nature, our mother, who is also a cruel stepmother? My experiments involve no suffering and are not really cruel. To-day's experiment indicated no pain, even when a third of the body had already disappeared; and now the tentacles are twined about the shoulders, and only the head emerges free. As in the other cases, it is only when a tentacle presses upon the brain that life becomes extinct.

"November 21, 1918, seven o'clock. My experiment to-day is conclusive proof. The child, which had reached more than three years, ought to have been able to understand that he was being absorbed and disappearing, and yet he never uttered a cry, his eyes betrayed no fright. It was not resignation nor anaesthesia, for he felt the prick of a pin in his neck. But plainly there was no agony. I conclude that assimilation into a vegetable organism is a thoroughly normal thing, although not hitherto understood by scientific men—a fact which lends support to my theory of the eventual enslavement of the animal by the vegetable kingdom.

"Animals could be destroyed to-day upon our planet and life would continue for some time, but it is childishly obvious that if the vegetable kingdom were to disappear suddenly, the animals would die a few days afterward. The true life of nature is in the vegetable kingdom, whose roots like long and slender antennae grope through the earth, not merely for chemical materials, but for emanations, radiations, inspirations, and vibrations; waves which sweep out from some mysterious reservoir—of which to this day we know nothing—of psychic matter that feeds our own brains. In the peace of the night, while man's brain is dulled in sleep, the vegetable kingdom, the conscious dominator of the world, breathes over the animal kingdom and especially over man, the great currents of thought that little by little change the thought of the world, currents that, fermenting in one brain or another, ravish with their fantasy the thought that we think free. It is through the vegetable kingdom that our spirits receive the ideas that open to us paradise or that plunge us into the shadows of pessimism. They are tyrants, these great trees that tower above us, despots playing dice with our human destinies.

"November 21. The expression of this child seemed to change. It is too bad that I could not understand what he said. He must have been the child of some Flemish refugees. It is strange that after having cried for ten hours on the way back in the automobile, he should have grown calm and still the moment he was in the power of the *Drosera*.

"November 22, four o'clock. I must have gone to sleep for a few moments, after having watched the experiment for twenty-seven hours, for already a branch of the *Drosera* is creeping over the face which was free at my last observation."

But resistance to sleep has its limits. Hartenstatter made one experiment too many. For when, on army business and under military orders, I penetrated into his great greenhouse in spite of the opposition of his terrified servant, I found Dr. Hartenstatter with his head held as if by a vise in the grasp of three enormous branches of his *Drosera*. The monstrous plant had already thrust two tentacles under his shirt and they, no doubt, were assimilating the shoulders of the scholar, who had evidently been surprised during his sleep.

When I came in he was wide awake, perfectly able to think, and fully conscious of the danger that threatened him. At the same time, I observed what remained of the body of a poor child, scarcely half of the bloodless face; and knowing that many children had disappeared in the region I understood at a glance the atrocious drama, of which the scientist had been at first the author and then the victim. And so when the doctor begged me to cut the branches of the *Drosera* with my sabre, my indignation bade me let his punishment take its course.

Faithful to my military duty—to make a report of everything— I noted down all that I had learned, and went out, taking the key of the door, to consult my military superiors. Unfortunately, during the few moments that this task took, a servant who was more curious and less disciplined than the others got into the greenhouse, I don't know how. He called for help, and the furious people clubbed to death the botanist, held in the vise-like grip of the monster, his pupil. They smashed the greenhouse. They covered over the *Drosera* with oil and burned it alive. Among the ruins I found a few pages of his notebook, which had been three quarters burned— unfortunately, for it would have been a fascinating thing to read.

Who is there now can doubt that Professor Hartenstatter is dead at last?

The Malignant Flower

Anthos

Lala Daulat Ras had finished his story. For a while he stood there, stiff and straight as a statue in front of the Englishman who was immersed in deep thought. He measured him with a glance in which the mysticism of ancient wisdom of his native home and enigmatic cruelty were mingled. Then he left slowly with measured steps.

Sir George William Armstrong started up from his dreaming and gulped down a glass of whiskey. It was perfect lunacy what the Hindoo had told him, and yet, and yet one had to believe him word for word, for Daulat Ras was a Yoghi, and a Yoghi never lies. But he wanted to, and had to settle for himself whether occult powers abided in these strange men, who hate the European and very seldom bring to light the "nature secrets" of their land. Sir George was well off and without any ties. No sport was strange to him. He could certainly start the undertaking, but he needed a re- liable as well as taciturn companion. The native servant familiar with the ways of the land, to whom he disclosed his plan, said he would sooner be thrown alive to a tiger or be buried in an ant-hill. So he had to turn to his faithful old John Bannister.

In the long full years of their connection, he had become more than a mere valet. Indeed, he was a sort of confidential friend. True and watchful as a dog, tenacious and indefatigable in hardships, courageous in danger. His skin was like parchment, no red blood seemed to flow beneath it, but in spite of his 65 years he was mus- cular and had a constitution like iron and steel. And Sir George took him into his confidence. But this it was which Daulat Ras had related:

Some ten days journey from here, in an accurately-indicated little valley of the Himalayas, which is about 200 yards long, there is a curious little bit of earth, a ravine hedged in by three high per-pendicular walls. The only access is on one of the four sides, over a sort of quagmire or pond, out of which poisonous vapors rise. You had to row closely along the edge of it in a boat in order to avoid the poisonous gases. The ravine itself, completely overgrown with flowers, is the home for demons, mischievous satanic forms, mixtures of man and woman, against whom all the weapons of civi-lization are useless. In spring and in fall they reveal their mysteri-ous power. Woe to him who treads upon their reservation. Death and insanity is his fate. If he escapes the destruction alive, he re-mains dead,—as far as earthly love is concerned. Mark this,—death for all earthly love.

John Bannister smiled sneeringly. His master stood immersed in deep thought. He thought of the blonde fiancée, whom in this very month he was to take to her future home. Near Calcutta, in a picturesque suburb, is a charming bungalow, which was even then being erected in feverish haste according to his directions. Then he would be at an end, once for all, as a restless globe trotter and adventurer. But till then, Harriet Richards was to suspect nothing of the goal of the journey, was not to be given one second of worry or of anxiety. He would pretend a business trip. And he laid out his plan. The railroad went part of the way. He would buy reliable maps of the country, would get provisions and a little row boat, would use porters until he would get to the entrance of the ravine. In the bright mid day he would enter it, while this last bit of the journey, he and his valued John Bannister should conquer alone. John rubbed his hands in satisfaction. He was satisfied with the party. . . .

The Hindoo had spoken the truth. The ravine was there. Be-hind dusky black marshlands was a bright tropical carpet of flow-ers in the most gorgeous colors of the young autumn. The goal was reached. The porters pushed the boat into the swamp and lay down trembling in a little hollow. Three hours of waiting was assigned them, enough time for the adventurers to go all over the little valley which was to be explored.

Countless little bubbles rose. The air was filled with strong biting vapors as the two discoverers glided along the edge of the turbid and scum-covered river. On each side the bare cliffs were in curious contrast to the blooming flora which awaited them in the valley. A quantity of withered thorn bushes, with dried and crooked branches, rose on the edge of the stream, which thickened steadily. The sun poured down obliquely. No wind stirred in this silent afternoon siesta of nature. As they got out of the boat, a heavy veil of vapor stretched over the upper valley. The atmosphere seemed to brew sultry over all and purple lightning jerked over the landscape. A hedgehog sprang up before them. Fearless and confident, he sized up the unusual visitors, trotted alongside of them for a while, then sat upon his hind legs and nibbled at an artichoke. Their shadows fell before them, dumb, trembling companions, while the adventurers, between bare cliffs, dropped down into the valley of the flowers, which stood in their second most exquisite bloom. Sir George forged ahead, carefully watching every step. Directly behind him came his companion, and both were armed to the teeth.

A wonder garden spread before their enraptured gaze. Flower after flower, each of inimitable brilliancy of color, pictures of never glimpsed dimensions, ever thicker, ever higher, rather trees than flowers. A whole forest through which it was only with difficulty that one could make his way. Orchids of the most varied kinds were here on the frontier of the highest giant cliffs of the world! Wary, dreamlike, gigantic flowers, with heat-trembling calyxes, covered the whole ravine, cutting off all vision beyond it. Brusquely and undeterred, Sir George forced his way forward and onward, and his companion had more than once to warn him to look out for unknown dangers. What would rise up from behind or between this colored scenery? What kind of beings lurked behind it all, waiting for them?

There was nothing to be seen but flowers and more flowers. In feverish excitement they observed the size of the strange forest with its great plant growths as high as men, whose flowers in silent and majestic quiet were throned upon their stems. Nothing moved. Once only a Himalayan fox moved past them like a streak of lightning, and again there was the silence of a graveyard. Only the overcoming perfume of these myriads of blooms increased, and further progress seemed to oppress the very senses, and the two wanderers were overcome by a fantastic dreamlike mood. These flowers, these giant butterflies, or magnificent dazzling color, fluttering around them—were they not all satanically beautiful beings, which resembled reasoning creatures, benumbing the senses with a whirl, while they simulated the human organs—ear, eyes, lips, and tongue? Sir George gave free reign to his imagination. These ruthless beings which emitted this perfume out of their great languishing calyxes, at once seeming to have unsatisfied longing and dreaming, were they not half-flower, half-animal? Like slender white giant candelabra, their bodies rose upward. What kind of a secret did they hide?

And he began energetically and impatiently to forge ahead. Already he was easily ten yards ahead of his companion, half of the length of the valley through which they were walking was well behind him. The black, bare, steeply-rising cliff, which might have been poured from sealing wax, and which closed the valley, seemed to vibrate far in the distance, John Bannister started to run in order to catch up with his master, but his progress was ever retarded by creeping plants or round rock boulders, and now a sudden thicket rising from the ground cut off his steps and his view ahead. He forced his way through laboriously and found himself in an open glade nearly at the end of the ravine. And the sight that met his gaze. . . . "But such a thing is impossible!" thought John Bannister to himself, as he rubbed his hand over his eyes. The unheard-of wonder did not vanish, but stood in a monumental quiet. In the middle of the glade a colossal flower rose up to a height of nearly 10 feet, the stem nearly a foot thick, looking like an immense hemlock cone. From the top five or six great leaves, resembling leather,

reached down to the ground. From the blooms there dropped a fluid
of overcoming strength of scent. And he saw Sir George William
Armstrong, sunk in wonder, standing close by this queen of the
valley. John Bannister involuntarily stood still. Something had
moved. The pair of blooms of this great flower which hitherto had
hung down, stiffened themselves visibly,—the piercing sweet perfume streamed out of them overpoweringly, and the three-fold
thorny lips with their colored pattern trembled in the atmosphere
back and forth, while the Doric column of the stem, dark yellow
and sprinkled with black spots, seemed to curve upwards, showing a labyrinthian net of blood red veins. What was this frightful
spotted viperlike body, whose spots swelled up to thick berrylike
eruptions?

Whatever it was, it meant danger. And John Bannister screamed
out with the full strength of his lungs. "Sir George, take care, for
Heaven's sake!"

But even then the awful thing came to pass. The flower slowly
opened, and something bright and flesh-colored shot out of it. What
dated so suddenly? Was it the sucking arms of an octopus? Was it
the soft arms of a woman? From Sir George there came a scream
that cut to the very marrow, and John Bannister, frozen stiff with
fright, saw his master lifted by his shoulders, up, higher and higher,
saw him hanging for a couple of seconds in uncertain balance, and
finally disappearing slowly in to the calyx of the atrocious, malignant flower, whose petals once more drew themselves together with
a start. In this way Sir George celebrated a symbolic marriage with
nature, a festival more overcoming, but also more horrible than
that for which he had prepared himself. Over the whole scene horror seemed to sweep on dark bat's wings.

There was the fraction of a second only, and John Bannister
had remained his senses. He hastened to the flower with giant
paces, drew his knife and tried to destroy the tough tentacles of
the plant, closely clinging to each other. The knife went to pieces
like glass in his grip, then he seized the axe, and accurately and
carefully delivered blow after blow, which swelled up to a sort of
clangor, as if a bell were cracking. After ten minutes of strenuous

work, he had freed his master from his dangerous position, literally peeled out of a sheath.

Pale as death he lay before him on the grass, a grim and frozen smile as if half of supernatural pleasure, half of the fear of death was on his rigid features. But he breathed, lived, appeared uninjured, and allowed himself to be dragged away as if lifeless.

The return journey was silent and oppressive, first going back to the waiting porters, then the whole party returned to civilization. Nothing could induce Sir Armstrong to open his lips. He stared before him as if his mind had completely left him.

Later when Harriet Richards can to his bed in the hospital, he at first failed to recognize her. Then, while foam appeared at the corners of his lips, he rose up in his bed and with a frightful, piercing yell, he pushed her away. . . .

And Sir George has not led Harriet Richards to the altar. Fourteen days after the catastrophe his hair became white as snow. A broken man for the rest of his life, he was taken to the City Insane Asylum, lingered there a year and a half until death set him free.

Returning from the burial, John Bannister suddenly saw Daulat Ras, the Yoghi, who seemed to have risen from the ground as by magic. "You had your warning," said he, and an undefinable expression played about his lips. "But how was it," cried out the other, "that Sir George rushed to his fate and to destruction, while I was spared?" On the features of the Asiatic lay the impenetrable mask of the Sphynx. With his forefinger he touched the parchment white face of the old servant. "Blood," said he, meaningly,—then he glided back and disappeared in the crowd of mourners.

Three years passed. Harriet Richards moved to Liverpool, and managed the household for her brother Jack, the ship-owner. Life resumed its usual way and even in her memory, the frightfulness of the events gradually paled. One evening, as Harriet sat in the comfortably-heated sitting room opposite her brother, the winter storm howling over the Atlantic, her glance rested on a column in the "Daily Telegraph."

Instinctively she took it up and read: "The Life Memoirs of the recently deceased Professor Dr. de Palfi, known as a botanist and explorer will soon appear. The professor's greenhouse, with their orchid cultures, situated in Vienna, his adopted home city, have enjoyed great European fame for the last ten years. In his memoirs, the professor tells in an impressive way of his extended explorations which took him into the most distant regions of all the continents. With the permission of the publisher we can quote from its contents today the sensational information that de Palfi on his last journey in which he reached the interior of Madagascar, actually came upon the much debated 'Man Eating Plant.' It is supposed to be a very rare variety of *Cypripedia gigantea* belonging to the class of the giant orchids, and is the largest flower on earth. These plants, growing in certain remote valleys, have described to them the power to seize small and also larger animals, and even men, who come within their reach. In the spring and fall, always according to de Palfi's observation, the pericarp, or seed container, forms a sort of natural trap. It thrusts out a quantity of sharp clawlike points, which, as they sink into the flesh, are strong enough to hold the large animals prisoners. Within, the plant is covered all over with suction caps, containing a sort of resinous gum that acts like birdlime in a bird trap. By virtue of a certain plant stimulus, a reflex motion back and forth sets up, enabling the enormous orchid to draw into itself even the body of a full grown man. The plant, it is understood, is a pure flesh-eater. It feeds itself principally on large animals and men. Sometimes the victims can be freed from the embraces of the flower after the murderous attack of the plant. Otherwise the captured individual is completely absorbed and fourteen days later the bare skeleton is cast out."

COACHWHIP PUBLICATIONS

COACHWHIPBOOKS.COM

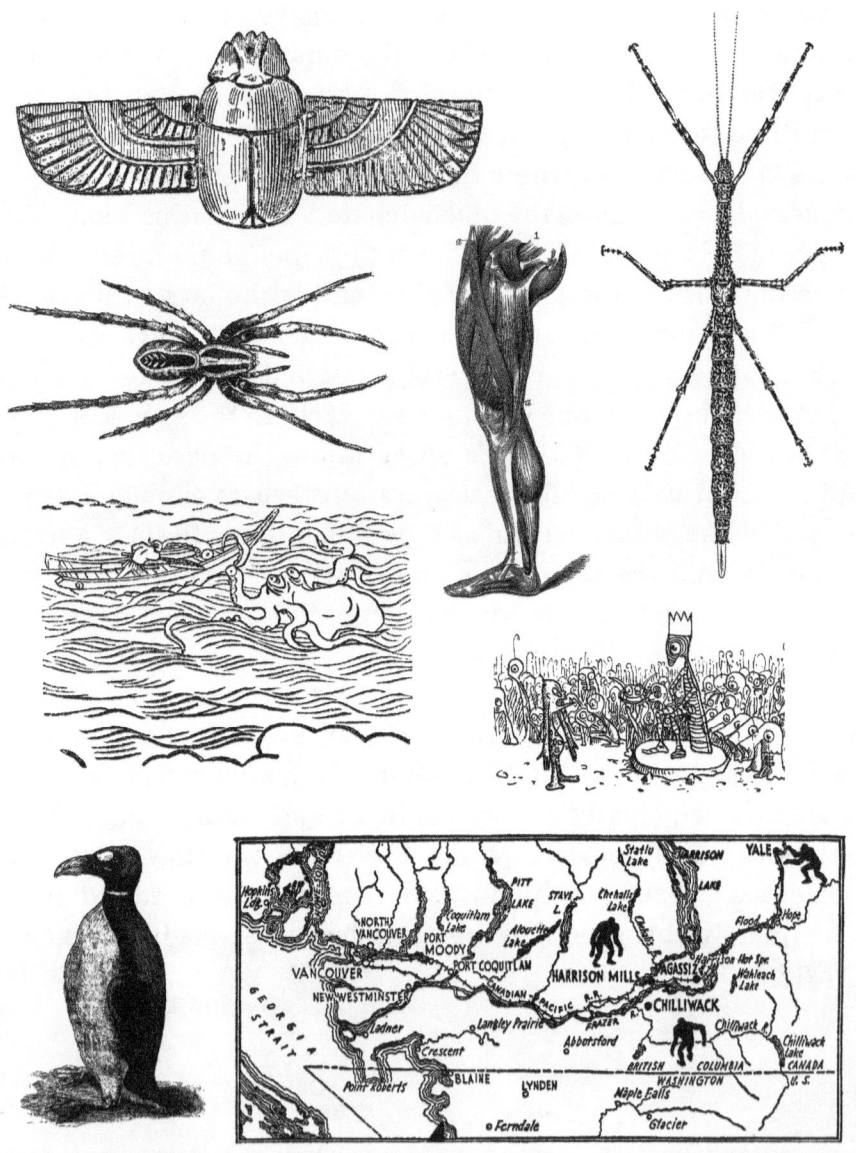

COACHWHIP PUBLICATIONS

ALSO AVAILABLE

Flora Curiosa

Cryptobotany, Mysterious Fungi,
Sentient Trees, and Deadly Plants
in Classic Science Fiction and Fantasy

CHAD ARMENT, EDITOR

Additional Stories of Botanical Marvels

Flora Curiosa
ISBN 1-930585-56-X

COACHWHIP PUBLICATIONS

COACHWHIPBOOKS.COM

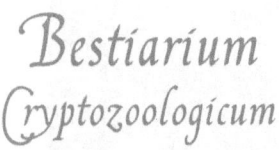

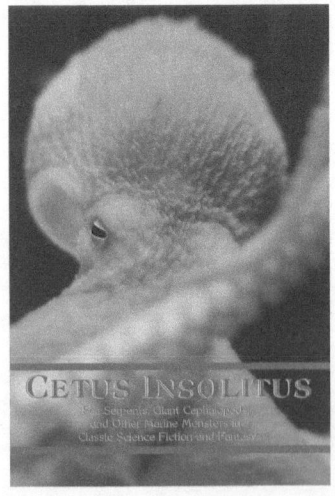

Unknown Creatures and Monstrous Beasts
in Classic Science Fiction and Fantasy

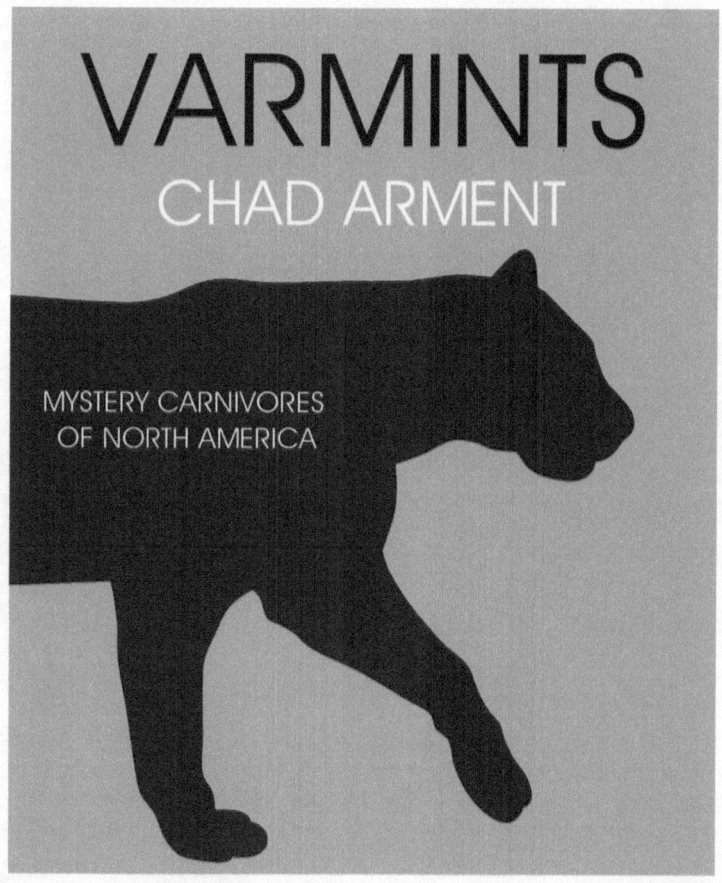

VARMINTS

CHAD ARMENT

MYSTERY CARNIVORES
OF NORTH AMERICA

Varmints: Mystery Carnivores of North America
ISBN 1-61646-019-9

www.ingramcontent.com/pod-product-compliance
Lightning Source LLC
Chambersburg PA
CBHW030959260626
47169CB00002B/620